Alderelm

By

Ellis McCauley

Cover art and Illustrations by

Rain McCauley

Thistlethumb Publishing ❧ Edwall

For two faeries and a dwarf

Library of Congress Cataloging-in-Publication Data

McCauley, Ellis

Alderelm

ISBN 979-8-9926228-1-2 Paperback

ISBN 979-8-9926228-0-5 Hardback

ISBN 979-8-9926228-2-9 Ebook

Library of Congress Control Number: 2025902635

Thistlethumb Publishing

Edwall, Washington

❧ Table of Contents ❧

Prologue I

Chapter 1 1

Chapter 2 19

Chapter 3 26

Chapter 4 36

Chapter 5 52

Chapter 6 60

Chapter 7 88

Chapter 8 99

Chapter 9 121

Chapter 10 131

Chapter 11 149

Chapter 12 161

Chapter 13 175

Chapter 14 199

Chapter 15 209

Chapter 16 225

Chapter 17 236

Chapter 18 257

Chapter 19 261

Chapter 20 265

Chapter 21 284

Chapter 22 296

Chapter 23 313

Chapter 24 323

Chapter 25 335

Epilogue 344

Appendix 345

◈ Prologue: Of Trees and Treeans ◈

There is a Tree named Methuselah high in the milky clouds of the White Mountains, where the wind howls hauntingly, innocent for its own cause, carrying echoes of the past. At well-nigh five millennia, she is young to any recollection of her parents' memory, who lived tens of thousands of years themselves. She stands strong, albeit with haggard bark and grotesquely twisted limbs, revealing scars of more than elemental cause but of tumult from generations ere, borne in the hope that the consciousness of time, in which so much has passed, will ne'er be forgotten and thus always exist. However, within her well-marked spirit, there resides no pity of past or present and no resentment of condition or cause. She waits patiently. Leaves rustle into the wind, the distance, and the past. The starlight of the sun intones lamentations immemorial while conjointly winging the light of hope upon the Earth. For Methuselah's soul, up to this very moment, hums with Earthen kin across the lands; this Tree, the very crest of life, of no great height or size, unless quality be marked, is one of the sagacious keepers of all knowledge, the descendant of the Ancient Ones, preserving stories of the beginnings, and the traditions of the virtuous and wise.

◆❦◆

In Earth's waking breaths, Methuselah's ancestors tasted the sweet soil with their sapling roots. With insatiable hunger, these anchorages ventured far and wide. Thick canopies hung heavy with leaves, a cathedral of reverent majesty upon a newly greened world.

Of swells and swiftness, Zephyr beheld the Earth's new ornamentations and tugged upon their great boughs. The Trees trembled. What was this? They knew naught, and a stillness of timidity took them. 'Twas as though an early winter had put the spell of dormancy upon them . . . and therein within their quiet, for their roots had grown substantial, entrenched far and deep within the entirety of Earth's mantle—they heard it.

Horrific the vibrations! Churning and rumbling, a land of sway in some deep and distant place—the seas and oceans. Enormous in breadth, rich and full, the creatures within chanted haunting wails and warbled in clicks and thumps. Shuddering in fear, the Ancient Ones threw the continents of Earth into upheaval, and for many thousand moons thereafter, they lay petrified in the wait for calmer days.

'Twas during this age, when looming mountain peaks touched the stars of multitudes, that wisdom began to emanate from the impressive shades of the giant Majesties. Time might even recount a blossom or two sprouting upon hidden twigs. The Trees were learning Her ways—the moods and motions of Mother Earth—and, at last, settling under the sun and stars. Only time could have introduced them to the temperamental wind and the turbulent bodies of Earth's abundant waters; within both, a rhythm of comfort was realized.

Still, the Ancient Ones hid within their shell of isolation while they hearkened the songs of sea creatures and put all to memory. Oh, how they desired to sing with their sea-dwelling brethren! Yet, as Nature produced a flourishing garden of mysterious creatures around them, the Trees remained mute. The grass and flowers, the elves and faeries, the sylphs and seasons, the rivers and lakes, all held the Great Ones in muse.

A faerie kind of wingless form was a favorite for the Trees to behold, for they brought laughter upon the winds as they made their homes within the nearby brush. And too, every full moon, the curious creatures stared up under the massive canopies with smiles of wonder and decorated the great trunks with flower-ridden wreaths. Full of dance and joy, the Trees were pleased to be nigh their presence; only more did the faeries' merriment entice them from quiet solitude.

Inevitably, one Tree, as bold as she was broad, could forbear her desire no more. Mightily, she bellowed forth all the pent-up passion within her being, beginning a chorus of reverberating song from the north, south, east, and west. The Great Awakening of the Ancient Forests had begun. One by one, the seven Ancient Forests called out in reply, and henceforth, the soil of the earth has ne'er been silent.

Yet a day of ill arrived and for aye changed the innocent garden of Earth. The Veriha, the Seven Wonders who breathed life upon our world, were leaving. Gently, they kissed the lands and children ere ascending to the stars.

Thus, did Laughing Tempests gather to fill their void and hold the glowing strands of the sun afar. Growling clouds and firelights were strewn across the lands, threatening to fell every last memory. Within their ominous presence . . . the Trees quaked; ne'er had they beheld anything such as this.

The wingless fae strode beside the Magnificent Majesties, hearts weeping for their beloved Trees as they whistled calming melodies beneath their trembling canopies. Boughs crashed around them in the howling wind, yet while other creatures hid in fright, the fae held unwavering. They would not let harm befall the Trees and with no matter of it, took fierce a stance in a message of will where sharply chiseled shafts were sent flying.

Thus, courage was gifted to the Trees, for they realized they were not alone. Together, flesh and Wood held tightly, facing the torrential surges of black tumult. The Ancient Ones ground their roots firmly and sent triumphant resonations of tranquility and peace reverberating throughout the whole of Earth: soil, water, and air. The tempests recoiled.

The dark day brought light; the Trees were bestowed guardians, and the fae were endowed with a place to call home. Within the boles and upon the boughs, the fae became as interconnected to the Trees as the Trees to the fae. The Ancient Ones called their spirited new relations, Treeans, and so became their calling to all kin across the lands.

❧ ✦ ☙

As is the circle of life and the way of the world, the Trees of Harbored Memory eventually pass to the stars and leave fresh seeds of life to grow anew. Unto the world, the saplings unravel their burgeoning leaves to the gentle touches of familial roots and tender Treean care. However, amongst new life, the Treeans themselves found none; they were dwindling, and none knew why. Long since had their Lastborn entered into existence.

◄ Chapter 1 ►

'Twas a night of foul intentions,
Beyond reason—twilight tempests.

—The beginning of Klickitat, an oral story that every Treean remembers being told in their youth

As the sun shone upon the end of its full breadth across the day's sky, well within a new spring, a young Treean finally found her Tree wakening against winter's spell of dormancy. Most of the curled and bent branches strode well above the Forest fog-mist below, and Leaf, as was the Treean's primary calling—attributed to her delicate and diminutive stature—sat comfortably within the canopy of immense proportion. A view of splendor rose and fell before her as the breeze lapped upon and so swayed the Sacred One's highest and most outer-hung twigs of new greens. Under such comfort and set so well within this vantage, the Treean could not help but gaze intently onto those lands well beyond her dear Tree's ample reach. The white caps that had lain snug across the many mountaintops all winter were receding with each lengthening day, and her gladness on the coming of the burgeoning

1

season of new buds and flowers was without bounds. So very long, as she thought it, had her Tree slept; the poor Treean had thought she would ne'er wake from the heavy slumber. Leaf's unconstrained cheer was heartily expressed and let loose under Treean whistle songs—clear, sharp, and softly melodious. The Ancient One listened, bent her outermost boughs, and tenderly embraced her young Treean; the sun was settling down amongst the distant fields, warm and soothing, yet the breeze was crisp, still pinched with a hint of winter. No matter, for the Ancient One and her Treean were most content.

Leaf paused her melodies and breathed in richly as if she might inhale the euphony held within the pinkish hues upon the horizon. "Not much to catch you up on, geesh Miriam," she said, sighing, the color of her complexion draining from the lightest sparkling green to a dull yellow-white haze. "You're well aware of the lack of goings-on in Alderelm, not the least, in winter."

Miriam's grumblings, so old and deep, brought boughs beneath Leaf trembling even before her full protests could be made. The young Treean laughed and whistled between tongues of the old and new language, reminiscent of a chit-chattering marmot. Leaf's aspect, always friendly and bright, was also bit with a savage curiosity and independence rarely seen in Treean kind. Her eyes lit with affection and immense joy; Miriam was having her way all right, and she had missed it. Warmed to be by Miriam's waking side, Leaf's smile fell faintly away.

"All right, all right, steady now," said Leaf, adjusting the coronet of buttercups wound within her mottled, brown plaits and around the burgundy brambles of her head. "I'll tell you all that's not happened while you blissfully slept."

Miriam's low, multiphonic bellows now resonated from deep within the earth. She was not a Tree to waste time. Leaves quaked heavily in clear objection to dialogue spent off course and, in so doing, disturbed a squirrel that barked in irritation. Leaf was surprised to see the creature barked at her and not her grand Tree, who was the result of its irritation, after all.

Leaf skewed her mouth to one side and squinted her emerald eyes down the bole of Miriam's heart. "Irritable and a tad touchy when you awaken, are you not, my dear Miriam?" she said as she rested her head against the Great Tree, the nettle brambles around her locks now curling in on themselves, the security of the fetal bud reclaimed and her mind beginning to whirl.

Many kin always came upon the borders of Alderelm, all welcomed fully, but the elves were her favorite, for they captured her imagination in truth of pure presence. Their kind was the oldest of all kin, save the Treeans, and they were well-skilled in many crafts. Listening to Treean talk oft where she ought not to have been, she had learned more about the elven ketyls and their distinction from one another than the Ancient Trees would have preferred for her age.

Ah, yes, she reflected. There were the Coyotls—the elves of transformation. Whether such a power was possessed in truth or not, she was uncertain, but she liked to believe it so. This poor ketyl was regarded in as lowly fashion as elves could be considered—their fascination and association with the fledgling kin, humans, their apparent downfall. Most kin were convinced that these humans would lead to corruption. Of what kind, Leaf did not know or understand. She perceived such words as unjust accusations rooted in jealousy against newfound alliances and friendships.

Also laid within her memory, although more freshly, was an elven ketyl represented by three who had come to Alderelm five solstices before during the Season of Colors. 'Twas upon a day when the sun found difficulty breaking between the clouds. An opportune time to search the mind in quiet solitude, but in no mood for it, she had decided to walk upon the northeast trails. Nigh Bigdebar, the Gentle Giant of Oaks, unfamiliar voices did float. Curiosity, led more by mischief than wonder, found her treading gingerly until a soundless bound found her safe within her friend's thick foliage. Aloft, she beheld them, dark yet fair to behold—Raven elves. She knew well their look by History's description, those whose hair was as black as obsidian and did dance in iridescent rays with the music of their native tongue. Those whose eyes, those windows to the spirit, were obscure in a penetrating depth, save for an occasional flicker lit as though the stars exploded and dissolved within their irises well-etched folds. She had been utterly incapable of not gaping upon them, and a peculiar tingling in her quills made her feel sure they were keenly aware of her presence. Still, she stayed in her place, even after the mysterious elves had long left, until sleep claimed its place with her. Leaf smiled to herself as she remembered.

Then, there were her favorite, the Puman elves. Tales of their daring feats and adventures followed them whithersoever they went. They were said to be "of the Wood" and were rarely seen in casual nature. Widely recognized for their superb skills on the battlefields and their adroit nature with the bow, they had long since captured her imagination. She was fortunate to have beheld them while not hiding and had considered their appearance contrary to their reputation.

Their skin tone was easy, like autumn leaves from the Elder Trees, a dark golden color that complemented the elves' russet hair. And like their Puman namesakes, each strand of those tawny locks was of a differing hue, blending and looking akin to the dried, late summer meadow grasses, save for the oldest Pumans, who were well-marked by bundled strands of dusk-red streaks. Yet above all, Leaf felt that the most identifying characteristics were the effortless grace within their taller, noble frame, the limpid gold eyes that fell lightly upon their subjects, and the sincere smiles appearing frequently with little effort. The Pumans held the most peaceful presence she had aye observed. Lethality seemed present only upon seeing the weapons they carried.

Glimpses of gleaming knives at rest in their scabbards, worn both on their legs and the back of their waist, and flight bows rumored to send arrows soaring over nine hundred paces under the skill of their masters tormented her mind with excitement. How desperately she envisioned many a feathered arrow soaring through the air. But alas, they stayed tucked away in their quivers.

Legend told of the sylphs, those winged elements of the sky, gifting the Pumans with the sense of approaching danger, but the Trees relaid no details, although neither was the tale refuted. The Trees, and thus the Treeans, spoke little on the topic. However, what was spoken was the ketyl's willingness to take up arms for others, of their staunch defense of the weak and helpless; Leaf supposed therein lay a hint of why such power might have been gifted to them.

Miriam's impatient rumblings pulled her back from her thoughts. "Elves, Miriam! Wapiti elves! Bristleton met them on the border march during the first moon of winter. They sojourned for trade, and trade they did! We acquired two choice bows inlaid with mother of pearl in exchange for the ceremonial Wood of the Ash. I shan't believe it. How could the wisest of elven realms think this is a fair trade?"

She felt Miriam's echo beneath her feet and heaved a sigh. "I know, I know—sacred. Still, I think the bows are worth far more than we comprehend. Their bowyers spend eight seasons making them, Miriam. Eight! Their time and skill result in bows that possess no weight—as if naught but a feather be grasped within one's palm. Yet they are as strong as mammoth tusks," and so saying, she fixed her sights, pulled upon an imaginary bowstring, and beamed as she watched the arrow soar, but the farther out it flew, the more distant her countenance became. "You know . . . I missed the sight of them. They'd gone before I arrived. Elves don't stay in their place very long, huh, Miriam?" She grew quiet, her mind's eye momentarily disappearing into the yonder. "Eh, no matter," Leaf murmured, repeatedly intertwining her fingers. "I can tell you they were clad in glimmering cloaks bearing the mark of the white elk.

Bristleton said he could see no purpose for their raiments to have flashed about the way they did, but nonetheless . . . I'd have liked to have seen it all."

She grew quiet again, pondering the elves and the lands from whence they traveled. She soaked in self-pity as her heart welled with yearning to journey yon lands and behold them not from a Tree. Gazing out over the eastern hills of Nemus, she watched as two great herons flew over the remote regions of the Feiko Steppe. *Rare a sight*, she thought briefly. Then, leaping down two of Miriam's gnarled boughs, she began muttering. Knowing her all too well, the Old Tree cooed in comfort, and a smile spread across Leaf's speckled face, set to a darker hue under the sunset. She sprang to the earth of the Forest floor, rivaled only by the annoyed squirrel in agility; she ignored its chirps of agitation.

"Let's see, what else? Naught of much more importance. Bristleton has been more serious than usual. I'd say cranky, really. Knowlton has required much of him these last months, yet our borders lay dormant. 'Tis a wonderment, but I suppose the elders are made of tenser fibers when a great majority of the Sacred Ones"—she paused here for effect—"go . . . to . . . sleep."

An echo rose from the depths of the earth, rising and pulsing through Miriam's trunk and sending her fledgling leaves into violent vibrations. Leaf fell over, laughing, then continued her journey around her giant's domed canopy.

"Aha, I've got it! During the winter solstice ceremony, Pinyl—" She stopped and stood high in alarm. Within seconds, she had scampered hot-footed atop Miriam's highest bough and stood, scanning the horizon; she beheld many birds flying in the same direction. Her heart pounded. "Not good, not good," she said, panting, a terror rising within her. The brambles of her head arose in hackles, looking at once like thistle sage and catch weed within a spinney of matted tresses blown upright against a windstorm. Her fingers gripped tight on Miriam's bark, and she shivered. "Smoke," she whispered, the brambles now flattening tight against her scalp, "I believe Felts Field is afire."

☙ ✦ ❧

On the outskirts of Alderelm, Bristleton and his command ran upon the east path's tenuous height to a rocky outcrop on Peller Peak. Here, a view of the twisted Wych River sought an audience, but to little avail, for on this occasion, Treean eyes searched the skyline.

"It comes from the northeast!" cried one of the border guards.

Bristleton leaped onto Cory, the nearby Limber Pine, and there saw such horror that hardly could he fathom it. Rampant walls of flames burst higher than he had erenow seen, swarming the prairie. The season was none too dry, and there was little fuel to flame this beast. An ill taste dried his mouth, and he swallowed deeply.

"It'll be all right, my friend," he whispered, patting Cory's cinnamon-grey bole, his keen eyes straining over the lands.

The ravaging torment burned the green of his spirit and induced pain upon his being. He could feel this fire's heat and sense the cries of bark and flesh alike.

"The Ancient Ones are safe; the fire tries the outposts," cried Bristleton to his company, his tone deepening with sadness, "but there are surely those in need." Murmuring Treean blessings to the lands under the siege of smoke, he took one last look upon the surreal scene yon and jumped squarely to the earth. "We were given word of such strangeness from the Wapiti—the smoke—'tis too thick, and even more, it does not rise. Ne'er could I have imagined—and so close to our lands. We must deliver word to the elders. Council will be called. All guards to march the borders. We will no doubt be receiving guests this evening," and so saying, he hung his head low. "No wreaths should be laid upon the boughs or boles of the Ancient Ones this night. Place them upon the streams to be carried where we cannot touch at this moment but with our hearts."

❧ ✦ ☙

Leaf left Miriam's side, and in the descending twilight, the bell-shaped flowers of the borealis vines delicately lit her steps down Alderelm's labyrinth of paths with the merest blushing of radiance. Yet, although the Ancient Forest resided within its familiar beauty and calm, there was naught to be heard but the soft sounds of gathered Treeans murmuring amongst themselves. To the center of the Sacred Forest, where Tumoil's nectars burbled forth from under the earth, Leaf stared up under the Tree canopies. Many leafy undersides there glistened upon condensing moisture to become a silken reflection of the stars. Yet, there was not even a breath of breeze: no Treean melodies, bird songs, or insects chiming. She became more distressed with each breath. The hushed voices of Treeans grew louder and louder within her ears, her heartbeat a metronome of irregularities. *Enough of it!* her thoughts screamed, and so thinking, she rushed to find Bristleton.

Bristleton heard swift approaching footsteps but was not alarmed, for these fell in close succession, and he knew them well. Always an eager young Treean did sneakily follow him on border rounds. If no harm was of it, he allowed the young one to believe herself of such stealth to have gone unnoticed. Though on occasion, Bristleton had called Leaf fore, a sheepish grin emerging from the brush. Erelong thereafter, an onslaught of torrential questions would assail him. Bristleton oft thought Leaf's mind and mouth to be fed by a storm-packed river. Ne'er a matter made, he felt akin to her in spirit and had thus committed himself to bear the bond of life and blood to Leaf's wellbeing, even though the little Treean was not of his branch. A father of blood doth not a father make.

And so, a corner of the marchwarden's mouth tilted upward slightly, which was more than might be witnessed by anyone else, as Leaf rounded the bend with careless, breakneck speed.

The young one halted before the marchwarden and stooped to catch her breath.

"So winded? What hurry brings you, Little Leadfoot?"

Leaf looked up at Bristleton, the intermingled shadows of the growing eve casting eerie highlights on his sharp features. She reckoned not for the first time the extent of forbidding quality Bristleton could hold.

"Leaf, are you all right?"

"The Forest feels . . . irregular," said Leaf, squinting, frustrated by her inability to describe feelings so weighted upon her.

"Aye," replied Bristleton, looking at once harrowed.

Little else was spoken as they walked the edge of Alderelm. Patrol was thick with many Treeans, alow and aloft, standing guard. Visitors were greeted warmly, most known well through their travels to Alderelm. Still, the twilight brought an uncharacteristic change to the Treeans' demeanor. Their smiles rested upon faces of strain, and their eyes shifted restlessly where normally an even calm reigned. Further was their talk much of naught, yet polite and brief, their attention returning again and again to the dark paths across the border as though some unwelcome presence might venture to pit itself against them at any moment.

"The gloaming is at an end," said Bristleton, breathing out. "We need be heading to council."

An owl made its whoo-hoo-hoo softly heard, and Leaf rested with hope in her heart. "Bristleton, did you hear that?"

"Aye."

"Perhaps the Forest finds herself again under the light of stars," Leaf offered. "Ah, what precious sound amidst all the unquiet."

Bristleton demonstrated none of Leaf's relief and joy. Instead, his gaze hit the dell of the south hill, intensity in all manners marked not lost upon her. She concentrated, her face squirreled up, listening as hard as possible while trying to detect what she might not hope for. She perceived the slightest deer-like crunch of footfalls. Bristleton placed a hand on her shoulder.

"Greetings," said a high-fettled voice of curious nature.

The marchwarden scowled into the shadows below, asking Leaf, "How many suppose you?"

"One, I figure, an elf."

Bristleton brightened under her reply. "Well done. We shall make you a border guard yet."

"Osiyo!" called the voice from below. "I represent the Coyotl elves and have come to talk with Willow Elder of Alderelm. Am I not welcome?"

As the speaker stepped cautiously forward, light shone on the stranger's face; Bristleton's countenance curdled. "That depends on whether the one asking hath forsaken old friends."

At once, the Coyotl elf's face lifted. "Bris!" cried he, breaking into a run and extending his arm. "I am well met by the Forest of Alderelm!"

Bristleton interlocked his hand around the elf's extended arm and then pulled, with no great gentleness, the elf's entire person nearer in a firm embrace.

"Hath been long, where've you been about?" Bristleton asked, studying the Coyotl's face. "Even the Trees couldn't catch wind of you."

"Bris, I dare not tell you—too long would it take. Good powers that be 'tis fine to see you—just fine. Although," said the Coyotl elf, his expression as solemn as stone, "I wish it were under different circumstances."

"Mmm, then the Forest rumors are true?" asked Bristleton, putting his bow to sleep within its casing.

"They are true and more," the elf answered in a heavy and hushed tone.

At this, Leaf stepped out from Bristleton's shadow. She stared up at the elf in fascination, waiting to see if he might change or act in some curious, elven way. The elf stared at the youth. Quiet held sway amongst the three for a moment.

"Osiyo, little one. Sage is my calling." The elf squinted down at her playfully. "Don't mind Bris; he was ne'er fair with greetings . . . or such formalities." He whirled a calloused finger in the air, and a crooked smile appeared upon a face wincing in thought for a word or perhaps in constraint of one.

Leaf wanted to step toward him, but instinct kept her close to Bristleton's side. This elf was very different from the others she had encountered. She felt no distinct presence about him. Rather, his air was ever-changing, and although his eyes held kindness, they also bore an unsettling hollowness.

"Ahhh," said the elf, raising his eyebrows and skewing his mouth to one side. "I see she's as full of speech as you, Bris."

The furrows etched upon Bristleton's brow did soften, although his staunch demeanor did not waver. "Sage Lagacious, this is LittleLeaf LeadTree . . . our Lastborn." The latter words lingered. "And Leaf, afore you, the most peculiar . . . and truest elf you will aye meet."

The Coyotl knelt before Leaf and bowed his head with dignified purpose. Unease crept under Leaf's skin, and she looked to Bristleton for comfort, but the marchwarden would not meet eyes with the little Treean.

Leaf took a deep breath and a timid step forward. "You are elf kind," said she, with a lilt of insecurity, although her eyes held their purpose. "Should I not kneel before you?"

The Coyotl looked up but stayed upon his knee, gazing well behind the green depths of Leaf's eyes, the windows to her spirit. There, he took in the heart of her nature and found it true. He was well-pleased and replied, "The thought of it means more than the action, even when entirely unnecessary."

Leaf shifted her weight and smiled.

Bristleton swept up the moment's energy with terse functionality. "Come," he commanded, already moving back up the path. "Many have already arrived." Leaf did not move, and the marchwarden called back. "Leaf, are you coming forth?"

"I'll be there shortly."

Bristleton nodded while continuing his expeditious pace; Sage took to his side. The soothing touch of the night had decided to wake the Forest, and Bristleton thought Leaf better revel in it than rush to a council of worry.

Sage leaned close to Bristleton; their footfalls matched. "Bris, many think this," and so saying, he tapped his head, "is not set squarely upon itself, but heed my words, there's greatness in your little one." His voice dropped. "And my good Treean, it doth not blossom in this Forest."

Bristleton's long strides did not falter, although his jaw tightened, and his teeth gritted hard. He knew the truth that lay in the escaped utterance. He led his friend up the twists and turns of intermingled trails, as natural a landscape as the Trees themselves, the scent of Pine and Cedar whetting their senses, and the gentle babble of unseen rills soothing their ears. The night birds clicked and clattered within the bracken while crickets chirped, and the frogs croaked their jests within the Forest choir.

The Forest became more alive with every approaching step the pair made. The elf was captive to the vast beauty present. Higher and higher, they strode up the White Mountain, the only peak along the range whitened not by snow but by the bark of the Ancient Ones, which grew hoarier and starker with age.

The ground leveled as they neared the gathering place, and their path opened into a glade. Here, vivid and brilliant, the starlight did shine as though drawn to a pond of modest proportions but of ultimate splendor—the Tarn of Lumen. Fed by the Spring of Tumoil, the cool waters of restoration and wisdom urged the rivulets to the river far below.

Sage gazed up at the sky and held the palms of his hands pressed together in front of his heart. "Ah, Aelin-lumen, I am long last at your serene side."

There was a secure feeling when one looked up at the infinite night sky under the shelter of the Trees. He felt like he had come home.

THISTLE SAGE

Thistle Sage. 1. A whitish-wooly annual herb with vivid lavender, bilaterally symmetrical flowers that appear in round clusters on the top of leafless stems. It looks like a thistle, but it is not. *2.* Recent Age. The physical description is the same. Salvia carduacea is of the Lamiaceae (Mint) family. Insects and hummingbirds love its flowers. Other birds and small mammals are attracted to its seeds. It is more closely related to Chia (S. columbariae) than thistles.

Ellis McCauley

CATCH WEED

Catch Weed. 1. An annual, fast-growing, herbaceous weed with sticky, tiny hook-shaped spines on its stems and whorls of eight leaves with tiny white flowers. *2.* Recent Age. Galium aparine, also called "Cleavers," is a species of Bedstraws whose roasted fruits can be used to make Cleaver coffee. The young leaves can be eaten raw or cooked.

BOREALIS
TWINFLOWER

Borealis Twinflower. *1. Evergreen plant, also known as "bellvine", whose white, bell-shaped flowers contain a bioluminescence that glows at night, this plant often harbors Flumbaran faeries, giving the flowers a look of twinkling and changing color in addition to their natural luminescence.* **2.** *Recent Age. Linnaea borealis. Creeping evergreen plant having pink bell-shaped flowers.*

❧ Chapter 2 ❧

There is no grace in the art of falling, even if well practiced.

—Battle-hardened dwarven maxim

Leaf peered down the moss-trodden path that led out of the Forest. So many had come this eve from whence a grandeur reigned of impossible possibilities. Imaginings of far and away places—of senses—of literal actualities meant to be experienced: taste, touch, smell . . .

Oh, distant abodes of my heart's mind, how will I ever really know you from the margins of Alderelm's protective graces? Leaf thought.

The freckles within her eyes were seared in sharp glints as the first night's breeze brushed enticement across her face. 'Twas alive with sentience, nipping and tugging playfully at her, invigorating her spirit. She turned back and faced the snakelike path that returned to Alderelm's heart. The wind's ever-wayward breath was not deterred, giggling joyfully through song. Leaf pined to join the wafting sprite, but this was not the Treean way; they did not leave their Forest.

She eased her spent frame upon her knees and lowered her head. She sat there for about the time of a three-cricket chorus when, at once,

her awareness was drawn to the lower slopes. Standing to her feet, she
scanned the lower Woods.

There's naught but Nature's course of creatures, she told herself, still
casting her eyes below while listening to see if Bristleton's voice was
perhaps being carried on the breeze from above. Silence beyond the
breeze tickling new spring greens was all she heard.

Far below by the riverbank, she thought she espied movement,
brisk, swift, and effortless as a sylph swimming the upper currents of the
sky. Promptly standing, she strained to discern the presence. The
trickling rivulet to her side and the rushing river farther away made a
wash of any distinct sounds. She listened for approaching footsteps;
none there came. Shadows quickly appeared and faded, playing tricks
upon her senses. Frustrated, she looked to the sky, but weighty clouds
taunted and teased, allowing only brief, intermittent peeks of moon and
starlight.

So engrossed in the yon Forest, she started when Loyla, the lone
elk, settled silkily to her side. The massive deer's attention was also fixed
on the river outland, and Leaf rested her palm upon the sorrel coat that
twitched beneath her touch. Nostrils flaring, Loyla took deep draws of
the air, a chill growing there. Her head was high and alert, perfectly
motionless. The smell of earth rose from her warm fur, and Leaf dug her
fingers into the elk's thick and shaggy mane. Loyla snorted, purging her
tension as she held her pose, eyes radiant.

Above their heads, a goshawk glided noiselessly beneath the canopy
save for the rustling of the few limbs it dared glance, which stirred the
yon Trees into canorous, low-toned chants. Loyla snorted and pawed the
ground. Her ears pricked forward—not even a breath swelled her chest.
Then, in an instant, she was off, bounding down the slopes with the
grace and soundlessness of her kind.

Leaf hurried after her, trailing the elk's direction while staying on a
secure path. One switchback, two, three, and there, it came into sight,

the antiquity that was the mighty Bridge of Telldon. Her footfalls drew to a halt. To cross this sanctity was to cross outside of Alderelm's borders; Muse contrived with the Tempts, calling the Treean closer, playing upon Leaf's mind in cloudy drifts.

Contemplating her course of action, the burbling of the Notturn Guards averted her attention. With overwhelming delight at her presence, the four Bridge Keepers, the Umbra Trees of the Braemarian borough of Notturn, brought from the MiddleLands as saplings long ago, tickled her toes and radiated greetings throughout her nettles. She smiled.

The bark of these lordly Trees revealed the truth behind tales considered a myth. Long ago, and deep within the Lethoss Mountains, the Umbra Trees had once grown to mighty sizes, needing barely any water, sun, or even the tonic, earthly air to sustain them. They only required the mysterious light of Etherea, a stone-art replica of the dragon who long and peaceably shared the Braemarian's residence within those long, endless halls, even miraculously raising her young aside theirs— with not a single casualty on record.

The statue's realism in all appearances and proportions was startling, but more, it was chiseled within a single lifetime from the hands of a solitary, blind Braemarian maiden. Carved out of frost—with granite mined from the Black Caverns—the statue cast a luminance of such brilliance that 'twas an inexplicable wonder under whose light the Umbrae blossomed in plenty.

Alas, this tale comes to a grievous end. The late First Age, by the MiddleLands calendar of reckoning, found the Northling Braemarians battling growing hordes of goblins for occupancy of the Cavern Cities, central amongst which was the borough of Notturn. The Umbra Trees fell rapidly under cruel, quick axes. The Trees were known to scream so audibly as to echo far outside the caves. Nature was silenced in horror.

Hence, the end of myth and legend finds the last of the known Umbra Trees residing as wards of Alderelm, where these sentinels now blossom under the sun and stars once again. Strange and perfectly domed canopies mark them as unique, but their preference for work and duty over keepings of history mark them as an oddity within the Ancient Forest.

In perfect accord, the very day of their arrival, so freshly brought from Notturn, their hard-working whims of nature were exemplified: a bridge over the confluence of tributaries was ever being reclaimed unto the earth, safe passage could barely be made save by creatures small. The four Umbrae collectively burrowed their roots in eager anticipation of a job at hand. And so, they became the four Bridge Keepers, where green-blue planks and boughs now make up the Bridge of Telldon. The Notturn Guards, as the Treeans refer to the gentle sentinels, thus found sanctuary from extinction within the honor of a duty they perform to this day.

Berries of blue upon the quinque vines offer reassurance to those wary of crossing the bridge over the deep gulch; meanwhile, the climbing tendrils, swooping in arches of elegance, adorn a traveler with many braces of handles. Waters greet with laughter, lapping the turns and crevices of crumbled rock, eager to join the Sasa River. All life here relishes amidst the misty spray tossed about from the cascade's turbulent joy. Any appearance of harm is not to be had as the Guards of Notturn are a most welcoming entrance to the flower-lit Mountain of Trees.

Leaf's head was full of conflict. What drew her here? And why did these feelings of both hesitation and eagerness pull upon her spirit? She made her mind firm, then set foot onto the bridge. A bough cracked and groaned as one of the Umbra reached out and softly touched her.

Leaf smiled. "I'll be okay, Edassa; I'm not alone." She looked to the other side of the bridge. Loyla was over there, and the Treean felt a new confidence swelling within her. "I'll be back before a nut can fall on the Forest floor."

Edassa objected and held her fast. The sentinel giant could do naught to aid the little Treean across the border.

"Edassa, I'm nigh a full-grown Treean, so no doting . . . or communicating to the others. Please let me cross quietly. I must."

Edassa answered with whimpers that reverberated through the soles of Leaf's feet, but her boughs resumed their course upon the bridge. Leaf sighed in relief, knowing it well within the Tree's ability to protest with deafening bellows. The gentle giants of Alderelm, eternally more tender than their immense size would predicate them to be, proved time and time again a predominance for subtle tones of softer voice.

She could sense Edassa's entreaties, resonations soft and repeating, echoes underfoot spreading through the tips of her fingers as she descended further, impelled onwards into this foreign Woodland. The new sensations, sights, and sounds held her captive. The tongue of this wilderness was foreign to her; the twinkling lights of the borealis did not play amongst her feet, and more, the Trees were ever so still and quiet. She could smell the moisture of the Sasa, and her heart beat faster as each step brought its sound of rushing water louder upon her ears. She was very nigh, if not wholly and altogether, forgetting her purpose, her eyes desperate to view the river, excitement palpable upon her tongue.

The ground was becoming increasingly like rock melded into the Earthen crust, creating a promenade that smoothed over and swelled like a crested wave just broken, ever so worn and smooth, sinking back into the soil from whence it originally appeared. The dark evening hid the reality of the danger beneath the Treean's feet that even now maintained no small height over the banks of the Sasa, the rocky crag staying silent as she shuffled and crept.

Catching a glimpse of light cast upon these rushing waters would be a beauty to behold. But then, to hear the colliding march of water and rock might be good enough for now, Leaf thought.

Alderelm

So much sound to fill the ear, a rumbling, deep-throated roar she could ne'er have imagined. Complete and utter captivation entranced her. Her flesh turned ivory, her vine nettles curled in tight spirals, and she momentarily lost her breath, for there she beheld her! So swiftly, the Sasa's water did flow, glowing brightly as her green iciness set off sparks of light in pools and eddies. The Sasa did not need the moon to highlight her caresses amongst the battered boulders; her brilliance lit the banks as if stars themselves lived and shone from beneath! Leaf forgot herself, so lost was she in the river's misty dance, and lived for the first time, purely, in a single moment.

Loyally, the Treean's ears and eyes watched and listened to the dance and song before her, but her feet could not stay true—many small stones of eroding sediment crumbled beneath her. In an instant, the Treean was on her backside as loosening earth gathered momentum around her. Sorely caught off guard, her stunned mind came around to reality. The instinct to right herself provided enough time for a hopeless slide. Her mind sharpened, realizing too late its error. Frantically, she grasped for a hold of a branch, root, or rock, but her clutching fingers found only disintegrating debris. There was naught to hinder the descent into the rapids below. Inevitability whispered.

Ellis McCauley

QUINQUE VINES

Quinque Vines. 1. *Trailing woody-stemmed plant of slender yet extraordinarily strong stem possessing many small, blue-berried fruits and often found growing in and forming a non-random shape. Of the first class of acutely sentient plants.* ***2.*** *Recent Age. Unidentified*

❧ Chapter 3 ❧

Father, son,
Though not bloodborne,
Ne'er fight, ne'er fight,
And be by will,
In the day and night,
That you always stand together.

—The tender entreaty of the Black Cherry Tree of Epahius, Eowyn, to the Raven wizard Lyle of Longcast and his son Durmyne, who did not know Trees could communicate before that day

'Twas just as Bristleton predicted; many had come upon the borders of Alderelm. Most of the travelers stood, too unsettled to casually sit and converse. Perceptive to each and every tension beholden in the air, Sage's gaze swept around the others and settled on the waters of Lumen. His eyes followed her path. Gently, she tumbled down delicate ledges of algae-covered rock into a smaller tarn of starlit gleam. Casual whirls of dance were her delight as she followed her course to the narrow confines of a rill. He listened intently to the peaceful sound of her grace, giving him respite from the wrenching suffering that rang endlessly in his ears.

Long life was his fate, the fate of his kind. Within his life, many seasons had passed without account. Time was worth naught, for what it brought was too terrible to recall or forget. Sensitive an elf as ever there was, his was a battle ceaselessly fought. Yet in such moments when Nature performed her chimes of tranquility, he became one with its ethereal essence.

Bristleton fixed an eye upon the elf and took to thought. *Sorrow etches itself deeply about his face. Why must it plant itself upon him so permanently? From whence did such sorrow arise? Yet those eyes, although streaked with the wild itself, surely, are still the eyes of overbrimming cordiality, windows to a heart most plentiful in empathy and compassion. Aye. Sage's openness to emotion is the very quality that makes him the most loyal of friends, but also the saddest of companions.*

Bristleton sighed and touched his dear friend's shoulder. Sage shuddered under the realism of the moment cast upon him so abruptly.

"Aelin-lumen, tukyle mei," Sage softly murmured, carrying elven breaths of renewed vigor, which enveloped an essence of reverence known only by those beings of the earthliest spirits.

The crystalline Highness of the Lumen did answer with a sovereign suspiration of tender tinkles upon her lambent edges and then released him. He was sorry for it.

"Come," said Bristleton, ushering Sage hence, "the Hall of Alderelm awaits."

There, a procession of many kinds descended out of sight upon rock steps that entered the depths of a corridor's deep recesses. Cracked and broken by age and the intrusion of mammoth roots, the stairway appeared held in place by naught save the lichen that covered it. However, wary travelers upon weary feet needn't fret, for ancient stones were settled securely upon roots of tender and purposeful poise as water droplets echoed amidst an otherwise quiet atmosphere.

Around the second turn of soft darkness, a cool air arose, as inviting as the scent of rain not yet fallen. The hall was nigh. Sage took pause and held a humble hand to his heart. Others passed him with little notice, the many footsteps mixing with the echoes of his memories. As he thought it, a dilapidated mind such as his ought not to enter a place such as this, and though delighted to be embraced in Alderelm's charm, he took his first steps into the great hall consumed with the difficulty of retracing old footsteps.

Then there, gaping amazement distracted his memory's thoughts. Ne'er had he thought it possible, but the beauty of the place had grown! The once enormous Trees were now astoundingly colossal, stretching up effortlessly through the top of the cavern. Giant burls and knots of outgrowth upon the titanic boles supported the golden glow of many a candle, thus giving beholders glimpses of the excontalitus stones set within the vine-ridden walls. These stone prisms reflected the taper light cast upon them, thus adorning the council with a vivid spectrum of rainbow-colored light.

With a reserved politeness and formality, Bristleton bid Sage to sit. Four carved Tree trunks fashioned as long council seat benches of varying lengths were a sight that change had not visited. Some familiar faces were about, but most he had ne'er seen.

Bristleton excused himself abruptly, and Sage cast a suspicious eye upon his friend's retreating footsteps. To this end, utter dismay held the elf with many successive groans laying barely quiet beneath his lips as he watched Bristleton approach one of the Treean elders—one he knew well—Knowlton Hophornbeam. There was no use in desperate wishing, for Bristleton had already bent over the Heartwood's shoulder; he began to speak, a punctuated stillness thus arresting the well-aged Treean's frame. Sage watched. Seconds passed, and Knowlton remained rigidly unchanged. Sage held his breath and considered the lack of a revulsive response improbable, unexpected, and more, verily impossible. Yet the balance of the natural world was assured and restored, for the old temblor sprang from his seat with an impressive start. He turned toward the elf, eyes narrow. What else was a Coyotl to do but smile and wave cheerfully? And oh, how innocent an act did elicit the old Treean's vigor; Knowlton clenched his fists while his face seized up, distorted and reddening; his eyes narrowed to minuscule slits of harshness; his craggy fists shook in the air. Sage was contented to have prompted such a response. Still and all, the elf's resultant pride began to shift into dismay as the Heartwood fussed and spat with rabid, unutterable exclamations until, at last, the swollen-faced elder lost enough breath to force his attention back to his closer comrades.

Meanwhile, Bristleton strode back to Sage in an airy, if not highborn way. Sage held fixed eyes of disbelief upon him, but still, the marchwarden said naught and watched the council room's goings-on. The Coyotl could not decide which emotion should take him, so wholly bemused was he by the audacity of his old friend's actions.

"Bris." Sage broke out in a loud whisper. "As border guard and Treean, I know you feel my stare upon you."

Bristleton raised an eyebrow, but his gaze remained fixed ahead.

"Was it really necessary to tell old Ironwood of my presence? You know he doesn't consider me on any high account—obviously."

Bristleton replied in a tone firm but soft, as if a touch of the elementals lay distantly amongst his heritage. "You'd be surprised to what account you're held, and aye, it was necessary."

The elf sighed, his expression one of resolute dejection, but his voice and manner remained amiable, albeit infused with sarcasm. "This should be a fine gathering."

Council had not yet begun; much was going on about the room, but the discussion platform was beginning to draw more and more attention after Knowlton's outburst, for an intense dialogue with marked heat was unfolding amongst the four Treean elders. Knowlton stood to speak. Although small in stature, he was tough and doughty. The utmost respect was given him from all kinds across the Wood and

Field, for many stories were his to tell and true to the spirited nature of Treean calling.

"The way of the Treeans is to stay within the borders of the Ancient Forest. There is no other way; we are the guardians!"

"Yes, Knowlton," replied Freemont, the elder of the Cottonwoods. "Guardians, we are by choice, but you know none have aye desired to reach outside the Forest."

"And now we're presented with such," added Hardtack, the elder of the Mountain Mahoganies, a branch of the Birch house—Knowlton's House. He looked to the elder, Willow, and back to Knowlton. His gentle spirit was of great concern. "Do we dictate what one's desires ought to be?"

Freemont nodded, his tall, broad frame a mountain. "We've ne'er done so in the past, nor is it our way to do so."

"We honor what we are," growled Knowlton. "Our spirits are tied to these Trees. Our nature is to stay rooted and protect the repository of knowledge and history they hold. This cannot be ignored."

The elders quieted and began to ponder the issue at hand deeply. Silence fell upon the hall. Sage grew fidgety in his seat, and as it happened, Knowlton looked toward him, irritation plainly seen. Their eyes locked. The wily elf could not fathom the need to weigh such an issue so heavily.

"Hauumph," Sage said. "Excuse me."

The low rumbling of shocked whispers floated around the hall. All eyes were on him.

Aghast, the bark of Knowlton's neck thickened, and the long branches of his head crackled as they rose out from the depths of his mane. "Council has not been called to order! And what would a non-Treean have to say on this matter besides?"

Sage knew only one way to speak—forthrightly—though the technique often lacked tact, and he was pleased to be asked the question.

"Everyone knows your kind are dying."

Indefensible gasps spread around the hall. Although a fact well known, to have made such an utterance with such nonchalance was, for most, too much to reason upon; Sage found the effect enthralling. Bristleton's lips were drawn tight, and his jaws flexed, but no surprise was found in his overall expression.

The Coyotl's plight encouraged, he continued, "Why do you argue about what is not yours to decide? Leaf, as I assume you speak, will be a grown Treean soon and one without her people. Her desire to reach outside your confines will benefit her, if not all of you."

Knowlton snarled. "These matters aren't your concern."

"No, quite the contrary—they are!" said Sage, evenly matched in ill temper. "Why do you quibble amongst yourselves on this subject . . . over your Lastborn? How can there be no discussion on your dwindling kind? Look at yourselves—so few! Far fewer than my sojourn of late. What will happen to the Sacred Ones when you all pass? Look what is afore you! Why do you not defend yourselves? You defend the Trees readily! What madness makes logic of this?"

"Defend ourselves against what exactly?" Knowlton snapped, gesticulating wildly.

"The dark approaching shadow! You must feel it."

"We feel it more than any," said Knowlton, near becoming an ox in searing irritability.

"Your people are the Guardians of the Great Trees, which all here love deeply," said Sage calmly, gracious in tone and posture, rising to his feet while extending an arm in deference. "Much respect is given to you for this. But we all have a stake in this Forest, these lands, and our common beginnings."

"No stake is greater than our own," insisted Knowlton, his chest swelling like many a superior-minded male full of false wit and arrogance on their way to confession. "We alone are the Guardians of the Sacred

Trees! You have no voice on such an issue!"

The cavern echoed as Sage boomed, "Knowlton Hophornbeam!" His eyes glinted as one with death dripping upon his blade. "Many have fought and died fighting battles for Alderelm—friends as you call—though not did Treeans take up arms and fight if crossing your flower-lit borders came to call! How does one measure stake in blood? Is a Tree's sap worth more than all, even yourselves? Let all here be granted voice and worth."

Knowlton did not comment, nor had he chosen to meet the gaze of the Coyotl of Tirades. Unspoken contentions from history past were bringing forth unsettled issues long staved. Torrential emotions laid bare two unyielding personas of beckoning passions.

The Lady Heartwood, Willow Elder, of the branches Elder and Willow, and residing additionally over her distant relations of the Hawthorn branch, nodded ever so slightly to the rough-stalked Hardtack, who turned to the elf and spoke, his voice heavy with empathy. "You must understand, most Treeans cannot psychologically leave these lands. We are as much a part of the Trees as the Trees are of the land, with roots that spread deep and vast within the soil of Alderelm. The bond we share with the Sacred Ones is nearly as two beings sharing the same spirit. You know this, Lagacious. Why do you press us?"

"As you said, my Heartwood. Most."

Somewhere in a distant reckoning, Knowlton comprehended these last utterances. Deep furrows upon his brow were the design of an exceptionally brilliant mind resting heavy on haunting words, and the sunken tunnel of the past produced tears that collected within the windows to his spirit. Sage beheld this and was taken aback. He strode forth to the old temblor and knelt before him.

"The intensity of such pain upon your person I did not desire. Forgive me, My Heartwood, I have bled with you on occasion."

Knowlton nodded. "You must fight now, even if outside the borders the fight calls you . . . or your Lastborn."

"Even if you traveled beyond the vastness of your imaginings," whispered Knowlton, visibly shaken, "you could ne'er fathom the torture of watching those you hold dear die from afar—or worse—wonder whereabouts they are—did they survive? Does he coil alone in suffering? Will he return?"

A dark and brumous shadow rested upon the elf's countenance. "Returned he has." It was the first time in many an age that Sage had beheld those deep brown eyes, and he was humbled to see how dimmed they had become beneath the grey fog of advanced age.

The old Ironwood put the Coyotl's hand within both of his; they became fixed with a palsy-like tremor. The feathered catkins that formed his hoary beard wafted and curled under his softening emotions, loosening their downy tendrils with each exhale. "We can hold no loyalty beyond the Trees and, thus, beyond Alderelm herself."

Sage lowered his head in a surrendered dismay and let loose a chuckle blended with a deep sigh. He scratched his hair in exasperation, tethered to a patience reached well inside himself.

A faerie of the Flumbaran stood up. He garnered much attention for the action, not least for the disturbance created by the rapid pattering of his wings. His quickening footsteps approached the elder's forefront while his head held a questioning tilt. And as he spoke, his voice crackled like old fallen leaves under the whirl of wind. "Forgive me, but this be not entirely true—ye have defended others beyond your borders a time or two. 'Tis been a while, no doubt about that, I can feel Father Time's passing in me bones. But indeedy, you here Treeans haven't always just watched. Why do ye hide these there particulars?"

His words paused while his head moved in bird-like fashion, to and fro, and his wings fluttered rapidly; then his footfalls halted, and his wide eyes blinked the mysterious spirit of faeries. Inching closer to Knowlton, he cocked his face as he spoke. "There be a few of ye I might even recognize who have taken cause with others. Many an arrow soar'in high into the air on behalf of not a single Tree," and so saying, the fae bowed deeply.

"A frightening experience to have beheld, for few arrows ever missed their mark," said a low melodic voice.

Sage recognized the voice forthwith and swung around. Ell'oyn, long lived in loyal command to Yor'el, stood with her kin, the sylphs. Regimented wings of brown-spiced feathers lay tucked but ready for ordered flight behind her.

"Forgive me for speaking," continued she, "but there holds little tradition to this council."

Sage gazed in no less amazement, even relief, at the old Ironwood Hophornbeam, who himself brushed away her words with a shrug. Sage became overwhelmed with more than some assurance.

"Nonsense, fanciful talk," Knowlton grumbled.

"It be legend, pardon me speak'in," said another Flumbaran.

"Ullot," growled Knowlton, turning around to Nimott while keeping a finger aimed at the other. "From the same mold of Nimott do you sprout, yet be it possible, thou art twice as bothersome."

"Oh sir," replied Nimott, "we're families of distant but distinct purpose, indeedy. No relation assured."

"If you must torture us," said a haggard yet strangely amused Freemont, "then for welkin's sake proceed to your point," and so saying, he raised his eyebrows eagerly. "Please."

"Ah, yes. Thank ye truly. Ye see, I grew up hear'in all the stories of the Treean warriors! A secret league—"

"Bah! Bedtime stories ... Treean warriors!" said Knowlton, laughing with a starchiness that pointed to more an accurate account of the bedtime stories than his outburst would have preferred to permit. Willow lowered her head, and Sage distinctly saw her hiding a subtle smile behind her hand; for the discourse being outlandish or Knowlton being caught in a truth well hidden, Sage had a bemused and rightly guess.

"And they com'in ta defense of those good and true; they do indeedy. But by gaw, if thou'st not pure, make ye path wide round Alderelm, for no truer shot be had, than from high in them yore Trees, if ye be'in bad. Them's tha stories littlies are told, yes indeedy."

Willow Elder came off her seat as gently as the morning mist rises and evaporates before the sun's fingertips. She was the oldest and wisest of the Treeans, and although age had set to work, it had merely succeeded in refining her. Silver hair shone with the brightness of life, and the leaves within it were green and vivid. To the center of the hall did she stride, the lightest tinkling of her garment softening the look of her eyes, akin to an eagle's: piercing gold, alert, and sharp.

"All here," she began, "hear me. Life is born of one seed . . . to many variations. Diversity and its inherent complexity endow us with great gifts in our turbulent existence. And, too, let us not forget our commonalities. From the most fragile flower to the stoutest Tree, all have a purpose, and none is greater than another's."

Then, Willow Elder turned to the elf and elder and paused. The silence crept painfully around the growing tension it produced. Her gaze tore them down, and the two became instant expressions of scolded children. Yet, her voice was forgiving.

"Sage Lagacious and Knowlton Hophornbeam, darkness begins to befall around us; let it not fall within us. Deeds here have not been forgotten. Both thy hearts have always been in keeping," and so saying, her eyes swept the hall. There were none her gaze did not meet. "Let ease take hold of this council, each in each other—'tis all we truly have."

❧ Chapter 4 ❧

Fury of the heart,
Light of the day,
No act of vile can be had.
Bound—now fey—a Haevonen leads the way.

—Cinnabar Moth tells Field Cricket of the Haevonen stallion's death

Leaf's descent came to a jarring halt, and her shirt tightened hard around her neck. Her legs struck out furiously; she was gasping for breath, choking, flailing in search of the object that snarled her. She reached behind her for a hold of anything to grasp and pull herself up, her mind envisioning an exposed root. Yet, she did not find a root.

The softness of warmth took hold of her arm, and with her airway free, gulping breaths encompassed her. Tilting her head backward, she beheld, albeit upside down, a sedate smile, the smile of an elf. She clasped her hand around his arm and worked to swing her other arm to his. Time slowed. The Fierce-Eyed Elf was reposed, granting perfect tranquility—he had to be Puman. In a situation as desperate as ever she had known, instant ease saturated her.

The elf worked to pull her up while her feet scrambled for solid footing; only one knee was to find it, and most unfortunately, in the form of a jutting rock. A flash of headlong agony interrupted all concerns of her plight as a pain of blinding proportions seared through the joint. An eternity passed, but Leaf could finally pull her foot atop the blood-stained protrusion. She heaved herself upward, bits of dirt and rubble falling and catching in her eyes. While debris distracted her, she found another bit of basalt, footing enough to enable the elf to clutch her fully and pull her to the level Forest floor.

"Thank you, thank you," she breathed, a cold shiver shaking her.

"Take better care; being splayed is unbecoming, to be sure," returned the Fierce-Eyed Elf, more preoccupied with their surroundings than with Leaf, who herself sat perplexed at how completely and utterly unimpressed he appeared after her nigh demise. "You've beheld the smoke?" asked the elf, looking her in the eyes for the first time.

Leaf nodded numbly.

The elf's brow furrowed. "Hem. A quality adrift draws me here," and so saying, his kind yet ever-so-flashing eyes took her in for some moments with a sidelong stare. "Perhaps," he mused, a sly smile breaking the tension upon his countenance, "the azure tips of the mighty wind drive forth, which might save thy hide?"

Leaf simpered, trying to get to her feet. "Perhaps."

Southward, on the other side of the river, a flurry of birds took flight, and the Fierce-Eyed Elf pulled her back down to the ground from which she had just attempted to rise. She gazed wearily at him, but he did not now pay her any mind. She wondered if he might have derived some sinister pleasure in the action, for the brutishness behind it seemed entirely unnecessary. Her nerves were still wayward in recovery, and her breath was hard-pressed to match her heart, yet the soil was rich and sweet and mixed harmoniously with the elf's presence.

The little Treean mustered the best of herself. "I have felt drawn here as well."

She felt ridiculous when he did not reply. She stared up at him in no small wonderment, and at last, he turned his gaze down to her.

"I'm from Alderelm," she said. "Do you know of it?"

"Alderelm!" replied the elf in reverent astonishment. "A guardian of the History Keepers, a Treean, graces me?"

"Yes! Ah, well, not quite." She sighed and shook her head in frustration. "Yes, I'm a Treean, but graced you are not. You saved my life. I don't know how to thank you."

"You honor me with your words, but it was not me," countered the elf in almost a whisper. "More than chance is at work this night." He glanced at Leaf's wounded knee and then to the river. "Stay here. I'll return to help you back to Alderelm with all possible speed."

"No, wait!" implored Leaf, struggling to her feet.

Her words fell empty, for the elf had left her side before they were spoken. Only could the Treean watch as he flitted away into the darkness. Blood trickled down her shin, a pitiful reminder of her enraging predicament.

Eternally left behind, thought she, and this so frustrated her that she dared place weight upon the foiled appendage. *Tolerable*, she reckoned with a wince and went hobbling after the elf.

Elves and Treeans are equally light-footed, still and all, Leaf's injury hit her with jolts of mind-numbing pain. Limping is a slow process, and it interrupts the natural sounds of the Forest. Even so, Leaf was nothing if not made of a determined mind. Thus, she was not long on his coattails. Sensing her, the elf drew up and turned to face her, holding up a hand. She halted, realizing they were only a few paces from the riverbank.

A somber air fell upon the character of the place, and she swallowed hard. A deep groan broke the air with a cold quiet left behind in the sound. Leaf envisioned childlike nightmares of a grotesque misshapen or otherwise tortured beast, and so scared was she, her body was as stone, heavy, and immovable.

For the elf's part, nevermore was his keenness thwarted; his gaze was concentrated, his grey-white eyes blazoned.

Eternity is itself, time, yet time is still set to pass save for now, Leaf thought, so slow it seemed to dredge.

Anticipation dripped. Then, at once, the suffocating stillness was split on the far side of the river. A shadowy figure, immense but faltering, bespattered the Sasa's dark confines with halting footfalls. The quality of the air held Leaf and the elf tight within a viscous abyss of acute wonder and sorrow. Burdened breaths, strained and wet, were a life force of quality diminishing despite its strength of will. And if the river were not so loud, Leaf could have sworn that under these breaths of death's arrival arose the softest chant of lamenting song.

The elf walked fore, gently parting the scrappy brush within the rock-riddled mush. Leaf's overwhelming curiosity endowed strength of courage against her fear and hesitation to follow the elf's strides.

Phew, whew, phew, whew, arose an erratic, labored wheezing within the shallows of the middle river waters. And therewith, the lightest whisper of gentle wind ushered away the mist enough to reveal a surreal sight of pathetic nature . . . and the most beautiful creature Leaf had aye beheld.

"Lawks—he's of the Haevonen," the elf whispered reverently.

Leaf recollected the horses of Haevonen, a mystical breed of equine. Yet she knew no more, for she was too far from the Ancient Ones to absorb their knowledge. She gaped.

The Haevonen lay upon his side, yet even then, he was both formidable and gallant. A stallion of massive proportions, his nostrils flared with each breath, and his ribs heaved with terrible effort. The feathered hair upon his legs was matted with Forest debris, and blankets of dried blood entangled his mane. Leaf's eyes followed the curve of his neck to the windows of his spirit—they shone defiantly, but their light of life was waning. Sorrow consumed her heart while fear abandoned it, and she approached the Black Beast. As she did so, she felt a lapse in the flow of time while a mournful hum arose from the plumes of faerie dust. The atmosphere was a haze of synchronism, a trance of the otherworld. Blending with this, a low, menacing growl arose behind them. Very slowly, she turned around, and the pendulum of time resumed its course.

"Life comes in large size outside Alderelm," Leaf murmured, tugging at the elf's jerkin.

A timberwolf of enormous proportions moved stiffly toward them, and every aspect of the creature was intense: appearance, gaze, movements—its energy rippled. Hackle hairs extended from the nape of the creature's neck to the tip of its tail. Rigid, the timberwolf stalked, baring its yellowed canines in fits and starts as it snarled and salivated.

"Na tan naka," said a voice of nectar.

Leaf turned to behold a figure of grieving stance. She had appeared from a blending of the air. Plush as the petals of faerie rings was her look. Gold, red, and yellow were the blends of her hair—as in the most vivid autumns of Alderelm or a late winter sunset. She strode to the wolf and lay a hand upon the grey head. It softened under her touch; however, the glaring eyes of distrust would not let their captives go, keeping their focus on the elf and Leaf. And though the growling had ceased, its dagger-like teeth remained loyal to their fearsome display under a tightly curled muzzle.

The elf's eyes were fixed upon the lady, bared to the spirit. He stood as though the entrancing spells of times forgotten held him fast and not so unwillingly. Profound feelings of ardor opened an abyss of emotions as his focus turned to thoughts of the inward heart rarely traveled by his guarded nature.

The loud pronouncements of unkind voices crashed upon the yonder side of the river. The lady took notice of naught but the sad creature, once of full might and glory, beginning now the quiver of imminent death. Gently humming, she knelt beside the Shadow of Nights, and as hums turned into a melodic language of color, the voices indicated that the dreadful wake of their persons was fast approaching.

In guttural groans of pain, the great stallion attempted to get on his iron feet but merely succeeded in lifting his giant head. The Lady of Soft Dirge urged him back down. Gentle words of glittering rainbows mixed with tears. Freely, they flowed down her cheeks and landed on his great neck. His quivering muscles began to relax, for alas, his effort had been too great; he took one last breath and no more.

The Lady of Golden Sunsets looked up at them slowly, deep-seated pain within her eyes, but also a strength ingrained therein, so profound as to have etched itself forever in Leaf's memory. Time's heartbeat became irregular, and the lapses in this constancy intermingled with the voices of afar now bestriding them.

Leaf looked to the elf whose hands had found their comfort, in no wasted time, upon bow and arrow. He was at home within his weapon's grasp. Of no second nature was its course, being an extension of his very self; the killing instrument was primary, having proved a staple of survival in wayward journeys. And now, the glistening horn bow, knotted and well-traveled, marked its sights yet again toward those of threatening purpose, human kind on this occasion.

The look of menacing reproach did not seem the men's proper semblance. There was a nobleness to their posture, but the sight of what Leaf and the elf had just witnessed allowed little negation for ill intentions. Four held ground to their fore, and as far as Leaf could tell, three drew nigh from behind. Soldiers, sentries to Seayr, each bearing its mark—the City of the Sea. She had not heard of conflicts arising from this land and was puzzled by all about her.

She saw that these strangers possessed steeds not unlike the one growing cold to her side. A frightening lot of equine masterworks, stamping and snorting about, yet beautiful, verily. The commotion that ensued was thunderous, with clanking metal and shouting. One rider rushed her, and she fell backward, staring at giant hooves brushing the air. She had not expected such an affront but was quick to scamper aside and out from under the crashing hooves that now stomped furiously about her person. No slight stretch of space separated her from the uncivilized brute's massive head, for from her view, his stature touched the firmament. The creature was a pillar of flaring nostrils and champing teeth, and the rider was its spire.

Wearing a red cloak with fringed edges, Leaf figured the horseman a man of some weight amongst his people, for although the cloak was soiled and well worn, it was of regal appearance. Yet then, she decided 'twas not the cloak that endowed this man, for on most, the garment would surely look like a tattered hood of peasants, but instead, the man himself possessed an innate quality of stature. And although Leaf did not hold a whisper of fondness for the man, an aspect in his eyes called for respect.

"Move aside!" the horseman snapped.

"You find your feet upon the foothills of Alderelm, the sacred realm of the Ancient Trees," replied the elf, grinding tight his jaw. "You would be wise to find your courtesy."

The horseman narrowed his eyes. "I care not a lick about Alderelm or its supposed Great Trees. We come with direct authority from King Orrin's—"

The elf broke off the horseman's reply, disregarding that he was even speaking, by turning his attention to another one of the men. "You've encountered this little wolf?" the elf said, grinning and gesturing toward the timberwolf crouched in menacing silence within the shadows.

"Ah!" the man yelped, both at the remark and at the sight of the creature. The man's arm seeped blood over torn remnants of cloth.

"Little wolf! That creature is of the Dark Realm!"

There was an incorrigible nature astir in this wolf, only slightly tempered by the Lady of Wold Reflections, and the soldier's outburst set the creature to work on guttural growls of terrifying pitch. Of all the foes within this collection of conflicted individuals, she was the one looked upon with the most caution. Her growl arose as if out of the fire realm itself.

The horseman dismounted with a robust huff, glaring quickly at the other who had spoken out of turn. The lady left the side of the fallen steed to face him, each of them. One by one, she stopped and looked them straight through, her scrutinizing eye causing each man to shift his weight uneasily and hang his head low. Her presence was ineffable; the moments that passed were like a dream overlooking the ever-changing waves of the sea. When she arrived at last before the red-cloaked horseman, long did she stare into him; deep did she bore.

Her intrusive regard for his person was a double-edged knife cleaving his spirit, and with no small effort, he found his tongue. "You have stolen from the Land of Seayr. We have been commanded to bring that creature back with us," said he, looking past her, his pride beginning to push aside his discomfort.

Still, the gentlewoman did not move, and Leaf felt the tension unbearable. Tears the Treean did not expect poured like an unguent for the spirit, and she ran headlong toward the horseman. Many swords came forth to halt her progress; their tips lay eagerly against her face. The Leaf of Alderelm turned as rigid as the needles of the Old Pinus and as ashen-white as the dead. Behind her, the elf's bow creaked.

"Lower your weapons," breathed the elf, his piercing grey-white eyes veiled with a glowering ferocity.

The horseman was, for a moment, held in disbelief. He glanced around him and laughed outright. More sniggering spilled from his companions while three more in hiding seeped forth from the brush behind the fallen Black Beauty.

"You stand alone and outnumbered," said the horseman, laughing.

"He's not alone," replied Leaf.

The leader chuckled as he stared at the puzzlement before him. "What would you fight us with, little one, a stick? You're young and full of spirit. Do not wish to die on this day. You know naught of what you're up against."

"We are up against treachery and wickedness from the Land of Seayr. A dying horse, a woman—why would men seek after such if not for ill?"

The elf recognized a mettle in the small Treean, and his eyes shone with delight to see it.

The horseman's smile faded, his haughty demeanor now swirling with vexation. "None of this is your concern. The creature is a chattel of the Seayran Lands. The king's lordship decrees it."

Then there, Leaf felt the strength of ten oaks in the arms that shoved her aside. Little stability raked within her body to resist the force thrust against her person while depending almost solely upon one of two legs, and thus, she fell hard and quailed. Pain obscured her sight except for the long, schlepping strides headed toward the seraph corpse, the horseman's swagger a bitter taste on the tongue. The elf rushed gently to her aide, cursing under lip in his native tongue as the lady took to the horseman's side; there was no doubt relief upon the horseman's sweating brow that no challenge befell him.

"Then it is done with this one," the horseman said. His voice was callous, but his expression was layered, managed under pretense, and unable to hide the rueful mask under it all.

The Lady of Golden Sunsets stared at his face; his discomfort rose. The thought of his men seeing him quiver because of a woman was not within his dignity's tolerance. The woes beset upon men were now his alone, as he felt it, and as his gripped mind failed to marshal the situation, an instinct of the primal seeped forth, clouding the very best of his wit. Hastily, his arm grabbed her, that heroine even now taking his heart, as his sight became blinded within shock, for the wolf had laid sweetly into him.

One of the soldiers let loose an arrow upon the rabid creature, but the Fierce-Eyed Elf splayed it with his own before it left the bow's string. He was the quintessence of speed and aim; two more fell in a breath. And near the wilted soldiers, he espied a stick the length of a man's average measure. The elf gazed on the petrified sapwood, blithely musing, and swung round his new weapon, leveling three more of Seayr's valiant to the newly fertilized soil.

Leaf missed none of it. She stood wavering like the green ends of spring clover, both revering and fearing the lethality of her new friend; there was no doubt of his Puman descent, and she recognized the inherent tragedy of their kind. She turned her attention to the lady. The horseman had released his grasp on the gentlewoman in no long struggle, for the timberwolf had wrenched him off his feet and was shaking him from side to side. He was as hapless as a dove in the talons of a kestrel until a lilt of strange utterance passed the lady's lips, and the timberwolf withdrew.

She knelt and took up the horseman's dagger, which had fallen to the ground, and her eyes focused like a wild animal's in hunt. Proceeding to his wretched side, she dug the knife firmly into the tender layer of his neck. The horseman lay shaking with exhaustion and anger. All fighting ceased.

Of the soldiers, three were left standing. They held their weapons ready, but none had the want or heart to test the elf further. Time stood still and waited on the lady. She was a raging river of barely suppressed emotion, and the horseman's mighty person lay in her soft hands. Blood trickled down his neck. The dagger rested tighter and tighter against it.

The lady's voice was sweet. Her lips nearly touched the horseman's ear as she spoke. "There is a part of thy heart, the nethermost part that you forbear . . . it aches to watch the guile, the wickedness upon your land." She drew back and knitted her brow. "Still! You abjure the truth and feign that naught is amiss . . . cooped to fealty for a king who hath benighted thy wits. Tell the king, this mortal man whom you so dearly love, that the stallion of the Haevonen's spirit lives," and so saying, she released him, "And ask yourself, does your lord's?"

The horseman stammered to his feet, clasped his throat, and looked at her in disbelief. His pride had been trampled, and his duty to the king was left unfulfilled. His thoughts searched for acts to save his sullied honor. Rashness overtook him, and he moved to draw his sword. The sword ne'er had hope of awaking from its scabbard. At once and sooner, the elf's new wooden weapon pressed against the horseman's neck; there was no time for the other three to act. The horseman coughed out strangulating breaths.

The Puman's eyes spit flames. "Do not wish to die this day; you know naught what you are up against."

The man would not relent; his thoughts were hardly clear. The timberwolf had gouged thick chunks of flesh, and he was bleeding richly. Chills began taking him as he pondered his chances of striking the elf with the dirk sheathed upon his thigh. *Yes*, he thought, reaching for his leg. *Call this elf to the stars with one thrust.*

The Puman pressed a knowing grin of disdain into the horseman's spirit. A quiescent glimmer lit within the corner of one eye, peculiar if not downright unsettling, not the least for its sudden awakening but for the taunt it elicited. The horseman swallowed hard, his body quitting the fight, dejection gripping his disgrace.

Leaf seemed to be the only one to heed the creaks and cracks of approaching Forest steps. She hoped to see Bristleton and the border guards, but more human kind emerged from the Wood. Yet, they were different in look and garment. Their skin was darker, possessing the hues of Ponderosa bark, while their hair was as dark as a moonless night. They made no hesitation in turning their many lances toward the three and their leader, and Leaf sighed in relief.

"Yolkai Estasan," said one of the dark hairs, the only woman within the new company. "The hawk told us of your need, and the elk led us forward."

The lady nodded and bowed. The newcomers returned her bow simultaneously, though none took their eyes off the foes before them. The Fierce-Eyed Elf released the horseman, who staggered to his mount. The others picked up their fallen companions and backed away. No words were spoken.

All atop their ill-tempered steeds, the Seayran soldiers returned across the river. A sight of tiredness and defeat, none looked back. The elf watched fixedly until the Sasa expelled them entirely upon the yonder bank.

The dark hair faced the elf and held her hand in a fist at her heart. The elf received the gesture with a softening expression and a bow of his head. "Your coming was timely and most welcome. You and your companions are Dauns?"

Her eyes lit up. "True it is. Far from our homes, we find ourselves."

"That seems to be the case for most of us. I am Noblien of the Puman."

"A Puman elf?" she asked, eyebrows raised. "But you look as pale as those who flee. I imagined the Pumans" - she paused, noticing the elf's flinch of disapproval - "forgive me. I am Tullkaee."

The elf replied with genuine geniality, but it was no small struggle for him to have swallowed the Daun's comparison. "Pleasure."

Meanwhile, the Lady of Wold Reflections knelt before Leaf and examined her swollen knee. The Treean stared at her in wide-eyed wonder. The lady smiled.

"The blood hath clotted, but the wound is foul with dirt. Come to the water's edge."

Gingerly, the lady tended to Leaf's wound. She smelled like honeysuckles, and her touch was as soft as ginger clover. *Resplendent in their shine, her eyes reflect the Forest hues, but deeper still,* Leaf thought, *is borne much more.*

"Thou art most brave. What is thy calling?"

"LittleLeaf LeadTree."

The lady smiled and, with utmost delicacy, placed a hand around the back of Leaf's head. Her touch felt like the tingles of gypsy moths, and a rush of heat filled the young Treean's ears, which rang with the bells of the Feeorin. The lady drew Leaf nearer—brow to brow—and the light of life breathed within the Treean's chest. The lady's doe-eyes closed, but Leaf's remained wide. Deep an inhalation did the lady take. The moment held itself against the passing of time. To Leaf's unblinking wonder, the lady reopened her eyes to reveal their brown depths changing into golden amber, the colors stirring in and amongst one another as her pupils narrowed to mere slits and then dilated abruptly with the broadening of her smile.

All watched silently. There was a difference about the lady that none could wrap their minds around. Leaf was unsure what had happened, but the experience had bestowed a soothing comfort and ease most heartily accepted.

The Puman placed himself by the Treean's side. "You, my young friend, have just been formally greeted by a season." Each syllable he uttered was deliberate, well-measured, and held a weight of respectful consideration, and too, accented a smile hidden in the corner of his mouth.

"A season?" Leaf repeated in astonishment.

"Her name is Niveus," he said.

The lady cast her gaze on the elf. 'Twas indescribably steadfast and intertwined with the elf's tender regard, so as together, neither lady nor elf could be described with any adequacy. Leaf had ne'er seen aught like it. One could have combined all the songs of love and ne'er come close to expressing the emotion that flowed between the two, all in simple silence. They stood like this for many moments until her hand stirred, touching the side of the elf's face. Tilting ever so slightly into her palm, he placed his hand over hers. They spoke in brief, in the Elvish tongue. Then the beamlets of her smile shone, and she parted from him, turned to the Dauns, and looked suddenly worn.

"Thank you for your aide. Your people hold dear the language of the Earth," and so saying, Niveus, that Season of Wold Reflections, sighed and looked at the majestic steed's lifeless body. "She groans under the weight of man . . . your coming gives me hope."

Over the corpse, she wavered as pieces of his mane lifted and fell into the water. The wolf howled a long and haunting lament. No one spoke or moved. Too beautiful to be lifeless, the Lost Stallion looked as though he might rise to his feet at any moment, and all wondered why violence sought such unnatural ends to life.

A voice of radiance resounded thick with grief but exultant in hope; the season had taken to song. Harmony melted into the ether of the heavens as the shimmering multi-hued carapaces of the Barsil Orbs swirled around the Fallen One. Then there, unfolding before their hearts of sadness, reflections of a lost life stretched out into a full gallop upon a land of red fields that lay upon the sun's rising fingertips.

"Haverdome," Noblien whispered to Leaf, "home of the Haevonens."

Leaf was full of wonderment and rubbed her eyes. The vision before them was a clear doorway wherein the clouds flowed at half their speed, and infinite seasons roughed out the landscape in wisps of flurried light. Was it a vision? Indeed, it was all impossible. The clouds sped up, and the sky turned from light to dark in rapid succession. Then, it settled under an expansive starlit sky. Fields of greens and reds waxed and waned in synchronized folds of color, and where nigh two hundred stones of weight once lay, amaranth took root within the river rocks of the waterbed. The fallen steed had vanished, all upon one last bloom of spring, and transformed somewhere far away. Yet henceforth, wherewith the group mourned, life would remain where the swamp of death had once claimed triumph . . . in the form of a single, red, unfading flower.

The season's song diminished. The doorway began to fade, and in all his majesty and splendor, the Beast of Beasts now marked the group out and whinnied proud and shrill. From now on, the strength of the Haevonens would forever support their backs.

AMARANTH

Amaranth. 1. A red four-petaled flower with compound heart-shaped leaves found in shallow water, riverbanks, meadows, and forests also known as the unfading flower. **2.** Recent Age. Amaranthus is a cosmopolitan group of more than 50 species of plant or shrub, annual or perennial. Some species are cultivated as leaf vegetables, pseudocereals, and ornamental plants and characterized by oval or elliptical-shaped leaves of either opposite or alternate patterns; they have been used as a food source since prehistoric times, such as by the Aztecs.

◆ Chapter 5 ◆

The sun sets, and the stars shine,
A circle renewed time after time.
Sprouts burgeon, and Trees grow,
In this is found comfort to tree roots below.
Beauty is life divine.
So, farewell for only a time.
That is until the sun sets . . .
and the stars shine.

—The last lines of Forest blessings to the departed

The unassuming Tumtum Tree is an oft-used symbolic representation of all the Ancient Trees in totality: 'tis an amalgam of many Tree families, with peeling thin-layered bark, lustrous multicolored leaves, and a delightful vigor. And its many corkscrewed limbs display an array of leaf shapes and sizes. Most importantly, it is the culmination of traits within the core of the Tumtum Tree that leave it well-suited as a symbol of the Ancient Forests, for within it rests the secrets of energy and spirit song. So, while the little Tree's upper canvas is hardly vast, and too, provides little in wonderment or shade, as with the most important aspects of physical existence, 'tis not the outside visible self where what resides should be marked of most note; it is what resides within. The spirit, the consciousness that emboldens ideas to take shape in thoughts and feelings, is what truly matters in the world. The Trees know this truth; thus, even the biggest and boldest will bow humbly to the most unlikely subject one might consider. What we cannot see, evolving from impressions of life's most extraordinary possibilities, manifests a reality of the spirit's deepest intentions. And that is what is honored in the realm of the Trees.

There can, thus, be little wonder about the esteem and symbolism placed on the alabaster sculpture of a Tumtum Tree, which graced the center fountain within the Hall of Alderelm. The statue was a gift from the Ancient Forest of Lemnoss, and it stretched out its many arms to those in attendance, reaching as a child for a parent's embrace. Heartwood Willow stood beside the small semblance and delicately broke off an elder leaf from her soft spun hair, setting it afloat upon the pool of trickling water flowing around the sculpture. Perhaps magic was bestowed on the leaflet, for the water's liquid life began to shimmer with boundless radiance. Hereupon and with care, the elder withdrew the freshly awoken Nephyr stone from the Tumtum's marbled base.

The Nephyr stone was as old as the very first Trees, and it bound hope and comfort to the union of all kinds by heralding the Trees. Through its waking, ringing yawns, the atmosphere charged with energy that built upon itself and enticed the Trees to join the call for council. The Nephyr's ringing and Trees' intonations sounded together like a warm crackling fire under cricket-sung skies on a cool summer's eve. Tidings were brought to Llaurantis, and the council had begun.

Knowlton arose stiffly, yet he retained an abrupt quality. He nodded to Willow as she rested her figure upon a throne of boughs and boles.

"Greetings," said the Ole Ironwood. "Many kinds are represented this night, but we have little time for formalities. Has anyone seen or heard from those not with us?"

"The guards have not caught sight of any more than those here residing, my Heartwood," replied Bristleton.

Knowlton held his head high, but the heaviness in his heart was evident. In Treean tongue and whistles, he let fly the blessings of all kinds. Sage held tight his fists and ground his teeth.

"There is a new creation: one of fire and smoke. And more." Knowlton sighed. "The Sacred Ones have been unable to discern even the faintest echo of one of their kin across the Utswana Sea. The Ancient Forest's worrit is awakening. Sage, Coyotl elf of the Lagacious house, friend to the Treeans, long an age has passed since your last sojourn here. The timing of your arrival can be no mere coincidence. What say you?"

Bristleton turned to Sage in expectancy and sympathy and noticed that his fist was clenched hard. Blood oozed into the elf's breeches, wicking into the fabric and spreading slowly outward. It's no less a metaphor, the marchwarden thought, for the day's unfolding and the tension he felt emanating from his friend. Trouble was tripping right along their heels, and he knew it. Nevertheless, the marchwarden squeezed his poor fellow's shoulder in a gesture of reassurance. Slowly, the beleaguered Coyotl rose to his feet. Now was the time for Sage Lagacious to speak . . . on matters he ne'er imagined would ever need to be uttered, much less discussed.

"Yes, a long age has passed. I've been afield, across the Eastern Seas in the MiddleLands; my journeys led me to Lemnoss. I've returned to Alderelm during ill tides not by coincidence alone—'tis verily true. With heavy heart, I relay a message from Heartwood Rowan, Treean elder of the Ancient Forest of Lemnoss, as he so committed me to bear word for word:

"Alderelm, our dear sister, hold tight. Always have seven Ancient Forests stood upon the earth. Grievous beyond comprehension, no more—we stand one less. Surgyle is destroyed, the Ancient Woods and all within, a lay of ash. Lemnoss is under siege—we hold, but for how long, I know not. Yet more need to guard your hope, for Emerus, the singing Tree stone, has fallen into the dark, and its condition is unknown."

The hall abounded in dead silence. A dagger had cleaved into the heart of Alderelm's very essence; everyone was stiff in dismay. But as the Trees absorbed the knowledge, groans of grief heaved the earth in an agony of sorrow unknown since the beginning of time on Earth. The haunting stillness of those in attendance endured as they listened helplessly to the Forest's grief. *I wish only for this to become a memory and be over*, thought Sage, eyes welling with tears.

Heartwood Willow was in shock. "Ne'er has our Mother known less than her Seven Keepers. And Emerus . . . has fallen into the dark? Nature's balance . . . how can this be? If the stone has died, the Earth will be a place of madness."

"Are you certain, Lagacious?" asked Freemont, the yellow-green leaves of his head curled tight. "The equanimity of Nature, oh dear woes that betide us, will find frequent and more desperate her struggles, in the very least, if such tragedy be accurate."

"Then, without Emerus," muttered a voice within the hall, "there's little hope?"

"Do not falter," said Sage. "Llaurantis is the very essence of hope. The gateway to the underworld lies within the Obsidian Fields—upon our doorstep! All the lands upon Earth have believed Llaurantis cursed . . . but not me! We will march into the innards of that sphere of omens and restore balance ourselves!"

"You're mad!" rumbled one of barely decipherable speech.

Sage searched the council for this new critic; his eyes quickly found him, a lliath of immense proportions who thrust his fist hard upon his wiry-haired chest. Sage received the gesture willingly and rushed upon the lliath with sharp strides and a wry expression.

"No simple matter is it to enter the realm you speak of!" cried Knowlton, interrupting the elf's course. "Pythium is Geul's realm. Ne'er has one journeyed there and returned as any semblance of their former selves."

"Nor is this our only concern," added Hardtack, the elders looking to him in tacit agreement. "Time calls on us to divulge rare knowledge with our kin, but to those who listen, a burden shared will be imparted," and so saying, the elder paused and looked at everyone; the energy in the room was not without immense distress, but there also hung an undeniable electricity in the air, an excitement in sight of what may yet become worse. "One of the Ancient Forests harbors the Sakatu," he continued, "a fruit of the Ancient Forests; it is a World Tree Seed. Within it, the very knowledge of Earth is carried, a seedling made up of every Tree to have ever lived. Geul cannot quell the laws of Nature as long as the Sakatu exists."

"It is a myth," cried one of the council.

Hardtack's eyes danced. "The Sakatu is no myth, but indeed, only the Forest in which it resides knows its whereabouts—the whereabouts of what has been kept safe within Alderelm's paternal graces for many a hundred moons."

Breaths of disbelief fell around the council as the elder Knowlton began to speak, raising his voice upon each further syllable, allowing no time for further gasps. "Understand fully, we not only find ourselves upon the threshold of Geul, but we must also protect what Alderelm possesses—the Sakatu—an object as hallowed as Emerus."

"Then we should hide the Sakatu," said Nimott. "We can take it to the faerie hills!"

"Better still, the grumbies of Shee could hide it," said Ullott.

Nimott nodded adamantly.

"The Feeorin!" cried an elf. Much distress took him, and he slipped repeatedly into the Elvish tongue. "Keep safe such a precious relic from Skloi? You doom us with such talk." He was lord of the Raven ketyl, and against the candlelight, many a strand of his black hair reflected the mysterious blue hue of the sun's late beams, so rarely seen from the earthly realm.

"Nay, no use of these quarrels," said Hardtack. "The Sakatu has but one bearer—"

"Our Lastborn," interrupted Willow. "LittleLeaf of the LeadTrees. Without her touch, 'tis naught but an empty shell."

Sage twirled around to Bristleton in astonishment. Bristleton bowed his head in affirmation. Sage swallowed hard and slunk low in his chair, chin cupped in his hand, and took to an inner deliberation.

"We've traveled full circle and find ourselves at earlier disputes," said Knowlton with an eerie vexation. "Letting LittleLeaf venture apart from the security of this Forest goes against every Treean instinct, for not only is she a guardian, but she is also the Sakatu bearer."

"Much a task," muttered a voice, "falls on Llaurantis."

"What of Lemnoss?" asked Freemont.

"We mustn't give up hope," said Willow.

"And we must send aid," said Sage, rising again. "The Bandas may offer their backs to lift many across the sea. We can be there before the new moon."

"Bandas?" asked Gemyne, elf royal of the Wapiti. "Rumors are not so strange as the reality that follows thy heels."

Yor'el, sylph of the Wygets, long an age serving as friend and ally to the Sacred Trees and elves, rested upon a staff which served as both longbow and lance; his legs were long ago injured forever. His wings held the unarguable arch of nobility, though he was descended from not a drop of royal blood. Fierce upon the field, none would dare venture toward the sylphen cripple, but more, his counsel was of gracious wisdom.

"The sylphs offer themselves to Lemnoss. No time is had. Let our wings serve this purpose, and our talents serve the fight."

The Treean elders bowed in acceptance.

"But what of Leaf and the Sakatu?" asked Hardtack.

"We could enter dormancy," replied Freemont. "Naught could touch the Forest, or the Sakatu, within that spell."

"And leave the lands on their own!" shouted Hardtack, creaking. "Abandon them?"

"Ease yourselves!" replied Knowlton.

"Fine, fine," grumbled Sage. "Plan protection for the Sacred Ones, but you have little time to decide. I witnessed today's fire, and I've seen such flames before. Alderelm will soon be under siege. Knowlton, we can fight. I come with knowledge of these dark forms. Should dormancy be the Treean decision, the Trees may very well awaken to a land of blackness on which only dark-hearted beings roam, beings who care nothing for the Forests or any Wood. Who or what else does the Forest serve if not the beings of the Earth herself?"

Willow looked to Bristleton. "Commander, you are in charge of our borders and hold much respect, but you have remained silent this evening. What thoughts have you?"

"I am of the arrow," replied Bristleton. "Many here know my deeds, but ne'er have I desired the fight. Yet, too long have we lain dormant. We're fading, and I think it is not the natural way of the world. Listen well; it will not only be the Treeans who die a slow, meaningless death if the council decides on dormancy. I do not wish to sit by and watch another Forest fall or see other lands besieged. My bow is calling while my knife loses luster. Under a peaceful coexistence, this is welcome, but do not let us continue to wither away. The sylphs go to the aide of Lemnoss. This is good. Foes will shudder at the sight. Now send a company to defend Llaurantis, Alderelm being the main stand. We need to defend ourselves alongside all kin and kind. And respectfully, I tell the elder Heartwoods that LittleLeaf must be allowed to follow her heart and leave the Forest—even as holder of the Sakatu."

Agreements were plentiful, and the council nodded until Knowlton cleared his throat. So doing, silence fell as a suffocating sheet upon the gathering. His atmosphere was a thundercloud, still and quiet but full of power yet unleashed.

"Bristleton, you speak well," acknowledged Knowlton, tipping his head with as much grace as pride, "and your thoughts are respected."

Bristleton nodded and curtly bowed; his guardian nature was acutely attuned to the fact that after the tumultuousness of the day's events, the subject of their discussion ought to be considered. Few noticed his subtle departure.

"Let none here consider the Treeans so passive as to be naive," barked Knowlton. "Mind ere the fist, duty first to the Trees. Whichever path council decides upon, 'tis essential that we ensure the survival of the Great Trees . . . even if this means our precious Lastborn is to follow the wind."

◆§ Chapter 6 §◆

Reasoning with someone in love,
Is like reasoning with the winter wind.

—Ancient Daunan proverb

"Beyond recall—ne'er have I felt such oppression," muttered Noblien. "The woes of the Cimmerians are upon us."

Tullkaee wagged a finger westward. "Over the whitecaps, fire blazed the steppe."

As Noblien and Tullkaee continued to speak, Leaf switched her attention to the sounds of discourse within the Daun's companions. Their voices were strong and deliberate, and their native tongue akin to the Forest, raw and beautiful. She supposed that these were formidable folk, for, in addition to the power residing in their speech, their every movement seemed to ripple with purpose; no action was wasted upon them. The Dauns held an authentic, even visceral oneness with all they spoke to, looked at, or touched. She was utterly fascinated. She deemed them a proud people who held high esteem for the Earth.

Their raiment was soft and supple, and the crafting upon them was meticulous. Angular designs of minuscule beadwork ornamented the legs and sleeves. Leaf mused at the love poured into such intricate creations; receiving such works of art was a great honor. *These*, she thought, *must be the Daun's most esteemed.*

Their dark hair had a depth of richness cast from a multitude of black hues whose copper highlights created a mirage of movement within plaits reaching effortlessly to their waists. Save for Tullkaee's, whose mane flowed free with three large feathers tied therein. The feathers rose and descended in the breeze with an expression of regal confidence, settled with the feminine powers of subtle balance, as though the feathers elicited the spirit of the bird from whence they came, a keenness found only in the wild, resting upon this woman of might and prowess. Leaf respected the aura about her, about them all.

Tullkaee turned to speak to her companions and then back to Noblien, returning to common speech when addressing the latter. It was clear that she was the only one in her group to speak it.

"There is concern for our families. The fire was unnatural, and some here believe the smoke, Kongoni."

Tullkaee's companions tensed visibly. Noblien did not understand.

"Tymen a vell . . . Skloi," Niveus whispered in Elvish.

Leaf was not completely confident in her mastery of the Elvish tongue, but she knew the word Skloi well and trembled under it. Here was no distant spirit of tales or myth. Geul was a tangible existence, an immortal monster! Spiritless, malevolent, and pure evil. A tyrant eternally bent on laying waste to the beauty of the world. Hitherto, he had stayed ensconced deep within the recesses of the Underworld.

"Aucks!" spat Noblien, and as he said the word, he sprang like a snake uncoiled when it strikes.

Noblien now comprehended and recognized their fear. Leaf watched him closely and felt the tiny leaves sprayed over her feet curl back into their protective stipules. There seemed an eclipse dimming the abyss of the elf's clear and tranquil eyes. The Treean searched them, desperate for an answer to their peculiarity, but without success, for Noblien closed them tight in an attempt to will what foulness must not come to truth. When the windows to his spirit reopened, the tranquility had returned within the varied folds of reflective greyness.

"Let us all hope not," he murmured.

Leaf's heart sank amidst understanding, and she pulled at his arm. "Noblien, the smoke from the fire did not flow with the wind."

"Yes," added Tullkaee. "Even after the fire burned, the smoke cloud did not move. The smoke was angry, and like a bear, it growled. We could not cross the fields. The hawk guided us south along the river toward Alderelm, which we have seen only through the tales of our foremothers' minds."

Leaf's face grew pallid, "Alderelm! I must head back—no one knows of my crossing."

"Ah," mused Noblien, surveying Leaf's wound. It was cleaner now but no less sore to look upon. He then considered the noble Dauns, but words became an unnecessary conclusion for Tullkaee's marshaled necessities.

"Kongoni soils the land, and my people lie vulnerable. My brothers will return home," and so saying, she flicked her wrist with a curt nod.

Wordlessly, her kinfolk directed a bow to the season; one bent a smiling eye on Leaf. Then they were gone, as quickly and quietly as when they had first appeared; weighted hearts dampened steady footsteps.

"I will go," Tullkaee continued, "with LittleLeaf to speak to her elders."

An audience with the elders of Alderelm is hardly a matter requiring a request, yet the directness of the statement took the elf aback. He felt an audacity therein, which produced a stiffening of the elf's posture and subtle dilation of his pupils. Yet the Daun did not diminish. A proudly set jaw and determined gaze meet the Fierce-Eyed Elf squarely. The two new acquaintances held each other in tacit odds.

"I am glad for it," Leaf replied, amused at the stiffness between the two. "And your company."

The sentiment satisfied Tullkaee in no short measure and softened the elf's rigid resolve.

"Then let us move with haste," said the Fierce-Eyed Elf, gingerly setting Leaf atop his shoulders.

Treeans find immense comfort in places aloft, and Leaf took a swift liking to the view upon the elf of higher vertical proportions. For the elf's part, the Treean's lightness was startling; she was made more of a bird than of faerie kind.

A steep path was their course, and the group was silent, guarded, and unnerved. Any of their next steps might bring misfortune, more than the norm for the days in a life of the past. And the day to come, always unknown, was fraught with dread, as though already benighted by dark shrouds. Feeding further upon unspoken fears was the breeze, for the mild Zephyr should have possessed a tinge more warmth for the time of year, yet it was chilled, empty, and hollow.

Niveus was worn. Nevertheless, she conveyed none of it and moved lightly upon the fallen leaves and needles of pine. Tullkaee took up the rear and held strong but was consumed with worry about what signs had been presented that day and for the future of her people. Noblien was of many simultaneous thoughts, which was a constant elven predilection, but above all, his musings took to the mysterious pull that had ultimately beckoned him here. A fetidness was resting in it that remained fixed within his nostrils, though neither beast nor mortal had yet to detect it. In all, the mixed company desperately hoped time's course was not venturing toward the greyness of the past—a past so long ago suppressed by departed stars.

The amber hues of the borealis twinkled ahead and up the high track. There was a comfort in beholding the plants' illuminations, and the group's footsteps quickened. In no time at all, the river was rushing loudly below them. Here, a narrowing of the canyon attempted to press the Sasa into submission. Her reply was a tumult of free abandon and relentless power—a grand view of ageless wonder—the cliff of Leaf's fall.

Leaf held her breath. She would like to forget the incident and bitterly hoped that Noblien would not pause or bring her near demise up for conversation. The elf did not. His pace remained steady; not even a glance took him. She felt relief and sighed deeply after they passed the cascades, but the moment of respite was brief, broken by a peculiar laugh, deep, with a hint of momentary mischief, and then again, quite warm. Leaf and Noblien turned to behold from where and why the laughter arose, their breath turning shallow as they observed the season.

Her face was lit in a smile as she balanced herself on the fragmented tip of a craggy edge while her eyes glinted between momentary breaks of enigmatic shadow. An effortless grace was hers, far lighter afoot than an elf or Treean, and her gaze darted from Leaf to the Sasa. Noblien placed Leaf upon her feet, restless in anticipation of the season's intent.

"Did she speak to you?" Niveus asked.

"She?" Leaf replied in dismay.

"The river," Niveus said with childlike amusement.

Leaf looked to the ground and felt her face grow hot. "Yes," she replied, "she did."

"For few doth time stand still," replied Niveus, bowing her head in respectful acknowledgment, her voice as honey to the tongue. "You touched the Sasa as an Earthen creature of her spirit because you walk the path of thy heart. May you always do so."

The elf crossed his arms and raised an eyebrow. "Indeed, walk the path of your heart, but diligently retain your wits if you desire to maintain a solid tread." And so saying, he ticked up the corner of his mouth in a charming and mocking smile.

The season's fair face lightened with gentle regard. "Heed a Puman's counsel with judicious regard; their words embody wisdom."

Noblien's expression was much to judge—a mixture of incongruous and distant etchings scored his countenance. One could derive many conclusions from such a look, and for Leaf, she considered at least two: that Noblien was quite taken aback by the comment and that his innate nobility perceived it as an undue compliment. Leaf considered, not for the first time, what strange and curious creatures the elves were. Their reaction to life was so wonderfully peculiar and beautifully complicated.

Niveus turned her focus back to Leaf. "Many a magi swirl visions of mispaths. Listen to thy heart, trust thy intellect, and be faithful to the truth." Her voice turned to whispers, and her eyes penetrated the essence of Leaf's spirit. "And let it be that you find what you seek."

"Her's is the vernacular of refuge," mused Noblien, peering out over the water's wash; Leaf felt uncertain as to whether he spoke of the Sasa or Niveus.

Worry was allayed for the briefest of moments as the group watched the waters flow rough and free through a silver maze of molded stone. Frigid tickles lapped the shores in a tease of wakeful life. The Sasa was strong and cold, yet gentle and warm to behold, a hypnotic combination of Mother Nature.

As the retinue continued, talk deserted them, and minds wandered. The river's gurgle grew faint as rills replaced the river's textured songs with lighter and thinner melodies. And though the Forest was lit with many a small warm light, their ascent was cast in the shadows of the giant Trees looming in the near distance.

Tullkaee could hardly believe their sight. The Ancient Trees upon the White Mountain were immense beyond tales or wildest imaginings. She was one of the few who did not find their appearance welcoming; her warrior spirit found threat before comfort in the unknown. Yet, she was not unreasonable and trusted the Treean in attendance. She was still grateful to be taking up the last place in the line, a vantage affording leeway in what tension she reckoned could be brought to bear from behind. Also, the path they walked was confining and lined with too much brush and brake that could conceal hidden dangers.

Across the next bend and rill was an open clearing marked by four Trees with a menacing posture. Giant, vaulted canopies richly covered in leaves of a willowy guise beset by cruelly twisted boughs of smooth, scale-like bark. Tullkaee swallowed hard, for the umbrage of these Trees, indeed, the limbs themselves, slithered and snaked about. *No doubt a trick on the eye*, she thought, but a shiver ran down her spine nonetheless. The Daun twisted and swirled the shaft of her lance to the right and left in rapid, uneasy succession—her restless palm sensing an increasing tension within her muscles.

Intermittent light flashed out against Tullkaee's eyes, and the Daun realized the bark of these Trees was reflecting the light produced by the swirling, silver-tipped point of her weapon. A breath of astonishment escaped her, and thus did her suspicion of the place grow. As she saw it, towering totems of Wood such as these were void of any goodwill.

"Aha, look! The Bridge of Telldon," Noblien said in reverence. "Such beauty made of Trees has there ne'er been." Tullkaee gave an unstifled snort in response.

Leaf, for her turn, sought the reassurances of the Notturn Guards with great eagerness. Yet not even Edassa's old grumblings greeted her. The Treean's stomach fell upon the eerie hush.

The Umbrae were no belters of monumental song, yet neither did the commonplace ever find them muffled. She twirled a Treean whistle under her tongue, shrill on waves of frantic longing, ringing across the Forest. Naught was the reply; the entire Forest was of cold silence. The reverberation of trumpeting songs echoing deep waves against her heart was utterly mute.

Leaf placed a quivering hand upon the Puman's shoulder. "Noblien, please halt. The roots of my feet need to touch the Forest floor. The Ancient Ones are quiet."

Noblien wasted no time in compliance, his face burdened, too, with worry.

Barely a breath of the Treean's personage had been set down before she flitted in a hobbled sprint, her pained limb unheeded, to the nearest Umbra—Edassa. She let fly, fluttering chirps of whistles interspersed with notes stretched long and melodic, all becoming more strident and intermittent—an outcry of a young one in distress. Her breath was panting as she concentrated on answering resonations underfoot. Nothing. She stared up under the wide canopies. Once more, she whistled, if it could be called, for the sound of her desperation now shot through the ethers like an ear-piercing shriek.

At last, a resounding reply did rumble, building on itself in waves felt as pressure pushed against the body, growing to an infinite height. The invisible roaring then exploded with a boom, expanding every molecule of air to do so. This was not a reply from the Notturn Guards. This was utterly primal, deep, and measured in oldness—a wail from one of the Ancient Ones further uphill.

The Fierce-Eyed Elf knelt in earnest deference, Tullkaee following the action to his side.

"The Trees are grieving," Leaf whispered.

Niveus walked over to her side and placed a palm on Edassa. "Come. We will find answers amongst your kin."

For more than an hour, the company strode amidst a surreal view of dark and light as an insidious cover of fast-sweeping clouds intermittently obscured the gleaming light of the stars. However, the rills of the White Mountain paid no mind to the welkin storms and continued to spring forth hope within, percolating melodies of the fluent world while the animals of night, tucked tightly away, joined her in song. Even within the Trees' sad silence and the raging storm skies, Alderelm held tight her grace.

The group had been caught between Mother Nature's calm and

turbulent extremes. For while the borealis glinted dimly amongst their feet, a salvo of thunder shook the wide air with a heart-pounding effect. The overwhelming disquietude set aside Alderelm's native and unrelenting charm, leaving wary visitors much to consider. To this end, they were startled when Bristleton ran up from across the glade.

The marchwarden's face was harrowed. His pace slowed to a predatory walk. Upon seeing Leaf, he took a sliver of ease and gazed wonderingly at the newcomers.

"Bristleton!" cried Leaf.

Bristleton beheld Leaf's wound and drew tight his bow—arrow marked. Taut was the tension of the air. The marchwarden looked at each group member, who respectfully bowed a head in turn. Bemused, much of his guardian wares began to dissipate, the pull of the bowstring slackened, and when his eyes fell upon Niveus, the arrow forgot what mark there was or had aye been.

"Curious is the company," spoke Bristleton, "who dare to stand afore me holding my youngling with a wound. Is there more than meets the eye?"

The marchwarden's eyes were a flash of challenge and temptation of character. Fixedly, he stared at Noblien and Tullkaee, no pleasantry, no nicety. Neither took his bait. He thought, *Quite the kin of quality who can reply to my manners with naught but humility.* The marchwarden had measured them up and decided with a nod.

"Welcome to Alderelm. I greet you … with greatest hesitance. Heed my words," warned Bristleton, locking eyes with Noblien, "let none move too swiftly, least till the thorns of my nettles find some ease." Niveus smiled, and this captured the marchwarden's gaze. "Long an age has passed since the sojourn of a season. Aforetime, I would have delighted in the honor of your presence, but now simple pleasantries are rarer."

Her smile faded, and the emotion behind its lapse now resided within her voice. "There are some named as seasons, who have oft walked amongst you within the Wood of Alderelm, though how does even a Treean recognize the Wood for something else? Forgive the absence of formal tarries, but know, ne'er has Alderelm past a solstice without the tiptoes of my kind amongst you."

Upon hearing this, every crease on Bristleton's stern features broke into a crescent of gaiety. A rare expression for him. Yet as a wave crest does inevitably crash and return to its melded source, so did his countenance return forthwith to its set of grim and chiseled rock. And while endearment for his beloved Leaf was indeed upon it, when he spoke, it was brusque.

"LittleLeaf, you are injured. Speak now—what happened?"

"I fell."

"Simply stated," huffed Bristleton, inwardly reassured by the rebellion proffered so plainly within such a lack of detail. "Are you sure there's not more to relay?" and though he asked, he did not wait for a reply. "To the tarn, let us tend to your—"

"My leg has been tended to," broke Leaf, pushing his hands away. "Why are the Trees grieving?"

"Let the Lumen soothe your ails," Bristleton urged, a plea resting within the inflection, "then we will speak."

Noblien ground his teeth, his eyes painfully sharp, squinting in anticipation as he and the others followed the marchwarden. Bristleton glanced back, and as their eyes met, no doubt remained that the weight of the report forthcoming was heavy indeed. Noblien cast his eyes to the blue pages of Tumoil's spring water parchment. Tullkaee was as a hawk in attentive stillness.

Bristleton cupped his hands and poured the Lumen's spice over Leaf's wound. Dwelling within the glittering waters was a vulnerary derived over eons from the Ancient One's roots, a mysterious elixir that gave the Spring of Tumoil its sentience and which healed the soft injuries so easily inflicted upon creatures of flesh and bone. Comfort swept over Leaf's pain, and the swelling slowly subsided.

"Short time will have you careless again," said Bristleton.

"What of the Trees?" asked Leaf with increased agitation.

Dark was the shade that fell over the border guard's visage. "Tragedy. An unfathomable tragedy. The world is as beautiful as it is cruel. One of the Ancient Forests . . . has fallen."

"Fallen?" asked Leaf.

"Yes, little one," Bristleton answered. "She exists now only in memory—she has been destroyed."

"This cannot be," breathed Niveus, her complexion losing all color.

"Aye, my lady," confirmed the marchwarden. "'Twas Surgyle," and as he spoke, although he appeared steadfast, a tremor resided in his voice. "And Lemnoss is under siege. An eclipse begins to settle upon the balance of the wild."

A leaf fell onto the water. Noblien watched the ripples disrupt the sheen of reflections. Sadness filled his heart while his innate Puman wares were drawn to Niveus. He sensed a terrible difference; her spirit had become still. Before his very eyes, her vitality was diminishing. Leaf saw it, too. "Niveus," Leaf called. "Niveus!"

The season's eyes submerged beneath a lifeless haze. She gave no response, no blink nor breath. Noblien rushed to her side. His eyes searched her face for the fight of life, the flicker of inner fire that burns within all kin, small in normalcy but able to ignite brightly when all else fades. Hers was lit; he felt it. Yet, as for her will, she had surrendered it.

"Chinook!" cried Tullkaee, clutching Noblien's arm and pointing into a blustering grey.

Noblien turned and breathed through a gritted jaw. The Trees began to creak and moan. There was hardly time to blink before a shadow of reeling brush descended on them. Savage blades of stinging tumult forced the group into a crouching stance, save the entranced season and the Fierce-Eyed Elf who shielded her.

Noblien snuffed in the scent of the blustering air. It smelled strongly of the sea. This gust was also warm, like a living creature, and its bites were cutting, choicely so. Not in the least, within it resided bravado. The elf's eyes narrowed, and a taxing irritation rose fast to anger.

"You cannot have her!" he yelled.

Wincing in the gale, Tullkaee and Leaf returned looks of bewilderment.

"Follow me!" shouted the marchwarden.

"Nivia!" pleaded Noblien, calling her in the elven tongue. "The Haevonen did not surrender to the challenges lay afore him, not even to his last breath! Do him honor! Fight the battles within you!"

A flicker of life broke through the glaze over the season's eyes before withering. Noblien shouted in frustration, whisked her into his arms, and took flight after the others who had stopped and waited for them, crouched against the wind on the stairway.

"Go! Go!" he shouted. "Descend to the hall! Descend!"

Tullkaee did not follow the elf's command. Instead, the mighty Daun held steadfast, her lance ready for combat as she waited for the elf, who flew past with a nod. Only then did Tullkaee turn and run right on the elf's heels. Looking back over her shoulder, her eyes widened in disbelief as the twisting gale trailed them.

Astonishment and many gasps met the group as they entered the cathedral of the council cavern. Knowlton and Freemont jumped to their feet. Hardtack rushed to Leaf, the hairy plumes of his spreading crown of more note than the fact that such a lumbering old frame could spring so quickly into action. Willow stayed in her seat, looking keenly at each new guest. Tullkaee drew up the last and took to Noblien's side, standing strong and looking fierce.

"Thou art later than expected," said Willow lowly, as if to herself and with near imperception.

The Fierce-Eyed Elf watched the words on her lips, and his

expression became one of utter puzzlement. He opened his mouth to speak, but naught of any adequacy came out. The lady elder's eyes smiled, but as she settled her attentions on the season who rested limply in his arms, her benevolent countenance drew in on itself and became taunt.

A fierce maternal love was this elder's trait, well-proved this eve, for the Heartwood rose with the fury and elegance of a storm wave cresting high and haltingly upon the sea, while resultantly, many a leaf upon her pleached, crowned head did teeter to the toad-croaked earth. She held up her hand and closed her eyes; the descending woe of howling wind halted. The hall became perfectly still. Save for an odd ave of tiny sorts, fluttering lost and misplaced within the gem-lit confines.

"Zephyr!" cried Willow, her voice seething. "Why've you come here masking your presence as a whirl of blusters? You are in the Court of Alderelm, and she is not yours—show yourself!"

A blue current of wistful dust swirled madly in a fabulous show of odd-colored orbs, celestial trinkets, and nautical fervor before taking permanence in the form of a well-aged man: bearded, robed, and bolstered by all the eyes upon him now.

"You cannot leave me bereft of duty to mine own kin. Niveus hath no place within your courts. She is my niece, and what I want will be!"

With this brash assertion, the truculent spirit of the West wind found many a weapon aimed upon his personage. This gathering was wrought with worry, and his prideful utterance had been most unwelcome. Although much revered, Zephyr's impetuous instincts had not served the root of his cause. He had mismeasured the leverage of his authority and thus assured his intentions were waylaid before he could storm about.

"Zephyr," snapped Knowlton, the old, hardened tendrils of his back cracking as they hackled. "You'd be wise to consider your position most carefully."

Zephyr lowered his gaze from the sturdy trunk of a Treean and scanned the council with utter contempt. He had realized his error and thus stayed in his place, but he did so with a hissing cold, chilling anyone who met his gaze.

"By strewth!" Knowlton scoffed, dressing Zephyr down at once. "West wind of all the earth and sky and see us this behavior? You are a royal sovereign! An elemental of the highest regard, acting as a ludicrous child who knows no better." The aged temblor's entire demeanor looked rankled. "Tush!"

Zephyr disregarded Knowlton's scolding and tried intimidating any he might with an icy leer that bit with arctic wintriness. Knowlton was further incensed and grumbled incoherently. Willow disregarded them both and turned her attention to Niveus, who was desperately resisting the urge to scurry in flits and flights to secure notes on high within the welkin blue. As a being of the elements, she was a tender compilation of all the world's sorrow in a day.

"Ah, the seasons," breathed Willow, casting a sympathetic eye toward the Gale King. "The pulse of raw Earth herself. Your kind . . . destined to absorb the streams of Earth without cessation. You are as outworn as anyone I've ere beheld. Niveus, although it has been many an age since we have seen one another, dear child, whither is thy heart of passion I so well knew?"

The Lady of Wold Reflections raised her head to reveal eyes of a blood mist, a frightful display of quiet grief—and death. Though shocked, Willow held fast her gaze, stroking the season's hair. Faint recognition glowed at the sight of the Treean elder, and the season struggled to her feet with fixed determination. Yet even in standing, her person appeared crumpled.

"Oh, dearest," clucked Willow. "Much sadness have you beheld this day."

"None more than you, my Heartwood," replied Niveus.

"The impact and assault on all our spirits has been to full test this day. Fulguris hath struck, but though stricken, we do not lay low. No. Niveus, daughter of Nivom, elf of the Eastern Lands, and Boreas, the North wind, you are unlike any season of our age. Tell me, what imparts your nature?"

Niveus closed her eyes. Her lips barely moved as she chanted to herself. Willow smiled fully and clapped her hands together. The council watched with peculiar interest and no less apprehension.

Noblien could feel Leaf's growing unease and turned his lynx eyes on her. She found immediate comfort within his gaze. "Here it comes," he mouthed, taking her hand.

Suddenly, the hall swayed, and the ground appeared both there and not. Mental acuity became a viscous endeavor, slow and tasking, while vision bleared. The bizarre sway in the clocks of time had resumed their course just as Leaf had experienced when she first set eyes on the great horse.

The chants of the elementals filled every crevice of the hall with a tranquility one could taste and smell. A deep density of baritone intermingled harmoniously with the rhythmic waves of watery reflections. Time, past and present, blended and became synchronous with the future, and in this wondrous, infinitesimal moment of infinity, Niveus opened her eyes; limpid and melodious, the colors of summer twilight, they burned once again with strength and hope anew.

The season could have easily been mistaken as a narrow cloud mirrored by the sunlight's rays over still waters. Her composure was Nature's grace, and her aura was alive with purpose. This is how Leaf saw it. For Noblien, there is no account except for Leaf's description, which is left now as an impression within the cores of Methuselah's rings. However, much is lost when translated into the common language: *The highest reverence and most earnest intensity could ne'er hold compared to the devotion I witnessed that dreadful council day—and all the more beautifully, it resided within a simple expression.*

The season wiped away tears and began to speak, but naught did Leaf comprehend.

"Nictile de fume, Nevi purdesai . . ."

The Coyotl elf gasped loudly and bent a knee. His head was lowered, but Leaf saw tears drip to the earth.

"'Tis the speech of the elementals," Noblien whispered. "The Poem of Turkhyle, the last spoken words of the Veriha, is only spoken within the tongue of the seasons. And whether one hears it or not," and so saying, he smiled gently, "to be nigh such words so uttered is a humble honor. She gifts the council mightily this day."

"Sect ha fur tume, ti vile dege ca sela," sang Niveus, bowing her head graciously. She pursed her lips and said, "What imparts my nature? Long sith thou hath asked me this query."

Willow tittered. "Long to you. You have spent your youth. Yet not so long to me, for I now spend my elder days. You know, the wisest words spill from the mouths of littlies, still snuggled to the truths of Earth's womb. Do you remember the answer thoust gave so long ago?"

"I could ne'er forget."

"Aha, good," responded Willow, in a manner well-pleased and with an expression having expected it to be thus. "The treasure of new life is—"

"Is," Niveus interjected, "the mystery of infinity which has granted my reason for being and given me strength."

Willow's pleasure radiated. "My dear, you hold well your youth. I am most pleased. The green of the wild beats more freshly within your heart than ever I've seen. Tell me, do you still feel the Earth's heartbeat? Strange a season you were, not a breath of solstice within you, but more, the breath of all creatures. Still so?"

"Still so," replied Niveus, pausing and furrowing her brow. "Yet, my Heartwood, this new burgeoning season is wrought with ills—more than you know, I'm afraid."

Zephyr grunted, and Niveus became shushed. Willow flashed him with a look of unmeasurable crossness before redirecting her gaze back onto the season.

"Words spoken upon these sacred grounds can bring no harm. 'Tis forbidden. A season's view of life upon these lands is unlike the perceptions we are endowed with. Please, your words are welcome, whatever they may be, and I hope they benefit the decisions and strategies laid out during this gathering. Speak with full heart, I implore thee."

Niveus turned her eyes to Noblien, the ground, and Willow. The Fierce-Eyed Elf was warmed but perplexed by the action.

"My time of leave is nigh," said Niveus. "I will say what I can."

Noblien's jaws gritted, but he held his head high while Willow took to her throne of spindled, weaving branches. Freemont and Hardtack followed suit, though with the tenuity of sparrows under kestrel-ridden skies. Knowlton stayed his ground, hand resting upon the handle of his curved-edged blade, damascened with the intricacies of aged bark.

Leaf missed none of it; she measured it all. Bristleton observed her acuteness and swallowed deeply. There was both burden and relief in observing the young Treean use, so naturally, his teachings on awareness. More than enough comfort, he hoped, to grant himself the strength to release her fully to what lay ahead.

Niveus walked a few steps to the tarn, addressing everyone. "With the lengthening days, a shrinking of the wild has tingled my fingertips. The fibers that link all kin are quivering . . . or absent altogether. The prophecy of Fulvetr stands at our doorsteps."

"Ah!" said Zephyr, flushed and swelling. "Spurn a seasonal behest? Defiance!" And after he said the words, his posture shifted as if beginning to uncoil for a lunge.

Knowlton did not miss the subtleties and, in all probability, recognized the ensuing intention before Zephyr was cognizant of it himself, for an emotional reaction is, at best, a blind instinct of the mind. And so, the West wind was promptly introduced to the blade of the Tree Lord's forebears. Knowlton pressed it snugly against Zephyr's belly. Yet the action was taken with such grace and dignity as to have gone widely unnoticed by the gathering. And forasmuch as this courtesy was executed, did the blade sting even more cruelly, carving out pride above the flesh.

"Have you noticed Ama's last hold?" continued Niveus. "I tell you, not of a season's design is the lingering winter. More sense now . . . my wanderings. Many creatures are filled with distress. Nigh a moon has had me restless breathing life into the newborns, for of late, they do not do so on their own."

The attendees rested with quizzical expressions. Many had ne'er seen a season, although all knew of their existence. But of their kind's dealings with the newly born, this was a curiosity.

She smiled. "Although I'm claimed as a season, I am different. Traits I share with my kin surely. Yet ne'er have I enticed an autumn or summer to reveal their tempers as do my brethren. I neither persuade a flower's opening breaths nor place a Tree to slumber upon the shortening days. Rather do I foster life where I might, by breath."

The council sat enthralled but no less confused. One individual made a loud, cooing purr. Leaf was a bit taken aback to see from whom the sound radiated, for it was a tall, solidly framed lliath, even in measure to their kind. Niveus met eyes with the hairy giant, her pupils widening into diamond facets, her eyes becoming an ever-brightening orange. The lliath responded with a gentle, throaty gurgle. Yet, for all else, the season was still presented with baffled expressions, begging for understanding. She nodded her head at the lliath and took pause.

"This is not easily related by speech," explained Niveus, at once closing her eyes. "Let me show you."

To all, the moment's sensations were heightened, yet the perception of it was slow, as if a waking dream had carried away the council. Henceforward, when she spoke, there was an emotional transference of clarity near transcendence; it was a communication comprised of colors and feelings, as integral to conveying thoughts as words and actions.

"Recall the scents and sensations of your earliest memories. These memories rest ineffable, borne deep, yet not wholly recollected—no past—no thoughts of the future. Only the core element of your being in its ultimate simplicity is made aware of existence by the warming comfort of breath . . . after breath. This is the fluidity of Nature, Earth, and her relation to the stars. Do you remember? Do you feel it? It is within this realm that I maintain vigilance—to the soundness and protection of the untamed younglings. Do you now understand? I've been imparting breath into what new life I might, for as their bodies first feel the air, they breathe, not its qualities.

"In this effort, my roams of haste found me in the Woodlands of Seayr three days past. There, I meant to take pause and rest. Yet a disquiet about the place sent me to shivers. I listened, and a wave of high air lurched alow. Carried within this breeze were cries barely censured. Had my senses run amiss? Was I so weary? The grasses of ribwort scratched at each other. Then there, the earth beneath my feet trembled in a fashion no less than the booming of thunder that vibrates the inner core of one's being. And ere I knew it, many hooves were upon the wold, crushing the stinging bunches of nettles and all else underfoot. Shrills of tamed wildness filled the air, and nausea hit me hard. But upon the sight of man kind commanding the horses of Haverdome—the Haevonens themselves—was I filled with such hopelessness that dry were my tears beneath anger. I lay flat on the ground, the elemental form escaping my capabilities, waiting to be trampled.

"The Haevonens galloped all out with chaos as their course. There was no kindness to look upon, either in rider or steed. For the riders were cruel, lashing their mounts with unrelenting vigor. And the horses reared as they ran, striking out forefeet and biting aught within reach, even the black earth itself.

"Pain slashed my heart—the lovely beasts of Haverdome searched the soil with their stomping feet for the familiar feel of their native lands so far yon. In physicality, they were bound against any ability to return home. Who knows if their spirits were even alive? For me, the horses seemed empty vessels of agony, no more. Hanging loosely around their high-arched necks were tattered remnants of the rope that had surely imprisoned them; plaited they were with the stems of a thorny plant.

"I did not know why death was stemming from new life. And I did not know why or even how the Seayran had captured the horses of Haverdome—those grand steeds known in legend as the Marrow of the Wild. All I knew was where the stinging ribworts scratched the secrets—Seayr.

"The Haevonens and their captors had passed. I had gone unscathed and unnoticed. Being in my physical form, of no significant difference to those of human form, I thought answers to heavy questions recently roused might be discovered within the borders of the Seayran city. And so, I went.

"Ne'er have I experienced the like: Gaiety was not of these people's presence. Any hint of softness upon expression was met with an unwelcome glower as they further shrouded themselves within the shadows of their inhospitable cloaks. I elicited the touch of the elementals, beckoning the spirit of each Seayran inhabitant I encountered. I was met with hollowness.

"The result hit me blindly . . . I was succumbing to their sickness; with each attempt to make some contact with someone—with each inquiring venture—I slipped into a reluctance to try or even care. Their bitter nature was becoming my own. Fading from my memory, the breath of the elementals.

"Yet more was at hand than mine own, for as my spirit began to drift away, I came across a barn door that hurried an inviting breeze, sweet with the scent of hay, to awaken my senses. Behind the high hay, not far inside, I heard singing, soft and quiet. From song might come answers, I reasoned and stepped inside in search of whom the tune did flow.

"My eyes fell upon a man, combing the snarled and twisted mane of a steed, tied hard and fast but standing beautiful still, independent in spirit from the bonds that bound him. The horse was indeed a Haevonen, impressive even compared to the majesty of his kind. I stood still and numb. But the man, the first Seayran whose spirit did not pain me, smiled with a youngling's warmth. He saw straight through me, the season I am, as though any typical day might bring the likes upon him. Then, after a fair greeting, he forgot my presence and returned to a simple song. I asked what he knew of the horses.

"He said, 'They're right and proper. Right and proper. They'll be send'in this one to the heavens erelong. Not right, no, not right at all.'

"Asked I, 'Are you saying this horse is to be put to death?'

"Answered he, 'Aye. He's a grand one he is. Too grand for the king. See, he's free. No one can tame 'em. My brother will think of sum'thin. He'd not have this. But . . . I don't know where my brother's at,' and so saying, he paused, not as a man, but with the curious innocence of a youngling. 'Like to drench my soul—the look in his eyes. By gaw, ya think he knows?'

"Said I, 'His sulk stems from more woes than thy tender heart might imagine. As to what he knows, ah, listen. He knows every intent behind thy touch, every meaning behind thy looks or gesture. Remember this well, understand?'

"Said he, 'Savvy, good, and clear.'

"My path had been guided by the unseen pull of a strong yet subtle tide sweeping me far off course before I had even noticed. My only hope was to swim with the current, for I couldn't abandon the Haevonen, and I had no time to enlist aide. My mind was a whirl for a swift scheme.

"Asked I, 'My dear sir, what is your name?'

"'Sessile,' answered he.

"I thought about this gentleman and wondered.

"Said I, 'Sessile, you must search for your brother over in the yonder wold. I will watch this charger.'

"Then I did hold my breath for his reaction and hoped for the exceptionally innocent nature I observed to hold through and through. No need for worrit. Off he ran, no questions, no farewells.

"To the steed afore me, I stared upon a statue of fortitude expressed beneath glints of wide, wild eyes. How do we proceed with such distrust and hope of death over conquest? Barely breathing, I neared to touch him, to release the bonds, but he would not have it, thrusting high his head, striking out with his forefeet, and snapping his gums against the open air. The shaggy tufts of his ears lay flat against his great head. Trembling, I kept my course slow and steady, hoping the Celestials' songs would soothe his wiles. With tender care, I reached the tie that held him fast. His body pivoted, his nostrils flared, and he snorted with a coltishly high whinny. I took to the Elvish tongue, so soothing to the creatures of old, until I neared close enough to unclasp his tie.

"The release of his barbed entrapment let loose then blood now running loosely over his face and my palms. I blew breath upon his wounds and ignored the gentle stallion's curiosity in me. In and out, his nostrils blew with excited inquiry, no longer deeming me a threat.

"I took the opportunity to reach for his muzzle, soft as a limloch's downy petals.

"Dusk was upon us. Torches were being lit. Voices approached. Quietly, I crept beside this one of even, heavy strides and led him to the high Wood until enough distance did part our chance to flee in speed.

And there, at the very highest point, nigh the Forest's edge, he turned back and whinnied. Shrill was the call to his kin below, and far did it carry. 'Twas not long until I felt the red-tipped grasses of his homeland curl upon receiving it. Once more, a brief whinny—none answered.

"Urging him on in simultaneous tongues, he relented. His head hung lowly while his iron hooves clanked like the evening calls of bitterns; the shadows of the Forest enveloped us. He halted again, huffed the sweet night air, and swung his kindly, feral face around to me. Deep the breaths of solace did we share.

"Growing in number and tone, voices below scattered amongst the town in rushed retaliation. We were pursued, and hotly so. Right on us from the beginning.

"For three days, we fled and were once encircled. A wolf pack, bound tightly within the familial bonds of Earth and quite glorious amongst their kind, came to our aide. Had they not, we would not have escaped. However, they suffered dearly for it.

"Thereafter, we traveled at the pace of snails and agony. The encounter had left the Haevonen's body broken. All I could do was walk by his side in tender song. Our pursuers had been delayed, and I gained hope enough that we might reach the White Mountain pass and find sanctuary between the Sasa and Wych rivers. With what strength I do not know, the stallion of the Haevonens hobbled forth.

"Of fortuitous chance, the hawk, Aiko, made a pass overhead. He screeched our plight throughout the Forest and guided the Dauns to our aide. As to this noble elf and most brave Treean, I do not know whether Aiko or Fortune sent them.

"Over the watercourse of the Sasa, the Haevonen went down—he did not rise," and so saying, the season lowered her head; she was silent and trembled.

The council all felt a shift of pressure within their bodies. Simultaneously, their senses of sight and smell became distant and numb. The brilliance of color collapsed. The sharpness of smell deflated and became dull. The all-inclusive melding of the senses, the transference of clarity and beauty, had been released. It was a jarring brace of realism against the effervescence of the realm of the elementals. The attendees of the council collectively sighed. Niveus lifted her head with a tilt and bowed to the council with her eyes.

"My Lady Heartwood, some foulness has found its way onto the shores of Llaurantis, with Seayr caught in its brunt. I have relayed all I can," and so saying, she glanced at Noblien.

Her eyes spoke fields of many tongues. The Elf of Noble Heart held high his head and looked hale, but the gleam within his glass spirit was somberly lit.

"No more time do I have," Niveus continued. "Long and too far have I stayed from the source of elemental fire. If I do not return to the welkin blue soon . . . I will diminish."

Leaf felt the breath of the elf change. It began to heave with a measured steadiness, the energy supplying its life-rhythm shaking, yet the elf held himself as still as stone. The Treean perceived an unspeakable sadness in him, yet she also felt comfort and newfound confidence standing next to the strength that kept him in place. She could not puzzle out all these curiosities, but she understood that she derived hope from the proximity of his presence and, therein, a strength she did not want to lose. And to this, Leaf hungered more to be near his side.

"Forgive me," Niveus said, and to this, Leaf felt the elf's breath stop for an instant altogether.

Willow's countenance was challenging to discern. She smiled, and it was genuine, but it seemed to rest upon a layer of cracking ice, thin and strained.

"Niveus, there is no need for forgiveness—humble gratitude," said Willow, with the expression repeated throughout the council.

Alderelm

Swiftly, the air did whirl—and she and Zephyr were gone. Leaf's heart sank, but for the Fierce-Eyed Elf, it ached.

RIBWORT

Ribwort. 1. A type of grass having lanced blades with minuscule serrations within which white, spiked flowers protrude, common upon the Lands of Seayr. **2.** Recent Age. Plantago lanceolata, also known as ribgrass, a weedy plant with lance-like leaves and a dense spike of small whitish flowers.

NETTLE

Nettle. 1. Hardy, prickly shrubs that grow wildly in an intertwining, vine-like fashion and bloom in vivid, unspecified color rotations. A favorite of birds and insects. **2.** Recent Age. Urtica is a genus of flowering plants in the family Urticaceae that grow as annuals or perennial herbaceous plants of which several species have stinging hairs and may be called nettles or stinging nettles. These plants provide shelter for insects, and their fibers have been used historically by humans for clothing, fishnets, paper, and sailcloths.

LIMLOCH

Limloch. 1. A class of *Ginger clover known for its large size (up to five feet in height and width), blue-tinged color, and long shafts of downy petals.* **2.** *Recent Age. Unidentified.*

◆⊰ Chapter 7 ⊱◆

Crystal pages burning blue,
Watching the firelights fade,
Of wonder is the elf's far look,
While colored orbs fade away.

—A verse from a poem by Snow-mallec, a Tinker faerie, here describing
the lights of a line storm discharging over the ocean

The season's departure was so abrupt as to have left the gathering in a
stagnant state, ineptly acclimating to the change of the moment. To this
effect, Sage perceived discomfort and awkwardness residing more plainly
on the elf and human who had arrived with the season. He ached to see
it and, knowing too well the feeling, spoke with enthusiasm and
mischievous delight. "I say! This is a fine gathering indeed." He spoke as
both a distraction and because it suited him.

The Puman elf tore a sidelong glare at the Coyotl that might have
stopped the heart of a lesser elf or one with a mind toward caution and
good sense, of which Sage had neither. And thereafter, the Puman stared
at him in a sort of quizzical wonder as though trying to recollect a
memory. Sage, however, only nodded with a full grin and a wink,
swallowing in satisfaction rather than fear. Knowlton's tendrils cracked

and popped, but this, too, was met with Sage's eager, gratified expression.

The sylphs held the form of statues, but more than all were their countenances sullen. Yor'el limped forward, his staff tapping the rhythm of destiny.

"Did she say Fulvetr?" Yor'el asked.

"She did," confirmed Willow, with little emotion in her voice.

"Aye gracious," wept Ullott, "methinks we're all doomed."

Soft and steady was the voice that followed Ullot's pronouncement—'twas Willow's. "No, dearest fae. Calm yourself. The Sakatu is still in our keeping, and spring hath arrived. Leaves burgeon, flowers bloom, and new life is born."

"With a bit of chill and trouble," snorted a lliath.

Sage eyed him carefully, and therein, a glint arose. "Ah, more the challenge. Where's your heart? You're an ol' beast. Certainly, much of naught stirs your fear?"

The lliath's reply was a snarl of contempt.

"Will Alderelm," interrupted Yor'el, the tips of his sylphen wings nearly touching the ground, "go to dormancy?" The manner in which he addressed the question was earnest in quality while delicately placed. "Given the unprecedented news of this eve, certainly you must know?"

Knowlton's twig-burdened brows furrowed, and the deep wrinkles therein folded in on themselves as his face puckered in concentrated speculation. The council held its breath. And like water pulled away from the shore before the rising wave of a tsunami, the air around the hall began to grow taut, grasped and retracted by an intangible element that tightened the atmosphere. Then, a whoosh of air blew, a vibration riding on it, heightening and building. Council members began to look at one another.

"Buuohh!" thundered a booming, trumpeting call. "Buuohh!" Arose another and another. The Ancient Ones were calling!

Alderelm

The crushing cadence of sonorous resonance forced a few council attendees to hold their hands over their ears. Others smiled dumbly in wondrous disbelief. Undulating waves of sound bombarded the Forest from every direction, a cacophony of deep, low rumblings pulsating the particles of ether itself.

Knowlton picked up his battered flute. His eyes closed, and the creases of his face vanished, an arthritic softness resting upon his countenance as he began to play; eerily haunting was the tune. Willow and Hardtack joined, and so on, until Treeans, throughout Alderelm, tapped flute tops in perfectly blended melody—a cohesion of simple harmony. Alderelm became a symphony conducted above grief for the sight of hope.

And just as the melodies began, they faded. One by one, each Treean halted their tune. And one by one, an Ancient One let their resonations fade. A last note wafted, holding its pitch until it melded back into the musical phantasma from whence it came.

When Knowlton opened the windows to his spirit, the Coyotl met his eyes. Pleasant relief and apology diffused across Sage's visage. There was no sanctimony or haughtiness within the elf, only the genuine feelings of a heart that loved Alderelm. Knowlton smiled with the tender bounties of clover lilies, perhaps more stiffly than those nimble stems, but no less light upon the world.

"I believe the Sacred Ones are not for dormancy," said the old Ironwood.

"Now," said Willow, focusing on Sage. "What can you tell us?"

Endlessly energetic and swift to accommodate change, the elf took a breath and went straight to business. "Much and little. The fire you witnessed today was no ordinary Earthen element. It was a type of shade—kin of the MiddleLands call this kind, the Ashindi. They are specters who plummet down upon fair lands and wreak their havoc thoughtlessly, receding upon seeing the gloaming. Yet do not despair, for they retreat from the stroke of weapons and can, in fact, be vanquished."

Spirits were lifted upon hearing these words, and heads began to nod amidst a rising gabble around the council. However, Knowlton's look was grave, and like Willow's, it remained transfixed on Sage, who struggled over the babble to continue.

"However . . ." continued Sage, but few heard him. "Listen!" he shouted. "The fires still burn, and the smoke does verily choke." Silence befell the hall. "Yet that's the least of our concerns. Under their attack, we shall become one another's worst threat if we do not keep our wits, for as the smoke sinks and darkens the land, friend will look like foe."

"What! What!" shouted a frantic Ullott. "Oh, this worries me, oh, it worries me."

An elf of the Hawkens, garbed in the airy cloaks of his ketyl, turned his piercing eyes upon the poor Flumbaran fae with not a leaf's weight of pity. Ullott stood firm in his shivers, and the gold eyes released him to the solemn question for council.

"How do we fight an enemy who possesses the powers of fire and smoke, and if that were not enough, take the shape of our brethren?"

"Ha! Again, some good news," cried Sage to a now distrustful and muted audience. "The elves!" A bewildered hush befell the air as the Coyotl continued with childlike enthusiasm. "The smoke does not choke us nor take our form."

This was not news the elves were joyed to hear, and they who had been so quiet now stirred and whispered amongst one another.

"There's more," said Sage. "After the withdrawal of the Ashindi, creatures named the Gauss do arrive. Foul and curious—of the palest flesh—no warmth occupies their innards."

"Oh, oh, it worries us!" said Nimott.

"Now," Sage whirred in a loud whisper, his sudden brevity of speech making his words portentous. "You know what to expect. Let not their look detain you, or swift, heavy clubs will hearken the crush of your skull. Move fast. These creatures are powerful but lack agility and extraordinary weaponry skill."

Council was much astir. Messengers went out forthwith, and elves were sent for with great haste to take a stand by Alderelm. Sage spoke in various circles on ideas brought forth by Lemnoss. Discussions were held throughout the night. There would be an excellent chance to hold off an onslaught if word could be sent out in time and aide came quickly. Still and all, Llaurantis was vast, and exactly how long it would be before ruin swung for a second swipe could only be guessed.

By the pink of morning light, the council was largely dispersed. Knowlton stood with the determined grounding of his namesake and looked about those who remained: LittleLeaf, the elders Willow and Hardtack, The Coyotl of Tirades, and the bizarre elf and Daun who arrived with the season. The latter two he knew not of, but noble were the Dauns and elves, and so he skirted his inquisitive nature and clung steadfastly to his intuition, although he observed the elf with curiosity. It was exceedingly rare to meet a Puman if that was, in fact, this elf's ketyl.

Knowlton mused on the thought. The elf's raiment did indeed match the typical Puman wears. His lean locks possessed the smooth blend of the Puman's late summer hues and the many red streaks of ripened age—a hallmark unique to the Puman ketyl. Yet those eyes, the windows to his spirit, had no gold inkling of the great cat. No. Rather were this elf's eyes grey, nearly translucent. Haunting. The old Ironwood suppressed a shudder.

"Best be we rest," said Hardtack.

All nodded, stretching their legs and backs, and headed for the stairs. Sage stayed in his place and followed their steps with words.

"When more elves arrive, Alderelm will be able to defend herself from the Ashindi. I then mean to head to Pythium."

Riled, Hardtack and Knowlton turned on the Coyotl rapidly, speaking over each other, incensed and emotionally exhausted.

"Best be," Hardtack said, "if you are going to behave as a lollylob—"

"Lagacious!" Knowlton protested.

"—to travel to Shee!" Hardtack said.

"Shee?" Sage repeated.

"Hardtack!" Knowlton spat. "Do not give him thoughts for Shee as well!"

"For 'tis," Hardtack bellowed, "the quickest route for a fool!"

All eyes widened, for Hardtack was the slowest of the elders to raise his voice or rise to anger.

Knowlton bolstered Hardtack's notion. "How might you just march up to Geul's front gate? Imbecility!"

Not an inkling worse for wear, the Coyotl mused. "Shee. Not had I considered such a course of action."

"Ack! No, no!" cried Knowlton. "Blasted Hardtack! Why did you put such a thought in his thick, empty head?"

"You know," Willow pondered, "As the last of the mages, the grumbies of Shee might be able to confirm whether or not Emerus is destroyed. They might indeed be able to offer other insights for us as well. Although the veil of Shee is closing, such a venture would be a terrible risk."

"Why?" Knowlton asked, massaging his temples, "Just why, Lagacious? Would you go to Pythium—what are you playing at? You would not survive this time."

"No," replied Sage flatly, "but I would succeed, and Geul would be no more."

Willow interceded, continuing her cause. "If 'twas truly realized that Emerus was not forever lost, it would rally our spirits beyond measure."

"Of course, Emerus is not lost," Knowlton grumbled. "We would not doubt our condition if the balance of Nature were destroyed."

"Hmm, perhaps," replied Willow thoughtfully, wisely. "Yet the balance of Earth may unravel before us. The kin of Earth, even the Treeans, would deny what was before their very eyes, so terrible, so unfathomable the condition of our fate. Here." And so saying, Willow gestured to Leaf. "We have the knowledge of Earth within the Sakatu, our Lastborn's delicate embraces, and Emerus—the balance of Earth. Knowlton, we do not know whether Emerus lies broken or lost. And I think it is no accident that Shee was introduced into our discourse. I believe if Sage is to run a hero's errand, then the outcome of a messenger to Shee would serve us better."

"I will go with you!" cried Leaf.

"That you cannot do," countered the Coyotl, within a blink of breath and more sternly than he meant. "You, my young friend, are the carrier of a precious gift. Not within a veiled realm would I take two such precious treasures, not to Shee and certainly ne'er to Pythium." He eyed the Sakatu hung around her neck, so small and unassuming, and smiled; weren't all the very best effects of life just like this—small and unassuming? "You have a luster akin to the stars, and those stars wait with anticipation to behold your deeds, but now's not the time, not the least with the likes of me."

The elf's words struck the Treean hard, not so much from hurt or anger but from sheer frustration, and she ran unsure how to contain or display her emotions. She ran as hard as she could, tears welling up and running down her cheeks as she caught the breeze of the fresh morning air outside.

"You would travel alone to the Gateway of the Underworld?" asked Noblien, incredulous.

"Aye. I've thought it all along," answered Sage, concentrating on the fletchings of the Puman's arrows rather than his face.

"Nay, Lagacious," said Hardtack. "Pythium is a pointless task for thee. Geul may have started all this, but his death would not end it. In suggesting you journey to Shee, I meant only to counter your outrageous plan with one equally preposterous, but Willow has tipped the point. I reckon now that I should urge your insanity to take you there."

"Your lack of good sense is contagious," said Knowlton gravely. "Best be if you are determined to face this newfound threat on your own, then perhaps you should confront it through the nuances of Shee's strange talons. These are desperate times. I cannot believe I concur—all of this is complete madness. Yet, the grumbies' visions may aid our needs, for they see what the Trees cannot." Knowlton sighed resolutely. He had made up his mind. "Do not go to Geul's realm . . . Alderelm needs you. And once again, she asks no small request." The elder's eyes softened beneath their brim, and his voice broke flatly but was dogged. "Enlist the succor of Shee."

"Aye, my Heartwood. I'd not defy a request of Alderelm," and so saying, Sage bowed his head. "I will travel to Shee."

"I'll journey with you," said Noblien. "I've had dealings with the grumbies and am familiar with the land."

"You've had dealings with the inhabitants of Shee?" interrupted Sage, raising an impish eyebrow as he noted a small sigil upon the elf's hairline at one corner. "And they say I'm wild for such ventures," and so commenting, he sized the Puman up, an incredulous grin spreading upon his calloused face.

Noblien's expression remained earnest. "If you accept my company, you must know I'm an exile of my ketyl."

Sage tilted his head in a feral curiosity teetering on disbelief, although his expression remained impassive. "Listen, my good elf, I care not as long as you can use that bow you carry." And he meant it.

"I will join this journey," said Tullkaee, plainly and with the rigidity of a mountain wherein all understood that her pronouncement was not a suggestion.

Knowlton took in the three, his face unmoving, unreadable. To each in turn did his gaze fall intently. Hard was his look, edged with the lines of burden many years pent. "We cannot send thee to task without at least knowing of thy callings?"

Noblien, at long last, smiled, and the Daun put a fist to her chest and bowed her head. "I am Tullkaee, representing my people, the Dauns. Our meeting is an honor."

Knowlton rumbled, hemming and hawing, his voice old and throaty. "Greetings. I am Knowlton Hophornbeam. Before you are the Heartwoods, Willow, and Hardtack."

Sage said, "These are Alderelm's elders, Noble Daun."

Tullkaee bowed again as Knowlton's voice burbled forth. "You are the first of your kind to step within Alderelm, though we know of your people and keep well their accounts. The Ancient Ones express warm regards." He finished, lowering his eyes upon Noblien. "And you, exiled Puman?"

"An honor unmet, Lord Hophornbeam. My calling is Noblien."

The old Ironwood waited for more from the Puman but, seeing the cause hollow, hemmed and hawed respectfully. "Ah, well done, well done. Knowlton will do, sir elf. We thank you both for your high merit."

Willow stepped forward and kissed the Daun's brow. Then, she lightly kissed the Puman's cheek. She stood face to face with him, commanding his attention.

"Truly much later than expected," she said, inhaling.

Noblien's expression begged for clarity. Yet the Heartwood only smiled, radiating a calm kindness that enveloped him.

"Sage Lagacious," said Knowlton. "You vex me. In recollecting, I've reasoned that we've spent more time at odds with one another than not," and so saying, he rested for an instant in his thoughts. "But," he continued with a snorting huff, "this is because you are worth the effort.

You're as good and kind an elf as you are a contentious pain in my stump, which is saying much. Notwithstanding all sense of truth, thy heart holds the wealth-well of honesty. I dare say you have justly earned the love and respect you hold on this White Mountain. You are no less than a Treean," and so saying, he pulled out a blade from under the wicker-withes that made up the bottom half of his long sleeve. The instrument was a small, vicious little sword, curved in a sweet, elegant fashion; it whispered against the sliced air. The elder caressed its engravings patterned nearly the entire length of the blade.

"Timbriel?"

"You know it is," the elder scoffed.

The elf's crooked smile lengthened across his face. "A fair sight, my Heartwood."

Knowlton grunted in agreement and stared for some time at the blade. Sage, too, admired it, but his countenance had become one of questioning and even worry, for the old Ironwood was acting out of sorts, which made the Coyotl uncomfortable.

"This sword records my family lineage, no small measure to account for. It was conferred to me by my mother. Its heritage is proud."

"Yes, my liege," concurred Sage, agreeing emphatically; he knew the truth behind Knowlton's legacy.

"Sage Lagacious of the Coyotl ketyl, you are no less a son of Knowlton Hophornbeam, Heartwood of Alderelm, than if you stemmed from my own branch. I bestow upon you, Timbriel."

Sage stumbled backward, holding his hands to his chest, mouth dropping. Knowlton's face grimaced. He was fighting back much emotion, the corners of his mouth arching up.

"Stand up straight," he growled, but the elf sank to one knee and lowered his head.

Knowlton pulled him up while quieting him by indicating that speech was unnecessary, or perhaps and more likely, undesired, his strict determination conveying the importance. Upon transferring the blade's mirrored edges into the Coyotl's palms, the Treean elder placed a heavy hand on the Sage's shoulder. Then, he turned away and headed for the stairs. He did not look back.

◆◈ Chapter 8 ◈◆

Night creeps in on the Soldier Tree,
Standing hard against wind and time,
Darkening walls, raging sea,
Hands clutch at the moon's shine.

—Words spoken by a lemure during the last stand of the Camelop ketyl
and carried on the wind whereupon they were discerned by the sylphs
and forevermore put to memory

Leaf snuggled into Miriam with heavily hung shoulders and a well of
tears barely withheld. She felt a loss inside herself, one she could not
cognitively grasp, and feeling Miriam's reassuring hums was comforting.
The Tree's old, weathered carapace expressed a sentiment of love most
rare. The speech of the Ancient Ones, the language of Anastomose,
conveys an unparalleled depth of meaning. For this small script of
history, Miriam's expression to Leaf is wholly inadequate, and it is in the
knowledge of this fact that one may grasp an intimation of its beauty and
weight:

"Scores of LeadTrees have borne the duty of guardianship. I have
known them well, a line of hearts true, each dear to me. The likeness

thou dost hold to thy lineage is evident. Stand tall and greet the changing winds with reverence—'tis an honor you are gifted. LittleLeaf of the LeadTree Line, time hath been good enough to grant us many suns together. To have shared one sunrise with thee, to have shared one sunset, to have felt thy touch for one instant, would I be grateful for, and look, we have shared far more."

Leaf rested silently in Miriam's company throughout the day, pouting between naps. The following day, as the sun approached its full height over the horizon, she saw Hardtack approaching. She wiped her tear-salted face and sat strong.

Hardtack was, by all accounts, the gentlest of the Treeans. He loved everyone. He was a Heartwood well-suited to the duties of his people, caring much for the simplest pleasures and little for the slightest sorrows. Of late, Leaf had been foremost on his mind. He sat beside her and looked out to the north, whistling softly. Leaf glanced at him out of the corner of her eye.

Hardtack sighed. "Well, LittleLeaf—"

"Hardtack," Leaf interrupted. "I'm tired of being the little Treean."

"Oh, hmm, yes, I see your predicament," said Hardtack, nodding in greatest empathetic condolence. "I was once young like you."

Leaf twitched the corner of her mouth in disbelief that Hardtack could remember being young. Hardtack smiled to himself and placed a blade of quillwort between his lips, softly chewing its tip.

"Yes, I was called Birchleaf—Birch for short."

Leaf propped her chin upon her fist and gazed upon the old, knobbed lines of Hardtack's face with intrigue.

"There are so many Birches. Even Knowlton is a Birch, you know. I didn't like my calling—not one bit. It indicated where I came from, not who I was. Birch! Humph. In my mind, this was no different from being called Treean! No, no, no. I was very unhappy. But no one listened. You know, I was the youngest of my family branch. Though I didn't stay young, as you can see, and I'm no longer called Birch, as you can see," and so saying, a percolating chuckle accompanied a fading sparkle in his eyes as he recollected the living past. "I grew up in one momentous day . . . been called Hardtack ever since."

Leaf waited for a tale of grand adventure, but Hardtack only began to whistle and gaze out far and wide. She narrowed her eyes and watched him. He suppressed a smile, choosing instead to chew on the blades of quillwort and pretend he did not realize she waited upon him.

Leaf could not contain her impatience and protested with a playful nudge. "Nooo! Tell the whole story!" How did your calling change?"

"Your ears are too young for such a story."

"Ah, Hardtack!" Leaf said, jumping into his stalky arms.

The gentle elder threw back his head and laughed heartily before sighing with the deepest of breaths and growing quite solemn. "When I was about your age, I had trouble keeping up with the others. And I don't mean grown Treeans. No, no. I mean those my own age."

Leaf thought of the prospect of having Treeans her age. *What would that be like?* she wondered. Hardtack's low, rum-rumbling voice brought her attention back.

"I'm a bit ponderous, you know, ne'er been nimble within the high limbs," he said, peering up under Miriam's arches. "Knowlton, though older than me, often stayed behind 'til I could catch up with the others, but there came a day when even Knowlton couldn't wait.

"For one day, high above Alderelm's crown, we heard the strangest and most fantastic screech-roaring. Oh my, all the young Treeans were jumping over themselves to investigate. I was slow and watched as everyone disappeared into the high leaves. I could only place their whereabouts by their eager laughter and cries of excitement. Heartbroken I was. From whatever those sounds had arisen, I would surely miss their discovery. So, I waited below, let happiness flood my heart through the Tree songs transpiring through my soles. Of course, I still listened for my friends in the growing distance, and I listened for more of those remarkable shrieks. The sounds had grown very faint, and I wondered what tales my friends would return with," and so saying, Hardtack paused and chewed more on his quillwort in dreamy satisfaction before letting burst an expression of mirth that startled Leaf completely.

"But I did not have to wait!" he roared. "Indeed! Ramming to the Forest floor was the most wonderful, beautiful creature, oh my! 'Twas a dragon! She had crashed right before me! Ohh, mmm, she was wounded, sad a sight. One ought ne'er to behold the life ichor issuing forth from such a magnificent creature. She was as white as the bark from the Ancient Ones and swung her neck side to side while snapping great, big, shiny, and very sharp teeth up at the air. In another blink of an eye, I had a second dragon afore me! He was bigger than she by twice a measure, enormous! Hmm, I'd say, in total height, he could've nearly reached Miriam's highest bough if not outright overstood her!" Leaf was fixed, mouth gaping and hanging on every word.

"So, there I was, watching these two dragons standing face to face, snarling at each other! That's when they stretched out their wings. 'Twas apparent they'd been fighting with one another and that this fighting was to continue, and as clear as Lumen that they'd not stop 'til one or the other, or both, was grievously injured! I abhorred the realization. These spectacular creatures of such power and grace—why? They could fly in the sky, cross the sea, and bend under and above Trees or cliffs with no more effort than my friends could whittle themselves through the deer paths of Alderelm. My heart hurt. It actually pained me. So I ran right between them."

Leaf gasped aloud, and the elder, encouraged by her rapt interest, continued. "I cannot fully explain why I did what I did—I just did. Oh my," guffawed Hardtack. "I must've looked like such a small and idiotic morsel of insignificance, waving my arms about, trying to speak in dragon tongue, crying 'Stop, stop. You'll kill each other!'" and so saying, he covered his eyes and shook his head at the thought, then looked back at Leaf with a chortle.

"The Sacred Ones told me later that's not quite what I said, but the meaning was understood well enough. Believe it or not, the two dragons took heed! The white one lowered her long neck and stared eye-to-eye with me so close I could see the flecks of color in her eyes! 'Twas a life-changing experience. A snort on my backside brought my attention to the other. He was a fine specimen, Leaf! Copper scales, golden horns . . . enormous talons! I'd no inclination to move, however. To both, I switched my gaze; what wonder, nose to nose, snout to snout with two dragons! I touched the white one; her fur was so soft, and I nodded to the copper one. They spread their wings, arched them over me, and took flight. I ne'er beheld them again.

"During this, the others had returned—caught sight of what had happened. Knowlton said that no one else would've been able to stand so still, so hard. He said I was as hard as the tack of the Ancient Ones, and the name Hardtack stuck."

Leaf hugged the elder tight; Hardtack stole back tears. How delightfully memories played before his mind's eye; so proud of the young Treean on the verge of full Treedom. So proud.

"You'll not always be thought of as LittleLeaf," he whispered.

Short-lived were future visions to perform their score; strange echoes had begun to fill the soil. Both felt it, but Leaf did not recognize their meaning. Hardtack was at once stiff, his deep-set eyes turning morose, even defeated. He was waiting, tense, hoping not to hear it—Miriam's call.

Shaking the earth of the entire mountain, the call did come. The great bellow was the first of many Tree proclamations of imminent danger. Every sacred root under the moss-covered ground echoed the same reality. Leaf had ne'er heard such as this before.

"Too soon," murmured Hardtack. "Leaf, climb atop Miriam. Climb high! Stay there!"

The Heartwood was not one to ever bawl forth in such a commanding tone, and she was at once dreadfully frightened. He boosted her up to get her moving, and she bounded higher and higher amongst Miriam's fresh greens with frantic speed. The elder watched as she did so. Once upon a lofty perch, she understood—the White Mountain was being consumed. Fire! Red, orange, hot, and cruelly vicious, the flames crackled and sparked, spreading like lightning streaks across a summer's night sky—the Ashindi had come.

❧ ✦ ☙

The blaze licked the Forest floor with a taunting approach on Bristleton's heels. He ran furiously toward the Tarn of Lumen. He knew he should be commanding the line of Treeans still waiting hopefully for the elves, and faster still, he raced; he felt an eternity in the short journey. Stopping, he turned, his eyes desperately searching. Deep the exhalation that took him on spotting Sage's lean silhouette upon the stone steps. The elf was tinged with an uncomfortable awareness, and staring past the Lumen's reflective shadows, he beheld Bristleton's face aglow.

"Sage! We have been caught ill-prepared. The Ancient Forest cannot protect her. You must depart now and take Leaf with you!"

Sage looked aghast as he eyed Bristleton's raiment, an amalgam of dirt and ash. "Where's Knowlton?"

Bristleton did not answer. Rage swelled within the Coyotl; his heart was stricken.

"I'll not leave!"

Bristleton pointed toward the mighty Treetops, and above all the others, Miriam towered. There, within her shelter, sat a frightened and pitifully small shape.

"We entrust our most sacred gift with you."

"It cannot be this way!" yowled the Coyotl. "Knowlton wouldn't want it!"

Bristleton shoved him away with a stunning force, turned, and disappeared within the smoke. Sage looked hopelessly for his friend, his expression a contortion of bewildered grief, but there was no use of it. Primal arose his urge to wipe clear these enemies, to ravage the Ashindi and let loose all the uncounted seasons of his wrath upon them. He looked around and all about as the Ashindi's magic caused the Treeans to look like horrifying specters. Yet to his relief, bows hummed, and arrows found their marks with sharp speed; they had remembered well his words, and the Ashindi were shrinking back. This was at least a bit of good. At that moment, a piercing and familiar whistle whipped across the air, arched with urgency. Whithersoever, the source of the call was no matter, for it elicited the fierceness within the tormented Coyotl to take flight to his appointed task and abandon the call of bloodlust.

As light as a drifting feather does inevitably settle to the earth, and for its weight land with the slightest permanency, so too did the soles of the Coyotl's feet hit the ground; not a sound to be heard as he dashed to Miriam's bole. He looked up into her immense leaf world, and for it, Leaf jumped promptly to his side, mainly taken by fear but having come to no harm.

"Conditions call on you to entrust yourself to me," said Sage, picking Leaf up within his arms and drawing out his newly gifted sword. "Timbriel," continued he, his rusty voice taking on the most velvet of hushes, "long since I've caught sight of you. May I prove half the skill and spirit of my predecessor, the Old Ironwood himself." He looked around one last time. A wild glint shone in his eyes. "Path of endless challenges . . . it will be a pleasure."

Wreathing in a serpent dance, the twisting curls of fire approached in all its wickedness. Leaf shouted for Bristleton, but Sage paid no heed and ran waywardly, ducking and darting to escape the flames. He could feel her rapid heartbeat, her small voice calling for her kin.

At the bottom of an embankment, the sparks near behind them, the Coyotl and Leaf slid underneath a copse of tightly woven shrubs. On their stomachs, Sage looked at her with dead-set eyes.

"Now is the time to gather yourself. You must stay silent if we are to escape. Though the devilish scowls do not know it, they hunt for you."

She looked at him, a mutated blur through her tears. The spitting of flames snapped and broke repeatedly against the Great Trees. The ancient bark held under the malice, but life upon the smoldering ground unraveled, disintegrating into the tomb of blackened earth. The sound of crackling laughter, empty and treacherous, muted her heartache and transformed it into molten fear.

The Coyotl pointed to a stand of ponderosas, and Leaf nodded in understanding and compliance. Yet any further progression of escape was deterred when Sage heard a nearby cry of pain; he froze stock-still like prey, having detected the scent of a predator.

His ears and eyes keener than ever, he listened and watched. Again, he heard a cry, stifled within a guttural groan, and in a bare instant, he scurried away. Leaf found herself alone. Beneath her, the Trees spoke to one another, and she lay hard, clenching her fingers into the soil, their voices bringing her comfort.

Sage had only traveled a few paces from the Treean. Still, the murk of Ashindi, the bodiless forms enveloping, smothering, and strangling every living quality of the Forest, had settled close by, and she could not see him; only the elf knew the number of strides parting them. He hearkened for the little one to his rear and the sporadic throes to his fore. Blustering was the wave of heat that rushed around him; the smoke specters had detected him, but only more did he concentrate his intent and attention. He lowered himself evenly and slowly into a squat ever so close to the ground, his foreweight balanced on two fingers, silent and waiting. A sibilant whirring encircled him, the Ashindi beginning their devouring work, but Sage remained unmoving, straining to behold his hopes.

The suffering cry reemerged to his right, and there, his piercing gaze caught sight of a figure composed of fire . . . and a familiar elf to its side. Sage smiled devilishly, ever and always wryly and crookedly.

"Get down!" he cried to the pair, drawing forth his bow and letting loose three arrows into the reeking ash of smoke and oppression.

The Ashindi recoiled, releasing himself and the others from their heated maws. Flames erupted into tornadoes of whipping heat while angry fire claws clasped wildly at the air in tantrums—yet they did not approach any closer.

Running to, then kneeling over and inspecting what had previously been presented as a fire creature, Sage blew out a sigh and cocked an eye to the elf. "'Tis grand to see you, friend, but Tullkaee is a grievous sight."

"Aye," panted Noblien. "The flesh upon her arm has been badly weathered. And her breathing is of no good either. The noble Daun has inhaled deeply the acrid tastes of this foulness, and she seems to worsen rapidly. Is there clear air to be had nowhere?"

"We will find it on our descent down the mountain."

"What!" said Noblien, scrunching his face and shrinking back as though Sage's words were poison that might touch him. "We are elves. Alderelm needs us against this foe."

"Yes," agreed Sage, "they do. However, we cannot," and so saying with a sigh, he encouraged a young Treean from out of the brush. "I have a trinket of value thrust upon me and am enlisting your aide on the spot."

"Lawks," responded Noblien, stepping forward and resting his hand on Leaf's head.

"You may calm yourself, little one," Sage purred, "You now find yourself in excellent company."

Leaf gaped at Tullkaee, who was gasping on the ground. Then she looked back up to Noblien, the Fierce-Eyed Elf meeting her gaze with a serene smile. How he could look calm or even smile amongst the tumult surrounding them was bewildering, but the sight of him gave her an immediate mind of reason, and she gathered herself up steadily. Likewise, Noblien was glad beyond measure to take sight of the young Treean. His tall frame stooped low to gaze level into her eyes.

"Are you all right?"

"LittleLeaf LeadTree," Sage interrupted, "a mighty spirit dwells within you. Find it now, for we are in your need. You alone can speak with the Trees and know every measure of this mountain. We need a quick path to the western side—to the River Sasa. Can you do this?"

She felt like a mere limb shaking in the wind, but in physicality, she stood firm. Her mind sped, and she swallowed deeply. Dreadful were Tullkaee's groans. She felt a mounting pressure. She closed her eyes and concentrated, digging her toes under the soil, tapping into the mass of communication underground. One Tree after another heard her, quieting each in turn as they transferred paths of safety throughout the Forest; it was a concentrated task for all.

"I know a way."

It was a gulch, a wet choice for early spring, shaped by granite boulders buttressed by columned basalt. Foreboding perhaps, yet far favored over fire. She did not provide details, for it seemed trivial under the circumstances.

"Then let us be off," responded Sage.

Yet there came a hesitation in the Treean, a tug on the tip of her recollections, a memory she could almost touch. She focused on the Daun, the injured warrior making her way to her feet, the sub-flesh upon her arm sorely exposed. Leaf grimaced.

And as if drawn by reflex, she dashed off, calling out behind her, "I'll be right back," before either elf could grab her.

"Leaf!" Sage hissed.

She moved swiftly and did not glance back. There was a purple-flowered plant called the timtoss that could tend one's burns: burns were so exceptionally rare amongst Treeans that it was a miracle she had even recollected it. Broad were its leaves, and therein was the medicine she now sought. She knew of a cluster growing near the Rock of Many Holes, not far, though perhaps smoldering by now. *Yes!* she thought with relief as they came within sight. The plant was still safe, sheltered underneath a moist, rocky shelf. She gingerly picked three of its leaves and scurried back.

The disapproving countenances of both elves greeted her return. Unabashed, she proudly held out the leaves in her palm. Noblien squinted down at them and back at her with no small level of scorn. He knew the leaves of this plant well and was glad for them but was none too pleased to have obtained them at such a risk. He took the leaves to Tullkaee while Sage frowned in disapproval at her. Their silence of condemnation was more disconcerting than if they had verbally scolded her recklessness.

Her necklace hung low, the Sakatu dangling. Sage eyed it coldly, finding an outlet for his frustration. "Deign it proper to keep that piece of Tree out of sight."

"The Sakatu?" asked Leaf.

"Aye," bit the Coyotl. "These fiends want it razed from existence. Keep it from sight."

Noblien finished tending Tullkaee's wound and took to Sage's side. His tone was measured, yet stern, hoarsely whispered in the Elvish tongue. "She's a youngling. Not does she understand any of this, much less the powers residing within the vessel she conducts."

Responding in the same vernacular, respecting the discretion, Sage replied flatly, "Good elf, before the attack on Alderelm, our situation was grievous. Now, 'tis utterly, dismally grim."

Noblien scoffed in disagreement with a guttural release from the back of his throat. "I do not pretend to know your torments. But watch your mood around that little one. Let not the pains of this world harbor your heart where that Treean lies, or she'll bear more scars than need be while we are present—she has a lifetime before her to earn those."

Sage glanced at Leaf, who watched them converse with wide eyes of utter vulnerability and confusion, the epitome of fresh innocence. He frowned, then exhaled heavily, ruffling his hair in agitation.

"Better it be while we are present," Sage grumbled.

Noblien's face screwed up in disbelief upon receiving such a callous reply, but Sage had already disregarded him and administered directions to their leaving at once. Leaf touched the ground and absorbed it into memory. All were solemn to see it. Then they were off.

Leaf led them quickly, doggedly, down a fox trail. Not even a trail, as one would call it, but a narrow ribbon of delicately pressed vegetation, a trodden path for the smaller creatures. So many times, she had paced near here, secretly waiting for Bristleton's patrol to pass. Now, she ran flat out, dodging and ducking obstacles, an insidious urgency pressing each footstep. Just a blur, they sped by a lazy day reminder, a stone adorned with spiraled carvings and other etchings. Onward, they dashed. Bigdebar swept down in gentle touch and drew many boughs behind the group for protection as they fled. Nertle, too, brushed the Treean as she passed, but her awkwardly bent boughs snapped back against the others; deep gurgles of apology poured forth.

The gulch was just beyond the nursery of Cedars now; faster and faster, their feet pattered. Leaping high and landing low, they all met the stinging cold of the water. Leaf was thankful the gulch did not flow as hard as she had feared. Down and down they crawled and slid.

Looking back from where they had come, they could see the insidious smoke hovering over Alderelm. All their hearts were heavy upon the dreadful sight, but arrows were flying strong, and the three warriors were glad to see it. As for Leaf, she was sickened. She imagined she could hear Miriam calling out to her, but so many Trees and so far away, she could not be sure.

Swiftly, they descended, but it seemed an endless time to the bottom. The frigid fluid shared its space generously, but with a biting price. It was getting the better part of all of them. Thankful though they were for the gulch's sheltering cradle, they listened desperately for the flowing waters of the Sasa River.

In the time it takes a porcupine to climb Perchard, the tallest Sitka in Llaurantis, the river's sonance was finally discerned. Its burbling was a chorus of harmonic rustling twists; however, the sound caused Leaf to shiver through and through. The memory of her near fall into the Sasa's wild abandon, those enticing blue-green waters of cleansing purity, was all too fresh. Such strength as of the river is not to be trifled with, even for a glimpse of her exquisite beauty. The memory reflected itself within a subconscious action, and Leaf hesitated. Despite that, the gentle nudging of the elves kept her moving until the outlet of the gulch arrived. Surreal was the sight, for the gulch kissed the river from the air rather than the land.

The group surveyed the view before them, a steep drop-off of abyssal nature. Although the inspection was brief for Sage, it seemed his biggest quandary was the mud covering his clothing. He fussed and fussed, wiping here and there in neurotic disgust, wholly preoccupied with what was irrelevant to the others, when an unexpected segment of the gulch's sidewall collapsed and fell in beside him. With this, one of Nature's many unpredictable wiles, the Coyotl was instantly swept off his feet and fed over the gully's edge.

Leaf gasped, grabbing Noblien's forearm. Yet at once, the Sasa merely weaved the elf into her waters with lustrous caresses, gentle and soft, where a moment before had flowed more than the temperate, swishing waters. A wide, solemn peace rested upon the Puman's countenance.

"Do you remember my words about retaining your wits and feet?" he asked.

Leaf relaxed with a partial smile, but Noblien did not notice. He looked on at Sage with curious pity.

"Well, I'm clean now," Sage called from below.

The Coyotl melded into the blue and swam about as though trouble had not just been snapping at their heels. In tired wonder, Leaf observed the elf and contemplated: *Amidst so much tragedy, how does one accept respite, however brief?* The inadequacy of dwelling anywhere but within the gloom of depression seemed unconscionable, so she turned her weary eyes to Tullkaee. The Daun looked formidable, the mud endowing her with the qualities of a painted warrior.

"The Earth is our mother, a pleasure to feel on my skin," Tullkaee said, turning her face to the heavens while curving her toes over the precipice. "I wear her with honor. Now, I honor her daughter's call, the river," and so saying, she cradled her wounded appendage against her heart and leaped.

Leaf, aghast, stared in wonderment, the brambles of her hair pinned flat against her head as though they might hide. Noblien regarded her with patient cordiality, his manner and mood at ease within an acumen finely tuned to the environment and no less for the concerns of the little Treean.

At last, she spoke, her voice a bare whisper. "I care to keep my feet firmly planted and take a less carefree route to the river."

"Then let us descend."

Sage and Tullkaee were rinsing off their gear and clothing upon the river's shore by the time the pair had whittled their way down the hardhack-covered steep. The group remained largely quiet, each tending their accoutrements against a newly formed breeze, subtle and crisp, flowing over and atop the water as the pink-rose sun descended, tainted by a smoke-induced orange hue. Leaf felt numb, as in a dream, catatonic but awake. She sat back against a Linden Tree, its voice a tickle of purrs and buzzes, undecipherable as any language. Yet Leaf was well able enough to detect a pleasant personality within gentle tones and soothing inflections. This was a much-needed solace for the Treean, and she absorbed it all, closing her eyes and gradually allowing her breath to soften into deep, unforced inhalations.

She did not know if she had fallen asleep, but curiosity pried open weighted lids upon hearing the tink, tink, and rustling of movement. She yawned and stretched, observing the Puman sheathing two thinly curved war blades upon his back. His manner of movement reminded her of Bristleton. The elf possessed the same unwavering air and a tangible kindness nestled between steadfastness. He spoke only when a matter of substance needed to be said, taking often to leaving questions unanswered. These qualities granted reassurance as well as heartache. She sighed and turned her eyes to the Coyotl.

From face to foot, as well as she could discern, Sage was covered in markings, pale symbols of a kind she had ne'er beheld before. Their quantity was numerous, and their size minuscule, which seemed a physical attribute well-suited to his fidgety nature. Even now, his right shoulder sporadically ticked upward to his ear while each finger of his bow hand took turns tapping upon a thumb in continual rotation. His entire deportment was edgy and disheveled, although once he felt her eyes on him, these aspects were quickly negated with a smile, genuine if not innocently impish. He added a layer of silk in the form of a wink. She thought him an endless curiosity in the most wonderful of ways.

Tullkaee was Sage's contrast of day to night. For the Daun was a spirit fully present in the moment required, exemplified as she lay resting; her entire body complete in inaction, heavy upon and almost sinking into the earth, so limp was she. Yet if action were to call, she could heave herself to attentiveness with remarkable speed; there was no doubt.

And time was calling on action, summoning the Puman to the awareness of his kind's peculiar gift; his sense of danger caused his brows to knit after he sniffed the air.

"Some menace begins again to accost us, yet I do not know what kind. Come, it is time to advance upon our course."

"Ah, good. Then let us get on with it," replied Sage.

"What about Alderelm?" Leaf pressed, her voice an ice-covered limb creaking within the frozen fog under the weight and rigidity set against it. For all her wanderlust, she wanted only now to go home. The realism of the events leading to this moment and the totality of the journey at hand left her with a heartsickness weighted amidst an unimaginable emptiness.

"Oh, child," sighed Noblien, kneeling before her. "Alderelm has the finest warriors of every kin to fight for her—and the elves will soon arrive to her aide."

Sage's complexion tinged ashen. He uttered not a word.

"For now," Noblien continued, "we must seek answers—we go to Shee . . . keeping you and the seed safe and returning to Alderelm with good tidings."

"'Tis actually a nut."

The Elf of Noble Heart smiled narrowly and nodded in acquiescence. "Hold strong for a few days, and we will present ourselves at one of her entrances and wait."

The nettle brambles of her hair flattened. "Wait. Why must we wait?"

"Surely a Treean knows the answer to this?"

"No. We hold more riddles than history concerning the Land of Shee."

"I see," and so saying, Noblien smiled gently again. "The land moves. One ne'er knows exactly where it will appear or when it will vanish. It does not belong to the Earthen realm. And, as with all aspects regarding this land, finding one of her gateways at the precise allotted time in which she may present herself is precarious at best. She is a fickle land. Alas, she is our course."

Leaf concentrated on this, and the Fierce-Eyed Elf, seeing her, for the time being, emotionally satiated, turned to Tullkaee and the Coyotl.

"We must be on."

Neither questioned nor hesitated, commencing at once the reassembly of their weaponry.

Tullkaee slung a bow over her head, affixing it to her side with the striped pelt of a cave lion, the tail hanging as a jeweled pendant from her shoulder. Around her neck, a knotted leather cord dangled a knife encased in a sheath of black-dyed buckskin, ensuring handy access for more menial chores; its delicate quality a distraction from the ferocity of other blades presented upon her person. Although one knife, rough-edged and wide, was unlikely to be distinguished from aught until upon one's throat, for it was beautifully camouflaged upon her mid-thigh. And at last, while lamenting the loss of her lance destroyed during the attack upon Alderelm, the mighty Daun grasped her tomahawk, latching its sheath onto her waist belt with a heavy sigh.

Noblien strapped his arm and leg scabbards. There was a quickness in his actions, a sureness unfaltering, as though a thousand suns had seen this done. Another knife disappeared within his sleeve before, and at last, he mounted his bow and quiver upon his back. Sage placed a knife down his boot, which was held by a strap at his ankle.

Leaf observed every movement of the three in a tired trance but no less a craving curiosity. More weapons were upon them than she had reckoned a possibility. The wealth of hidden battlements instilled within her a feeling of some enlightenment while a piece of naivety, young and precious, seemed to shrivel away. In its place, there came a bold new vigor, indomitable and in desperate need of moderation, but a vigor, nonetheless. To this end, her attention migrated toward the Coyotl with a feral curiosity.

Sage was lost in the folds of preoccupation, whispering elven blessings to Knowlton's old blade. He stroked its shimmering edges, and as he did so, the silver sword turned intermittently aquamarine like the colored edges of free-flowing water. As if in an attempt to return home, refractions of its light met the river and, therein, spread tentacles of glittering life. Leaf came under its spell, eyeing the sword with a hunger formerly reserved for the expeditions unfolded within her mind; Sage's wide, crooked grin inferred an agreement of sentiment.

"We must find you a weapon," said Tullkaee, noticing the Treean's interest. "Every warrior should have one."

"Hmm, yes. I, too, can teach you what I know of archery—and the sword," added Sage.

"Bah," said Tullkaee, "A lance would serve you far better—a staff to start with."

Waving the Daun's comment aside, Sage stepped forward. "Rare an opportunity is given, for you have three teachers and styles before you."

Noblien rolled his eyes closed and gritted his teeth tightly. And while he had not yet spoken a word, the energy radiating off his person was felt, and the group fell silent. When he opened his eyes, he took a deep breath. The stony reticence in the air surrounding him was menaced by determined strides that placed him directly in front of the Treean with intimidating speed. Pitted against all of this was a lowered voice of many battle-fought ages, with an edge too smooth to be comfortable with. He placed a finger on her forehead.

"Here resides all you need." So saying, he turned to face the river, thus turning his back to the group and, in so doing, conceding to the disintegration of any point of purpose or significance of the moment.

The Daun and Coyotl stood mildly inept and slack-jawed at having had their previous moment displaced and more by craving the wisdom that had displaced it. Leaf, frustrated by all of life, kicked a pebble. Landing with a solid plunk into the river, the marbled crust of earth sank as surely as her spirit. What of this action incited the Puman's blood may ne'er be known, but the Fierce-Eyed Elf turned on Leaf with frightening speed.

"Show me you can use the weapon of your mind, and I will teach you the elven art of the blade and bow. They are a complement only to one's wit. One should not lust after these implements of death. Life is the greatest accomplishment there is in this world ... aside from choosing to live it," and so saying, he paused and searched the Treean's face. "Do you understand?"

Leaf nodded in complete composure and serenity, yet her green eyes danced. Seeing this, the side of Noblien's mouth ticked up with moderate displeasure. Sage laughed outright, cackling heartily. "The Treean will yet add to your plentiful red hairs."

QUILLWORT

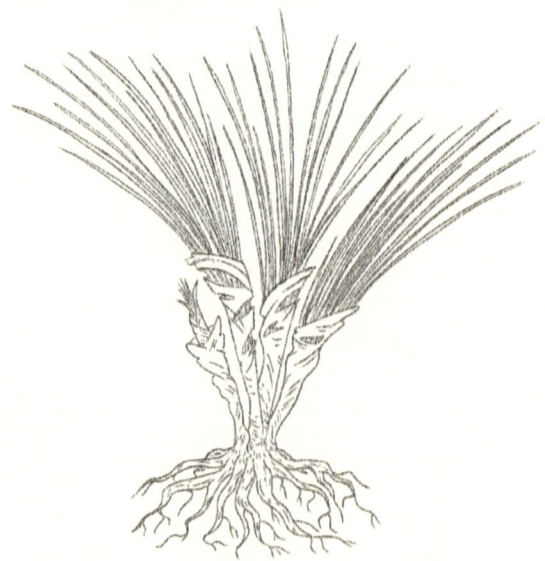

Quillwort. *1.* A common tall, blue sweetgrass of Llaurantis. *2.* Recent Age. A marsh plant of genus Isoetes.

HARDHACK

Hardhack 1. Woody plant having compound diamond-shaped leaves. Fibers from hardhack were useful in making fine fabric. **2.** Recent Age. Known by the common names "steeplebush," "Douglas spirea," and "rose spirea." A woody, flowering plant of the rose family native to eastern North America having pink-shaped flower clusters. The leaves are long, alternately arranged, and toothed at the tips.

TIMTOSS

Timtoss 1. *Purple-flowered plant of broad leaves medicinally used in the healing of burns. 2. Recent Age. Unidentified.*

❧ Chapter 9 ❧

Willow of the west,
Pine of the north,
Oak of the south,
Elm of the east.

—The Woodland's four directions, as taught by faerie kind

The company stayed on a deer path beside the Sasa River until the constellations migrated high into the night sky. They had not taken a rest and were weary. But Noblien pushed them onward, sensing a danger that hovered just outside his perception's grasp. The group moved on without complaint. Yet, as for the peril troubling the elf, while he could almost taste it, he could do no more than feel the insidious way it merely existed, lingering outside of explanation and remaining an indistinguishable force. And for all this, he could not get the group far enough ahead of it; he was unnerved in no small way. So, he pushed the group harder.

The stars had traveled nearly the entirety of the night's axis when, at last, the inevitable occurred: one of them took a misstep in their exhaustion. It was Tullkaee who tripped and fell hard. She winced in pain, not from the fall but from her burns stretched and torn in the act.

Sage's countenance wrinkled in a combination of empathy and worry. "She is still weak. Her wounds are too fresh." Tullkaee grunted in protest. "I meant no offense, noble huntress."

"What was that?" Leaf asked, staring into the dark Forest.

"I hear nothing," responded Tullkaee, rising to her feet. "Do your ears trick you?"

"No, I don't think so," answered the Coyotl, to both their surprise; his attention had been captured, and he, too, searched the innards of the darkness beyond the shrub line.

Noblien, meanwhile, pulled an arrow from his quiver and held its feathered fletching between his fingers. Sage followed by slowly pulling out a long-spindled dagger from its sheath. He held its tip, ready for a long throw.

"Noblien," Leaf whispered. "What's out there?"

"Just the Wood," replied the Daun.

The elves did not add to Tullkaee's answer nor acknowledge that the Treean had even asked for one, as they were too focused on the distance.

Keen and still, Noblien notched the arrow and pulled the bowstring to its haunting place. His hand tightened around the grip, and his bow hummed under the tension.

"Noblien?" Leaf pleaded, insecurity enveloping her.

The Puman still did not answer. The bow was eager for the shot. The ping and hum of the resolute and trusted bow joined the silent whoosh of the departing arrow. No sound was heard thereafter, yet Noblien held still, his eyes fixed in the direction the arrow had flown. He felt a mild tension dissipate with the satisfaction at having marked what trailed their course, along with an irritation at it having had no effect. He sighed a shallow sigh that echoed as more of a feral growl. Sage raised a brow and looked the Puman up and down.

"Speak, friend. Lay out your preoccupations; we are with you."

Noblien did not answer. Sage tugged his sleeve, and the Puman's eyes met the Coyotl's before a genuine breath of any depth escaped them in tacit recognition of their stress and tiredness.

"We need to rest," Noblien stated flatly.

Sage nodded eagerly in amused agreement. "Let us follow this channel away from the river."

The canal lacked the energy of the river's flowing threads, but a far larger sound emanated in its wake. Following the Coyotl's steps, the company drew forth, his spirit animal almost visible through his choppy, casual stride. The steady gush of crashing water greeted them as they approached the outer mist of a tall and narrow waterfall. It tumbled and sprayed with warm hisses, and Sage grinned ear to ear. He beckoned the group forward with a wave, the loudness of the falls blocking the sounds escaping his lips. He strode up with a narrow footstep into the cascades, hugging the wall, and then, leaning forward, he ducked behind the cascading curtain, the waterfall's thick protective shell. One by one, the group followed.

Behind the flowing water shield stood the surroundings of a cave echoing with the falling splashes and droplets of moisture that smelled of musk and minerals. It was a surreal sight: petrified Trees decorated the chamber's expanse, and white crystallized monoliths shone with the luster of the sun on newly fallen snow. The cave was so old that the Ancient Forests might not even remember its advent.

"A water cave," Tullkaee said, marveling. "You elves carry the spirit of the mother close," she continued, nodding in approval and touching one of the calcite trunks. "It is good."

"How did you know?" Leaf wondered, spellbound by the petrified wood's smoothness under her fingers.

"I very well didn't," Sage lilted with a chuckle. "Just a hunch. Although," he paused, "perhaps I did." His voice trailed off as he concentrated. "Well, in any case, we have a secure place of rest for a time."

"Thank the Sasa," said Tullkaee, offering a devotion of gratitude in her language.

Noblien said little and was swift to investigate every slit and chink of the dignified cavern. His movements were agitated and squirmy, as though suffocating under some phantom menace that bristled behind his every step, breathing down his neck, ravening after his blood. Leaf took note of his restive behavior and wilted deportment, which had been, up to this point, confident and even proud. And she thought there was no slight misconception in the belief that the wild cat might choose shelter in a cave when 'twas no less than a cage to its mind. For Coyotls, perhaps comfort was induced more in plenty from a den environment. But for the Pumans, at least this one in particular, he was undoubtedly chapped in these surroundings . . . unless an alternate passage out might be found. So the Fierce-Eyed Elf was keen to discover every access to escape.

A wide crack in a giant slab of basalt opening in the back corner satisfied his itching, and with little matter to it, he commented that he would be back shortly. The Coyotl followed his trail.

"Why do elves do that?" Leaf asked as Tullkaee sat to tend her arm. "Just disappear. When elves leave Alderelm, they often ne'er even say farewell. They simply vanish."

Tullkaee looked at her with earnest steadiness. "They are elves. Their spirit animal is strong in them and guides much of their actions. Remember that Noblien is Puman and Sage is Coyotl. They are, in many ways, the wild itself. Let them be free. Accept them as they are, as they accept you."

❧ ◆ ☙

In good time, Noblien returned with kindling. Shortly after, Sage returned with food, his arms cradling a grand and colorful assortment of nuts and mushrooms and several mar-mar berries, an exceedingly hard-to-find Wood fruit that grows underground throughout the winter and appears just beneath the soil upon the dawn of spring. Hoarded greedily by the faeries, whole underground networks were rumored to exist, but only the fae knew their locations.

Leaf and Noblien's eyes widened in delight while Tullkaee's spirit sank with the harsh bite of reality—they had been forced to leave Alderelm with no provisions. The Daun desired to go hunting, yet the elves insisted this was not prudent. She grumbled much in protest, yet her heart was not truly dissatisfied. She was sore and worn. A peaceful abode for the coming hours would be a comfort.

Noblien set about stacking the kindling for the subtle warmth of small flames when Sage stopped his progress with a look and shake of his head. "Treeans do not find comfort in the creation of fire, my good elf."

Noblien turned his gaze to Leaf in a tortured expression of remorse. "I should have presumed this to be a possibility. LittleLeaf, my apologies."

Leaf pulled her shoulders close to her ears, feeling apologetic and insecure, while Tullkaee moaned and roiled in anguish. "A fire will bring warmth," she pleaded. "It is not of dark purpose."

Sage shook his head. "No, noble huntress. Would you subject a Treean to the element of fire?"

"How is it that Treeans stay warm?" asked Tullkaee, her voice thin with disbelief.

Leaf smiled. "We do not require warmth, only the Trees."

Tullkaee filled the cave with the grumbles of a bear, and Sage laughed to hear it.

"You may light a fire, though," Leaf continued. "'Tis alright. I'll be fine."

"No, dear one, this we will not have," countered the Fierce-Eyed Elf.

Tullkaee continued her grousing, but the group was learning that she grumbled much and often, and there was ne'er much to make of it. "Well then, little Treean spirit," she huffed, "would the lighting of my pipe be unsettling?" Leaf smiled and shook her head. Noblien and Sage met eyes with broad smiles. "Ah, the elves laugh at my expense!"

Sage held up a hand and gestured a measure between his thumb and index finger. "Only a little."

The Daun let loose a surprising thunder of a laugh, deep and rolling, contagious to even the temperaments of the heavy-hearted, at least for the moment that her mirth hung in the air. Tullkaee then pulled out her tomahawk, lighting the narrow top side of the hatchet after carefully stocking it with a sachet of pipeweed. Leaf watched as astonished as she was engrossed.

"Th-this is your pipe?" she stammered.

Tullkaee grinned through puffs while graceful spirals of timid smoke began to ascend. The spicy sweetness of pinyon pine and desert wildflowers filled the water cave. The scents calmed Leaf's senses, and the tiny fern leaves upon her brambles folded, stretching wide and drooping down the length of her tresses. The energy of the group had at last taken a deep inhale.

Sage began to eye Noblien mischievously within this environment, for comfort brought such moods to him. "You remind me in no small fraction of Bris."

Noblien stayed at ease and did not reply.

"Sage," Leaf asked, "How do you know Bristleton?"

"Ah, we met long ago when Knowlton did not have a grey hair on his head," Sage replied. "But more would put us all to sleep." Diverted but undeterred, Sage regarded Noblien once more. "What of you? What's your story?"

"You've hardly completed your own," Noblien replied. "Besides, I've no story."

"Aha!" Sage yelped. "Everyone has a story."

Noblien looked unamused. Tullkaee and Leaf hunched over and listened with intrigue. Sage continued his sibling-like prodding. "Your eyes aren't like any I've ever seen."

"Sage," Noblien replied, "You should not behold me in such ways. How long have you been without a companion?"

Sage laughed with the group. "'Tis been a while, but do not wish to hope for such particulars from me."

Leaf grinned to hear such conversation.

Sage kept on at Noblien. "You don't possess the gold eyes of your Puman kind. Yours are as grey as a morning fog or sheet of summer rain."

"Poetry now? Be off."

The Coyotl turned to Tullkaee and Leaf. "Ne'er scoff at a poet. Indeed, there are ballads of old traversing all the elven realms about Thai Mielle, the Grey-Eyed Elf."

Noblien rose with a resigned sigh and walked back to the corner of the cavern and lay down, saying, "You, my newfound comrade, miss a lot, yet you do not miss much."

Sage eyed him closely but could see no signs of the reaction he had hoped for. Looking like a sulking child, he perked up upon deciding to recite one of the aforementioned songs; it was, after all, on his mind. He spoke in his native tongue, and the words flowed as dried leaves whirled in a light breeze in late autumn. Leaf's eyes were heavy, and the Coyotl's voice became distant, tranquil. Her mind slipped into the blending world of dreams.

Camas and beetle runes,
Welkin blue and cricket tunes,
Honeysouke, sweet the air,
Sunset waters, mountains fair,

Alderelm

Of leaves and shadows and willowy shapes,
Comfort is brought in the time it takes,
Preferring peace under a night sky,
Whither all the world's wiles abide,
Grey eyes—doth he hide in Forest deep?
Under leaf or canopy?
Or rocky crags above the hills?
Unions of elves, behold!
Now captive upon crimson rows,
Light will gleam upon the cresting moon,
Unsullied on the morrow,
Look upon the land today,
No need to gaze with sorrow,
Thwart the fate of elven spirit,
Behest the ban be naught but lyric,
Vestal vow under Tree flowers,
'Tis that time of waking hour!
Veriha! Veriha!
An adamant he doth possess,
Given as a treasure,
Veriha! Veriha!
He'll save the Realms of Haverdome,
And last the days forever.

MAR-MAR BERRIES

Mar-mar Berries. 1. *An evergreen plant producing leathery, alternate, elliptic leaves and having a complex network of rhizomes. The fruits are subterranean purple-red berries that grow during the winter months and ripen in early spring. Warning: Guarded greedily by faeries.* ***2.*** *Recent Age. Unidentified*

DESERT WILDFLOWER

Desert Wildflower. *1.* An annual herb used by humans throughout Llaurantis and the MiddleLands for pipeweed and teas. It grows from a basal patch of leaves divided into pointed segments, producing erect stems, each bearing a single, bright yellow flower that blooms throughout the spring season and does not have a scent. *2.* Recent Age. Identical in physical description as above. Called the California Poppy, Eschscholzia is native to the western United States and grows in various habitats below seven thousand feet. It grows after spring rains and may bloom into the fall. It has lime green, lacey leaves, and a bright orange cone-shaped flower. It is a nervine that encourages relaxation and reduces stress and anxiety.

❧ Chapter 10 ❧

Grandmother, Grandmother, Grandmother Toad,
Your beauty is mystical, your kindness unmatched.
Please tell us the way,
We are lost! We are lost.
Long and plaintive, she croaked in reply,
Go fore and keep to,
and do not look back!

—Fignaut faerie story rhyme in The Tale of the Mushroom Mouse

Leaf awoke to the soft gleaming of light filtering through the waterfall's silver tendrils. She had slept hard in dreams of Alderelm and expected to find herself cradled in Miriam's gnarled boughs, high above the clouds amidst the endless blue sky, where the morning breeze would gently rock her to wakefulness. Floating there, she would listen for the soothing flutes and whistles of Treean folk welcoming a new day. However, she heard naught but the sound of rushing water, and she lay confused. Beginning to place herself, she clutched the Sakatu and exhaled deeply. She yearned to smell the crisp mountain air, yet there was only the damp cold of colorless rock. A rush of nightmares forced themselves into the nethermost abyss of her unwilling spirit. She moaned in recollection. The Great Trees had called beneath her feet in pleas she had ne'er before heard. Baleful were the cries that fought their greatest terror—fire.

Her bristles quivered as she remembered, and her body shuddered. A tear escaped her eye, and she viciously swiped it away, hoping she had reacted quickly enough for no one to have seen. Gazing around, she found that only Sage's presence separated her from being alone within the looming, calcific bedrock. He sat with his back to her, his hands tucked tight under his legs. Moving over to his side, she looked up under his curling, brown locks of unkempt hair and stared at his face in curious wonder. His expression was as fixed as stone, pinched together as though stuck in a split moment of pain. But more unsettling were his eyes. The windows to his spirit held no glints of mischievousness, no twinkles nor sparks—they were flat and empty. The pit of her stomach dropped.

"Sage?"

There came no reply. Tugging the elf's arm, Leaf called his name again, and for this, Sage clenched his fist and held it in front of his face as though struggling with some unseen force. She jumped and scurried backward, falling upon her side. The Coyotl elf stayed stock-still, his fist frozen and his lower jaw jutted. Gathering a fray of courage, she approached him again, studying his fixed features with no slight distress. Desperately, she wished to behold one of his aimless gestures, his ever-expansive smile, or even the benign bravado that defined his peculiar humor. Yet he did not move. He sat there like an eerie, dead Tree no longer lithe in the wind.

Meanwhile, Tullkaee and Noblien stood within a small glade adjacent to, and on an incline from, the jagged opening at the cave's crown. The sunlight filtered through the morning haze. *Beautiful*, Tullkaee thought. *Even peaceful.* However, she did not believe it. Studying an odd finch of speckled color ruffling its feathers under the streaming warmth, she tried to enjoy the moment's comfort. Yet Noblien was restless, and his movements irritated her. 'Twas not long before he headed back to the silver rocks, murmuring inconceivably as he passed her. There was an eloquent power in his movements, the stealth and grace of the great cat. She appreciated such aspects but sighed as the elf disappeared beneath the crevice. 'Twas as if the cavern had swallowed the elf whole, and it might be that she inwardly wished for it. Indeed, the statue of her form lacked any excess of concern. Only was she rueful that this peace was soon to end. Tapping down a new bowl of pipe leaf, she lit her pipe, knowing that Noblien was indulging his worry somewhere beneath her feet. To this end, the Puman drew to Leaf's side.

"I'm sorry, Leaf. I shouldn't have left your side while you slept."

She stared at Sage. "What's wrong with him?" Noblien did not reply, and she turned to him with frustration, reddening the reflective green of her cheeks. "Why don't you answer me!"

"Forgive me," answered Noblien, swallowing hard.

"Is this how elves sleep?" she whirred.

"Only to those who choose life over death brought from grief. It is rare to see—I respect and pity him for it. He has slipped into the depths of his mind."

"His mind?" she asked, doubt etching the furrows of her understanding. "Will this happen to you—will you do this?"

"No," he comforted, repositioning his person to speak to her dead-on. "I will not."

"He is not wakeful then?" she blinked in some bewilderment.

Noblien ground his teeth, his jaw flexing as he decided how best to answer. "He is not awake upon the earthly realm."

Leaf's energy skipped a beat in the enthusiasm of curiosity. Noblien detected her change and thus diverted further conversation right before she was set to speak.

"Come!" he commanded hoarsely, gentling his voice after that. "Let us venture outside these cavern walls for a spell. 'Tis best to let him be.

He will come around soon. You'll see," he said. "Best, he thinks no note has been taken of him."

Leaf nodded and followed the Puman toward the misty, filtered beams of twisting sunlight—thin, cylindrical rays that outlined the high egress as though the cave wore a glorious, shining crown in the darkness. The Treean was momentarily awed, but devoted preoccupation pulled her gaze back toward Sage. A subtle smile lifted Noblien's visage upon beholding this, for an empathetic spirit is the mark of a sensitive individual whose mind is driven under the heart's guidance. He bent to give Leaf a leg up, but the Treean did not notice and alighted effortlessly through the high-pitched outlet. He then smiled fully to himself.

Atop the hillock, the green of life poured into the young Treean as does freshly fallen rain fill the roots of beings belonging to soil and earth. She looked up into the sky. The air was heady with pine and sprig, very much like Alderelm. Yet how strange to feel naught beneath her feet— no vibrations or resonations—no calls or grumblings. The day held such beauty, while elsewhere, the green of life was shriveling under an encroaching darkness. The day was either a gift to be protected or a deception to resent. She felt a truth in both.

Tullkaee greeted her, and the Treean forced a smile. She believed the Daun to be a woman of great strength and posture—a warrior in her prime. And of great contrasts was this gallant woman made. Even now, the lissome Wood sorrel that flourished upon the glade, soft and fair, wisping between sunlit beams in a circlet of eaves, only served to highlight what was the bastion of Tullkaee.

"Are you hungry?" Tullkaee asked, handing her a piece of shriveled, dried meat. "Charqui. Take it. It is good."

Leaf knew the elves did not eat meat, so she glanced at Noblien. He caught the gesture; how she endlessly delighted him. Her courtesy in this regard, however, was not necessary.

"We'll travel hard," said Noblien. "Take what you can now. I don't know when we might eat again."

Leaf graciously took the charqui from Tullkaee's hand and took an eager bite. It tasted more of salt than meat and was hard to chew. Very hard. Tullkaee watched the Treean with eyes of delight. "I think she likes it! My daughters made it."

Leaf smiled up at her, chewing desperately but making little progress. "Ahh, you have otters?"

"Yes, two," the Daun said, puffing with no small order of pride. "They are with my people to the north."

"Daughters?" repeated Noblien, gaping. "Lawks, you must miss them terribly."

"Yes, but they are accustomed to my absence. I have led the hunts since they were young."

"What are their names?" asked Leaf.

"Oshk and Maunt," she replied, eyes dancing. "Twins—close to your age in growth."

Noblien handed Leaf a handful of berries as he spoke. "We will see you back to your family."

"Elderberries?" Leaf asked, swiftly throwing them into her mouth.

"Do not chew or swallow them," Noblien warned. "Those are henbane. Their nutrients are had from the outside. The inside is likely to make you sick."

Leaf quickly spat them out while Tullkaee indulged in a glut of laughter.

"Hardly worth the risk," said Leaf with a hesitant smile. "Are you not hungry?"

"No," he replied gently. "More comfort do I find in the intermittence of dining than not."

Leaf scrunched her face, incredulous. The lines of Noblien's lips softened into a smile. "Eat the berries, LittleLeaf. They are a gift in uncertain times."

"LeadLeaf," she replied. "Niveus and Sage call me LeadLeaf."

He raised his eyebrows. "Ah, yes. And I presume you approve of this new calling then?"

She smiled broadly. "Aye."

"LeadLeaf is a strong name, to be sure," Tullkaee said before training her eyes on the elf. "Do all Yaguarás refuse meat? I saw Leaf look to you when I offered her charqui," she added, nodding at Leaf in response to the elf's surprised expression. "And I notice that you do not relish talk of the hunt. I do not understand how your spirit animal does not influence these ways."

"'Tis not only all Pumans," Noblien replied with a carefully considered breath. "'Tis all elves who do not partake."

Tullkaee's countenance darkened and then reddened in astonishment and incomprehension. "I do not understand. From what I've seen, the elves lack no skill."

Noblien chuckled. "It is not because we cannot hunt. Our ketyl animals gift us many traits, but the consumption of flesh that they themselves require is not one of them." The Daun's expression caused him to continue laughing, albeit with a grace of gentle quiet.

Leaf let out a squeal and ran over to some shrubs growing within the shadows of the Forest Trees. She squatted then turned back to her companions' now attentively rigid figures, lifting her hands in the air to reveal the plumpest of plump toads. Her face was beaming.

"What is it?" she blurted in fascination.

"You would simply pick up what you do not know?" Tullkaee asked, disbelieving. "And wait, how do you not know about such a Forest creature?"

"A Forest creature?" Leaf repeated, blinking widely. "It is so odd. It doesn't seem real."

Then came a familiar laugh, a gaiety light, and gesticulating from behind the three. "Now you understand why we marvel at you!"

"Sage!" whooped Leaf.

The Coyotl stretched his arms in a yawn. "Noble huntress, the seven Ancient Forests do not have toads."

Noblien directed a quick and narrowed gaze at the Treean. Leaf understood and checked her excitement.

"Did you sleep well?" she asked innocently.

"Well enough," he said, puffing and continuing undeterred. "But to toads . . . Grandmother Toad is the keeper of all the secrets regarding herbs, and she is quite proud of that fact. She and her kin are quite vain, you see. And the Ancient Ones are not keen on doling out excessive praise. So, Grandmother Toad declared that no toad should reside within the boundary of any Ancient Forest. Still, we should revere their kinds—for aren't they perfectly beautiful?"

Throughout Sage's diatribe, Tullkaee's mouth slowly dropped open. "You are absolutely . . . peculiar."

Sage did not digress. "Have you noticed what else the Ancient Forests do not have? Mushrooms!" Noblien rolled his eyes. "The stout, diminutive peculiars, being neither plant nor animal, also grant gifts of sustenance . . . through medicines, spirit journeys, and other faerie realms. Yet, the Ancient Forests do not need them. Is that not profound?"

"Utterly," Noblien replied flatly. "LittleLeaf, you might consider returning the round wart, lovely as she is, to her endeavors. We must bore on."

Leaf nodded, still captivated by the creature, and gently placed it back in its wild, large world. She watched it for a few moments, then gave a whimsical sigh. Maybe the toad thought her a shrub or Tree herself, for it leaped back onto her, and they stared at each other. The Treean beamed and renewed her effort to disembark the lovely creature.

"Goodbye, Grandmother Toad."

"Have you caught a sense of Shee?" Noblien asked Sage.

"Other than it shifting in the dead of night?" scoffed Sage dejectedly. "No."

Noblien sniffed high in the air, musing. "I feel it has trestled itself within a nip of the air. But the Treewood abounds with the smells of spring."

Sage nodded. "'Tis indeed distracting. Which way do you reckon this nip of air tugs?"

"Northward and parallel to Alderelm," Noblien replied, without complete confidence, watching Sage try to catch a whiff of the land himself. "Do you sense it now?"

"Och aye, now I do. Well done, Thai Mielle."

The Puman's glare manifested with a savage pestilence. "You are a carking scourge rare and bold. It is a sorry distinction to call you a friend."

"Noblien!" Leaf shrieked, astonished more at the momentary lack of restraint than the insults he catapulted.

And then a realization hit her. His stoic disposition was not derived from an innate attribute of his nature but rather from a hard-fought discipline that mitigated his reactionary impulses. Under this recognition, she began to respect him all the more.

Sage looked pitiably stung, and it wounded the Puman to behold—his countenance thus softened. Yet, the result of the Coyotl's expression was so instantaneous as to show how the previous was merely an act.

"Mightily. Consider me a friend, do you?"

Noblien submerged the fatigue the Coyotl's antics produced, and his ever-stalwart heart instead marshaled compassion for Sage's lighthearted spirit. In this regard, the irritating Coyotl was indeed a gift, so he began to walk away, but not without reproof. "Let off your preoccupation with the color of my eyes."

Sage lackadaisically ruffled his shaggy hair, cocking an eye at the Puman with a confounded intensity unsuited to one so recently scolded.

His broad and crooked grin returned. He was overly pleased with himself, and this caused Leaf concern, more for Noblien than for Sage.

"But," the Coyotl said, "you did call me friend!"

⏣ ✦ ⏣

The group's adjusted track took them away from Alderelm on an oblique, the Great Forest remaining painfully visible through the mountain peak's stellar height and from the patched pillars of smoke still rising from within. The view of the blue sky that met the land before them belied the truth of their journey's weight. So heartsore was the company's energy that any life and spirit within proximity ran and hid as the death of their quiet stillness passed. Each in turn, and far too often, Noblien, Sage, and Tullkaee would set sights on the Treean with an encouraging and affected smile, checking in without words. *What a comfort and a torture*, she thought. The metronome of the repeated pitter-patter of the company's footfalls eventually took her deep within her mind's eye, where she drifted into daydream memories:

She was resting under the bower of a Linden Tree, its heart-shaped leaves a messenger of vernal tides. The polestar, the first to introduce the eve, began to shine, and the starkly fresh smell of approaching rain tickled her nostrils. Thereupon, low as the far ebb of the tide and as soft as the delicacy of starlight, was the voice of Willow Elder.

"Now, LittleLeaf, what have you learned from the chronicles of Nirmossa?"

Leaf shifted her weight, sighing. "The elves are treasures, touchstones of the Earth. I wish I knew more than from accounts of old."

A scowl momentarily crossed Willow's features. "Why, LittleLeaf, do these creatures so enchant you? When they call upon our borders, you're ne'er far."

"More than any kin I've learned about, the elves live by their hearts.

They do not live for self-attainment."

"I see," said Willow thoughtfully, biting her lip. "You know, some of us are made from flax, others from cotton, and fewer from silk. Yet all creatures quail for their own needs afore others."

Leaf shook her head as several flower-stemmed fiddlenecks in her nettled hair curled tightly with her rising frustration. "Not the elves, not like other kin. The history we sit on is full of such truths. Surely you see it?"

"Every creature on Earth lives by the flashes and charges of the storm," said Willow, exhaling with cautious patience. "Life is a function of the attraction and repulsion of this power. However, the elves possess a curious current, for theirs is equal and similar. They are of a strangely aligned reasoning innately propelled within their core as fiercely as the line storms we lay witness each equinox."

This was the most Willow had ever spoken of the elves—or any kind in such a manner. 'Twas her prerogative as one of Alderelm's Heartwoods and one of the seven stars of the fae. Leaf was riveted and hungered for more while grasping little of what she spoke. Yet the young Treean knew—she felt—within the depths of her heart, its truth viable.

Willow smiled. "LittleLeaf, all of this combines to make them sad creatures full of unwanted violence."

"Unwanted violence. Within their near presence, one can feel the sadness they hold. And none of this is to do with themselves, but forasmuch as us! They could endeavor to live with overrunning peace and happiness if they isolated themselves from other kin like the grumbies and Treeans do. To witness death as they have—what toil must weigh over them."

"Verily," replied Willow. "What has inlaid such an impression within the empathy of your heart?" And though she asked, she did not wait for an answer. "The sun has long since set," she cooed, her voice a salve to a spate of woes. The air was wilting under the growing night sky, and Treean tunes were subsiding. "Look, the moon bestrides us. Not all can be accomplished in a day. Let us retire to the Lumen's side. Perhaps you might play a tune or sing?"

"I prefer your voice."

"Not a Treean in Alderelm desires not to have all hear their song—but you," said Willow, amused, tittering gently. "Alright . . ."

The aery will of courage
The sylvan spirits of the wild
The seraphs of the glebe of Earth
Now, a mere trace of Zephyr's tide
Scimitar and Camelop
Losses of immortal kind
No answer from the black mast sail
Or the Veriha who left behind
Noble hearts who defended
The defenseless and those in need
We must ne'er forget the losses
Of immortal kind
Oh, the Battles of Nirmossa
Scimitar and Camelop
The aery wills of courage
We remember well, remember well
The sylvan spirits of the wild
Who took to the Veriha's side

"LittleLeaf, this dream is spent. Your heart is free; go to the side of your beloved elves."

"LeadLeaf," said Sage, with a clap of his hands, "your daydream is spent!"

"Pfff, leave the child alone," said Tullkaee reprovingly. "Let her mind wander. This is healthy, you, not so much."

"Humph," Sage grunted, fiddling with a long blade of scanty grass. "None of you talks. The travel is dull."

Onward they progressed, and toward the end of the day, the sun replete in the satisfaction of its spring-warming tasks, the landscape's features began to transform. The ground had grown rockier and the grass shorter. The smell of the air subtly changed, if only here and there, and the scent of brine was within it. Leaf's nose tingled when the ethereal currents, grown stronger over the last hour, whiffed the new scents upon her. The group's direction put them directly into the wind's course, and it howled the harder for their effort, but at least now, Alderelm was beginning to turn to their backs.

To this end, the Coyotl elf's restless agitation could no longer be endured. "I must go back."

Leaf and Tullkaee halted, utterly shocked. Noblien spun around, surveying the entire group, perplexed.

Sage's face brimmed with guilt. Yet to his mien, was there only a bellowing stubbornness. He was a wild, tame creature on the brink of bolting, every fiber of his being ready. He swallowed his regret, took a deep breath, and focused on Noblien, shifting his words away from the common tongue and into the vernacular of the elves. "Smoke still rises above the White Mountain—"

"Enough talk," replied Noblien in Elvish, lips tightened in worried anguish. "You are in charge of Leaf!"

"I'm a waif," replied Sage, shifting his footing. "She takes to you."

Foreign tongue or not, the Treean heard her name, and her heart wrenched. "I want to go with you."

"No," both elves replied simultaneously. Then Noblien said, "This cannot be."

"Neither of you can tell me what to do," said Leaf, and turning her focus on Sage, she bit in hard. "You told me that Bristleton requested you take me away from Alderelm. Why are you going to leave me?"

Noblien raised his eyebrows. There was not a day between moon and sun when his respect for the Treean had not grown. And more was he pleased that the burden of attending such inquiries was not his alone.

Sage scowled. "Alderelm is the closest place I have to a home. I must see. I hope for the chance of a miracle."

"Alderelm is my home!"

Sage winced but refused to argue. "I will go at haste and catch up with you," he said, addressing Noblien. "They'll require rest breaks. I will catch up. Three days, give me three days."

"Blatherskite!" Noblien replied, visibly shaken but successfully reining in any more emotive outbursts and mastering a conciliatory tone instead. "This is no light matter—safeguarding the Sakatu and the Treean's Lastborn."

Sage's head tilted in thought. His visage became placid, although his eyes still glinted with mischievousness and endlessly daring mysteries. "Yes and no."

Noblien let out a great exhale and rubbed his temples.

"Hear me out," continued Sage. "Willow Elder laid her lips of gold upon thy cheek. If ill intent rested within your heart, a scar would've appeared where her touch did graze. Thy heart is naught but true, as is our huntress here."

"Impetuous Coyotl!" the Puman shot, maintaining his composure only within a halo of seething disgust. "Dare not taunt me! The Treean elders, what would they say? Two unknowns, wards of their most precious gifts?"

"Slake your temper, Thai Mielle—"

After this utterance, the Puman shoved Sage hard. The Coyotl slipped back a step, recovering with uncanny ease, his face lighting with an infuriating smile. To the Elvish tongue did he return to taunt. "You think I've not noticed?" And so saying, he scrutinized Noblien's face, whose eyes now held question. Sage's expression settled smugly while he whirled his fingers in an air dance alongside either of the Puman's long curved ears. "Confide much and little, do you not?"

Noblien knocked his hands away; Sage's posture stiffened, and their energies hackled against one another, eyes blazed—Noblien's glacial, Sage's feral— both just as menacing.

"Why belie us Thai Mielle? I reckon—"

"You reckon too much," spat the fierce-eyed Puman. "Tend to your own matters, which are of plenty."

"Seeing our predicament," Sage said, laughing dryly, "you reside well within my matters, indeed! And your sharp tongue," he continued with a smirk slithering across his face, "sees me verily on the mark. Ah well, time to furbish our hearts with spears," and so saying, his already beady eyes narrowed. He plopped a heavy hand on Noblien's shoulder while the latter ground his jaws. "Worry not! Your gifts are far more than I'd hoped for. My mind's a fool's. Steadfast enough to travel to Shee, but of Leaf . . . the task was not meant for me."

"Your mind is no less trusted than mine," said Noblien through clenched teeth.

"More is that youngling Treean's," said Sage, "than both of ours I deem."

Noblien grunted in reluctant agreement. "I share this gift of burdens with thee."

"Good," said Sage, a determination fixing across the creases of his face. "Then I mean to return to the Realm of Trees."

Noblien cursed in the Elvish tongue, low and guttural. At this, Sage's side-bent grin spread across his face, settling in strange harmony with the crookedness of his teeth.

"Ah, you'll miss me then?" he said.

Leaf's newfound and disbelieving despondency interrupted his self-humor. "You mean to really leave us?"

Sage shrugged, hapless. "I'll be back, quick as daisies."

"That's not an expression," said Leaf.

He winked and smiled again; it was exasperatingly comforting. "Trust me." And so saying, he loped off into the wind's direction.

Noblien rested a resigned hand on her shoulder. "He's on a course of action he is willed to follow."

Tullkaee approached their side. Noblien acknowledged her with a mournful tilt of his head.

"He is not right in his head," she mumbled.

The three stood in union, staring after the sinking figure of the Coyotl disappearing over the horizon. They felt a void in his diminishing presence. For Leaf, the elf's departure was acutely felt. A sensation of uncomfortable heat meshed with a terrible, clammy chill that seemed to swallow her. The feeling had no welcome to it. She desired to speak, yet words could not be retrieved. Only did her heart gasp and clutch in turn with each beat. Sage traveled with excruciating speed. He was becoming barely visible more quickly than she realized she had dreaded. And then, he vanished. She had only blinked, and he was gone.

"Come," Noblien grumbled. "Shadows follow us—within the very air about us. We must be off."

"We have not rested all day," said Tullkaee.

"Soon."

Meanwhile, Leaf rubbed her eyes and refocused them to catch sight of Sage again. There! In the furthest reaches of the Treean's yon vision was the silhouette of a coyote. "Did you see—"

A staccato yip-howl traveled faintly within the wind's graces. Could it be? Tullkaee and Noblien continued to talk unaware, but she sensed that the call gilded the very brace of her posture with an odd and familiarly erratic nature, a psychological armor. All at once, the previous wash of ill ease swept away. Her breath let out, long and regained.

WOOD SORREL
SOUR GRASS

Wood Sorrel. 1. *Predecessor of those delicate plants known in the recent age.* **2.** *Recent Age. Various plants of the genus Oxalis, having three heart-shaped leaflets and either yellow, white, or pink five-petaled flowers.*

Ellis McCauley

FIDDLENECK

Fiddleneck. 1. *An annual herbaceous wildflower named for its flower stem that curls over at the top like the head of a fiddle with its many goldenrod flower blooms.* ***2.*** *Recent Age. No change from above. Of the genus Amsinckia*

HENBANE

Henbane 1. *Bush-like plant having a mixture of green stems and bark, oblong leaves with serrated edges in opposite pairs and producing wrinkled, dried berry-like fruit whose outer layers are rich in nutrients.* **2.** *Recent Age. Known as Stinking Nightshade, a poisonous plant growing upwards to thirty-six inches tall with a foul smell and funnel-shaped flowers of pale-yellow color and purple veins, which has been used medicinally in various ways.*

❧ Chapter 11 ❧

To be loved—to have known love,
Is better than breathing the air,
All else becomes glorious and insignificant,
The seas are no challenge—mere droplets of dew,
And dreams, an opportunity to soar amongst the welkin blue.

—Excerpt from the sylphen canticle, O'Merrus

To the lower lands, the curving heights descended into the depths of rock-ridden fields. The terrain outlined and funneled them onto the fringes of a Woodland. Therein, Trees of stout proportions but no exceeding height emanated their serene and longevous spirits. So was the scape of the western side, wide-open clearings and assorted timberlands as points interlinking a veined and repeated pattern.

Leaf did her best to keep pace with the Fierce-Eyed Elf while Tullkaee took up the rear. She focused on a bright silver feather mingled within one of the Puman's fire-ember locks. It swayed, ne'er settling under the persistent footsteps. Or was the strand of hair silver and the feather red? The wee Treean was too tired to know anymore. Yet, in

149

truth, the silver feather was instead a sliver of hoary rock come from the Blue Cliff of the Puman's birth, made of shimmering accents of the rarest minerals and borne so long within the elf's hair as to be bound and twined as one.

Often, the Puman stopped and gazed back, waiting with watchful eyes. Yet, he always returned to the hectic pace. This matter progressed into the evening until Tullkaee's long, easy strides passed the tired Treean and swept aside Noblien.

"I have watched the bear star shift many times," she said. "A straight track you do not lead."

"The whims of Shee are a challenge."

"Leaf is tired. We must rest—and eat," she said, crossing her arms. "The time is now."

"Aye pertayai," replied Noblien distantly.

Tullkaee was perturbed. Although she did not comprehend the language, she was offended by the tone and indifference lain within. "My people revere your kind, but I now see tales powerfully true. Are you so at peace with solitude that you lose sight of what's best for others?"

"I prefer solidarity, but that's not why I make such a push. I sense an ill. No more can I describe than Leaf is too near it."

"Yaguará, a fight is coming. On such a quest, this cannot be avoided. Let it come. Better than to leave a trail smelling of fear."

"Fear?" said Noblien, gasping, his eyes wild. "Your huntress spirit carries you, but keep this thought tight. We are not ready for a fight."

"And we will not be if you continue beating us down at this pace. Great tales will be told of how we sacrificed ourselves for the Vultures of Delight," she scoffed as Noblien's eyebrows rose. Her obsidian eyes narrowed. "We rest."

Her obstinance could not be avoided; he respected it. "You

hold to thy matters," and so saying, he bowed in concession.

◦3 ◆ 6◦

The weary travelers settled upon the fringe of a Cedar grove. Beneath this grand manor were strewn layers upon layers of pine needles, sublimely softer than the prickly sheds of the regal Blue Spruce or the tar-ridden sheds of the majestic Ponderosa, whose calming cinnamon trunk could ease the heart. Yet for now, the Cedars offered the company's shelter, their scent spicy to the nostrils in a woodsy, balsamic way.

"The Sunillum flood was not of this age," Leaf blurted.

Noblein raised an eyebrow. "No, indeed. But you, a Treean, would already know this."

Leaf's honesty could not restrain her point of purpose, and she looked pitifully woebegone.

Noblien laughed. He did so rarely, and it struck Leaf as almost phenomenal. It was a cascade of cool warmth, although she was unsure if she was comfortable with it. Characteristically, his warmth was granted quietly through the melancholy of his silver eyes.

"You're curious of my age?" he queried. "Well, that glacial flood was afore my coming, but of Sage, lawks, although he doesn't look it, I believe he's an elf who's seen eons of stars come and go and was likely witness to it."

"As aged as Miriam?" Leaf asked.

Tullkaee looked confused. "Miriam?"

"The greatest, most beautiful Tree that there has ever been! Although she can be grumpy. And she's a bit gnarled and coarse around the edges. Miriam is one of the last of the First Trees—the ones who saw the Earth awaken! We are bound together. She's my family."

The Fierce-Eyed Elf momentarily lost his breath. Only the innocence of the young could make such an utterance so earnestly while speaking so profoundly in a matter-of-fact way. He reckoned that all the lessons of his life in total summation would not equal half of what he had already learned from this unassuming spirit sitting beside him now. And so, a subtle smile rested, for a fleeting moment, in the absolute of peace.

"Indeed," he continued, swallowing hard, "'tis quite probable that he is as old as your Miriam."

"What kind is she?" Tullkaee asked.

"Well, the Trees of the Ancient Forests are an amalgam of every type of Tree on Earth, but I'll admit that she carries many Sitka traits."

Tullkaee seemed impressed. "The Sitka," she repeated in awe.

Yet Leaf was pining to know more of Sage, and her inquiries would not be deterred. "How do you know of him?"

Noblien took a long pause, his face distant in heavy memory. Nearby, a small, brown-spiced ave lilted a throaty trill. Noblien grimaced and squinted at the bird.

To details small and far do the Ancient Ones transcribe and preserve through root and woody whorl. They are, after all, the History Keepers. And they thus comprehended the hesitation taking hold of the Puman now.

"I know only faintly; to this end, I cannot be entirely sure. But it is only I of him—he does not know me . . . though he endlessly tries." The Fierce-Eyed Elf drew a breath and sat back. "My youth was spent upon the cusp of Mulheteämult, by elven reckoning, the Age of Ursham nigh its end of glory. Changes blew swiftly; I felt them coming, nigh the brink of waste and want I could ne'er have imagined," he said, voice thin and drifting. "The delight of the Puman spirit is to venture afar, but we found many of us ne'er returning. Our home, the Blue Borough upon the Crag of Leda, along with the elven way I'd always known, was fading, and I hung close to my Da. He spent much energy venturing into deliberations concerning your kind," he said, nodding to Tullkaee and grinning wistfully.

With a sigh and glazing eyes, the Fierce-Eyed Elf looked for the briefest moment as a youngling, vulnerable and innocent. "It was the Even Tide of Hanging Lanterns during those short summer nights when it all fell apart. My Da—" and so saying, his voice broke as the padded footfalls of his story unraveled. He closed his eyes and concentrated, restarting. "My Da . . . rushed upon me, breath hard one night. His words are still a blur. He was telling me to leave and wait for him outside Leda. And then, he left. He just left me there, the lair effused with the whirled air of his departure. I clutched my bow, not an arrow drawn or time to tie on my quiver, and I hurried after him, barely keeping on his dust. I ran harder than I'd ever run in my life.

"I had a feeling . . . that I should not lose him. But I did; he vanished afore my eyes. The Foehn wind rode the tail-gust that went with him. I recall the sky lit blindingly bright. I was running hard, and I fell. I fell upon where his bow lay; the Charlock cradled within his footprints."

"The Charlock?" said Leaf. "Are you saying . . . your father was Flumen, the Elven Archer of Faiyum?"

Leaf's question gave the distracted Puman renewed vigor. "The Trees know of him?"

"Aye!" answered Leaf emphatically, incredulous that there would ever be a speck of doubt over the matter. "You are then a Troyelle? Son of Flumen!"

Noblien did not respond. He seemed to stare through her, his expression rigid.

"What did you do?" Leaf whispered, empathizing with a fate she knew she would one day encounter herself—to stand alone amongst the remnants of her kin.

"I hid," Noblien said flatly. "Hid nearby where I last glimpsed my

Da, within a hollow nurse log. 'Twas not long ere our Coyotl ran upon the scene, whispering to himself, much distressed. He looked as he does now, rustic," and so saying, a wistful, delicate smile graced his expression. "And he looked like a safe place to be, yet hidden I stayed. He picked up one of my father's arrows. The only one left undamaged. I remember that he looked at it for a long while. And ere he left, he placed it and the Charlock atop the fallen trunk from where within I trembled."

Leaf eyed his arrows.

"Yes," Noblien said, nodding. "Here it sits, awaiting its time."

"Why did you not go to him?"

"I don't know. I was young, confused, and afraid—my Da had just disappeared. I acted the way of the Puman. Eventually, a ravaging hunger enticed me out, although I ne'er returned to the Blue Borough. I lived alone and off my senses for a long time.

"Noblien," said Leaf sadly.

"Well 'nough," Noblien replied, resting a soft hand upon her shoulder. "My nature was carved out from those beginnings. They are the core of who I now am. I cannot regret them." And so saying, he paused, a concentrated torment lingering upon his face. "'Tis time," he said, giving an exaggerated exhale as if delaying some inevitable, awful consequence, "as has been ruggedly pointed out by the Coyotl of whom we speak, for me to open up more about myself."

Noblien's jaws tightened, and he hesitated for a long time thereafter. Leaf and Tullkaee waited with gentle patience. Noblien pointed and circled his fingers nonchalantly around his head.

"My hearing left the moment the dust of my Da began to dissipate. I'm naught but an eavesdropper on the constant din of wind. Little else fills my ears save the occasional groan of Earth." He searched his companions' faces expectantly. "I ought to have revealed my reality sooner. Forgive me."

"You are deaf?" Leaf asked, incredulous. "How—"

"Your lips tell most, your expressions the rest, and the Puman sense has saved my unworthy hide aplenty."

Leaf and Tullkaee were quiet, absorbing the reality of the truth he revealed. Their minds revisited the previous days, and now that truth be known, they each wondered how they could have missed the signs. Tullkaee's mouth moved to speak yet stalled, her expression curious. The realization and acceptance that gradually lit their faces held no resentment or anger. Only and amazingly, as Noblein thought it, did their expressions evolve from shock to wonderment, settling and fixing in a renewed high regard, for he already held their respect and admiration. Yet for the Puman, he was awed by their reactions.

"You hear nothing?" Tullkaee asked. "Nothing at all?"

"I hear a roaring, like a stormwind."

She contemplated the matter. "Well, is there no better way to communicate with you?"

Noblien laughed. "Naught has changed, dear huntress. Although if you are willing, I can teach you both some hand signals that may be of benefit if I am not close enough to read your lips or the situation calls for silence."

She nodded. "I see advantage in what you speak," and so saying, a satisfaction made her muscles relax. "The elves cause me to wonder over many thoughts. But you—*you* cause me the most wonder."

The elf's smile was bare and gentle, changing the perspective of every feature on his face, even though it was barely noticeable. From grey eyes to fair skin, he was generally unlike the Puman kind. Yet more intriguing was the air about his person, the mysteries he carried in every essence of his being, whether it be his expression or manner of speaking. He seemed to be the physical manifestation of the firmament beyond the stars.

"But Noblien, what of your father—what was the light, the wind, what happened—why haven't you asked Sage—I don't—"

"Leaf," Noblien interrupted, shaking his head. "You seek answers to questions I've spent my entire life merely getting ready to unravel."

The elf's grey eyes, silver as birch bark under the half moonlight, passed over Leaf, becoming fixed in that peculiar Elvish fashion when the riptides of other astral planes tug upon them, and all they can do to converse in the here and now is remain calm and focus. The Treean sensed a deviation in his presence, although she could not reckon precisely what presence, or lack thereof, she sensed or did not, so curious was it all. Only could she absorb the wonder of the elves.

"I'm the last of the Troyelle house. Rumors say that we are cursed." He looked amused at Leaf's rigorous frown. "Nay, nay, do not fret," he said as a wry darkness crept beneath his countenance. "This arrow waits with me."

Relief surged through Leaf, not for the first, second, or third time that Noblien was friend and not foe.

Noblien looked at the Sakatu hanging around Leaf's neck. "Some questions are more important at the moment."

Leaf nearly lost her breath, for the Sakatu responded to him. It pulsed under his gaze!

Noblien continued, unaware. "And I'm not going anywhere." The intensity of his eyes softened, and any hints of past pains or lethality melted away. The mysteries that made him up became a refreshing security in uncertain times. "Lawks, I'm spent."

"Ha!" Tullkaee cried out. "It is not footwork, but the mouth that calls the Yaguará to rest! Leaf, your presence will be invaluable on this venture."

Noblien turned a hawk-eye on the Daun. "My kind has not been just to yours."

Tullkaee's lips pouted around the edge of her pipe, the fragrant and delicate wisps of smoke wrapping around her sun-weathered face. She took a long draw, the faces of her ancestors resting over hers. "You carry much guilt. Now you will carry guilt for the injuries of human kind? Yaguará, no one is entitled to bear such weight. I have witnessed Sage's sufferings and learned of your own. The whole world suffers. We are made of suffering. But there is beauty within it." She handed Noblien her pipe. "Let the pipe warm your tongue, and I will tell a story."

Leaf nestled in the grass, the sun's morning rays beginning to warm her, while Noblien remained a rigid statue, his eyes distant upon the slipstreams of memory yet focused on the moment unfolding.

"Long ago, in the old days, my people were alone. Darkness surrounded them. They were naked and cold, and they cried. The great blue howlers of the sea heard them—found them out—and sustained them with their haunting songs. These creatures were my forebears' first warmth and company.

"When the howlers found my ancestors, they swam beneath them and carried them upon their great backs. 'You are land creatures!' the howlers cried. 'Created from the depths of our world but belonging more to the solid soil of our cousins, the Legged Ones. You are meant to hear the land waters: the glaciers, the lakes, the streams, and the rivers, as well as the wind.'

"My forebears agreed it must be so, and the howlers crested above the waves near the shallows, letting my peoples behold the light above the fluid world and push them to land. Upon the solid earth, they opened their eyes. They had never seen such bright, searing light. They had to shut them. They were blind. And once more, they felt alone.

"But the Legged Ones, tender in their touch, took the hands of my ancestors and embraced them warmly as newly found kin. When my forebears shivered, they clothed them, and when they cried, 'We are alone,' they replied, 'We are with you.'

"Strengthened, my people grew quiet and listened. They heard the land waters and felt the wind. They opened their eyes once more. The

157

Legged Ones pointed to the north. There my forebears traveled, calling it the First Lands, the land my people even now call home."

"I don't know this story," said Leaf. "The Legged Ones, were they elves?"

"Dohiyi Elonna," replied Tullkaee, remembering in deep concentration. Leaf looked to Noblien.

"Aucks!" said Noblien. "The Crone-Sages of the Scimitar!" His voice fell, rasped, and drawled. "Better be they find peace. Your people are older than any human kind I have heretofore known . . . ere their loss—the loss of the Scimitar ketyl. Your ancestors must have come across the Crone-Sages near the end of the long days from whence they yearned to rest and gambol in the wealth of sun-dried fruit shining red as anklets of larkspurs worn in assurance the sea fruits would reseed. There are many songs about those beautiful spirits—and they were most gentle and wise."

"Why do the Trees hold no history of this?" asked Leaf.

"Without a doubt, they hold it, LittleLeaf—though this is a loss too new and excruciating for them. Thank you," he said, bowing at Tullkaee. "More of the feminine spirit would better this world, I believe."

The Daun's eyes lit with appreciation, although she merely nodded in acknowledgment.

Now, time slowed and allowed the company to rest. Solid sleep and deep dreams took the Daun and Treean far within their spirits, while Noblien stood alert and ever watching out over the dell from whence a strange sense befell and followed them.

"Would it not be nice to spot a fleeting glimpse of nobler days, when many a creature no longer seen upon this fair Earth did stroll within a comfort of safety," said he, beneath his breath.

Looking back at the two, he thought about Sage, his whereabouts, and his condition. Then, his swift gaze turned to the bens of his homeland as his mind walked into the past. His clear eyes reflected the sky while his whisper settled within his native tongue:

"Dear Oreads on high, upon steepest rock and over deepest precipice, take care of my mountains, for I am gone."

LARKSPUR

Larkspur. 1. Long, flowing sea plant of deeply lobed and pointed leaves and clustered brilliant, red flowers within which the edible fruit was harvested. **2.** Recent Age. Toxic plant of genus Delphinium, having spurred, multi-colored flowers of vertical arrangement up to 2 meters tall.

◈ Chapter 12 ◈

Day end of the First Age,
The longest aye Earth held,
The Age of the Veriha,
Leaving of first friends.

—Passage from The Chronicles of Seasons

Sage felt dread seep through his being as if it were a physical presence mounted on a throne of eminence, staring down his sulking shadow. He looked at the clear heavens, yet to his mind, was there a monstrous storm of ominous grey-black clouds mounting an insidious, creeping attack on Aura, the fair spring breeze, who was floundering under the storm's suffocating assault; her fresh draft diminished steadily, and in its stead, a stale air refreshed only by a sneering downdraft of vile stench was delivered. He watched the sky's white cloaks determinedly fight to honor the sun, but they could only shine briefly beneath the darkling's stifling mass. And at sad last, within his mind's eye, the great expanse of sky was bedimmed.

He grumbled. The storm pelted wave after wave of gusts against him while ghouls fought for access to the realm of his mind. Still, he beheld the White Mountain of Alderelm in the distance, her crown lighting beneath shrouds of high-wisping, unsettled mist. He strained for the merest glimmer of the Trees' silver-barred boles and sighed heavily in worry, knowing not whether Alderelm's Great Helms still stood. He persisted forward, arriving at the Sasa River, the tink-tink of hailstones muting her rippled greetings. She welcomed him lovingly, but he saw only an incorrigible spinning of turbulent wiles made more frenzied by the melting snows.

The wind bawled; it was deafening now, and his inflamed mind drifted to the conundrum of elven wake-dreams where past and present became simultaneous. He fell to sleep, contained by this place, cradled within the scents of Aman:

Aman, Earth's foremost and longest era, held an unimaginable, sweet beauty that was concise in every aspect of pure measure. It was a time when the Veriha, those supernal wonders who made full what was empty, lived among the rest of creature kinds. They were the first, the very quintessence of Nature, and now, what is so-called is only the merest hint of their remaining essence, a diminished echo. The Coyotl had experienced Aman's bliss, but for a moment in a day, his beginnings resting on the last, the Eluvium.

They had begun it. Those malicious entities who, for no reason, were bent on marring life. Those beasts and elements whose characters delight in the languishing cries of innocents and even each other. They created blighted flavors and ill scents, icy nights and searing days, carnage, mayhem, and the cruelest deaths. The mixture seeped upon Earth's innocence, creating a breath in the spiritless void. The breath swelled putrid and became a rank wind that reaved in the conception of Geul, master of all evils, creator of naught.

Penetrating the pristine of Earth, his breath sent forth unfathomable misery under a maddening scream of wrath, and the insatiable craving of his maw sent tremors to the core of her heart. So began the glutting of fiends, gulaugs they were called, feeding off each other until Grimaul was spawned, the vilest of them all, servant only in the presence of Geul's altar and then only with snarling contempt.

The rogue tempests and unbreathed winds, those elements without Nature's natural compass, flew with the bitter-filled, hateful gulaugs. They loathed their place in the world and spurned the Veriha for not saving their moldering spirits. Full of contempt for their existence, the elemental and fiendish malignancies began their feasts of flesh, gorging until their bellies were grossly bloated with the slurry of their kills. They howled and gurgled with what may have been laughter, snatching whatever they might and roiling the innards of fairer beasts, the remains of their havoc left for rot, the smell of decay and fear pleasing them.

Sullied was the Veriha's empyrean-bourne. Not could the Wonders live, nor could they perish. Their departure was nigh. All of Earth felt it.

Heartrending was the cracking of skies—the Eluvium had come. Creatures wailed in grief as the Veriha melded into the very breath of the Cedar-spiced Earth. The softest sonance blended with the wind, carrying plaints to the heavens of whence they did hie, till a star above shone for each. Thus, the lights of myth, the auroras, were beheld in truth; henceforth, the apotheosis of blessings upon a darkening world.

Treean and elven lore relayed similar accounts. Sage relished the details of both while holding tight to his own. The tides could not be steadier than the memories returned to him time and time again. A haunting song was of them. 'Twas the song of the Last. The last Veriha to depart. The Wonder, who hesitated.

The resonations of her voice shaped a blurred figure of stirred dust that intertwined into the fading illuminations of the setting sun. Love was cast from her sorrowed eyes as she sang an invocation of hope. A quiet repose that the malicious entities could not grasp was hers. She was unlike the Veriha who had ascended before her, and the wretched fiends and elements were, for the first time, frightened.

Creatures of the wild recognized her difference, six taking openly to her side: Wapiti, Puma, Raven, Hawk, Scimitar, and Camelop. Her eyes narrowed, and the crusted gulaug scabs and elemental shadows shivered.

Faint words to beloved creatures preluded a fine dew of tears as the sparkles of her eyes were extinguished. She had once replenished all the lands with less effort, but now, as the last sacrosanct droplet fell away from her cheek and entered the disaffected heaviness of the world, a preternatural hum transfused the air, and she diminished.

The malicious entities, thinking their time had come, whorled and lunged, but the six, so loyal by the Wonder's side, picked up gifted staves and became the first elves of Llaurantis, henceforth and for aye unique amongst their kind. Touched by the grace of the Veriha, they were bound to each of their animal's spirits, the path of sacrifice seared into their souls.

Yet of Sage, well, his memory begins with the Wonder's last tear, the small insignificance whipped away into the dirtied skies:

The Tree of Cassen beheld the wayward teardrop, and even as the unbreathed winds blew their chilling talons down upon the hardy trunk, its sap stayed its warmth in greatest joy, for the Veriha's hesitation had created a teardrop of thoughts and living reflections!

Anon, that gallant, stout-hearted little Tree, surrendered its magic greens, and to this end did Zephyr, the Wind of Winds, rush in defense of the beset Yellowwood. The unbreathed winds waxed intense, and Zephyr could not tolerate the uninvited gales beating down upon his lands. Fierce and hale, the King of Winds rushed upon his opponents, who squalled under his assault. More the luck, for the newly shed greens of the Cassen Tree were wisped toward the wayward anomaly, that lone teardrop of beating pulse, and therein, able to grant a lee of shelter ere the teardrop was cast away from the eaves of Llaurantis.

Long a flight, the tear-babe suffered, whorled within the madness of the cross-gales, lungs fighting against the seething pressure, its life nigh over ere it began. Yet a will of countless eons resided within this little one, and as death flicked and flared, the tender cherub ensconced within the balm of leafy greens displayed a vigor and hunger for the wild fight of life. Knowing naught of their stow, the scuds spat the new tear-babe upon the gnawed lap of the Barren Lands, a region of red sands and many a broken and cracked rock. The cherub cried, and the leaves of the Cassen Tree manifested a tonic of calm for the blurred babe's eyes— the jade glow, sweeter than the lullabies of Fignauts. And indeed, the tear-babe was soothed, holding tight his cries even as the sun became a torment.

The leaves did what they could, but the balm of their protective suppleness was brittling. Desiccated against his tiny newly formed flesh, the sheltering foliage imprinted all the intricacies of love onto the tear-babe's soft skin. The sensation this incurred tickled, and in response, he outstretched his extremities, which waved aimlessly like jellyfish tentacles upon the ocean current. The sands sensed the babe's movement and shuddered while the babe sought comfort in desperate, slurping sucks upon his fist. The sands closed in, rippling beneath him, snakelike in form, beautiful if not for the menace behind their undulations. The end was close.

Yet fate sent an unexpected creature to his aide, one as adaptable to circumstance as the air and very nigh immune to the fickle tempers of any situation. So it was that the pattering of paw-steps and yip-howls approached with long, easy gaits while the red sands began to swarm around the youngling. His cries hit the ethers with squeals of terror, but a warm, rhythmic breeze swept across his cheek, and a soft wetness sniffed the entirety of his form. His cries quieted, and the sands retreated. Moist, drudging breaths nudged against him, and a gentle pressure encompassed the back of his neck. The babe snuffled between tired gasps as he was lifted, a rocking cadence moving the land beneath him.

Sharp was the yelp etched into the babe's memory, and harsh was the fall that flung him upon the thundering earth once more. He rolled many times, the hot sand sizzling the flesh of his arms and face. No longer could he hear paw-pads pattering or the yip-yippering that had previously chorused. He could only hear an ear-numbing screech growing louder with each gust of sandy wind tearing at his skin. Yet there existed a stronger will in his saviors than the fell spirits set against him, and no long moment passed ere he felt a familiar, soft wetness touch his face. Wild-gentle eyes gazed down upon him, and again, he was tenderly buoyed, although the gait that had previously rocked away his woes was now halting and uneven. Blood drool flowed down the mouth that delivered him, determined eyes fixed ahead.

The sun was setting on the last day of Aman. The limping creature continued to take her begrimed foundling to sweeter lands. And when at last she felt they were safe, she placed the babe down, his unmanageable arms miraculously finding her cold nose as her long, lolling tongue expressed concerned affection in the form of many caressing licks. The babe beheld the grizzled creature; she smiled at him with dancing eyes. He would ne'er forget their gold-green depths. They spoke a language he innately comprehended and revealed the anguish from the loss of many kith and kin. She cocked her head, sniffed, and nudged him. He was quiet. She yowled, and the babe replied with wet giggles. He would survive. He would learn the creature's way—the way of the Coyotl.

So became the seventh, the seventh and last spirit bound to the elves, believed to have faded from life long ago. However, the Trees knew otherwise, and for many eons, the maternal wisdom of the Ancient Forests shielded him by keeping his truth in silence. As keenly astute as he was naïve, he was a tender anomaly of the complications that mystery evokes, and the Trees and Treeans loved him.

Metallic was the taste that came to bring Sage around, his wake-dreams ending. He wiped his brow and reclaimed his whole self as best he could.

"I shouldn't have come. Thai Mielle spoke the wisest."

He eyed the further riverbank. He was close to Alderelm, too close to turn back, but he had a peculiar sense that an aspect was out of place, and he could not figure out whether or not it was simply an aftereffect of his tortured mind. He stood still, thinking, and made a conscious effort to breathe.

The wind was calm, and the only sound was the crisp, crinkling taps of the flowing water. Yet he cocked his head and listened. Chanting? Yes, to be sure, there floated a droning song, the type that makes the spine stiffen. No intimacies did he care to embark upon, so Timbriel stayed sheathed, and he reached for his bow.

The intonations closed in around him. Grasping his bow tightly with one hand, he nocked an arrow with the other and breathed in and out slowly. He closed his eyes, concentrated, and listened.

Swift and to the left, he took a mark and listened to the bow's fluting energy propel the arrow with a whooshed, whistling course. He listened for an impact. Nothing. Opening the windows to his spirit, he gasped.

Lemures, beautiful and frightening lady guides of death, those who wisp the newly deceased to a more soothing place, stood around him. They existed on the precipice of dimensions, neither wholly in nor out of the corporeal sphere, and thus, these specters of cross-worlds appeared to fade in and out of vision like a full moon beneath a clouded night sky. Their cloak-covered heads turned toward him, where he caught glimpses of porcelain-fine features of unnatural pallor.

Said one, "You are restless."

Sage did not answer. He looked past the apparitions to a place where numbness was welcome and swallowed hard. Another raised a hand before his face, her violet cheeks sickeningly beautiful. He could not help but focus on her. A twinge took his fingers.

"You've looked death in the face before," she said. "Why now do you tremble?"

"Because it has ne'er looked more beautiful."

"Then you are too close," she said, stepping back. "You are to tend the living. You need to quiet your mind."

His face contorted. "Do you think this is not my daily battle?"

The lemure sighed with sympathy and touched his forehead with her hand. The contours of her face emptied beneath shadows, and her voice fell softly upon his heart. "Isis and her saints lay kisses upon thee. You are our lodestone. And there is truth in dreams."

Sage stood cold, frost smoke hanging on his breath as caterwauls hit the vapors of the air. The misty walls of Gehenna forced themselves into his mind's eye, and the lemures vanished into the air. He wondered why he was ne'er taken across the veil.

With a shrug of fortitude to push on, he turned to scour the river. An overhanging Tree branch caught his eye, and he leaped upon it with careless ease. From this vantage point, he was able to jump onto a middle river rock, and from stone to slick stone, he crossed the river until several rockless, elven leaps separated him from the shore. There was but one path now, and he entered the Sasa's frigid waters.

The river joyfully tested his balance against her currents. He smiled, wet his forelocks, and sputtered with a restless whistle. Once he made it to the shore, the grateful Coyotl blew the Sasa's blue hilts a kiss.

Myth is excellent at fostering fictitious accounts concerning the Coyotl elves. Indeed, more than not, their ketyl was flop-footed, as happens with those of a casual nature, yet they possessed as many gifts as all their elven cousins combined, the skill of silent Wood-walking amongst them. The Trees know of such truths.

Now, Sage enlisted his best footwork, and so calculating was he in still movement that even the Puman might recount him as one of their own best heroes. Tenderly, he stalked until an unnatural east breeze briefly stunned his progress, so foul was the scent it brought. His jaw flexed as he unsheathed Timbriel with menacing slowness. Sword in hand, he took three footfalls forward, halting abruptly when he heard a snuffling grunt, then more. He had nearly stumbled over an entire horde of Gauss, their stink obscuring his senses. Realizing his near misstep, he narrowed his eyes, attempting to penetrate what depth he could within his field of vision, their dank aura still fogging his faculties. Deciding upon the best course of action, his hands tightened around Timbriel's grooved hilt. He readied himself for a sprint of bloodlust, his muscles quivering, coiled, and eager.

At that moment, the Tree crowns rustled, whishing against a wind that had cleaved the air as their spindled fingers reached. Sage lowered his sword, recoiled, and listened, ears attuning to this new air-light ruckus. Distinctly, a bird's mewl rushed to the heavens. The screech echoed in a massive swooping circle as it chafed the mountain's core and resounded against sore eardrums.

The Coyotl grinned and kissed his sword, the sword of Ole Ironwood, its glimmer only an inkling of the illumination living within, the light of Timbrothiel. The Gauss were roused and searched the skies in confused alarm. And ever the willing bearer of additional confusion, Sage flung Timbriel long and far. The sword struck the earth with a crack and sang, the vibration of its hit carrying orotund hums of pure challenge across the ethers. The Coyotl smirked in satisfaction as the Gauss shrieked in chaotic disharmony. Looking up the White Mountain, he took a quick inhale. She was indeed a mighty hill, and his eyes looked upon her height under a slightly lowered head, a reverence of respect. Determined, he took off in a dash, up the overgrown spiral path of sentries long ago, Timbriel lilting on, pulsating with an emergent glow.

As he ran, he wondered with growing irritation if all was lost and whether he might find a watchguard before reaching the borders of Alderelm. There was no time for further wonderings, for he espied a homely, wide-eyed figure whom he jumped upon and grappled to the ground.

"Osiyo," the Coyotl whispered sharply, with a maddened, beaming expression of joy. "Tell, tell. Why do the Hawkens place their young at so critical a lookout?"

"You're an elf?" the shaking sentinel said.

"Ahh," replied Sage, laying a harsh, happy kiss on the elf's cheek. "The brilliant of mind, too. Ha! Listen, does Alderelm still stand?"

"Aye," the young elf stuttered.

"Look yon," Sage said, exhaling, nodding in one direction. "Concentrate."

"I don't see anything."

"Bosh!" scoffed Sage. "You don't look! Does the spirit of the hawk not give your kin keener eyes?"

"Wait, aucks!" rasped the young elf.

"Indeed," Sage confirmed. "Send word, a second front musters unchecked to Alderelm's southwest. Make speed nestling . . . and sharpen your weapons—they will taste blood tonight. Say naught of me."

He motioned the sentry onward. "Go hie. The soil will soon be whelmed with Gauss."

He watched the young Hawken scurry off, forbearing his heart's inclination to follow. "No mistake in coming, I see now, but to continue would mean me blind." He glanced downward in regret and caught sight of his stain-covered shoes. "These are always covered with the best grit of earth. The yearning of my heart is the tantrum of my spirit. This leather tells all."

He kissed his thumb, touched his chest, and gestured toward the White Mountain's upward sprawl before an eager glint mantled the gentle aspect of his eyes and turned them around to the brush below. A mischievous, long grin crept across his face. Then there, he sprang forward down the trail toward many a watery, waiting eye. He saw them all—those who lurked in the shadows and those who came to meet him head-on. And with cunning dexterity, he spat parting farewells to those foes who met his dagger.

The Coyotl's course was to Timbriel; it awaited his return. Several of the Gauss grasped the sword's leather-bound hilt and struggled to pull it from the earth, for its ringing ached their ears. But only did each shriek as their clamoring hands burned against its freezing surface, for no permission did they have to touch it. Time and time again, the magic grace of the blade's silvered edges sent punishing stings up the hilt against their insults. Cries and woes ensued while Sage, now of the finest fettle, rushed toward the sword's call, parrying each foe that crossed his path with the swift ease of his kind. Yet more enemies were beginning to take notice of him, more than he could bear up against, and he shot an aggravated look of worry up the mountain trail from whence he had just come.

Eyeing the Elf's struggle against the Gauss-at-arms, deep within the darker umbrage of night, squatted one of impressive bulk. Its face was calloused with a vacuous expression. Its lips moved like a bovine chewing the cud, and as it cowed behind the folds of night's veil, it watched the scene unravel. Passive inaction was the creature's plight, odd for a Gauss, but the wilted clover held within its clutches was odder.

The Treetops whistled and then swayed. The spying Gauss shifted its gaze away from the muster and sniffed the upper currents. It heard another hiss of air hit the Treetops, which again had begun to twist under the gust blown against them, and there beheld a silhouette of winged form slicing across the nebula of cloud and haze. For a moment, its jaws were still as it watched the heavens. Birds of such size were found in the MiddleLands, not those of the west, of Llaurantis. It looked back at the tiring elf fighting well against its fellows and pursed its lips. Further expression may have been minutely reflected within its eyes, were they not blurred under the ointment of its mucilage. So, with a seemingly blank expression, the Gauss tucked the clover beneath a fold of its plated jerkin and returned its maulers to their place of aggression on its club of poniards. No longer a statue of the night, the creature melded into the chaos.

A screech smacked the mountain ridges, and blasts of air whipped the brambles before the moment struck the present hard with quiet stillness. Distantly, quietly, arose a thumping, thumping. The sonance grew louder like a thousand kin arriving for war. Then, within a moment's silence, swooped a feathered beast, a sort of bird of prey, half the size of a coarsened-aged maple. It launched many a reeking creature up and into the air while arrows pierced the sky in glorious, hissing arches from high atop the White Mountain. The assault against the Coyotl began to fray in scattered, disorganized clumps. At *last*, thought Sage, *the mountainside is protected.*

The avian creature drew down tightly, a sweeping curve of speed turning directly toward the Coyotl. He saw it coming. Valiantly, he kept up the fight, but the plumage of plenty set atop him. The great bird anchored her position while muffled screams of anger fought out from beneath her. Yet only until the Gauss had all fled, did the bird's wings draw back to the sides of its royal chest and reveal a furious elf.

Sage looked around for the enemy, huffing and puffing in torment at not having seen them flee. "Leoness! You fluffy peahen!" He glanced toward the shadows from whence the arrows had toppled; they would soon come.

He ran to retrieve his beloved sword and, having drawn up to its side, pulled it from the earth and stroked its lambent edges. He spoke tenderly, the accent of Coyotls suddenly more marked. Timbriel shone in response, its radiance scattering light in gleaming channels like the rising sun of dawn. The bogged murk of the Gauss stench was dispersing.

"Dear Timbriel," Sage murmured. "So, they don't take kindly to the hums of Timbrothiel?"

A slow-gaited stride took him back toward the feathered beast, where his scornful gaze marked its mottled, hoary, and black feathers. Easily ten times his stature, the brute bird scampered nervously in tight circles upon its four-clawed feet and crouched in a posture of submission. Sage slowed and began to approach more cautiously, cooing softly. He laid the gentlest of war-scarred hands on the soapstone beak.

"Good to see you, odd girl. I very nearly lost myself."

She ruffled her rich feathers, telling him little else than he had been granted grace and mercy. His smile was at last serene, tainted with naught but pure affection. She let loose a honk less noble than her appearance and nudged him. It nearly made him topple over.

"Ahh, how I wish you could tell me of Lemnoss. Your swift return is worrisome." He sighed, patting her steadily in as much reassurance for himself as for the well-met banda of old. "So very good to see you." And there, a familiar spark, both mischievous and impatient, returned to the windows of his spirit. "Care to set me to flight, odd girl?"

CLOVER

Clover. **1.** A plant with compound leaves of four leaflets, tight heads of tiny purple flowers, and magical protection to ward off bad luck. **2.** Recent Age. A small, short-lived herb of the pea family, also called "trefoil," of the genus Trifolium, has alternate compound leaves of three leaflets and tight heads of small, fragrant flowers crowded into dense heads varying in color depending on the species. Highly palatable to livestock. Clover adds nitrogen to the soil and is used for soil conservation and improvement. In the Middle Ages, it was believed that carrying a clover would enable one to see faeries.

✥ Chapter 13 ✥

Truth rests, without doubt, within the corners of the mind, but more can be found dispersed amongst the articulations of the heart, traveled forthwith only with the utmost courage, hope, patience, and most of all, love. Let it not be traveled alone.

—Marked upon history by Manos, Elm of Alderelm, upon absorbing the fair blessing under the breath of a Wapiti elf maiden eyeing a group of Treean youth nigh the moon of Wardenhood

For a day and a night, the three traveled forthwith to the terrain between the Red Valley and the soft rolling hillocks of Seayran. The region was both sparse and thick, as though undecided whether it ought to be Wold or Wood. Over their shoulders, the ridges of the White Mountain range had faded entirely from view, blanketed from sight by distance, rolling hills, and lowland boughs.

Noblien had barely spoken since their respite under the fringes of the Cedar grove. He was preoccupied with worry, not in the least over the whereabouts of the foolish Coyotl. Ever more did he look distantly from whence they had come, halting intermittently to check in on Leaf while cocking his head curiously as if he could hear the land before him.

Could it be, his companions wondered, that the roars babbling within his ears granted whispers of place and course? Whatever the Puman's hidden facets, Leaf and Tullkaee would follow him to the netherworld. They had both decided, unbeknownst to the other, when a surreally peaceful pause took the elf so wholly that the heritage of the world was mirrored off his eyes, and the constellation of sovereigns was for an instant graced atop his head.

Yet, for now, the fantastical image was sundered under the long strides of Leaf's new comrades. The piteous Treean ran without stopping, nighing only their last and departing step, although the brick arms and stalk fingers of Tullkaee oft heaved her up to speed. Leaf knew what was at stake, and through will and worry, she was determined to build vim and vigor with each day.

As for the mighty Daun, she was always strong. Yet her mind fretted, considering what strange denizens might threaten them in these uncharted lands. At last, she could no longer refrain herself and turned to Noblien.

"Yaguará, how close are we to this Land of Shee?"

It was unexpected how the elf drew up his gait as if the question had been anticipated before it was asked. Taut were the Puman's lips in drawing forth their answer, and ominous was the tone in which the words were laid.

"We are right upon it. Understand, nowhere and everywhere is Shee. 'Tis the entrance we must find. Let's be off; a slower, more cautious pace needs take us, for we are close too . . . to the Bay of Horsemen." Upon the latter utterance, a bottom breeze curled the leaves of the Forest floor, and the elf's visage, sweet as it was soft, stiffened. "Let with care your footfalls."

Caution was ever the Daun's plan. She argued for little else.

Onward, the company proceeded, while a stray northwesterly breeze whisked twisting tails of challenge in misplaced delight. The airstream sprite was innocent enough, simply guilty of its given nature. The companions could only bear up against its onslaught, gratified in the knowledge that the wind's more maelstrom cousins were not beckoned towards their westerly advance as well.

The terrain of their course was becoming more lush, unruly, and thickly green as the landscape crept over and onto itself in flourishing wild layers, concealing the paths of Nature's creatures. Yet it began to feel hauntingly cold and seemed to swallow them. And more, the air within felt thick yet empty—the juxtaposition of it all was starting to unsettle the Treean. So, when the Fierce-Eyed Elf halted, Leaf immediately looked to him for answers; of late, the elf hardly ever stopped for aught. And although there was no doubt that Noblien felt his ward's gaze pierce his person, he held his look fast, solemn as it was, toward a colonnade of wreathed, arborescent columns that were covered and partially hidden right before them.

"Tullkaee, LittleLeaf, regard these timbers with rightful awe," Noblien said, exhaling. "The Silvern Woodland rises to greet us."

Enormous Trees made a staunch and wide keep of stately proportions. This Woodland was no fledgling Forest. No. This grand palace was a petrified relic of elven ways bygone. Once one of the eldership, it had become time immemorial, holding lost enigmas within the recesses of bark from whence a maze of boughs stood guard. Not even the Treeans could hope to fathom its secrets, and for it, the Forest was hauntingly vacant of what made a Wood seem a Wood.

Leaf reached to touch the Forest's phloem of spirit with soft words and trembling caresses. "Noblien, they're so careworn."

"Aye, LittleLeaf," replied Noblien, "but her countenance was once well kept. Her helms stand empty now, yet they do not relinquish their rank." So saying, his voice drifted into a breath of self-collection. "Rather, they stand strong. No will can smite the memory of these Woods. She'll ne'er forget." He paused and looked around the upward lifts of leaves, his features of reverent composure, although furrows deepened on his brow as one invoked by tragic recollections. Onward, he walked, speaking in a tempered tone full of Elvish inflections. "Respect her—we are but vagabonds on her part."

The palisades of the Silvern were dense but opened into many wide willow girths within, wherein the damp air, so onerous before, did now lighten. Therewith, too, the austere shadows became a mighty shield crest hung upon Forest ramparts in deference. Here, honor hung heavy in the air, as did the haunts of the unkept dead, the sense of it enveloped in captivating mystery.

Leaf was beside herself in wonderment. "She's a dream thread by the Wood spirits themselves."

As she spoke, a grove of Red Firs revealed themselves, no longer concealed behind the mustered Tree walls of the Silvern gates. Pious anchorites steeled against the erosion of time. Towering, weather-carved staves looking more like patricians, ordained and sealed for their part, stood fully garbed in amethyst moss. These were Trees of antiquity, very near, or at least so, the height and age of Alderelm's own. Leaf was enamored with the symbolism they stowed, in their cause and beauty, and not the least, in the chalcedonic music they whelped underfoot.

But for Noblien, a vile sense had befallen him, cloaked in the smell of blood and the stench of vengeance. His eyes narrowed, their gleam slipping beneath the intricate valleys of his spirit while his bow found a secure anchor within his palms. Following the Yaguará's lead, Tullkaee took hold of the Yew slung at her side, although she did not know for what she prepared or where to direct her aim. Despite all this, the Treean was oblivious, caught in the rapture of the Old Barks. To one, her eye was captured.

She was a white Oak, a testament to the gallantry of Trees. Her fissured trunk was hollowed into an enclave created by a devastating lightning strike. Still, the mighty Timber anchored and soared, indifferent to the woes of life. Leaf stepped past the circlet of Wood avens that had grown around her and entered the fibers of her belly unbidden. Rich were the patterns of the Tree's woodgrain, baked and sealed off from her offset core, her heart. The Treean's tongue hummed the vulgate of the Wood, and her touch glided smoothly over hardened incisions. But the white Oak, far out and above, bid Leaf take heed, her twigs in a twittering angst.

Noblien sensed the danger and rushed forward. "Leaf!"

It was too late. Down, down the Treean plunged. Noblien stammered at the sight. "Fie! Fie! The glebe's fallen in under her!"

The Treean shouted for the Fierce-Eyed Elf. She desperately wished for the Puman's help, for him to pluck her up like the day they had met, yet she plummeted until she landed hard. Stunned, her entire body aching, she began to move but froze at the sound of sniffling. Hoarse breaths crackled as her body was poked and prodded. She lay in an opossum's pose, breathless.

"It's a creaker," spat a sniveling voice.

"Creak-ur?" asked another.

"Creaker," said many other voices, hissing.

"What's us ta do with ah creak'uh?" scoffed one with a high-pitched whistle. "That is't no fun."

"Did yus daft wormed-holed heads not hear?" said the sniveling voice. "It's ah creaker. Been a hunnerd slopped rains down har since thar kind wur ah-bove. Its breed is tha hist-ry keepers," said the creature, widening its minuscule eyes, its voice sinking into a muted whisper. "Ist said theys can conduct speech with tha those Trees."

"Who cares 'bout that?" croaked one. "Wes can dig dirt."

"Ah, it's no gud to us," added another, gurgling in fits and pops within its throat and mouth. "Let's dangle it or' the Lethe!"

"Yeess, let its yeasty tongue taste the watur of ah'bliv-yun," wailed one to the creatures excitedly.

"Oh! Oh! Think it'll wiggle and squirm a bit?"

"No yuns toad-snouted cankers," snarled the sniveling voice again. "It's the key ta the daft Trees."

"Yer talk with cracked tongue, ya wooden-headed slug."

"And ya think with less," the sniveling voice sneered. "Get thes Trees ta work with us ah bit and more bait for the trappuns thou knows."

Now, one creature hobbled through the circle of cursing and spit. It eyed the Treean's form with a curious tilt of the head and a loathsome lick of the lips. Leaf stayed stock-still. Slurred and wet speech met her ear with uncomfortable closeness. "Trappuns have been slimsy."

"Listen har, fut lick'ah," countered the gurgler. "To the water with it! Free the burdens of its mind. Thars more fun in that!"

"Yeh," rasped many, taking to chant. "To the Lethe, to the Lethe!"

The sniveling voice became extinct within the mutated cacophony, which few might call a song:

To tha Lethe,
To tha Lethe,
String ya up, dangle ya high,
Wiggl'in squirm'in creak-uur die!

Their feet stomped to their hymn, and Leaf shivered in terror. She must get away. She must move. If only she could slowly slide away unnoticed. Forearm past forearm, reaching and pulling, she began to slither away from the numerous feet, although she did not know where; any place aside from this would do.

"Put a shiv in its gut," said one, spying Leaf's regress.

The creature stamped on her back and pulled up a chunk of her brambled hair, breaking several twig-like appendages. She screamed out in pain. Another knelt and licked its foot, which seemed to be a custom of pleasure, for the creature purred repugnantly before its barnacled tongue scraped across Leaf's cheek. Beady and unblinking were its red eyes, which narrowed as it took in its cringing victim.

"Let me go!" cried Leaf.

"Wee, it squeals!" the excited creature jeered, tearing the back of Leaf's shirt with its long, hooked nails.

There was naught Leaf could do to resist, though she struggled fiercely under the oppressive degradation brought so rudely upon her. She shrieked and yelled in helpless anger, but this only elicited the creatures' trollish excitement. Out of breath from her cries and struggles, she drew herself into a ball and whimpered with dry tears and frustrated hope for the talents of her friends to come quickly to her aide.

Far above, Noblien was in a fit of frustration. The pit of Leaf's fall was too small, and the crown roots too large for him to pass through. "Groundlings," he hissed.

"And we meet voices," said Tullkaee, nodding in that direction.

The elf's expression smoothed into an eerie calm as he turned toward where the mighty Daun indicated. He could pluck off these irritants before they presented themselves, but instead, he gazed toward the sky. The Daun, learning more and more about her fellow's nature, watched the Puman closely. Yet any further scrutiny was startled away when Noblien whistled in short, piercing bursts, fluidly expressed, to which the smallest of small birds flew past her ear and swished headlong into the Tree cave of Leaf's engulfing plunge. The mighty huntress's jaw dropped.

Noblien eyed her fleetingly and drew out his war knives. To this course, Tullkaee followed, choosing her tomahawk, and waited, turning an eye to those stalking their position, close now. Noblien spared no such attention and stomped upon the earth's moist palate here and there, searching for any spot of soft, weak soil between the labyrinth of roots. Yet the Daun's focus narrowed, alert and predatory, on the approaching voices.

Fools, she thought. *Too loud! Too loud for Forest wanderings.* She knelt, using the head of her axe as further balance. She was a vision, stunning in her strength and confidence, deadly in her beauty and power, and fearsome because the attributes were rarely appreciated together.

As to the cacophony under the earth, it had hushed abruptly. The punishing groundlings had become stone silent as they gaped, stretching out and shrinking back their wrinkled necks and blinking in some attempt to comprehend what sight was revolting to even these foul folk.

Leaf did not know what brought silence upon the scamps. She dared not look. Her fetal form shivered, and over and over, her mind's voice pleaded, *Do not let them notice the Sakatu strung around my neck. Twine of nettle, limb, and leaf, the Treeans ask your favor.*

One creature, more curious than cautious, touched the rough, bark-like skin of Leaf's back, albeit timidly. Her spine was etched in deep crevices that folded over onto themselves in malformed spindles, the inflexible tissue of scars, branded with infernal, scarlet hues. She shuddered, the wails of past trauma too horrific to remember beginning now to seep forth. The creature fell back. The others gurgled, taken almost with pity, their gruesome swallows overfilling with mucus, making their breaths sound labored as though filled with the oozing resin of a Black Pine.

Yet one tightened a hand around Leaf's neck. It squeezed for all the dissatisfaction life gave it, its face tightening with its grip. Leaf struggled, scratched for space between them, for one inhalation, but was falling away into unconsciousness.

"Don't go and ruin the fun," said another, slapping away the choker's hold. "Ya slug-slimed weasel. The Treeun goes ta tha Lethe. Them waters is ripe, right ripe." Its eyes briefly met Leaf's; they held a faint but defiant glint of sympathy, although the moral emotion dwelled deep in the pit of impenitent resignation. "To the Lethe with yun. Tie it!"

The Treean could feel the fetter applied was twine made of goat root, for it stung and dug into her skin, forcing the pivots of her joints into an unnatural form. She felt a need to roll in agony but could do little more than breathe as the paunch-bellied trolls hoisted her above a water pit whose dark fluid burbled, its odor envenoming the core of her being. Her consciousness began to struggle for recognition between the realities of the waking and slumbering worlds.

Faintly, there came a whisper to the fading Treean's ears, a song sung by the low, mellow voice of a young marchwarden. The hums arose from the darkest depths of her memory, a long-forgotten lullaby, as the stagnant slurp of frigid mush began to coat her feet. She wept. As her head became submerged beneath the indescribable watery filth, her last sight was a whirling finch flying by. Must be, she reckoned, that I am fading from the graces of life and meeting death.

The ave sped like lightning across a pitch-night sky down to the tattered tunnels of the groundlings. It brushed aside the Treean's sinking head with the speed of a peregrine falcon before thrusting itself up, up, up, and out into the fresh air. Tiny was the bird that enlisted all zeal to burst with its best speed but mighty was its heart. Richer cousins would have puffed with pride at the sight of their distant relation.

The Fierce-Eyed Elf lifted a finger to touch the whir that whipped past and ran to where the bird had emerged from the ground. Tullkaee, never having seen the bird of haste, swift as the tinker faeries of legend, intended to follow him, but three fellows paraded forth from the shade of the Woodland's columned gates.

A voice aflush with challenge shot the air with insolence. "Hey there!"

It was a young man, strong yet slight in stature, bearing the crest of Seayr upon his sleeve. Recognizing the insignia, Tullkaee grumbled. To his right, two more Seayrans walked forward, displaying more bravado than was within her tolerance.

She smirked. "A brood of bestial trolls step more quietly."

"Not enough," said the haughty sentry, "to intrude upon our terr'tory, but more, you seek to insult us?"

"Uh," Tullkaee scoffed. "The shagbark is beginning to yawn with boredom. Where, little sucklings, are your nanny goats? I hunger for a real fight."

"Nowhere does this discourse proceed," said Noblien, moving his person between Tullkaee and the three who grew bolder with the passing of every second; he had approached with such disquieting stealth as to have unnerved the lot of them.

"Do not lecture as though we're mere children. We're footmen well 'nough of age to serve the king's legion . . . and due the proper respect as so."

"Well, 'nough of age?" mocked Noblien, pausing to glance at the youth's unfilled boots. "Take heed. I do not care a jot about your age or service—only my course and purpose. I've no ill toward you; however, ponder your intent carefully and with haste, and then carry forth whatsoever. But let us hope you choose well thy conflicts, or well-nough of age will ne'er bring forth the season of the well-aged. Do you catch my meaning?"

"How dare you speak this way to a sentinel," hissed the young guard, inflecting the end of his statement loftily and in sync with the rising of his upturned nose. "You've no place here, elf," and so saying, he paused for some effect.

However, the moment fell hollowly, and the struggling youth slowly drew his sword as though such a halting course of action was more menacing than the simple act of unsheathing the killing instrument in the first place. Noblien rolled his eyes.

"Look around," the undeterred youth continued, "the bays of destiny have already called a just end to the burg of this Woodland. Pitiful an end, too, as would be expected from your kind. All that time left were a few blazoned tapestries and the wake of elven pestilence. Your kind makes me sick. As I speak, I should spill your entrails and be rid of your fair feathers."

"Forasmuch as your mouth does bloat, be on with it," replied Noblien, putting away his twin daggers to the wonder of all present.

There was a hesitation in the moment as everyone wondered whether each had misheard or mistaken the words and actions of the elf. They wondered whether this was a threat or a surrender, and how to react in whichever circumstance. The Puman stood serenely and waited. The world skimmed on. A bevy of birds delivering chirps on the wing flurried past. The sentry shifted their footing and swallowed nervously. And in a moment lost on everyone, Noblien knocked the sentry-youth off his feet. The action was harmless but of particular note, for the speed at which the elf had moved left the limbs of the shocked comrades frozen, unsure of how to proceed.

Pity rested on the countenance of the Fierce-Eyed Elf, whose energy and essence seemed to glow with a mysterious blend of the past and present. The once haughty youth suddenly beheld the ethereal nature surrounding the elf, and shame overwhelmed him, further whittling away at his pride.

"Careful your wit to mouth and hand to action. You might lie a bit differently on the soil in a different encounter. Even with the sight of our eyes, we can behold naught when anger blinds us. Follow what course you must, but necessity calls me off to mine," and so saying, Noblien reached out his arm and helped the sentinel to his feet.

Tullkaee watched it all, her face hot with anger. And after Noblien sprinted away, her tongue took to flailing them. "Unbelieving! I was not aware any cland existed that could raise such fools! Remember what mercy grants and who granted it. An elf. A Puman elf. The most lethal kind. You stupid fools! You still do not appreciate what you just taunted. Puumman. You would be wise to study their kind." She laughed, still astounded by the situation that had just passed. "His kind makes you sick? His kind? His kind swaddled your grandfathers' grandfathers. To turn a cheek after insults on the dead. No, no. This cannot be left unsettled. Come here so I may carve out your tongues as belt tokens."

❧ ❀ ❧

Leaf now tasted what bitter truths lay in legends, the Lethean waters. She coughed, choking, as the memory-erosive fluid spilled down her throat, filling her lungs. Her memories pinched the foremost regions of her psyche; they were being unraveled and torn. The little Treean fought to hold them tight, to keep her mind's impressions from dissipating into nothingness. She fought with a ferocity she did not know she had and with what had been suppressed for her life, *the Brekenridge Foils.*

The Foils began upon the Brekenridge, the southernmost edge of Alderelm. 'Tis a Wildwood of scalded beauty rarely ventured. Nonetheless, it claims an exquisite and transcendental splendor unequaled. On the verdure of a most noble spring, when Leaf was nearly twelve rings grown, the Nemean nerve of Alderelm snapped. The Ancient Ones hold onto the event's account, but Leaf always kept the incident sequestered in a distant corner of her mind.

In this rough encampment of memory, a young marchwarden ran with the spirit of the West wind, his heart pounding in as much apprehension as exertion. Alderelm's breath tightened for the marchwarden, and the faerie knots unraveled beneath his steps while the twinflowers dimmed behind him. An unconscionable sorrow tempted to burden his heart forever; all the Forest knew it. Onward, he ran, full hilt, to reach his brother.

Here, history turns to love, or more accurately, to the grief of it; for love can be a guileful creature and, in this instance, it had inflicted its best and worst upon a Treean's spirit. That Treean, the brother of the marchwarden who now ran for all his worth, had fallen in love with one of the ancient Trees, and she with him: Nirmossa, the highest devotion of heart and spirit among kin kind. 'Tis a duality between impractical ideals and rational illusions, the inside out of reality in perfect balance. Within this wondrous state, where a Tree and Treean found love, the first cataclysm was set in motion to unravel the beginning foil.

The Treean's beloved, the beautiful Kaurì, that Ancient One with glossy ocher bark and broad silvery leaves, could not gather enough strength to unveil her new greens upon awakening from the brume of winter's spell. The season had been too long and harsh, and now the shadow of permanent slumber began to rest over her.

Great was the sorrow that took her Treean love. And as the days passed, his sorrow devolved beyond grief into anguished madness. In this state of illness, he began the unfathomable slash work of hewing her towering vessel, her drying limbs shaking under the impacts—*the first foil.*

To the cracking of cherished ancient Wood met by an axe, the marchwarden slowed and halted, staring in horrified disbelief. In front of him, his brother hacked away, seized by the fury of heartbreak, while surrounded by seven of Alderelm's marchwardens who had bloodied him with half a dozen arrows. Sickeningly, despite the wounds, the brother stayed his strength through grief. The marchwarden wheezed in revulsion.

"Which of you dares to injure my brother?" the marchwarden asked in disgust. "Get away, all of you!"

He glared, halting further action for the moment, but none of his fellow border guards retired from their positions, and the creaking of tightening bow-wood menaced their resolve. The marchwarden fixed his gaze upon his brother.

"Bo, methinks a time ago, we'd have had them all easily."

The axe work halted, and the marchwarden's brother looked

around apathetically at the surrounding guardians. Only one surreal glance did he bend toward the trembling marchwarden. For a moment, they were young, playing roughly and challenging each other to dares. For a heartbeat, hope entered the marchwarden's heart. Yet then, his brother spoke.

"Might be, you ought to raise that there shoddy bow."

The marchwarden was taken aback but quickly fell to instinct and the comfort of their relationship. He was, after all, his brother—and the jab had stung.

"'Tis not shoddy."

"Tis a piece of scat, Bris. No one could shoot straight with it."

"I ne'er shoot otherwise."

"Nay, you've always shot off the mark; 'tis that crooked piece of wood that makes your aim appear clean. If you were to shoot with a proper bow . . . you'd miss," and so saying, the brother smiled, although the expression was eerily stolid. "I'll not be halted," he said flatly, spinning the axe in his hand; the marchwarden stepped toward him. "Do not advance on me, Bris. I will strike you down."

"Bodark?"

"You are right in your course, as am I."

"To mark my brother?" the marchwarden replied incredulously, almost pleading.

"I would have no other," his voice dropped, and with an unexpected rapidity, he leveled a devastating axe hit upon the Deciduous of Perpetual Beauty, his greatest love.

The marchwarden's reaction occurred within a single breath. His shot was pure and instant, before any other border guards could contemplate the discharge of a single arrow. He felt the fletching brush by his fingers and heard the brief hiss of the arrow. He closed his eyes and listened to the treacherous thud of its impact, ran to his brother as in a nightmare, and held him in his arms.

The Forest was silent. The grief was palpable, all by and against the wishes of both. In an instant, his brother's heart was beatless—*the second foil.*

And here, the scar upon the Lastborn took a hideous turn, for the beautiful Kauri's great vessel began to groan, whether from the sustained insults and turning wind or from the death of Nirmossa's love will ne'er be certain. All that matters is that the Sacred Tree fell—*the last foil* to begin it.

Here forth they came, the full recollections of the Brekenridge Foils, scraped from the rampikes of Leaf's deepest memories. The Treean's body shuddered, and a wake of stinging ripples spread through the Lethe's slurries. The scars upon Leaf's back tightened.

The impact of Kauri's fall produced an echo of silence as though a vortex had descended and taken away the surrounding air. How could a sound be both thunderous and silent? Whatever the answer, the mystery of it awoke Baal, the Spirit-Giver of the Veriha, who let loose a wave of anger rich and fierce upon the lands. For Baal had felt Kauri's legacy stripped from the soils, felt the heaving death. The reaction was guttural, a grief-stricken reflex, a sorrowful plague-curse spit out in a misunderstanding of circumstance.

Alderelm was swarmed as all manner of fauna became crazed, tearing and clawing at the bark of the Ancient Ones. Even as the Treeans were hunted, they mounted a brave defence, many falling in savage description.

LittleLeaf LeadTree, the Treeans' Lastborn of tender age, quavered near the brim of canopy shadow. Her kin had perished. Her frail form cried, yet her wind-wept breaths did not have enough air to emit any sound. Her vulnerability attracted death. Yet for what power takes on occasion to intercede in life's stakes, the marchwarden's gaze turned to her. His arrows spent, he took a staff and hurled it through the air toward the Treean of trembling leaves, effectively smiting the blood-filled mouth nearly upon her neck. Still, another and another encroached to take up the mantle of the last. The marchwarden looked on in horror, a tear of frustrated anger falling down his cheek.

"Hie, Miriam, Hie!" he shouted with all his effort. The grim, colossal Tree rasped and creaked. "Hie, Miriam!"

To the tender Treean did the Great Tree begin to bend, grasping as gently as she could decipher, for Trees lack the sensations of touch that the creatures of softer shells possess and, too, are not meant to bend except against the wind. To this end of miraculous events, Miriam saved the young Treean, but at a terrible cost to the youngling's flesh, which was gashed and torn across her back, the Lastborn's scars forever fixed.

The Treean sprout screamed in anguish while latching onto the Ancient Tree's large trunk for comfort and safety. The Great Tree gurgled a lullaby as her leaves quaked in peaceful, tinkling ripples of assurance. And at this incredible moment of love's defiant possibilities, Baal recoiled in a healed realization, halted at once the madness, and retreated into the ethers. There might have been shame or regret were it not that the Spirit-Giver was an inkling-thought in the foundation of life itself, and aside from the Brownian motion of sentiment or the power of life's determination to exist despite all odds, Baal was still an infant of the universe, unaware of result or consequence.

The events of the Brekenridge Foils were hidden deep within Leaf's core and had become an essence of her spirit more than a tangible memory. When the Lethe reached these sequestered experiences, it could not feed upon them. Instead, it became steeped in the marchwarden's fight and vigor and the Great Tree's bravery and determination, all a compilation of love, and all integrated into Leaf's wall of character and presence. The Lethe had lost its miasmic powers over her.

"It's fight'in the Lethe?" a groundling asked, bewildered.

"Ain't poss'ble," said another.

With one more suffocating inhale of the mongering waters, the Lastborn took it all back, every molecule of memory swiped and every chronicle she had aye forgotten was fully embraced for the first time in her life. With kicks and thrusting arms, she pulled her head above the water, coughing and gasping.

"It ain't fettered!"

"Get it now!"

"Ya go an put ya fingas in tha theres wuters, ya'd wormed-hole head, and see un what haps."

"Here it comes now."

"Reckon, it'll be good pickups now."

"Grab it!"

Leaf felt the sticky tips of their fingers as the world spun, and she gasped for air. Her mouth tasted the way a rotting carcass smells, and she vomited. Delighted, the groundlings clapped and jeered.

"Ah, creak-urs tasted it," said one creature. "So, what yun think?"

Leaf sprang forward, slewing past the imps and backing herself against the subterranean gallery. The groundlings' mock simpering had not the coaxing effect they had hoped on the rebounding Treean, and they blinked wide in confused dismay.

"LittleLeaf!" echoed the approaching voice of Noblien from a far-pegged conduit to the left.

The groundlings at once scattered, pleading for their lives amidst long, clean knife falls, Tullkaee's axe not far behind. In the clamor, Leaf scrambled and clung as close as she could against the confines, panicked and wild.

With the creatures in enthusiastic retreat, Noblien went to her; concern suffused over his face. "LittleLeaf," he whispered.

Yet the Leaf of Alderelm was not approachable, and upon seeing this fact, the elf's head tilted in pitied empathy.

He repeated his entreaty. "LittleLeaf."

"I know you," Leaf said.

"Yes," replied Noblien, placing his hand on her shoulder and searching her for wounds.

The deformity of the skin on her back was not to be missed, and his eyes reflected the anguish of it in empathy that Leaf had ever experienced it, more than of the wound itself.

"Oh, dear little one."

"Footsteps approach," Tullkaee said. "The fools make too much noise."

Leaf's eyes rolled back in her head, and with the celerity of his kind, the Fierce-Eyed Elf caught the Treean's limp body. He swaddled her within the warmth of his jerkin, his woven shirt of elven firmament hanging loosely now, without its war tackle binding it.

We'll take a chance," Noblien gruffed, while fitting knives and quiver back upon his person, "within these tunnels."

With Leaf in the Puman's arms, they chose a confluence of black walls bending centrally and downward. Upon one step, steep and uneven, the elf turned right, walked a short way, and halted. From the height of the hollow emerged three giant roots, and between them, trickled water that was wonderfully fresh in scent.

"Here," he said, setting Leaf upon the plateau of bent roots and retrieving a sachet of galingale, that aromatic sedge of the bitterroot range so sweetly aromatic as to bring wakeful peace from deathly sleep. "They'll be lost," the elf continued, placing the fine remnants of dried leaves near the young Treean's nose. He eyed the Sakatu, such an unassuming nutlet, even threadbare if he were to be honest. Yet, it carried the majesty of the Forest, of the Trees, and he thought at once how unworthy he was to even look upon it and cast his eyes away.

Tullkaee motioned to Noblien. The shouting of their pursuers was close.

Noblien winced in despair and shook his head. "These tunnels are a composition of illogical courses. They could be beside us and not know it."

Tullkaee grumbled under her breath and listened for the fools lost in the passages. She was angrier at their ignorance than at the fact that they sought them out.

Noblien sighed. "She has met the waters of oblivion—the Lethe. Smell its stench? As a Treean, I fear she has seen and put to memory what is a void of emptiness."

Neither spoke for a long time after that. Only did they watch Leaf and wait. Then, as though touched by a whispered breeze, Noblien gazed calmly and smiled at the Daunan huntress.

"The Haards dug this place out," he said, his voice barely discernible. "They hid from the hunts for their hide. Near the end of any countable number, the inhabitants of the land we now seek offered the claw-footed horses sanctuary. The Haard would flourish once again, the ancestral lineage of the flagbearers laid out.

"Although legend tells of a small-few number that did not enter the Land of Shee, for trust no longer existed within their doughty hearts. Instead, they learned to blend into the sun's rays and the stellar gleam. And to this day, in the last hours of one's life . . . they come . . . and with them is brought light, a spectrum of the celestial, lest any aye die alone and in darkness as their kin once did. And for those precious spirits of tender age or delicate wit, the Haards bear the brunt of death's nonharmonic chords. Speeding to the constellations of Elysium as radiance beams across the sky, they whisk the innocents away upon the iridescence of their silken hides. For my kind, the self-sacrificing pony stays with us through the haunted Weald apparitions, ever loyal to the lost. At least until Eternity awakens and realizes the elves were forgotten in its dreams," and so saying, the etchings of Noblien's countenance settled in a wistfully grave manner as one at peace by way of resignation.

"With a tale such as that," said Tullkaee, "there is hope for this journey."

"Hmm, I don't believe 'tis a tale," replied the elf gently. "And 'tis wit and will to be relied upon. Do not trust in hope."

"Yaguará, the will is strung together by hope," said Tullkaee, though not before the elf had turned away to survey the status of Leaf.

❧ ✦ ☙

Leaf stirred many times before rest, and the galingale did their work and returned her to the waking world. The Fierce-Eyed Elf was nearly beside himself when his silver-grey eyes met an interrogating choler within the green of hers.

Cautiously, he sought to perceive her spirit's condition. "LittleLeaf, how are you?"

"My head aches," she groaned. "Noblien, those waters—"

"No more," he shushed, his insides recoiling.

"But the Sakatu hums," she persisted. "What've I done?"

"Fear not, methinks the Sakatu stirs only in confusion, for 'twas submerged where memories are lost. But the waters of the Lethe are not so strong as to penetrate its shell. Its knowledge is safe and protected; I believe this with all my being."

A draft of fresh air brushed across them, and at once, the winnowed halls of the caves seemed to call the three henceforth. Leaf stood, her hand cradling the Sakatu hanging around her neck. She closed her eyes, concentrating. "Noblien. It expresses intent and hums the songs of Seayr. I believe we are meant to go there."

Noblien eyed the Sakatu, chewing on possibilities. To Shee or Seayr made less difference, while Leaf felt the energies of every Tree in totality call to her. He did not like that the Sakatu had shed its dormancy, nor did he take to diverting their course. Yet his gifts of guardian wares also felt a tug toward Seayr, though he had muted the urge. There was no matter for it; they were off, following courses of instinct rather than the plan.

WOOD AVEN

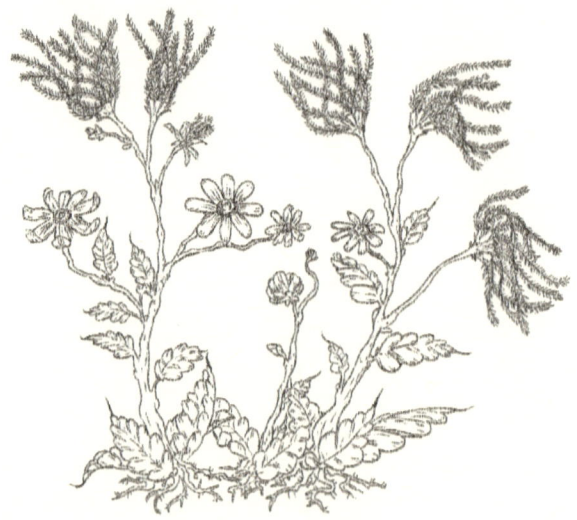

Wood Aven. 1. *Any of various plants having irregularly shaped leaves, white, yellow, and/or reddish flowers, and plumed seed clusters. **2.** Recent Age. Of the genus Dryas, a circumpolar species of the mountainous and arctic regions called "Mountain Aven." Also known as "herb bennet." The Mountain avens' flowers track the sun's movement across the sky, are relatively large, white or yellow, and grow upon leafless stalks above a dense rosette of shallowly lobed leaves.*

GOAT ROOT

Goat Root. **1.** *Plant with multi-stemmed hooked tendrils and deep, sharp, stinging roots.* **2.** *Recent Age. Also known as Shrubby Rest Harrow, Devil's Shoestring, and Catgut, a perennial herb with long, deep roots that grow one to three inches tall with pink and white or pink and pale-yellow flowers bunched at the top. Traditionally used to treat ailments such as rheumatism and tuberculosis. It has also been studied in cancer research.*

GALINGALE

Galingale. 1. A perennial grass-like sedge having rough-edged leaves, reddish flowers, and aromatic rhizomes. Used as a medicinal herb in rousing the senses. *2.* Recent Age. Identical to above. Also, in the ginger family, it can grow up to 1 meter tall and blooms from July to September.

❦ Chapter 14 ❧

It is a little-known fact that the number of flowers that bloom in Summer equals the number of bumblebee hiccups and butterfly sneezes in Spring.

—Lichen reveals secrets learned from Mushroom to Moss

Elevated from head to heel, the Coyotl was afresh upon the back of Leoness, gliding high within the ethers of the welkin. He was serenely soothed by the vespers the enigmatic banda drew forth from the filamentous cirrus wisps, and it would be a wonder to everyone but Sage that this feathered dragon knew this fact innately.

Circling downward beneath the high clouds, a landscape of Forests thick in the wealth of vegetation filled their view. Intermittent glades acting as outposts from the plentiful shade balanced the scenery's perspective. The glorious sight was an ode to the western slopes of the White Mountain range, where plenteous moisture flowed in ceaseless cascades upon moss-ridden rocks. These copious liqueurs of life brought such colors of green as to be at times more brilliant than the sun's light and at others more bedimming than night.

More at home within the sage and bitterbrush, the pines and vernal pools, the arid, dryscape of hidden treasures, the raw wind ever twirling to kiss the sky and Earth—more of the scablands was he. Yet he could respect the lift of spirit brought from gazing upon such a beautiful landscape as this. Still, he grumbled, for the abundance of vegetation, even as lovely as it was, had become a complication in the hunt for his three companions, and resultantly, the irritants pinching at his mind grabbed his erratic temper.

Leoness continued swirling lower as he scanned the view, and in so doing, he beheld a kestrel in pursuit of a dove. *'Tis unnatural for ave to prey upon ave,* he thought, welling in disgust. *Woe to the disappearance of the gryphons and the resultant travesties such as this,* and so thinking, he touched Leoness's soft neck.

He watched as the dove hit a nook hard. 'Twas an accident of fortune, for it was then concealed and rested stone still while catching its terrified breath. The kestrel sharply angled the pinion of its wings and, with a breath-stopping whoosh, slung its momentum upward to a Tree branch in wait for inevitability.

Nay, this isn't right, thought the Coyotl, *this rhapsody called life. Orisons are of no use when we are fordone within the jowls of death upon the moment of conception. Yet, before death, there might be some frays worthy of notice,* and upon thinking this, his countenance turned anew with mischief.

Leoness felt the Coyotl's intent, and together, they eagerly scoured the currents toward the Tree and kestrel. The wind stole tears from Sage's eyes, which stung salty and dried as they reached his cheeks. Catching sight of the pair's crazed approach, the hungry kestrel winged away in fright of its own death. Its wings pumped toward the sun, which hid behind a cloud. The Coyotl, much satisfied, turned the banda away from their pursuit and returned a keen gaze toward the shaking dove left under the cove in hiding.

"Yes, by will, there are still rights in the world, Leoness!"

Reveling in their perceived accomplishment, the Coyotl and banda yawed between winds, spinning and turning playfully, a hard-angled tilt opening the view of lands beneath them. At this moment, Sage espied such good fortune as to wreak the devil in him once more—his company.

Noblien had already beheld the two miscreants of the sky and was relieved that Sage had returned. Perhaps a twinge of this ease could be attributed to the knowledge of the Coyotl's wellbeing. However, not more than a blithe musing might Noblien consider in this regard. And so, he set a fleet of whistles to the air, to which a familiar ave came to sit upon his shoulder. Tullkaee was no less bewildered than when she first beheld the bird and perhaps even more appalled, for she figured such a thumbnail-sized creature ought not to be related to the paragon of a warrior's retinue. Yet the Fierce-Eyed Elf's grey eyes pierced the wee bird with grand affection. Then, with a jerk, the little creature returned to the air with all the valiant effort a mighty warrior heart could give.

What a sight! The hawk-in-miniature set in hot pursuit after the banda of considerably larger proportions. Poor, sweet Leoness, while fierce of spirit, was not the fiercer against the tenacious creature now making such a fuss upon her tail. Squawking in repulsed consternation, the banda alighted to the ground in aggravated fear, with a laughing Coyotl perched in precarious readiness to hop off and greet the company.

The view of the finch chasing after the banda would have set Tullkaee to complete fits of laughter had she ever seen such a creature, and also, if she had not underestimated the possibility of it truly existing. But the Daun had not either and thus stood mystically horrified at Leoness's honking figure as Sage approached the three unconcernedly and with an open smile.

"Leaf! You're looking worse for wear. Good granites, does the Puman not stop for thee? And where, pray tell, are your clothes, good Treean?" The Coyotl turned to Noblien and rattled off more. "What's all this? You're no doubt set to cross the threshold of Shee. What're you up to, Thai Mielle?"

Tullkaee, still grappling with what brute stood before her and whether or not they should all run or fight, cried out. "That monster will have us on a spit of fire."

"Aucks, monster?" replied a startled Sage, swinging around on the spot. "Listen here, noble huntress, she's a banda. Her derivation and presence are a blessing. There's no mild cross between a gryphon and a Halouse," and so saying, he cast an admiring eye toward Leoness, bent limb over wing, scratching an itch on her anointed head. The result of this wayward position caused her body to tilt to such a precarious extent that she and her shadow looked for a moment as one. Leaf and Noblien backed away. "Careful though, while she's surreal upon the currents, she's prone to accident on the ground."

She did, in fact, tumble over before regaining her balance with a ruffle of feathers and an awkward honk, which propelled herself into another maneuver of questionable elegance. She followed by gazing adoringly upon the Coyotl for what time her inattentive mind could spare.

Seemingly unaware of the great beast's latitude or lack thereof, Sage rounded back on Noblien. "What say you? What are you all about?"

The upper corner of the Puman's mouth twitched, and he answered with a degree of fatigue too early for the time of day. "We go to Seayr."

"Seayr?" said Sage, gawping. "Lawks, Thai Mielle, you've breathed the Obsidian Fields!"

"Stop calling me that," Noblien said, seething in a hiss of controlled but rising impatience.

"Right, right, as you wish. But clearly, our journey first takes us to Shee. Methinks Heartwood Willow—"

Noblien held up a hand and turned his face away. "You delight too much in your mouth. Enough."

Sage scratched his head, surveying the company with more care and caution than he had upon his arrival. The company was more careworn than when he had left them, and his worry heightened. He walked to face the Puman once more, though with more attunement to his needs.

"Noblien?"

To this, the Puman responded, "Only by way of more rest than travel have we made headway toward the border of Seayr since departing the Silvern Woodland," and so saying, Sage placed his fist to his heart and bowed his head briefly, the homeland of an extinguished elven ketyl given reverence evermore in respect. "Leaf has not been well," Noblien continued. "She will heal, but her body is spent."

As if to emphasize the point, Leaf lurched forward to expel what bile was left in her stomach. Over and over again, she heaved the emptiness of her gut, growing weaker after each attempt to rid any utterance of what before occupied it. The Puman's countenance expressed regret. Sage was quiet and solemn. No more words were said. The decision was unanimously conclusive, and each took a seat around the poor youngling at last asleep under the recent sunder and assaults of her body.

The Daun was soon to follow Leaf's path, her eyes heavy and her chin eventually nodding in heavy slumber. Heretofore, her deep breathing was the elves' conversation. Noblien waited. The leaves rustled, the sun strode through tumultuous clouds, and the silence finally broke.

"I was wrong, Sage, very wrong," Noblien said, nodding to Leaf, "to think we could protect her from the pains of the world. My friend, she's already met them—enough scars for a lifetime," and so saying, he paused and gazed upon the Coyotl who watched the Treean sleep. "She fell," Noblien said between gritted teeth. "Groundlings. I could not reach our dear Treean until she'd met much torment, the Lethean waters."

Sage's eyes widened as he ran both hands through his disheveled hair. Noblien gave Sage a moment to absorb the awful reality. The

Coyotl, after taking several deep breaths, looked over Noblien's face, winced, and then found his words with the deepest of drawn-out sighs.

"Then she's well considering."

"My friend," said Noblien, swallowing, "I've been mistaken under each of my steps."

"No more guilt is yours than mine," said Sage, with an unusually level-minded judiciousness. "Hereon, we are each other's boon," he said, placing a hand on the Puman's shoulder. "Yet tell me. Why to Seayr?"

"The Sakatu," Noblien answered, "has awoken in some manner of speaking."

"What?" whispered Sage loudly.

"Aye," continued Noblien. "I believe the Lethean waters awoke it. And . . . it appears to express intent through her. She says it hums for Seayr," and so saying, he shrugged. "So, that is where we go."

"Very plainly said," replied Sage. "You say the Sakatu has awoken? Are you quite sure?"

Noblien nodded, his lips thin and tight. Sage stared at the Fierce-Eyed Elf, who steadfastly held his gaze.

"Well, then, our course is Seayr."

Some time passed between the two elves in silence as they rode the mysterious slipstreams of their elven minds. Both frequently checked the sleeping rhythms of the Daun and Treean, their figures silhouetted against the day's backdrop. Rare a sight to see, a Puman and a Coyotl standing strong together; the Trees would put the image to memory's wood rings.

From the peaceful quietude, the ferment of the Puman's mind abated enough to venture further in conversation, and so, smiling awkwardly, he said, "I told them."

"Indeed!" replied Sage, his deep-set eyes alight. "Very good then. What did they say?"

"Very little."

Sage chuckled lightly. "This surprises you?"

"It does, yet I know not what reaction I expected . . . or if I expected one."

"Tell me, why don't you reveal your deafness to others?" Sage asked, leaning closer as if to hear a secret. "Do you perceive it as a weakness or perhaps an advantage?"

Noblien was quiet for a moment. "Much of both, I believe. But mostly, 'tis so much of who I am that neither do I consider it."

Sage was next to ponder in silence and concluded the subject with a measured nod of acceptance before mulling all the other matters.

"Why does their lack of reaction not surprise you?" inquired Noblien, breaking the silence with a curious enthusiasm quite out of character.

Sage answered without a faerie's breath of contemplation. "They trust in Thai Mielle and his arrows, not Noblien and his ears."

"Would be a compliment were it not for your ceaseless prodding," sighed Noblien. "I abhor being referred to as Thai Mielle," he said, rubbing his eyes under the strain Sage imbued on his person. "But you already know this."

'Twas unfortunate the Puman had even addressed the aggravation, for any attention given it only fueled the imprudent Coyotl, and realizing his error too late, he sighed in regret. Deciding to give no more fodder to the irritant, he halted his scolding and immediately moved on. However, Sage was already well-lit under an impish spark; he simply could not forbear any such moment, for it itched under his person. So. He spoke . . . again.

"The Faiyum are skilled archers—"

Sage had barely finished uttering the words before Noblien pounced, striking him brutally beneath the ribs. Sage coughed, flashing a moment's instinct of anger, having ne'er expected the rage he had just caught nor the vehemence he now beheld being so iniquitously cast upon him by those grey eyes that he could not help but adore.

"Aucks! Hasty to the fist for one who advises reliance on the mind."

"You taunt endlessly but do not think to reminisce about the Faiyum or claim me as belonging when such myth stories stole my youth."

"Indeed, thou art Flumen's son. Although, those are no myth-stories as you say."

"What know you of my father? Speak now, for I'm done with your pretenses."

"You carry two items upon your person that I would know anywhere. First, your horned bow—a rare accoutrement, the Charlock?" Sage posed this question with arrogance, and Noblien's eyes narrowed. "Yet more is that white-fletched arrow resting pretty and ne'er dispensed within your quiver." Here, Sage withheld a grin, for he did not want to experience another hit, nor did he wish to return the favor should a second opportunity present itself, but his eyes danced, nonetheless. "It . . . is . . . most familiar to me."

Noblien uncoiled, and Sage, half expecting the pitch, stepped aside to avoid the Puman's full wrath, although his eye was split open in the partial impact. "Indeed, twice!" he cried, touching the blood now streaming down his face. "Twice you have unleashed raw emotion. Do you now see how good I am for you?" and so saying, he shook out his arms ere tightening his fists. "I've known you and was most glad to meet with your request to aide on this journey. Very little do you hold the look of your father, but in your disciplines, aucks, Thai Mielle, do you resemble greatly. So come on, let's have at it!"

"I'm not," Noblien said, "my Da . . . nor Thai Mielle."

Tullkaee rose from her slumber, and the fortress of her person strode between them, her expression somber. "You share history. Work it out with words."

"Fair enough," answered Sage, nodding to Tullkaee and dabbing at his bleeding brow.

"You say you knew my Da? How—for what purpose? Why did you arrive upon his shadow, and why did you place this arrow atop my hide and leave?"

Sage's entire deportment deflated, and the energy that buzzed around him fell inward on itself. "You, you remember me? How long—"

"You ne'er relent!" said Noblien with a snarl. He then lowered his head and leveled his gaze, which burned cold. "I'd have sat on our matters for a time deemed appropriate, but you push and push. You want to talk about the Faiyum and bring up my Da? Then let's have it. What know you?"

"I arrived too late," said Sage. "I was too late to save him. His child was better off far away from the likes of me. I placed that arrow," he said, nodding toward the snow-white singularity resting in its abode over the Puman's shoulder, "atop your hide in a gesture of honor that you might one day suspect and hopefully realize, that I knew where you hid—silly cub-child, of course, I knew where you hid."

Noblien's gaze held a predator's focus and penetrated the air with untamed emotion. "Save my Da from what? What happened to him?"

"You do not argue that your father was one of the Faiyum?" asked Sage.

Noblien nodded. "This is well known. And this arrow signifies the end of them; he was the last."

Sage hemmed and hawed. "Why do you presume that your father was the last of that noble cause?"

"I've seen naught of the Faiyum since my Da's disappearance."

"So, if you don't see the deeds of the Faiyum for yourself," Sage said, flinching, his composure shaken, "the Faiyum no longer exists?"

"Enough, Sage," Noblien pleaded. "I care not a jot about the Faiyum unless 'tis regarding what happened to my Da."

Under those words, Sage beheld the youngling of his dearest friend as though many hundred seasons had not passed, and he blinked, realizing his cowardice. "Your father," he began, his mouth already too dry to swallow, "succumbed to the venality of a wizard triad in Rhovania who were corrupted by their own sorcery. Either they learned of the Faiyum's inherent magic and considered it a threat, or they desired it for themselves."

Noblien's jaw clenched in fresh anger. "My Da was killed over the Faiyum's supposed magic? Where are these wizards now?"

The pain in the air was palpable as the corner of the Coyotl's mouth flinched and his eyes twitched. "Dead," he answered, his voice carrying not a breath of emotion, though the brown abyss of his eyes had darkened, and the danger presented therein told all that needed to be said.

Noblien sank back, his spirit fallen against a frustrated introspection, and further conversation diminished while Sage's mind explored the crevasse of time. Only the dull rhythmic thudding of the Coyotl's boot-tip against a crumbling rock pillar sounded the rest of the day and prefaced the night wherein, at last, the elves' wake-dreams provided a soothing balm for the mental concussions of the forenoon. As the sun set upon another day, sleep swaddled the mighty Daun while the Treean continued to slumber as if under the spell of winter's dormancy, her body healing under the hums of the Sakatu.

◄§ Chapter 15 §►

Nature needs neither humans nor elves to complement its fruits and flowers.

—Faerie witch of the nomadic banshee clove

As the fresh sun warmed the soil the next forenoon, the scents of balsam spice and vanilla arose and imbued the place with an aroma so divine as to finally stir the Treean from her healing sleep. Leaf gazed around bleary-eyed, half expecting to find herself within Miriam's limb hold, so soft and warm was the secure containment she felt within the gentle rocking, up and down, as with the breeze. Yet as she awoke, blowing a feather away from her mouth, she began to realize her place and stroked the grand head of Leoness. The gentle banda, intending to protect and warm the Treean, had tenderly curled herself around the wee sleeping form, wherein her rhythmic breathing granted Leaf security customarily reserved for the new young of life held within the familial embrace of cherished tenderness.

The Coyotl turned an eye to her and smiled. "Oh, good powers that be—she looks upon us again."

Leaf returned the smile, yawned, and stretched. "You're back," she murmured weakly. "How is Alderelm?"

"I would not be yet returned," he said with a wink, "were they not holding strong."

She felt a lift in her heart over his enthusiasm as he chattered about Alderelm's good standing and hope on her behalf. Meanwhile, Tullkaee pressed her to eat, and Noblien insisted she take her time and rest. Sitting upright, she listened contentedly to the three talk to one another and marveled that a songbird sat upon Noblien's shoulder. The intermittent conversation offered the elf time enough to hum to the minute ave, the melody drifting across the surroundings like a thick, rolling fog settling in amongst the Trees, ethereal and mysterious. In response, the ave puffed out its feathers and half closed its eyes.

Noblien beheld Leaf's attention and smiled, eyes glistening. "Her name is Eyas. She's small in size only—of the heart is she mighty." And with a latent curiosity, he mused, "She has been my friend for time beyond her years."

As the morning turned to late day, the Treean studied the Trees about them. Nigh twenty Red Cedars circled the graces of a monumental maple donning the laces of high-tipped roots grown in an undulating pattern in and out of the soil. A Sitka Spruce was on the fringe of these, with delicate, curving tips starkly contrasting its formidable presence. All the Trees were glowing against the contrast of the sky, where grey-canvased clouds blushed into a sable-blue torrent of color. The scene was mesmerizing.

Leaf smiled to herself and felt for the Sakatu in its place of hiding against the heart of her chest. It was well-hidden under the jerkin and cope Noblien had, from his garbs, clothed her in. She could feel the newly protruding edges of burgeoning life. They were as soft as the fur-lined petals of a Wood nymph's wings. And under the green of her hand resting atop it, she could feel a faint thrumming, the delicate resonations tickling her spirit like a sneeze and a whisper.

Her thoughts wrenched back to the Lethean waters, and her hand tightened around it. Those heinous muds had rushed forward more than buried memories; they had awoken this odd sphere of bark and husk, its seal lock broken under the assault. She shivered. There was so much to focus on, not thinking about. And for this, she was decidedly done with the present moment's concentrations.

"I think," she said, wobbling, "I'm ready."

Noblien raised his eyebrows. Leaf had been through so much, and he worried for her wellbeing. Yet, there was naught more for the circumstance presented, so he stood.

"Then let us be off," he replied in a positive tone laced with dissatisfaction.

Honking as loud as a dozen unroosted crows, Leoness stretched, stood, hopped, and tottered while the group made straight their trappings. Sage winked at Leaf and smiled in grand admiration of the creature, now shaking off any remaining sedateness still clinging to her. And with that, the group was off, following the sun as it rounded the sky trail into the west.

The land opened before them, and the more downland they ventured, the more expansive the terrain appeared. The skies also changed, turning soft, light clouds into billowing monstrosities that rushed the breezes downward in robust tumults fresh with the salty scent of the sea. The group said little. That is until Noblien slowed and finally drew up to a halt.

His lips thinned, and the muscles of his jaw ground. "We have visitors."

"Do we?" asked Sage, searching the horizon. "Grand, then. We needn't seek out Seayr. They come to us . . . as they well should."

Tullkaee rolled her eyes. "With all that squawking," she gruffed, nodding toward Leoness, "it could hardly be less than surprising."

"Listen not to her, Leoness," said Sage, his tone taking the high and lofty air of royalty.

Leoness arched her neck, pleased with Sage's attentions; she erupted into a bevy of screeches most painful to the ear. Sage took to the Elvish tongue while three tantrum beats of the banda's wings revealed a squabble beginning to take place between them.

"This is meet," said he. "She'll not leave."

Leaf could now see riders approaching, an intimidating sight, and the ground began to rumble. She felt a lump in her throat. "It might be good to have her with us."

Sage flashed a hawk eye at Leoness, and with a snap of her beak, she alighted. The heavy whooshing of her feathered wings meant she was pouting in the action. He watched her until she was high in the sky before focusing on the new excitement nigh upon them.

The approaching steeds were sumptuously bedecked with colors rich and vivid, and they seemed to join speed and force within their marching canters to look at once as ridiculous as they were beautiful. Their sight caused Sage's face to pickle in a reddened heat. Noblien did not welcome the expression and murmured to him in the Elvish tongue. Sage responded by cooling, but only on the surface.

Twelve charged upon the company, checking their speed only at the last moment, a sign of distaste and rudeness. Dour were their stone-weathered faces. One, bleaker and more cheerless than the others, cleared his throat.

"You approach the threshold of Seayr. No guests have we invited."

His horse champed the bit and tossed his head, sending froth driveling to its ironclad hooves. Leaf stepped in closer and behind Noblien.

"We are representatives of our common lands," said Noblien, "sent to deliver tidings of darkness traversing our fair lands."

"Our common lands?" jeered the horseman.

"The common land of Llaurantis," replied Noblien.

"I share no commonality with any of you."

Noblien's jaws grit, but besides, the Puman had a serene composure. "My lord, we request an audience with King Orrin, friend and ally to the realms of Llaurantis for many a year. How and where might he be?"

Sage could not suppress a grin, for both elves knew who stood before them. And while he felt the incitation marvelous, it tickled a mild irritation that he had not been the one to have vexed the king in such a manner.

The horseman's eyes flashed, further steeling the darkness prickling around his person. Leaf watched in bewilderment, fully netted by the effect of the simple inquiry.

"I'm King Orrin," said the horseman angrily, lifting himself out of his saddle with a final hiss.

Tullkaee's eyes widened, and she looked around at the elves with a disbelieving horror that recognized their actions.

"Great the honor that betides us," replied Sage, with a bow and a smile revealing his thoughts.

"I beg your pardon, my lord," said Noblien. "We are well and humbly met," and so saying, he bowed, although lower than Sage and with a slow elegance only an innate regalness of character can execute. The effect poured over the king, drawing attention away from Sage's taunting insincerity. "Will you hear us or send representation for our common cause?"

The king's eyes veiled over in thought. Leaf hoped this was a prelude to a resolution, even if tempered by the stifling energy of the gathering itself. The horses stepped to one side and then another, becoming more disquieted with time and even more so as the Coyotl began to stalk around them; he stared up at each rider in turn, the challenge clear to each. Yet, it seemed Leoness was the one to drive the king over the edge, for as he watched her soaring, a shade swept across his face.

"Common cause?" the king asked, barely moving his body, the effect of one less than human. "Common cause?" he reiterated, drawing the latter out with distaste. "What do you behold here that might be of any commonality with your lot? Let darkness befall the lands of Llaurantis. It has already befallen Seayr." He began to lead his horse away, then stopped and turned his gaze back to Noblien as though half a thought escaped him, and some excitement was elicited from it. "There is one—yes, I shall send like kind for common cause with you," and so saying, his person was lifted out of his saddle under his enthusiasm as he shouted, "Captain!"

A muffled answer floated above from a horseman to the king's left, well hidden within the group. "Yes, my lord?"

"What's that daft ostler's name?"

There was a distinct hesitation in the horseman's response. "Sessile, my lord."

"Yeesss—"

"Mercy," said the captain, "he's of simple mind, innocent to the world."

"A representative they have requested, Captain, and one fitting of our interest to their affairs have I picked. Take them to Gabets. Deliver the ostler to them. Do not let them wander, and make sure they leave."

"Yes, my lord," replied the captain reluctantly, spurring his mount aggressively toward the Puman. However, the latter surrendered not a single blade of grass, the loathing between them apparent as they locked eyes.

The king's entourage turned and left, their diminishing echoes leaving the captain's frame in the dust. Leoness screeched from high above while Leaf took in the figure before them and gasped.

"Captain," said Noblien mischievously. "We've met."

Sage cast an eye toward Noblien. "You know this fellow?"

"Oh yes," snorted Tullkaee. "He is well-versed in retreating."

"He was one of the horsemen," sniffed Leaf, shuddering, "who chased down the Haevonen."

"Lawks! You?" asked Sage, rubbing his chin. "'Tis odd that you did not divulge to your king that here reside some of the individuals you'd ere encountered?"

The captain's face tensed, mangled with creases deep and taut as he dismounted, resolve expressed in every movement. "I've been true to King Orrin—"

"Yet, you begin to question him," said Sage. "Worse still, you'd defy him? How can we trust such an individual as this?"

"I suggest you do not," answered the captain without hesitation and in a frank manner much respected by the Coyotl.

"Not the answer I was expecting," Sage continued. "You make no defense for yourself?"

"I make no excuses," the captain replied impatiently, turning away and looking toward a western track of flatland as drizzle arrived. "I'll ride some ways ahead. Do not leave the path these hooves leave for you. Keep your pace; the night will approach before you reach Gabets." He looked back and surveyed the four. "Stay together. The king's greeting will appear hospitable compared to the village inhabitants of Seayr."

"What desperate strangeness has laid itself upon the lands of Seayr," said Sage.

The captain gazed down and back after his words, clucking his mount forward. The group remained quiet, watching him lead the way as the mist rain intensified into a sideways pelting of heavy raindrops.

After the full moon's glimmer behind the water-soaked clouds quartered the length of the sky, the Earthen sod, which had at first eagerly supped, became quenched and gurgled forth the excess rain, of which there was plenty. The deluge overstayed its welcome, even for the rain-loving Treean, whose brambled locks were soaked.

The glow of lights appeared in the distance, not so far now. Strangely, in the chill of the wetness, the glow did not seem even as warm as from a single candlelight. Yet it was their means to an end, and they carried on faster, Tullkaee's thunderous puddle splashes marked above the rest.

The captain's horse stood outside a large open door, and as the company approached, the defined scent of hay and horses wafted out warmly in greeting. Within, the group could hear two voices: the captain's, gruff and strained, and another voice of incongruously flat tone and lyrical inflection. Hearing their approach, the captain ushered the group inside between two doors, which, when pulled closed, met each other to form a seal. Bringing his mount within after them, the captain pulled a board, meant for this purpose, down to lock the two doors.

"Speak now," ordered the horseman. "What business is afoot that brings you here?"

Noblien glared, his color heightening. "Yearn for knowledge in a humbler tone or bring forth your sword."

The captain flushed, perhaps in anger or for being put in his place so swiftly; one could not be sure, but his tone was markedly tempered when next he spoke. "What kind of king would put at the hands of fortune a child's mind, as is that of the ostler's, to hear your cause on Seayr's behalf? Understand me, I would gladly draw my sword to yours, but for—"

"Then make it so," said Noblien, although he did not move to retrieve any of his weapons.

"Nay. You don't understand. I've no resistance to using my sword when required. Yet" - and so saying, he sighed as one torn between convictions - "for dueling when less than duty is at stake is too great a risk when my brother depends on protection from it." Then he nodded at the ostler. "He's my brother and in my keeping. As such, my fealty to the king has been recently forfeit."

Sage raised his brows. "Lawks, this is a prodigious unfolding."

"What's his calling," asked Leaf.

"Sessile."

"And yours, pray tell?" asked Sage.

"Downs of Scottia."

"Well, Downs of Scottia—"

"Downy."

"Well, Sir Downy—"

"Scottia of the Norwesterners?" interrupted Noblien, his countenance impossible to read.

"The same," said the captain.

"You are a Thessalian, then?" asked Noblien, approaching the captain with a tilt of the head as one observing in pity a creature unknown or perhaps not worth knowing.

To this, the captain stood tall and alive, where gloom had occupied his person before, as a flicker of light passed over his expression. "I am."

"Why so far from home?" asked Noblien, who had markedly stiffened.

"Thai Mielle," interrupted the Coyotl, not keen on the difference he was watching unfold in the Puman. "This dialogue is all good and well as etiquette follows, yet perhaps we might seek out why we've been called hitherto and then be on our way with speed." And upon laying out these words, he stared eye to eye with Noblien in a tacit warning against imprudence.

The captain, relieved by the Coyotl's diversion, took the opportunity to focus on his brother. "Sessile, gather your belongings; we leave tonight."

"Tonight?" cried the ostler, a panic beginning to choke his tender heart. "No, no, brother! The horses—"

As for the elves, Sage's request was met with a vacant stare past his noble intentions, and as the ostler pleaded against his brother's command, Noblien sidestepped around his fellow elf and headed straight for the captain. "Your brother makes a good point, and to that end, let us speak frankly, for I am fumed beyond measure in you and your monarch, not in the least for what you call your duty. Gramercy man," and so saying, he paused, took a breath, and turned away, the profound meaning of the moment nigh unbearable to him. "Seayr," he continued, his voice raspy with emotion, "has captured the very essence of the wild—the Haevonen. So-called are the feral, unbroken creatures you call horses."

"Hold now," whispered the captain. "This cannot be so. You speak of children's stories."

The Coyotl raised a brow. "Speak so he sees you, Thessalian."

To this end, Tullkaee touched Noblien's shoulder. He looked back, begrudgingly removed from his thoughts, yet tears had gentled his eyes. His attention regained, Sage informed him that the captain thought him misinformed about children's stories.

"By strewth, you're a proud, insolent, and foolish creature," said Noblien plainly. "Sage, can you not" – he wagged a finger in exasperation – "deal with this?"

The Puman then collapsed to his hands and knees as if to cap the moment. 'Twas somehow unbefitting of an elf of his air, and all were shocked to immobility. He struggled repeatedly to lift himself, but to no effect.

"Sage," Noblien muttered, "get Leaf out of here."

Sage was indignant. "I cannot get her out of here without getting you on your feet . . . unless you prefer being carried?"

Noblien winced and was so well rankled by the Coyotl's blithe noncompliance that he growled on the concerns of impetuous knaves. This utterance did not affect Sage in the least, but as these particular words were indeed well understood by the others, they did have some peculiar impacts therein, not in the least, a smile upon the noble Daun who found a small reassurance in the fact that the elf's current affliction was not life-threatening.

"Thai Mielle is no less than the Sakatu," replied Sage, which provoked a steady stream of guttural words derived from the Puman's native tongue.

Tullkaee placed Noblien's arm around her neck; in this way, Noblien was righted, though he gasped from the effort. Yet, the windows to his spirit sliced straight through the Coyotl in bitter disapproval.

"You must get him out of here," insisted the captain.

Sage turned around to face the horseman; his face skewed to the side in distrust. "And suddenly, you're full of care and concern?"

The captain shook his head piteously and in frustration. "I'll not let harm befall my brother, so he and I leave straight away. Follow us out; we can lead you up the safest road. But my brother will not be joining your company."

"Nay," said Sage. "We know our way; besides, we are bent on Shee for whenever and wherever we find her." Then he added, "But not without the Haevonens."

The captain balked. "And I'm . . . what said your friend? Proud and foolish?"

"Aye, you are," snapped Sage. "But alas, you and your brother are recruited, and our courses are now aligned."

"You're heedless!" the captain cried as Sage nodded in agreement, a crooked smile thus punctuating the affirmation. "Death pursues your company right on your heels!"

"Honestly, man, you've no idea," said Sage, who then bent his gaze toward the ostler and paused. He had recognized a distinction in this man of simple persuasion and, unlike most, did not revile him for it. As for his brother, the ignoble captain, he reckoned he was probably a man of noble character but one oft lost in the trait's pursuit. The Coyotl made an audible huff of determination, his mind made up. "We'll split into two groups. Will your brother part from you and go with my friends?

"He'd part from me, sure, but he'll ne'er leave that herd behind."

Sage's eyes flicked back and forth as his mind raced, looking for a plan. "Hmm. Then he goes with us."

"Us?"

"Hah!" said Sage. "Aye, together, the three of us will make our way to the Haevonen. My companions will follow us at some distance as we guide the herd to the outskirts of Seayr."

"Are there any of the Haevonen," Noblien grunted between breaths, "that holds respect within the herd?"

"What?" asked Sage and the captain at once.

"He knows what I speak of," replied Noblien shortly, nodding toward the ostler.

Sessile bobbed his head in confident affirmation. "I call her Atanta. She's a fine one, a bit weathered with age, but she's who the others look to when fear takes them."

"Your name is Sessile?" Noblien asked.

"Right as rain; my name's Sessile."

Noblien closed the windows to his spirit and made a single nod of relief before attempting to catch his breath. "If we can lead her, we lead the others willingly."

"And with them to the gateway of Shee, one calamity is redressed," added Sage.

"Sage," Noblien rasped, "you might need to bring forth Timbriel."

"'Tis drawn."

"My breath is stifled unnaturally," Noblien coughed.

Sage shot a glance at the Thessalian, who also drew his sword. "Whithersoever this insanity leads, until my brother is safe, I promise thee we are one."

To this pronouncement, Sage produced an unconscious grimace yet took the hilt of his blade to his brow in swift courtesy to the other. The captain saw the former action and respected, therefore, the latter even more, and resultantly, against even his repulsions, felt thus moved to prove himself.

"Where might be this Atanta?" asked Sage, gazing now only upward toward the rafters, which trembled and sifted dust. "Quickly."

"She's in yonder field, penned and locked," answered the ostler.

"What do we face?" asked Tullkaee, swinging her tomahawk end over end in one hand while Noblien slumped over in her other arm.

"I know not," the Coyotl answered between his teeth, closing an eye in thought calls for Leoness.

As for the Fierce-Eyed Elf, he found himself in no good state. Forsooth, only in body did he now reside with his companions; in spirit, he had been withdrawn into the quintessence of the ethereal, between the pith of rogue winds and the waves of the spirit forms, the Ylem.

The Ancient Forests learned of the Ylem many millennia ago. The Trees comprehend the strange force as a great veil of universal current that interacts with existent energies abound, benign for its part, yet a catalyst for much distress where conducted. The Ylem casts afflictions most upon the newly born or sprouted, its flexures drawn to life's foundling sparks. The unraveling that follows is an inadvertent snuffing out of the force that attracted its crinkling currents in the first place.

The universe, however, is expansive, and the Ylem rarely crosses paths with life on Earth. Yet, of late, it had hovered over Llaurantis. Perhaps the energies of the Haevonen taken from the realm of Haverdome were enough to set the enigmatic current upon the continent. And perchance, the Sakatu's awakening contributed to this moment wherein the Puman fought for breath to breathe. He could not have known that the unease he constantly felt nipping at the company's heels was the same as from his childhood.

Verily, the Trees recount the electric snapping of the Ylem's current when the youngling Puman fell onto his father's vanished presence. 'Twas the wizarding magic's aftershock that stole his hearing, but the Ylem that transformed his eyes' natural gold color. Ever after, they reflected the color of the Ylem's very substance, its undulating wave-rolls hidden in the folds of his iris, a veritable crash course of the Ylem and Earth's reality. To this end, Noblien was connected to the Ylem . . . if not a part of it.

Noblien braced hard against the weight of his breath, then relinquished it, finding the will to make his way again to his feet. His strength returned if he held his breath with a gasp here and there for air. And more, while in this state, could he see the Ylem. It looked like flowing water, and the world about him was presented inversely through a serous transparency. The sensation was dizzying, yet he was afoot within his mind, and relief joined his desperation.

So did he stand and bound upon the Treean, for the Ylem was rushing toward the Sakatu. The momentum of the protective act knocked Leaf off her feet, though Noblien caught her. However, his action had put the Coyotl on his heels in no kind manner against him.

"Off Sage," Noblien growled, flinging the Coyotl to the earth. "I am myself!"

Sage rolled to his side in Elvish curses, for the fall had hit him sorely.

"LittleLeaf, hold your breath." Leaf looked unsure of what she heard. "Do it!" Noblien commanded.

And as the Treean began to hold her breath, the Fierce-Eyed Elf placed the tip of his snow-fletched arrow over the Sakatu, where he beheld many root threads of the nutlet blent and at one with her collarbone. Upon beholding this, he was aghast, and it was no small task to maintain his focus; he was as vexed as he was caught off guard at every turn, and he found this realization as stifling as the suppression he now fought to protect her against. Nevertheless, he closed the windows to his spirit and began to speak, the coarseness of the common language silking into the salve of the Elvish tongue. Behind him, Sage slowly rose, watching intently.

A plundering wind repeatedly mounted against the barn outside, causing the rafters to tremble. Inside, it felt as if the air had been swallowed. Under this phenomenon, the Puman's fine strands of hair began to rise and float, snaking down an unseen current like the river vine tendrils of the Cocia Trees, whose long, supple limbs lapped within the shallow waters of Lemuria. Seeing this, Sage mustered his guardian wares against his curiosity and turned his back to the pair for their defense. However, the unfathomability of what he stood guard against confounded his nerves.

The barn door rattled, and the Wood grains splintered as though a hateful determination marked out the old, knotted rings. Sage crouched forward, bracing his stance, a fortune well met for an untethered gust swooshed in manically. Whirling, the coiling airstream gathered all the hay-scented air it could muster and threshed out, leaving complete stillness as its adieu.

All was silence in a spectral void of energy stolen. However, Life's tenacious pulse beat again. And slowly, Time joined her in their dualistically resumed courses.

Noblien placed the arrow back in its quiver. "It's gone."

Leaf wheezed as she pulled in a draft of breath, hugging Noblien with the strength of a Ponderosa.

"'Tis all right, little one," he soothed. "'Tis all right, settle now," and so cooing, a smile broke across his face, lean and pleasant.

Gingerly, he supported her as she righted herself and, deeming her well-being sound, turned to face the Coyotl. To him, the Puman cupped his hand to his heart and sent the gesture toward Sage in deference and apology.

Sage returned the courtesy summarily, then scratched his head. "What was that?"

Noblien hesitated, then answered, "I don't know how to explain it. The sense of danger that I haven't been able to wrangle out . . . it seems to be a force, an energy, similar to lightning. This sounds unbelievable. Do you have confidence in me?"

"Listen, I don't take lightly to being tossed about, so your present well-being is proof of my confidence," answered Sage, growing serious. "Your quick action to Leaf is a testament to the continuation of the Faiyum, like father, like son; that was the touch, make no mistake."

Noblien blinked, stepping back. "It was simply—"

"A reaction, right? I believe the Faiyum is not extinct, Noblien of the Faiyum. I like that; 'tis almost better than Thai Mielle."

Grimacing, the Puman turned to the captain. "I cannot explain all that has just occurred, but more than the capture of the Haevonen has been at work upon these lands."

"All that wind busting through here," the captain asked, gesticulating toward the roof's inner beamwork, "was that the force you described? You're linked with it?"

"I believe," answered Noblien, "we all are."

"The Faiyum?" ruminated the captain. "Thessalian history—"

"To the Haevonen then?" interrupted Noblien, dismantling the conversation.

The captain swallowed, narrowing his eyes before glancing toward his brother and taking a deep breath. "To the Haevonen."

❧ Chapter 16 ❧

*Always listen to your heart; any more than that will have you deceived, for
many a magi swirl visions of lure, and who is to say whether it be the truth or
not? Verily, the intellect sorts it all out, but only the heart, apart from the
mind's desires and dreams, the purest unwonted heart, tells one from whence
truth doth lie.*

—Euphrosyne, Aspen of Erato

The large barn door was opened, and the night's dankness encroached
upon the group. Noblien was as strengthened as he was wearied, his
senses more honed than ever before. With silver eyes aglow, he picked
up a shadow in the near distance, telling Sage that his attention must
also be drawn there. Casting his gaze thus, the Coyotl flitted off silently.
The Puman cocked his head and watched attentively. The shadow was
shuffling and hopping. Leaf and Tullkaee realized that Leoness had not
ventured far from the Coyotl.

Sage returned, Leoness hobbling along at his side. A crackled,
erruupp, was muffled by the Coyotl's hands and could well have been

mistaken by any listener as a hulking bullfrog. Noblien looked as though a rebuke rested upon the edges of his lips, but he said naught and silently directed the brother onward to lead them toward the mare, Atanta. The group followed the brother, a large man of soft quality. Weaving in and out of fence and paddock, shrub and rock, he halted and rested a hand upon the steed of quivering sinew. The others came up behind him and beheld the sight.

She was an enormously elegant creature. Her coat glistened, yet it would have shone as brilliantly as copper under the sun if not so set under the damp weight of the night. Her mane was thick yet strung in a hopeless labyrinth: broadsheets hung over each side of her neck, and her tail was no less than a tangle of tapered mats. Oh, to the days upon the fields of Haverdome, the windows to her spirit still flashing in defiance of it, wide and fierce, but as much for her condition, she gazed as lowly as the situation. She was shackled and could not move; still, her muzzle snuffed the air and flared. Her will was indomitable against any oppressions set against her, and she snorted for the flight of freedom. She was a Haevonen, the very Marrow of the Wild.

Noblien walked toward her. The mare stared at him and raised her head to show the whites of her eyes, teeth bared, and gums snapping. Still, the Puman continued his path. She whinnied to the herd, the strident pitch halting him to near senselessness, for within the windy din of his deafness, he discerned, however faintly, their calls. "Thank you," he whispered, and to his voice, she lowered her head, a sculpture of art, and pricked forward her ears.

"Sessile," said Noblien, "you've a knack with these creatures. Think you could unshackle her?"

The tender man nodded, his eyes ever soft and kind.

"You've done well caring for them."

"Is naught," the ostler shrugged.

"Sessile, my friend and I need you to go over there with your brother and my two companions and meet us just outside Seayr. The herd will need to see you're there. Can you do this?"

The man of tender heart halted, looked up at the Fierce-Eyed Elf, and took him in; he studied his face and nodded. "Atanta says 'tis fine, you're to be trusted," and so saying, he rubbed his hand over her shoulder and released her from the last of her shackles. "Guide them, sweet girl. I'll see you soon."

Leaf could not help but look around for the season. The last time she beheld a Haevonen was within her presence. There, time had slowed its course, as it did now. She looked at Noblien, who tilted an ever-so-brief return glance. Indeed, she was not alone in such sentiments of thought. Breaths were slower, every action bent in its course with careful purpose, and the hums of Earth's heartbeat set down her rhythm. The encumbrances now removed from the goddess of horses, Noblien looked over at Sage and nodded.

"Right then," said the Coyotl, turning and addressing Downy and Tullkaee. "Tullkaee, I'm sorry, but necessity per the human condition calls on you, Sir Downy, and his brother to travel back from where King Orrin's direction graced us. You'll remember the place?"

Tullkaee nodded, her expression indignant.

"And you'll meet us there?" Downy asked disbelievingly, a scalding hoarseness coating his question. "You think you can lead that entire regiment of horses without notice?"

Prompt and proud, Sage cracked a wide, untamed smile. "Humans possess many qualities. However, silence upon foot is not one of them."

Downy shook his head incredulously. "And Sir Elf, what of the silence of those many beasts?"

"Tish, not a problem," Sage responded joyfully, aiming to instill enough confidence to propel the man forward. He had grown impatient, revealing a more dangerous tone in his subsequent words. "We've no time; you need hie."

Downy, his brother in tow, turned away begrudgingly. Tullkaee stared hard at the elves and Leaf. Noblien turned his attention to her.

"Watch that the captain has truly forfeited his loyalties where previously laid," murmured Noblien, approaching and embracing the Daun's arm. "My heart feels he is naught but true to his brother, but to us, I would not rely. Leaf will stay with Leoness aloft," and so saying, he pointed to the welkins with a soft, reassuring smile. "We'll be right behind you. Be ready."

Tullkaee nodded to Noblien and then to Leaf before turning and plodding away, the honor of the huntress landing surely in each step until the blackness of the night veiled her from view. Leaf began to tremble, but Leoness swung her neck under the Treean's arm, a mystical reassurance flowing through her. She gazed up at the banda's reptilian eyes, foreign and enchanting. The intricacy of the light absorbed and reflected within their amber hues was the same unique quality she recognized within Sage's, and comfort enveloped her.

Noblien and Sage began to lead the goddess of horses to the bank of a steeply inclined pasture in elven hums. The copper creature pranced, but it was a placid cadence, her natural manner of waltz, set amidst an awareness of the current circumstances. The elven hymns further steadied her, the lyrics mutually understood. Leaf and Leoness followed from a safe distance.

Suddenly, Atanta reared sideways. Leaf gasped, fearing that Sage would be trampled under her heavy hooves, but the elf was deft in his movements and reacted the moment her muscles twitched. His voice crooned even as he escaped the danger, and the mare lowered her high-set neck, lulled under his confidence.

At last, stepping onto the same grasses as her herd, Atanta's eyes lit up with a ring of fire. Her body quivered, yet she stood motionless as the elves approached each of her kin to cut loose the hobbles that shackled them. Quiet was the procession that followed their release, each following Atanta, only an occasional triumphant stomp interrupting the night air, an astonishing sight to behold.

Sage rounded very slowly and carefully behind Leaf and Leoness, eyes ever vigilant to the herd's progress. "Time for you to fly," said he, murmuring more to Leoness, who clinked her beak in response. "Atop you go." Leaf blinked dumbly as he picked her up and placed her between the banda's neck and wings. "She'll not let you fall. Let merriment fly with you," and so saying, his crooked grin welled his visage, and Leaf saw for the first time, and with some astonishment, that the Coyotl's eyes were reddened and tear-filled.

Before Leaf knew what took her, Leoness lurched forward and heaved into the currents, bringing such a glut of air against them that the Treean momentarily lost her breath; how she could soar! Leaf could not believe the power and speed of the banda, who flew with bare effort, and at first, she clutched the feathers upon the banda's neck too tightly. Leoness shook her neck with a light squawk, and Leaf released her death grip.

"Oh Leoness, forgive me," she comforted, as her dazed fear transformed into a bizarre nonchalance even as the objects below grew small and passed with astounding rapidity. Height, after all, was a place of solace for a Treean. Holding her arms open and embracing the wind, she felt the fetters of her life drop away with each wing beat. The Haevonen felt it, too. Freedom.

Tullkaee and the others had made a good pace. It was quite a journey to be made on foot twice in a day. Silence had been their companion, the Daun taking seldom to speech and the captain with no desire for any. Only the brother broke the night with an occasional question or hum, which the other silenced quickly. Now they waited, and their eyes searched.

"Twas the captain who first saw the herd. He could not believe the elves had accomplished the feat, which made his past and present actions more acutely realized. He swallowed hard. *What are the repercussions of well-intentioned bad choices?* he wondered. *Can a remedy be found for their repetitions? And am I now making another poor choice that I think is right?* Frustrated, he sighed and watched the elves soundlessly herd the Legion of Horses. *Impossible. Verily,* he thought, shaking his head in respectful dismay, *'twas impossible! Perhaps, I'm finally finding my proper course with this odd company,* and so pondering, a weight lifted from his countenance.

Tullkaee, on the other hand, grew agitated, for she could not see the Treean, and many wonders took her. She fixed her eyes on Noblien, and the Puman nodded in return, his face strained but not distraught. The herd slowly halted, and she watched as Sage walked from the far side of the herd to the Puman's side. They conversed, albeit with many pauses, evidence of their concocting a plan. Noblien placed a hand on Sage's shoulder before Sage turned away and headed back toward Tullkaee and the others. His pace was swift and gentle like velvet weaving over sweetgrass. The Puman stayed in his place, stroking the mighty neck of Atanta but watching the Coyotl's progression intently as he concentrated on keeping the herd calm. It was clear that neither elf wanted the others any closer.

Tullkaee fixed her eyes on Sage as he approached, yet even as a swoosh of air and energy surrounded the group, she was still taken aback when he arrived. He smiled at her, in all probability amused by his effect.

"Noble huntress, watch me. I may lose myself."

Downy raised a brow to this pronouncement, angling his head in Noblien's direction. "Like your friend did?"

Sage quivered in a silent laughter that seized his body in light ripples, the outside corner of his eyes crinkling. "Ah, thank you, Sir Downy," he said, inhaling deliberately, stooping forward. "I certainly needed that," and so saying, the elf winked at the captain, whose face contorted into a confined puzzlement. "I'm unfortunately . . . much worse."

"So, this is an Elvish condition?" said Downy, now entirely bemused.

Again, Sage laughed, but as he did so, the glint in his eyes became ominous. "Pugnacious, a characteristic I well admire, yet perhaps this would be a good place for you and yours to depart and begin your life anew."

The words were challenging in tone but a well-meant warning, for Sage knew the danger the captain and the ostler faced with the company and, possibly, in the coming moments, even against himself. The captain, he thought, ought to be ready and willing or leave. Leaving would be the safest choice in Sage's mind.

The Thessalian mulled the idea over. There was an attractiveness to the words the elf spun forth. But Sessile began to rock from leg to leg, humming out of tune in a whine that rose in pitch as he swayed. The answer was already made; leaving this newfound company would not be their course.

"We stick by the horses," said Downy, sniffing and swelling in confidence of the decision.

Sessile's humming transformed into rich melodies, his lips forming a thin smile. Sage, too, was inwardly pleased with the choice. He had bet on the captain's mettle.

The Coyotl pointed to the sky. "Safe with Leoness. Listen, the gateway to Shee is finally upon us, and we must enter soon to succeed with the Haevonen. But her gateway is weak, so Noblien and I have devised some elven trickery to get us there." The last, he mumbled in thought.

He looked at Downy and lifted an eyebrow. "This task is dangerous, even without a herd of the Haevonen. Presenting the gateway to Shee will take nearly all of me, and even on a good day, I'm hardly stable." He chortled. "Make ready that lovely axe, noble huntress," he said with a wink, although Tullkaee did not move. Sage narrowed his eyes. "I'll take offense if you do not. You cannot let me lose myself or hurt anyone," he said with pleading eyes; Tullkaee reluctantly complied.

"My ketyl possesses the power of transformation," Sage continued, making eye contact with the captain and the ostler. "The idea is to use this transformational energy to bulwark the gateway as I change into my ketyl's totem under the weakened veil. You see, the energies derive from the same source, the Veriha, so in theory, my transformation should be absorbed by the veil, strengthening it enough, at least, for our passing through it. However, I'm unsure if this will work and what state I'll be in if it does. Will my head be a jumble? Will I even be in elven form? If you behold a coyote, trust 'tis me," and so saying, he turned away, then spun back. "Might be best if you both simply stand still. Do not in any way distract or present yourselves as threatening. Understand?"

"Completely and not at all," replied Downy.

Sage flashed a wry smile and began walking away, his physical form wavering. "I do very much like you."

The hues of their surroundings passed through his person. He had become a shadow of light, a whiff of essence. And as Tullkaee watched, she sheathed her axe. She thought using the weapon was a terrible choice and was, anyway, a woman of her own mind and decision.

Clarity was the Coyotl's perspective, brilliant in color and sensation. However, the cost of hovering between realms, those astral planes marked unique by those who inhabited them, was immense—it took his will and life force and teetered it on an edge he yearned to lean over.

Sage Lagacious loved and was loved easily; his lifetime knew much of it. Yet as the Trees discerned, he wandered the Earth unsettled. His life was bent on realizing the power of unrelenting love, too often without the presence of those for whom the emotion was created. Friends were his family; his well-open heart loved fully or not at all. Throughout the ages, too many had been snatched from the protection of his arrows. Thus, grief often consumed him for the better part of his long-lived life.

He exemplified humility and gratitude toward all life and reciprocated love equally, be one a Tree or an elf, a fae or a sylph, a flower or a river. The Trees cherished him for this and always attempted to hold him to the tides of this realm when his mental journeys flung him elsewhere. Yet, he was so innately spontaneous that the Trees found clutching him away from the brink of insanity nearly beyond success. The roots chortled to one another that the reason they are reverently referred to as ancient, for ancient from a Tree's perspective is quite a mute reference, is due solely to the Coyotl's enterprises and effects thereupon.

From his companions' perspective, an archway composed of water formed over his form; Sage had succeeded in presenting the gateway to Shee. Yet, he gave much of himself as a conduit to a weakening veil. The group could not know that he struggled to recall them, Leoness, Alderelm, or even the stakes against them. He was fighting for what memory had been withheld. Here and now, in necessity, the Ancient Ones speared his mind with images of their mighty boles of white and leaves of green, burst high between clouds and sky azure. They called on the Coyotl's spirit to bear up and behold the flickering lights of the borealis alow and listen to the flute whistles calling him home. He heard them. Now, even as the light of the Veriha blasted through his spent body, he would not collapse, not under the arches the Trees of Alderelm did render.

Sessile was the first familiar face Sage began to recognize, and for the poor ostler, were his eyes wide with concern. Nevertheless, Sage's recovery was bolstered by the reflection of the spirit within them, authentic and pure, acting as an anchor to his drifting spirit. And as he regained his awareness, he reached out.

Yet alas, his attempt at movement was met with the absence of progress and, more, the feeling of being tightly bound. This so instinctually angered him that he tried to swing with his other arm, of which he, again, found only immobility. Tullkaee, that strong Oak of the Dauns, held the elf firm. The restraint that initially drew out his feral instincts began to soothe and help him realize where he was. And there he saw it. They stood under the gateway to Shee!

"Thank be to the Dauns for their strong daughters," Sage hailed, relief hitting the infinite of the gateway's mirrored fringe; 'twas as a dewdrop's ripple set upon a still pond distorting life's colors and settling within and into themselves. "I lost myself?"

Tullkaee grunted in the affirmative. "You are a skilled warrior, but your fight is less focused when you travel the sunlight without the mother."

Noblien led the Haevonen forward, their giant hooves heaving into the gateway, shrill whistles and whinnies of raged delight joined the breeze set in motion by their passing, the smell sweet. Leoness spun lower and lower, spiraling in elegance and grace, quietly as the owl upon a night hunt. Noblien spoke in cooing intonations, the Haevonen nudging him as they passed, his penetrating silver eyes smiling. Yet through all this, the Coyotl studied the Daun.

"What do you mean, travel the sunlight without the mother?" he asked, his rusty voice broken.

She surveyed him, the flitting glances, the fidgeting nature, and sighed gruffly. "Father," she said, pointing to the heavens. "Mother," she continued, pointing to the Earth. "You are a free spirit who honors the connection to Nature around you. But often, you glow with the sun's light, without the mother, and become a wind dancer.

The Coyotl's features leered under the latter words. Tullkaee did not know the winds. The temperamental Zephyr had once been a mighty defense, but to the others, he could not utter without rage. She could not fathom their ear-numbing howls and deadly intent. To dance upon them was utterly unacceptable, and the eons of bruised fights ground out the Coyotl's jaws under a restrained tongue. The Daun was noble, as were her people. He would let go any reply or further thought on the issue.

Whistling for Leoness, he strode into the gateway. Tullkaee watched him go. She could hear the shaman's chant and smell the fragrant incense. The wise were patient.

⊷ Chapter 17 ⊶

You existed before you can remember that you existed, so why question existence
when it is obviously not for you to understand?

—Flumbaran reasoning

Entering Shee's gateway, Sessile felt a warm breeze surge against him. As he walked forward, it relinquished the gesture gracefully. Downy and Tullkaee followed, each in turn and likewise, taken by the difference in the air that rushed upon them. All were mesmerized by their changing surroundings.

The sun hung as a low orb on the horizon, its yellow-red hue radiating over stunted Trees of vast girth and peculiarly shallow canopies. They were deeply rooted in a silty land that leaned toward the barren edge of life. Speckled thereupon were glacier boulders of intriguing shape and size. Some were round, while others stood as stone pillars edged with shades of sweet jade and blush.

Taking their first steps onto this foreign terrain, the Haevonen stayed tightly banded together. Sessile, intent on their welfare, scanned the herd for Atanta. A shrill whistle, far and above the others, picked her out. She stood on the herd's far side, tossing her refined head, snaking her neck, her tousled mane casting copper-red hues on the glory of her outline. His relief and happiness upon her sight made him laugh in purest delight. She was as she should have always been: free and with her kin.

The moment was broken when Leoness and Leaf soared through the gateway with a shriek, the banda screeching sideways to a halt, wings outstretched for balance, claws grinding the coursed earth. The raucous sent many of the Haevonen back on their rear legs.

"Easy now, LeadLeaf!" called Sage. "You want ne'er to upstage an elf."

Leaf turned in the direction his voice had stemmed and discovered he was approaching them with a smile. Leoness roared many ear-numbing harrumphs, which were vaunts to her spectacular landing. Sage narrowed his eyes and stared her down at once, but his voice was ever so soft.

"Hush now, odd girl. I wager you'll have us both in trouble, although," he whispered into her ear, "your alighting was most brilliant indeed!" She rubbed her fur-feathered neck against his side as he continued to coo to her.

Noblien drew to their sides and placed a hand on Sage's shoulder. "Are you all right?"

Sage did not answer but briefly met the Puman's eyes and gave a subtle sigh. Noblien understood and pressed no further.

Leaf dismounted and· began turning in circles with excitement. "There's a Tree here humming! I can hear it!" She looked up at the elves, her face afresh and light-filled. "Very much like those of Alderelm!"

Sage's demeanor suddenly changed, almost collapsing in on itself. "The Tree of Cassen."

"Is this . . . not a good Tree?" asked Leaf, frowning.

Sage fixed the windows of his spirit onto hers. "Nay. Quite the contrary, 'tis a very good Tree."

A hollow tinge in the bottom of the elf's voice kept Leaf more restrained than she was wont to be. There was a feeling he was beyond the border of well-being, and she paid respect to this in silence.

"Is this the Land of Shee?" asked Downy, striding up and glancing back at his brother. "Are there inhabitants in this place?"

"Aye," replied Noblien, "this is Shee. As to the inhabitants, they'll be round. Patience, Thessalian." The Fierce-Eyed Elf turned to cast his luminescent gaze on Leaf. "In this place, we're safe. Few can find the entry, and those who do are hard-pressed to open her veil. Yet more are the long troughs that intersperse time's waves here. You see, the outside realm moves along with haste compared with Shee, which ruminates on the mere prospect of trudging forward.

"Nooo, this cannot be," said Tullkaee in marvel. "Are you seriously saying time moves slower here?"

"Aye," replied Noblien as Eyas, the mighty warrior of aves, fluttered between them to settle on the elf's shoulder.

This juxtaposition of a wee bird perched on the shoulder of a warrior elf while discussing the relative nature of time was too much for the practical Daun. She shook her head with a disapproving grunt while Noblien's eyes glinted.

"Look'in!" Sessile shouted, forgetting the task of fretting over his beloved horses and joining the group to repeat the announcement. "Look'in, look'in!"

Below an escarpment arose six cherublike creatures. Two were afoot while the others rested atop compact, draft ponies of dun coloration and short crescent manes that accentuated their thick, curved necks. They approached slowly and in wonder, their pace quickening as Sage waved.

Sage saw the confusion on the faces of Tullkaee and Downy and grinned broadly. "Shee is home," he mumbled out of the corner of his mouth, "to the grumbies who arrive afore you. They prefer the company of their own kind so be careful with your manners."

Leaf chuckled to herself. If only Noblien could have seen what he said, she was sure he would have rolled his eyes with a weary facial contortion. She reckoned that Sage's knack for making Noblien's face twitch and wince against his stoic nature should not amuse her. Yet, their interactions endlessly delighted her, and besides, there could be no harm in her secret entertainments.

"Their steeds," Sage continued, "are the mighty flagbearers."

Downy surveyed the creatures. "More hair than horse," he said. "With goat feet, no less! Hardly to be named as steeds."

Sage thought deeply and countered in no wasted time. "Do not underestimate the descendants of the Haard."

Downy crinkled his nose.

"Brother, look!" said Sessile, sputtering. "Those folks are walking straight up ta 'em."

Even as Sessile spoke, Downy beheld it. The two grumbies on foot hobbled, as was their way of walking, over and around the Haevonen with little caution. His jaw dropped.

"Might you warn these . . . grumbies of their inherent danger?"

"Nah, they're excellent healers," replied Sage with dry directness. "The Haevonen need them now, and should a grumby get tumbled, well," said Sage, shrugging, "as I've stated, they're excellent healers."

Downy was horrified. Sage delighted in the effect but could no longer torture the poor Thessalian. "I jest, man, though they may not look it, they're very wise. They know what they're doing." He paused, seeing that Downy did not believe him, and so added, his voice rising in earnest, "As did your brother."

Downy's eyes fixed upon Sage's. He studied the inner workings of the elf's spirit and finally released them with a sigh. Sage smiled to himself. *Underneath all that excess bravado is a good man*, he thought.

The rest of the grumbies made their way toward the company, their ponies in a high trot that might have been dignified were it not for the riders' excessive bouncing. And as they drew up their mounts and halted, one grumby frowned.

"Caterpillar guts," she spat.

"Now, now," Sage said playfully, "that's not nice."

"Noblien! Lagacious!" said another whose childlike voice, high and innocent, did not fit the scolding tone. "I should've known. Only you two could bring such big trouble!" and so saying, the figure pointed to the Haevonen. Although small, her presence was as large and penetrating as her face was weathered and wrinkled.

The elves looked at one another. They had known that each the other had visited Shee, but they had ne'er traveled here together nor spoken of such travels. The fact that they were being received as fellows-in-arms made the pair keenly curious. However, the reception was not enough to subdue the Coyotl's disposition.

Sage strode over to embrace the fellow grumby, grinning ear to ear, even as she sat on her steed, so low in height were both. "True 'nough old friend."

The elf's embrace was mightily returned, and the grumby's scowling face transformed into open-mouthed joy. Noblien stood tall and waited. When the grumby fixed her attention on him, the Puman bowed at the waist. The grumby cordially received the gesture in a manner equally reciprocal to the Puman's modesty; she knew well the differences in the personalities of these two elves and responded to each respectively. A wise aspect to a creature kind of such turbulent emotions, able only to demonstrate one at a time.

"The seeing of you both is good," said the old grumby, her eyes twinkling. "Much have we missed you, though not at once do grumbies expect to see."

Sage smiled and nodded while Noblien took a turn to speak. "'Tis good to see you too."

The grumby grinned and looked back at Sage. "You'll be wanting to see her."

"Without a doubt," replied Sage, his eyes turning into minuscule slits between his crooked smile and the laugh lines set around his face. He patted the flag-bearer, and the pony turned an ear to him, nickering lowly. "Let it be till the Haevonen are tended and this company is at more ease; then I'll slip away."

The grumby nodded and turned toward the others with curiosity. "First to another's land is first to introductions."

Sage chuckled in acknowledgment. "My good company, this is the Land of Shee, home to the honorable grumbies."

As Downy and Tullkaee bowed their heads humbly upon this pronouncement, the grumbies began clucking their tongues. Excited at this, Sessile began to clap. Leaf watched wide-eyed while standing slightly behind Tullkaee.

"Afore you," Sage continued, "is Abi, the grumbies' chief alchemist."

Abi bowed in her saddle and then cleared her throat. "Now you learn of us. Esa and Alus are in the field with your ponies. To my right is Daggus, and to my left is Mione and Grundy.

"Our company is well met," said Noblien.

"You friend," interrupted the grumby introduced as Daggus, urging his flag-bearer forward. "Best friend. But are they friends?"

"Aye, they are," replied Noblien.

"Best friends?" asked the inquisitive grumby, pointing a little finger now at Downy's chest.

The Thessalian's complexion waned. Although half his size, they unsettled him. They were uncanny and unpredictable.

"Aye, without doubt, best friends," assured Noblien, puzzled.

"No, no, no," Grundy argued, dismounting and then stomping his feet. "He cares only 'bout building dirt. More and more dirt. No friends with grumbies."

"Building dirt?" asked Downy.

Abi eyed Downy doubtfully. "Oh, Lagacious, big trouble this one. Clothing of Seayr. Seayr building too much dirt. No friend to the land, no friend to grumbies."

"Ah, that's interesting," said Noblien, flashing a taunting glance at Downy.

Sage felt it necessary to intercede quickly. "Assure them you're a friend. Pull up your shirt and reveal your stomach. Hurry, man, manners, manners."

"What?" shrieked Downy, incredulous.

"Belly buddy, belly buddy," chanted the grumbies.

"Friend or no?" asked Abi.

"The jig is up. Come on, man," said Sage, enjoying every moment of the Thessalian's situation. "Show your grit. For the sake of your good and ours."

"You're enjoying this!"

"Indeed," gibed Noblien. "We are, so truly, enjoying this."

"What, the Pythium is a belly buddy anyway?" Downy snarled.

"That remnant of yoke between babe and mother," said Sage, grinning, "that most all you common folk possess."

"You're a sick rapscallion. You know that?" Downy snapped, his dander descending into an embarrassed pity. "What an absurd request."

Noblien placed a hand over his mouth to conceal a smile, a dram of pity resting in the corner, whereas Sage hid naught and cackled outright. However, the most deflating reaction came from his brother, who joined in the chanting.

"Belly buddy, belly buddy!"

Resigned to his fate, Downy at last lifted his tunic. All was quiet as Mione approached and touched his skin. Sage whistled while Tullkaee raised an eyebrow. When Mione nodded and called the others closer, the humiliation of the piteous Thessalian was complete, for an intense discussion supervened, and Abi was called over.

The development initially appeared tense, but finally, the strange and temperamental creatures gushed out cheers of "Outy, outy!" and "Best belly."

"You are friend," Abi assured. "Can always tell a heart by a belly buddy," and so saying, the paunchy alchemist reached up to embrace the unnerved Thessalian, who nonetheless accepted the affectionate gesture with a sigh of relief.

Grumbies are distantly related to Flumbaran faeries, although time and isolation in the Land of Shee slowly relinquished them of their wings. Yet, their antennae remained for many reasons, not the least of which was as an essential means of body language, which Abi now used to indicate that she would address the group. The spindled appendages pricked forward, their tips flicking as she outstretched her arms and held everyone's gaze in turn.

Leaf considered the grumby: Her bearing portrayed a rare level of humbleness, accentuated and exemplified by the angle of her head, which resembled a person perpetually looking out at the world from under a bower. Her smile was serene, basking in a radiance emitted by the energy of her heart and mind. And when she chuckled, everyone understood her meaning. It was as though she had reached out her hand and spoken to the group with her mind—and now, she desired introductions to continue.

Sage was not one to miss the message. "Honorable grumbies," he said, clearing his throat. "We are pleased to find you. As you are acquainted with Noblien and myself, let me present the rest of our company. We have Tullkaee, a Daun of brave consequence, Sessile and Downy over here are brothers from Seayr, and LittleLeaf LeadTree," he said, placing his hand on her shoulder, "a very special Treean from Alderelm."

"LeadTree," repeated Abi, her eyebrows rising. "Alderelm—"

At that moment, Leoness struck her foot upon the ground and made a honking screech of no little consequence. This blustering disturbance sent Eyas, who had been preening herself atop the banda's back, flying upward into the sky with a twittering dissonance.

"Ah yes," Abi clucked, "Grumby greets the bestest finch in Llaurantis. And Leoness, heir of the Halouse," and so saying, the old grumby took off her coned cap and bowed. Rising back up, she snortled and swallowed deeply, almost ruminating like a cow. Slow and tranquil was the action.

"Abi," interjected Sage, "there's much to say, but first, we seek your aide with the safety of these Haevonen."

Esa and Alus stood not far off and concurred with a nod. If naught else, Sage mused, their large ears were meant for the keenness of hearing. Abi responded to the two grumbies in kind.

"Yes. Come. Follow the leader," she directed, tottering toward her mount, clucking to herself as she went.

Sage raised his eyebrows and looked eagerly at the others. "Whelp, here we go."

The grumbies and their sturdy flagbearers directed the Haevonen with astonishingly placid ease along a sunken pathway of silt and gravel where the landscape yawned and stretched before the ridge began to drop away between rivulets of talus slopes. Bunch grass and sagebrush softened the terrain's untamed quality even as they grew in splotches according to their isolationist preferences. And wild irises further softened the rawness of the place. This realm was strong and fiercely independent, ne'er reconciling with the elements. Leaf took in every breath of the place to cherished memory.

As the path began to curve and decline, enigmatic basalt and granite pillars, standing like monoliths, revealed themselves. Towering sentinels, a Forest of stone Trees, echoed the surrounding sounds in low hums like the reverberating murmur made after the initial clash of two swords. Beyond these towering masts, the earth appeared to descend into the approaching distance and dance upon a blue lake whose farthest shore introduced the greens of plentiful Trees.

Many Haevonen whinnied at the sight, and everyone's pace unconsciously quickened. Plumes of dust rose along the sinuous path as the horses sat back on their haunches and sank their hooves against the sifted earth to keep it from sliding. Grasshoppers marked the coming of eve, crickling and sasping in chorus to the melody of the canyon wrens while the looming calls of the killdeers suffused the mix under the alpenglow of the coming twilight.

Ultimately, the pathway opened near the lake's gilded edges, and the ground transformed into a river rock bed where many coots looked back at the odd assorted company of creatures accumulating there. Their red eyes pierced Leoness with doubt and disdain, repeatedly squawking and arching their necks. The ungainly banda returned their favor with some of her own croaking honks and an arching of her neck that rivaled the definition of true elegance. The coots, however, appeared displeased and swam further out into the lake. Leoness snorted, and Leaf, having observed the encounter, touched her feathered forehead.

"Pay no attention to them, Leoness. 'Tis not fair that they should judge you on land while they sit in their element. You glide in the air just as gracefully as they do the water. Honestly, they're not so different from you," said Leaf. "Except you are sweet where they are rude."

Still, Leoness stared pitifully at the retreating coots and sat so squarely and far back on her rump that the underside of her feet were struck up and forward, her back legs being placed, resultantly, nearly beside her front. The gangly creature was heart-struck, and Leaf felt for her.

Abi approached and turned from the shoreline to address everyone with a smile that had apparently ne'er left her face. "Water tunnel takes us to village. Water tunnel named Bluefish Cave. Pretty, pretty. Fixes all," she said, patting Leoness. "Don't forgets to look at sky as we go through, bestest pretty," she continued as a translucent aura bubbled up from the lake and forged into a domed water walkway. "Line up. And remembers, little-talk in water tunnel."

"Little-talk means whisper," said Sage with a soft smile, stepping ahead of Leaf and behind Abi, leaning toward the Treean as he passed.

Tullkaee paused, scrutinizing the water tunnel with a frown. The lifegiving fluid continually rose and flowed over itself in a circle, yet there was naught she could perceive that held its course from collapse. *Magic*, she thought. She was not one to trust it and grumbled.

"Trust our course," urged Noblien, walking past her and beside Atanta, the goddess of horses. Tullkaee moaned and followed.

The flagbearers led the Haevonen placidly, their necks nodding with each front footfall, their cumbersome stoutness making a meditative pendulum of movement. The atmosphere was gentle, as if the Bluefish Cave was an elixir for transfiguring woes into the comforts of home. Downy walked like one in a dream, too spellbound to speak. Sessile stuck close by his side, mouth agape.

Leaf halted to touch a giant stone situated just inside the water tunnel. Water dribbled over its green edges. Plink, plink, plink. There she stood, surrounded by water, walking upon it, and the only wetness appeared upon this fist of Nature. Noblien cast his eyes askance at her.

"Later, will you please describe what it sounds like within?"

Leaf was shocked and stuttered her reply. "Yes, of course. I'll do my best."

The Fierce-Eyed Elf closed his eyes and inhaled deeply. "Thank you, LittleLeaf."

A cool breeze flowed through the water tunnel, which smelled faintly of earth, algae, fish, and leaves. Noblien's expression lightened as his spirit attuned to the incorporeal heart of the place. Leaf studied him. Elves, she mused, were the most wonderfully peculiar creatures. He felt her watching him and, with a sparkle in his eyes, smiled before walking on.

Leaf let out her breath in thoughtful whimsy and studied the setting sunlight flickering through the water's halls. It was like wavering contemplations of the ending day. And more, she considered, as though the sparkling reflections were many more miniature suns filling the sky distantly and that those dwarf orbs sought to organize a dance upon the liquid ethers on which they now extended and stretched. Their colors were cast with a vibrant intensity that was somehow soft upon the eyes. Perhaps, she theorized, this was because they had been reflected so many times within the rippling water.

Beneath her feet, the water was darker, a cerulean blue belonging to the realm of midnight. These deep waters were a rune of mystical meaning and beauty. Shiny darting objects glinted, one halting just long enough for Leaf to realize that it was a fish, schools of fishes, which themselves investigated the travelers. Another object, a shadow, then coasted ominously overhead, angular in form and slow in its progress, like a wraith. Closer and closer, it swam to the very edge of the water tunnel until Leaf could see that it was a titanic fish with a whiskered nose and penetrating tawny eyes. It swam aside their persons before drifting away as a cloud taken away by the wiles of the wind.

In the Bluefish Cave, sounds such as the clinking of hooves were amplified yet muted in clarity. The nicker of a horse or the whispering of Sage and Abi ricocheted like waves breaking on the shore, hollowed to the extent that the precise notes lost a decipherable location. Echoes melded together from everywhere, and their waves resonated up, down, and outward. 'Twas akin to a chorus but without directional distinction, a rustling bent around the air. Leaf imagined what she heard would be like huddling within a deep crevice of a hollowed-out Tree and shouting with all one's abilities against a windstorm.

The other end of the Bluefish Cave was nearby, and Leaf could see its shoreline rising into view. The smell of burning sweetwood tickled her nose as a siren-breeze twirled through the water tunnel as though pushed by the fire's amber glow, seemingly reaching out for everyone in eager anticipation of well-made greetings. The charms of percussive music accompanied the breeze and light so that those three elements clamored together to behold those who arrived. She looked over her shoulder to where Tullkaee and the end of the procession followed. Behind them, the water tunnel gently descended like a seceding wave fanning out and diminishing upon the water's surface, which, after that, lay placid.

Abi waited for each of the travelers to exit, greeted them as though days had gone between their recent introductions, and directed the group toward several waiting bonfires. As they walked and sat, Leaf stared up at the Trees. Their leaves were a vibrant green as though newly unfurled in youth. Their tops were round, and their girths were wide. In all, these Trees could not help but make her smile. Within their crowns hung huts. Their roofs were made of large, halved nutshells of some variation she could not discern. She felt the wee homes delightful, swinging in various painted colors: reds, blues, and yellows predominating. A Treean's home was made within the nooks and crannies already presented or in the ground within a root cave. This was beyond the scope of her imaginings.

Abi maintained a keen awareness of Leaf's interest, prompting her. "Flying houses, no?"

Yes, Leaf thought. *What a perfect description.* She nodded and half laughed, still amazed. Abi left her to her thoughts, pleased by the Treean's captivation.

Leaf tuned out the crackling bonfire and the joyous music to focus on putting this place to memory. Noblien, ever the guardian, watched her gently, for he knew the grumbies were close in nature to the Treeans, and this experience could be one of solemn remembrance.

However, Leaf was hit with an overwhelming curiosity. How, she wondered, did the grumbies hang those flying houses? They don't appear to be a creature kind that would be adept at climbing—even walking seems an endeavor for them—and those huts are mighty high in those Trees. There aren't even ladders or platforms to access them! Strange.

She marveled at the delightful, big-boned Trees and then observed in astonishment that the bud-shaped huts were held aloft by thickly knotted ropes. She nodded to herself. No doubt an unwieldy and challenging material to manage, or so it seemed to her, but certainly doable. She searched the limbs for abrasions, as any Treean would, where the weight of the dwellings might gnaw into the boughs, but there were none. Then, all at once, she realized the startling truth. The ropes were not ropes at all but living vine tendrils. Her eyes followed the whirling workings of the tendril limbs. She traced their variegated, spear-shaped leaves, scanned their wrappings around the smooth bark, and realized that the vine tendrils were growing from the Trees. *They were the Trees*, and they moved! Not believing her eyes, she squinted and stared. Slowly and methodically, they crept, moving the huts in a gentle but continual motion, up and down. She could not believe her eyes. And when a grumby waddled up to the base of a Tree, a flying house was lowered to the ground. *Spectacular*, she thought, beaming.

Digging her toes under the dirt, she wondered what the Trees' voices would sound like if they could sing. She willed them to say aught at all, but the vibrations of the soil around them were still. Their language was conducted above ground, lending helpful caresses to the abodes of their altruistic partners, the wise and childlike grumbies. Yet then . . . there was a tinge and tingle! She sat up straight, attentive. Yes. A rising din traveled from another direction, another Tree, not too far off, a solitary commotion.

This Tree's vernacular was entirely foreign to her. She concentrated but could only decipher its emotional underpinnings that rang out like the dueling ka-cows of two quail choiring against one another from their high perches in greatest indignation. And while the exact meaning was unclear, the emotion behind its connotation was without question - impatience. *Ah*, thought Leaf. *It's like Miriam.* Her thoughts, beginning to spiral into memory and heartache, were disrupted as Sage sat down next to her, shoulder to shoulder, nudging her as he did so, drink in hand.

"Take this," he ordered cheerfully. "Drink up. 'Tis of proper nutrition and will rejuvenate you." He imitated the action and waited as the Treean took a sip. "Tastes terrible, doesn't it?"

"Sage!" she spat. "You could've warned me!"

"Look around. We sit by the grumbies' fireside, they sing and dance for us . . . and they bring forth their food to share." And so saying, Sage eyed the drink; Leaf's face contorted. "That's right, that's their food," he whispered. "Did you happen to notice that Abi lacks teeth? Grumbies don't have any. All the alchemy in Llaurantis and no teeth," he said, giggling delightedly. "What's the use when you've this fine beverage!" and so saying, his wide grin, cracked at the sides, making Leaf smile too. "They're grand creatures, Leaf. Grand! They'll be our favor in these dark days."

Leaf's face fell upon those words. She would like to forget. If Shee was but a moment in Llaurantis, she could live a lifetime without thinking of it.

"I must at present go," said Sage; Leaf stiffened after the words. "I've a Tree to commune with," he said, looking up at her from under his mangled forelock with a gentle grin.

Her face lit up at once. "If the tendrils under my toes are still of any use, I can tell you she's quite keen on seeing you."

Sage laughed fully, and Leaf loved to hear it. There was an aspect to the sound, so utterly Elvish, like rain tinkling on water, calming yet unavoidably sad. Also, it carried a particular quality unique to him, as though he coffered all the secrets of the world and tucked in a taunt for good measure.

"That is why I must now leave," Sage said, kissing two of his fingers and placing them atop her head.

She watched as he bound away. 'Twas as if shadows played on his form, hints of the Coyotl taken in and out of the shadow of his movements. His gait was easy yet long and springy, vacillating between a loping trot and elven footsteps. His form flickered, and the Coyotl became the namesake of his kin in front of her very eyes.

Leaf looked to her right toward Noblien and Tullkaee, who also watched the Coyotl's departure. Sessile sat next to Downy on her left, where Downy concentrated intently upon the inner-lapping flames as Sessile joyously watched the dancing. Leaf sighed, and then Abi approached.

"What thinks a Treean from Alderelm that a Tree calls for Lagacious?"

Lagacious. She liked the way Abi referred to Sage by his second name. "I find it delightfully peculiar," she replied. "Although he has a history with Alderelm, I cannot say 'tis completely surprising. Still, 'tis intriguing. What type of Tree is it?"

Abi chuckled, her belly gently rolling with her laughter. "Treean more curious about Tree than about the how and why it calls Lagacious. Tickles Abi."

"Oh, well—" Leaf began to stammer.

"No, no, not judging Treean. No rights and no wrongs. Just-just." She raised her hands and flipped them right side up to show her openness; Leaf gave a reserved, polite smile. "Treean knows of Cassen Tree? Sage been visiting her forevers."

"The Tree of Cassen?" asked Leaf, to which Abi nodded. "Yes, the Ancient Ones know of this Tree. She's not one of the Ancient Forest Trees, but she is equally as old and wise. There's a myth that the Writs of Brighid are impressed upon each of her leaves."

"No myth," said Abi. "And each leafusses, yes, teeny writings on each. Powerful magic."

"The Tree of Cassen," repeated Leaf in wonder. "Abi, how did Sage develop this kinship with her?"

"Ready, setty?" Abi beamed. "Sage is the first Coyotl."

"The first?" asked Noblien.

"First," replied Abi. "Sage has no bellybuddy because he was born from Veriha as a tear. Cassen caught tear in her leafusses. Wrapped him tight. Cassen Tree leafusses hold tear in big wind until coyotes come and save him. This is beginnings of Coyotl kind."

"This cannot be," sputtered Leaf, trying to process the information just relayed. The brambles of her hair flattened hard against her head as she considered. "Then he's old," she mumbled, the hue of her skin turning intensely green and her brambles now rising. "He'd be almost as old as Miriam!"

Abi nodded. "Walk'in bones old."

"Noblien," said Leaf, gasping. "He looks about the same age as you! How's this possible?"

"Maybe Brighid writs keep him young," Abi speculated, shrugging. "Brighid powerful magic. You se'un his tattoos? Many little-tiny tattoos." The group nodded dumbly. "Imprints from Cassen leafusses."

"I'm unfamiliar with . . . Veer-i-ha," said Downy, faltering.

"Veriha," Leaf repeated. "These are ancient histories, long ere the coming of human kind. The Veriha are also called the Seven Wonders. They were the original inhabitants who made the Earth habitable. They're revered by all who remember. They reside now in the stars."

"I see," Downy said hesitantly. "I understand that elves age differently than humans, but if Sage is the original elf of his ketyl, how long has he walked the Earth?"

"Since the Veriha ascended to the heavens," Noblien whispered.

"And this is a long time?"

"Eons . . . *eons*," the Puman said, exhaling. "An unimaginable length of time to even an elf."

Downy scratched his head. "Forgive my continued ignorance, but what then is Brighid?"

Abi looked toward Noblien to answer. "The Writs of Brighid," said Noblien, "are the written representations of the first spoken language, believed to be imbued with the living spirit of their meaning."

Downy sighed in frustration. "This makes little sense."

"Words have meaning, captain," replied Noblien. "And the words of the Writs of Brighid have literal meaning. Even the words of the common tongue, of which you and I exchange now, carry weight under their intention."

"This I understand well; there's truth in it. Though I still doubt these Writs of Brighid, as you say, hold magical meaning if they even exist. Seems more like the flight of fancy."

Noblien's face screwed up in patient protest. "My Da told me bedtime stories about them. 'The Writs of Brighid hold ancient magic,' he would say. Only the Faiyum knew of their whereabouts, and they would keep safe the sacredness and power held within." Noblien trembled, his speech slowing as a realization swallowed him. "I would ask how the Faiyum knew where they were, to which he would ask why it mattered as long as the Faiyum was keeping its magic hidden and safe. To think now, his fellow was covered in the writs." He rubbed his eyes. "I told Sage that the Faiyum was extinct, that my Da was the last. I was so very arrogant and out of turn. All this time, he was the Faiyum. I'm blind as well as deaf."

Abi's eyes narrowed. Her face gentled in a tilt. "Lagacious has reasons. Many reasons. You no blame for what you think when he no speak. He no blame for no speak. He shields you. He shield everyone. Grumbies love Lagacious, but we worries for him. I sees that you will shield him next. This makes Abi happy. Sees this grass? Desert nettle. Tenacious. Grows out of rock, very much like Lagacious. You, all of you, are the rock. Understands?"

The group was silent, and the pause in the air held weight. Noblien's jaw gritted. "Aye. Thank you."

"No worries. Grumbies help."

"Abi," began Noblien, "we've sought out the lands of Shee for help with the Haevonen, as you know, but there is yet more to our need." He sighed, not knowing where to begin. "There's much to relay, and we ask for the grumby's vision and wise counsel."

The reality that they were finally in Shee and ready to reveal the chaos on Llaurantis struck Leaf unexpectedly hard. All she could do, caught off guard by the release of her pent-up turmoil, was stare at the ground, tears beginning to drip down her nose. Leoness, curled up and resting contentedly behind her, clucked and nuzzled her soapstone beak under the Treean's arm.

Abi placed a pudgy finger under one of Leaf's tears and wiped it away. "Abi knows. No more watering the grasses. The world make no sense a lot. We too small to see the big. Long as we make hope and not just hoping for hope, all be good. Now you rest. Tomorrow, we send the Haevonen home. Afters, we attend to the making of hope," and so saying, her crinkled old eyes nearly disappeared within her smile, which warmed with the beams of sweetest and kindest sincerity.

DESERT NETTLE

Desert Nettle. 1. A prickly plant that can grow between the crevices of rocks, having toothed leaves and stinging hairs with pale yellow flowers that bloom from spring to summer. **2.** Recent Age. Eucnide urens, also known as Desert Stingbush, consists of blooms with five-petaled, pale-yellow flowers and grown on cliff faces which are often fed on by Desert bighorn sheep.

SWEETWOOD

Sweetwood. 1. *A small evergreen tree that blooms vanilla-scented, white blooms in the spring and whose needles turn gold in the winter. Its pinecones are heated above a fire to infuse the air with a calming smell similar to a combination of rosemary, marjoram, and eucalyptus.* **2.** *Recent Age. Sweetwood is a common name for several plants, none of which are comparable to the sweetwood of Alderelm's time.*

⊷ Chapter 18 ⊶

*From Earth is grace brought, from the sky is patience given, from the day is all
forgiven, and from the night is it all forgot.*

—Coyotl adage

"Vell no 'ta bur'nighn," Sage said, holding his fingers aloft and touching
the clusters of the Cassen's teardrop leaves from under her outreach and
shelter. "For she is ever flourishing and strong."

Her leaves lit and faded, flickering to and fro with a tee-ta-tat, tee-
ta-tat as warm air rose from the earth into the cooling eve. The motion
cast starburst reflections in miniature from the imprints of amber motifs
laid within the leaf veins, mirroring the world around it like glass. The
Coyotl's heart and spirit overbrimmed with peace under the little Tree's
protective embrace. Unbuckling his quiver, he sank back against her
trunk, smooth as weathered river rock, and sighed long and heavy, his
woes of the world dissipating in her presence, with a sleep of the purest
kind cushioning the torments of his mind. The Cassen thrummed, her
contentment reaching Leaf's tendrils in purred resonances and settling
the distraught Treean for the night.

On the early morningtide, Sage stretched and opened his bleary eyes. The Puman sat cross-legged in front of him, apparently surveying his sleep.

"Thai Mielle," he said, yawning, "you ought not to stare in such ways—I'll think you've taken a flavor to me."

Noblien smirked, and perhaps just the hint of a smile emerged from the corner of an involuntary wince. Sage studied him. There was no ill look to the Puman's countenance. He seemed more composed of thoughtful temperance than his usual restrained irritation. Unease crept under Sage's skin.

"She's a beautiful Tree," said Noblien; Sage nodded. "Abi spoke much about you both last night."

"I see," said Sage, the corner of his mouth twisting in neither a smile nor a frown, instead giving a rather suspicious mixture of both.

"I'd ne'er have had an inkling of your beginnings. To be—"

"So old," Sage said, interrupting. "You're wondering if that's why I'm mentally off-kilter?"

"No, I'm wondering if you were ever going to let me in on any of your confidences."

"Thai Mielle, I'm old and the first Coyotl. Now you know."

Noblien rolled his eyes. He desperately wanted to express himself differently but found navigating his thoughts nearly impossible. "The Tree of Cassen bears a remarkable resemblance to your marks. I distinctly remember one on my Da as well—on his forearm—the sigil of the Faiyum?"

"Ah," Sage said, understanding but pausing in thought about how to proceed. "More aptly, a sigil of the person rather than of the Faiyum, each being unique." He analyzed the corner crest of Noblien's forehead. "Yours is loyalty. I see why she chose it for you. A noble word to carry. Your father's was friend."

"Why did you not set me straight?"

"I don't know," said the Coyotl, sighing. "I was avoiding larger issues after all. And besides, you were quite intent on the Faiyum being no more. There's a choice, you know. I was unsure if you were ready or even wanting. Besides, the touch of the Faiyum ... of the Writs of Brighid, cannot be taught nor practiced, so in this way, there was no need to," and here, with all the drama Sage could muster, he raised his hand and with a mock-serious voice said, "divulge your fate."

Sage paused, studying the Puman.

"The touch is an instinct driven by the heart's emotions. I suspect you reached for your arrow back in Seayr from an unconscious drive to focus all your intent through it to protect LeadLeaf. That arrow has significant meaning to you, and it always has. It channeled your touch, your magic, whatever you want to call it. Magic is an overused word carrying little meaning anymore. What is magic?" he scoffed. "Real magic is the giving of oneself. In this regard, call on caution. For once you give of yourself, 'tis irrevocably gone forever."

Sage's eyes sought refuge from the deepness of the topic in the undercarriage of Cassen's leaves, but the forenoon sun shining through the greens encouraged openness. "She saved my unworthy hide long ago. I'm a part of her." He smiled and paused, closing his eyes with a slow, deep breath. "In the courses of life, Cassen gifts a sigil, a word or expression most encompassing of the recipient. The mystery of why one is selected belongs to her, or for that matter, how one is chosen. The Faiyum is a credit to her and the Writs of Brighid. I am naught."

Noblien moved to contest the latter statement, for to his reckoning, the crazed Coyotl and bizarre little Tree worked in concert, but Sage had more to reveal and did not pause long enough for the interruption.

"Noblien, I've grieved that I could not save your father. He was my best friend," and so saying, his eyes reddened. "I loved him—the pain of not being capable of tending his child ... the likes of me—tch—you cannot fathom the torture." His body shuddered. "I left you there," and so muttering, he hunched over with his head in his hands as his body began to shake. "I left you," he repeated. Tears of pent-up emotions now escaped the prism of Sage's being, his entire body overcoming the protective rigor mortis of suppression. He was now a fluid portal of agony's affection.

Noblien preferred these ideas of the mind's heart to remain covered until they were foreign, numb sensitivities one was unaware of carrying, mere shells of the mind barricaded against itself. Yet now, Noblien knocked a tear away, and shivers began to course throughout his body. He swallowed and allowed himself to absorb the pain. They were two warriors facing vulnerability for the sake of confronting the truth and, therein, being the bravest testament of courage.

"I am who I am," said Noblien, leaning his forehead against Sage's, "because of your decision. You can't regret aught, for I could be no other. Sage Lagacious, the firstborn of the Coyotls, you cannot carry all the world's burdens."

"I can try."

"It's interesting that while you didn't raise me, we are so very much alike in our nomadic tendencies," said Noblien, smiling. "Our paths must have come so close to crossing each other's many times."

"And now here we are." Sage nodded. "In Shee of all places."

"With the Haevonen!" chortled Noblien. "No one would believe it."

"Now that's a story, isn't it?" Sage said with a snort, wiping his eyes. "Ready to return them to their homeland?"

"Indeed."

❧ Chapter 19 ❧

How does the wind grapple with the aftermath of a galloping horse blown by?
Where does one begin in the description when such a compilation of senses has
been put under assault? Horses, those representations of the grace and power of
Nature, invitations in the flesh to an experience unsullied. Exhilaration calls
the rational to recognize fear while the soaring spirit beckons the analytical to
be cast to the wind just left in the dust.

—Excerpt from the Thessalian horse master manuscript of Delevar

Abi was well-pleased to see the two elves approaching. They strode in unison despite the swaggering of one and the gliding of the other. *A good sign*, she thought, and smiled to herself. Sage cracked a wide, crooked-toothed grin, speeding up to a trot to join the company, leaving the Puman's side. Noblien nodded, his expression unchanged beyond perhaps a softening. Abi sighed in deep satisfaction.

The grumbies stood in a circle, and as Noblien approached and greeted everyone, Abi cleared her throat. "It's time. Ready setty?" So saying, she turned an eye to Leaf. "Grumbies are like seasons and sylphs, but we no use winds; we use ethers. Can't see either, though." She winked and then shut her eyes.

The other grumbies also closed their eyes. Then, they all faced the same direction, clucking their tongues—a ballad of the grumbies. Veroosh! Their surroundings were suddenly quiet, and the air seemed to withdraw in on itself. Leaf flexed her jaws, trying to pop her ears, while Leoness restlessly danced in place, her clawed feet breaking the compressed silence with a tap-tapping. Leaf looked to the elves for reassurance, and Noblien, ever on the lookout, felt her gaze. He motioned to his heart, bowed, and extended his hand to hers.

A rising scent evened the air with the home-felt warmth of rich, loamy soil. Yet there was no breeze, not even the slightest, and as the Earthen aroma rose, the air began to feel as if it were condensing, precipitating a narrow veil of dewdrops. The sensation felt like the sun's kiss on a cold afternoon when the colors of the sky reflected orange and pink against the dark, bluish-grey, water-heavy clouds. And as a light wind gathered around the Haevonen, they stirred from their contented grazing.

Most of the herd possessed copper-chestnut coats of inlaid gloss, an apparent gift from the sun. A few, however, were as black as obsidian. And as a roll of thunder split the sky, the herd marched in a heavy-footed dance that refracted all these shining aspects into a moissanite of color. Whinnies made of soughing breaths and gentle nickers led the hearts of everyone, even while the clangor of their hooves shook the earth. The hoofbeats were rhythmic, and in this way, even while the combined sound was impressive, it was also a steady metronome of the universe unraveling as it should. Through it all, Leaf felt the wisdom of Miriam, of the gentle Hardtack, too, and she heard the winnowing flutes of Alderelm. Thanks to the Haevonen's mystifying presence, Alderelm was alive in her, and this realization took her breath away. The Majesties tossed their heads, their eyes dancing as they pranced a soiree of essence, wild and free.

The four directions—east, west, north, and south—abruptly

brightened as they coalesced into one phantasmagorical circle, the scene growing closer. Then, a rush of wind whipping with rain washed through the orifice in a fleeting bluster. Behind the tumult arose the glow of a red-tipped sun accentuated by a warm, heady breeze from the land of Haverdome. The red-tipped hobnob grasses whetted the senses as the Haevonen bounded toward their homeland. Some leaped through the demarcation of change between Shee and Haverdome, while others haltingly paced through sideways, snorting with caution but also joy. The view of the rolling prairie was an ever-stretching grassland spectacular in scope. The colors, from the earth to the sky, were a collation of Nature's most fantastic, the blended and contrasted whims of an eccentrically refined character.

Leaf's attention was broken when the grumbies stomped upon one foot, then grunted and stomped on the other. Whoosh! The wind that had previously rushed inwards toward Shee now retracted back into the shrinking landscape of beyond. Haverdome began to fade, and Leaf cried out, though she did not know why. One Haevonen turned back. The eye that met hers under a forelock of airy fortitude was soft, gentle . . . docile. She was taken aback by the honor bestowed and lowered her head in respect. Reading the sinews of Leaf's being, the Haevonen tossed its head with a triumphant whinny. The message imparted was clear. We are with you; we will always be with you.

HOBNOB GRASS

Hobnob Grass. 1. A *pasture grass of red-tipped blades native and found solely within the lands of Haverdome.* *2.* Recent Age. Unidentified.

❧ Chapter 20 ❧

No other creatures crave the upper currents more than Trees and hawks.

—A musing from Notus

As the eves to the fields of Haverdome diminished, the energy of the air fell, and the distant humming that had crept like subtle tremors into everyone's bones halted. The stillness returned, but only briefly, for a robin scuttled forth and sang out brightly with all its worth in the effort. Leaf smiled. An aspect shone so triumphantly in the robin's rotund assertiveness. It was a sergeant of arms ready to boast a victory and rally all to good cheer.

The grumbies' merriment was plentiful, and food was cooked, shared, and enjoyed around them. Abi sat in a rock grove designed with a garden of granite bulwarks, slate and schist formations, and specially placed limestone columns. Eventually, she cocked an eye at the company.

"It's time for big talk," she announced. "Haevonen back home, is good. You did well. Grumbies happy to be a part of getting Haevonens home. No regular horse. They full of origin air. Special. Must be with their land, their place," and so saying, she looked at Sage with a heavy heart. "World is changing, Lagacious. Eves closing, and grumbies finding hards to open. We're soon to be in different worlds, no crossing. You's won't be able to return. No one will be able to see Land of Shee again."

Sage held his head high, although his rusty voice quivered. "Cassen informed me. Lawks, Abi, how I'll miss you all.

"You'll be missing Cassen," Abi said, her heart warm with understanding as though her proclamation would spare the Coyotl.

"More than can be expressed," Sage replied, his voice as gruff as roiled river rocks in floodwaters. Yet still, he managed to turn to Leaf and, for her sake, smile.

Abi nodded, swallowing. "Now, tells grumbies what's happened outside Shee, and Abi will tells you what Abi sees."

To everyone's surprise, it was Tullkaee who spoke first. She had not missed the devastation in the Coyotl's reddened eyes. Nor was she blind to his battles and pains. And for LittleLeaf, she understood the heartache of leaving one's people. She perceived, too, the Puman's attentions and concerns for Leaf and Sage, how he shared in their heartbreaks and suffered more than either could notice through their own preoccupations and pain fogs. The company was weary and heartsick. So, she would speak up; it was simply a reaction to necessity.

"The lands are under attack by Kongoni," she said, searching for the common word.

Leaning forward, Abi tilted her head. "Abi knows your language."

Tullkaee's eyebrows lifted. She was respectfully astonished. She reckoned that Abi's weathered all-knowing smile of serene contemplations hinted at aspects akin to the personification of Mother Nature, the crone shade of her moon cycle therein. This idea made her swallow over a lump in her throat and brush down the rising hairs on her arm. Blinking, Tullkaee collected her thoughts. "They bring smoke. Smoke that takes our shapes. They have attacked LeadLeaf's home."

"Alderelm?" asked Abi, with a narrowing and smoldering eye.

"Yes," Tullkaee replied solemnly but with an incredible assurance of strength resting well within the middle of her voice. "Another Old Forest has fallen, and yet another defends itself."

Abi clucked and humphed while weighing the Daun's words. Then, she peered at each company member as though accessing the outside world through their silent stories.

"I'll be closing my eye bulbs for a bit," said Abi, beginning to mentally traverse the astral layers of air-matter, the strata intertwining the ethers, in order to decipher their cryptic clues, those secrets bending the future toward probability. However, it must be said that the emphasis is on probabilities, ne'er absolute terms, for the push and pull of destiny and free will is fluid. This is where Abi concentrated.

The company was still; even the childlike Sessile and the restless Leoness waited in patience's shadow. However, patience was no friend of the Coyotl, and when the sun opened the wide breadth of its arms at mid-height in the sky, Sage could forbear no more.

"What say we have a match of marksmanship?"

"I'd say we'd be most rude, for here, the alchemist's mind toils away in the ethers for us," replied Noblien.

"Nay," Sage drawled. "She'd be but proud of our honest endeavors. Besides, she could go on like this 'til the stars shine."

Downy sighed upon hearing this. "Are you sure she isn't just sleeping?"

"Haha! Nay," Sage replied, amused at the captain's inquiry. Amusement was evermore the Coyotl's friend, so he shot back at Noblien puckishly. "I hardly see honing our skills as protectors of this poor, defenseless Treean as rude."

"I'm not defenseless," said Leaf.

Tullkaee attended Leaf's concerns by aiming a scornful side glance at the elf and casting him off with a hand gesture. "He teases you, LeadLeaf."

"Forsooth, you are our protectors, LittleLeaf," said Noblien.

Leaf squinted at him. "LeadLeaf."

Noblien scoffed. "I hardly see the advantage of being a leaf made of lead."

"Then we are decided," said Sage, eyeing the distance for a target. "Let us shoot for that yon woven container five score steps away by the greenish boulder cluster over yon. Do you see it, Thai Mielle?"

Noblien groaned. "Thai Mielle? Honestly, you're relentless. Which one of us is the younger?"

Sage's countenance was aglow with delight. "Well, based on your current temper, I am."

Downy stood and stretched. "My bow is made for the longshots. Might be you both rethread your raveled strings."

"You call that distance a longshot?" asked Noblien as the three assorted their bows and made ready their shafts; Tullkaee smirked, and Leaf delighted in the banter.

"All right, LeadLeaf," said Sage. "Watch the styles afore you."

"Sage," replied Noblien, "we should let the Thessalian go first."

"Aye, indeed," said Sage. "Sir Downy, take your aim."

"Gramercy for the courtesy," said Downy, clearing his throat, pride welling his person. He took his stance and loaded the bow with the arrow pointed upward. He drew on the right side of the string with his thumb, his index finger topping it, and twisting the bow slightly to the left with his wrist, he freed the shaft. It was a clean shot. The arrow hit the target squarely and silently. Sage raised his eyebrows and cheered while Noblien nodded in approval.

"The Thessalian can shoot!"

Next, Sage strode forward to take aim. "All right, LeadLeaf. Your stance is most important. Next is your posture. You must plant your feet firmly, stand tall, and watch that your elbow, hand, and arrow are in line. Find your anchor point. Hold your breath, close an eye, and release."

The arrow pinged into the target like a snare beat that made Leaf grimace. Sage grinned wide and crookedly. The white-fletched arrow had found its mark next to Downy's, and he turned around to the others.

"That was a fair shot," said Noblien, who now strode up to take his turn. With the bow in hand, he was at home, every aspect of his demeanor relaxed.

Sage switched positions with Noblien and stood next to Leaf. "Now, LeadLeaf," said Sage excitedly. "Thai Mielle's bow is named the Charlock. A fine bow—I know it well. Do you see those curves at each end? They're what give it leverage. While the Charlock is small, it is strong. The back is made of a horn, and the front is sinew. Strength and flexibility are its making," and so saying, he stopped and reflected on the Puman with a disapproving sigh. "'Tis interesting how Thai Mielle draws. Hmmm, yes. Watch. He places his thumb underneath and draws with the middle and index finger on either side of the shaft. I would think this technique flawed, for it increases the time required to mount the arrow, but as we have seen, the Puman is lightning fast, so we shall not fault him for his technique." Leaf grinned ear to ear to hear such critiquing of a Puman, masters of the bow, and Noblien no less, but the Coyotl did not notice, for he stared acutely at Noblien, studying his every move. "Now, do you see that? Look at how straight his wrist is. Also, he raises the bow on the draw and then rests it down to its anchor point. I do enjoy watching him do that."

"LittleLeaf," Noblien's voice rose as Sage's trailed off. "Look at where you want the arrow to go and breathe."

Sage scrunched his face. "As I've said, you've many techniques afore you. Might be you ought to start with mine?" And so saying, he smiled with all teeth apparent, gleaming wildly.

Yet then, Noblien's arrow left the Charlock's cradle with a hackle-raising hum and nailed the target with a haunting, resounding, and predatory thump. Its form was purpose; its song was lethality. Sage was for a rare moment quiet as it hit the wicker vessel beyond and splintered his own arrow.

"Come, Leaf," said Noblien. "Take my bow. Hold it. How does it feel?"

The Treean stood next to the elf and took his bow. She was filled with many emotions. The bow felt good, natural. Her hand curved around the grip, loosened and tightened again, with each of her fingers cascading open and closed. "It feels like I've held it before, but 'tis also scary."

Noblien smiled. "That's good. A weapon should be at home in one's hand and also respected." He handed her an arrow. "This is important. You want to position the arrow before you nock it. Hold the end here and place it on the bow. That's right. Your thumb is the shelf, and your index finger can further balance it by holding it in place. Now, follow the arrow back with your other hand, and, in one fluid motion, nock it. Yes, that's it. Push the arrow into the nock." He analyzed her progress and was well-pleased. "Nocking each arrow this way allows for more control and faster follow-up shooting. 'Tis a Puman technique. Now, pull the string with these two fingers. Your thumb is here. Good. Pull back," he said, leveling her arm and aiding, ever so subtly, in her draw of the string. "Keep your shoulder level. Good. Keep your eyes open. Now, the fun bit. Don't focus on the aim. Just look at your shot . . . and release."

Leaf opened her fingers, and the arrow left the bow when she exhaled. The moment felt aligned and perfect. The sound was a high-pitched twang rather than a swooshing thud, but she had made her first shot and under the tutelage of a Puman elf no less.

"These techniques may work for you," said Sage, pacing expectantly, "but by grace, I feel she ought to use three fingers."

Noblien did not see him speak. He was gazing out at Leaf's shot, concentrating and serious. "That was no sorry first shot, Leaf. Well done."

Leaf felt weak and numb in the knees, but she beamed under his compliment. There was much more to a bowshot than she had ever imagined, and she had imagined plenty. The Treean archers of Alderelm made it look easy, as did the three of her company. There was a finesse and skill to archery that was just like playing music. One had to feel, respond to, and reside in the moment. And drawing the string was very difficult.

"Tullkaee," asked Noblien, turning around, "will you not shoot?"

"I will take a shot," she affirmed, with a stretch and a grunt as she walked over nonchalantly.

Her bow was the smallest of the three and plain in appearance. It was made of Locust and Elm, Trees of stout spirits. She shot with her arrow on the left and did not draw close to her eye but drew to her chest with a short bow draw. Her shot gave a therump that was deceptively hollow compared to the power of the shot. Leaf took in every detail. Her shot was quick and straight.

"Is this the way all the Dauns shoot?" asked Noblien.

"Yes. We are brought up as children playing target practice this way."

"Then, 'tis an extension of yourself," Noblien said.

Tullkaee paused; her face was displeased as though she disagreed. "For the hunt, it is good. For the fight, it is not my weapon of choice. I prefer the staff for the fight."

"And that axe you tote around your waist?" asked Downy.

"I would choose my axe over this bow for the fight."

"At close range, this is good," Downy continued, "but for approaching foe in the distance—"

Tullkaee blinked slowly; she was bored, and the bulk of her weight shifted as she threw her axe without warning. It whirled with terrifying speed and precision, traveling further than seemed possible and hitting the wickerwork box with succinct accuracy and a touch of mirth.

Leaf swooned in admiration while Sage whistled. Noblien gritted his jaw, the corner of his mouth ticking upward and twitching. His thoughts were more of a mystery.

"Still, you only have one," Downy grunted, dissatisfied.

Much conversation ensued. The company was beginning to learn each other's ways, and even when they disagreed, there was an undeniable respect developing between them.

As the daylight began to walk with the twilight, the grumbies draped the meditating Abi in a blanket cape and lit the ground paths with firelights that sweetly underlit the mushroom-domed Trees. The group wondered what insights Abi might reveal and whether those inklings of future trappings leaned more toward the ominous than not. Worrit was a member of the company.

At last, Abi stirred. Her crinkly nose twitched as she sniffed and snuffled to full awareness, her catlike whiskers tilting on either side of the odd appendage like a seesaw. Now smacking her lips, she blinked her ever-easy eyes at everyone, but she did not smile, nor did her eyes dance with the glints of burbling joy that had earlier occupied them. Leaf's shoulders slumped, Sage sighed dejectedly, and Noblien ground his teeth while the grumbies gathered around and brought Abi a goblet of nourishment, which she drank at once. Satisfied, she rose, gathering the robed garment around her arms to drape around the left side of her neck.

"Walk with me," she said, a bubble of encouragement sleeping in the words. "Abi needs to stretch her old bones."

The company walked with her to the shores of the Blue Fish Caves. The wind gently lapped minuscule wakes onto the shore. There, she halted, and everyone looked toward the scene before them. Across the waters, the landscape stretched, its scalloped edges rising in striated levels atop one another where small, twisting Trees speckled the horizon in tasteful intervals as though purposefully placed and sprouted there.

The warm colors of the ridge exhaled a focus of truth and breadth of dimension, the hues of wheat and cream pleasantly enveloping the senses. This spot was a source of peace for the winsome grumby, who clucked and nodded to herself as if she was communing with the lake to get permission to access her source of wisdom, which resided on the further shore.

"Today, Abi no sees the world outside Shee. Abi tried and tried. Ether was testy, like wind bites and humming bees." So saying, her antennae momentarily drooped. "Shee verys close to splitting from Earthen realms. Grumbies will become myth. Eves to Earthen realms have been closing for some time. Using ethers to open doorway to Haevonen was hard, very hard," and so saying, she smacked her lips. "Now Abi sees time almost up. It's no safe for you in Shee unless you wants to stay." She cocked her head and waggled her nose. "But listen. Abi hears the Singing Tree Stone."

"Emerus?" said Sage. "No one knows its whereabouts or condition."

"Hmm. Wells, not lost," Abi nodded. "Changed."

Sage was beside himself. "Changed? But Nature—"

"Universe is living," interrupted Abi, looking at everyone. "All you sees around you, and even what you don't, changes as it grows. Ethers pull apart or together, just the nature of it," she said, shrugging. "So. Universe changing. If universe changing, then Tree Stone sings," and so saying, she pointed to Noblien. "You knows the waves of ethers. We grumbies call thems the Ylem." She saw that Downy looked confused, even doubtful, and shook her head. "Hard explaining ethers to kin that no sees it. Methinks your journey is good journey," she said, abruptly turning and hobbling back to the village. "Abi sees no knots."

The company followed her, Leaf stamping up to her side first.

"You's Lastborn Treean?" asked Abi, still trundling onward,

breathless in the effort.

"That's right," answered Leaf, the tinge of her skin washing out.

"LeadTree carries knowledge of all Trees? Of history?"

"How'd you know that?" Leaf asked, stopping dead in her tracks and looking down at the Sakatu, whose greens now spread to her neck. "What's happening to me?"

Abi goggled. "You's the World Tree Seed."

"What does this mean?" Leaf asked although she understood intuitively.

Noblien closed his eyes. *No, no, no.*

Abi turned to Sage, Noblien, and finally Leaf, smiling tenderly. "Means, to save Memory of Life, including grumbies, that LeadTree need take seed to white mountain, white mountain—very pretty. I sees it in ethers."

"Alderelm!" said Leaf, excited by destiny's prospect.

"Nay," replied Sage, shaking his head. "That's the most dangerous place she could go."

"Her safety and the protection of the Sakatu is more important than Alderelm itself," replied Noblien. "Going back is folly."

"Aye," agreed Sage. "I returned briefly on our journey; 'tis no place for her."

Abi squinted in concentration, then shrugged. "Abi knows what Abi sees. You comes for answers, Abi gives. Only sees white mountain, no mores, no lesses. Come. Let us sit by the fire and enjoy ours company before the grumbies open Shee's door one last time—"

"I mean no offense," said Downy, clearing his throat nervously, "but should we not be leaving at once?"

Abi held up her knobby thumb as if detecting the wind and concentrated briefly. "Abi, too tired, must rest befores lifting eve. Eves heavy now. No worries, much."

"Don't worry much?" Downy said.

"Yes, not much," replied Abi, smiling.

"She's a daeva," mumbled Downy under his breath.

Sage leaned in, having heard him. "She's . . . a grumby. They're complicated creatures."

"Then they're all daevas," said Downy.

Sage smiled. "I'll admit, the analogy is close."

Back by the sweet, crackling fires, all found a seat, and goblets of grumby mead were passed around. The company was tentative to try it, but the soothing sensation the elixir brought from the very first sip called for second sips and more. These beverages, made of lullabies and mysterious tales, were more potion than drink. The effect was almost immediate; the group relaxed.

"Lagacious," Abi whispered, patting the elf's hand. "We wills take good care of Cassen."

"Thank you, Abi," answered Sage, although he knew the Cassen would take care of the grumbies. "I'll miss you, old friend. I'll miss all of you. This place is sublime. 'Twas a good fortune to have you all in my life. If change is the lifeblood of the universe, 'tis bittersweet," and so saying, the Coyotl inclined his head and clinked his goblet against Abi's. "To change."

Abi returned the gesture and, in one gurgling swig, finished the contents of her goblet, smacking her lips in satisfaction. The Coyotl laughed. He would miss the grumbies, their perspective, and their world. Where Alderelm was his grounding rod, Shee was his reprieve. He was losing both. Moreover, the Cassen itched at his heart and the essence of his spirit. That bold little Tree was a part of him and him to her. Not could he fathom a life where she did not reside. But he could not think about that now. The moment was too gravid in torturous realizations of sad inevitabilities. Luckily, out of the corner of his eye, he espied a tantalizing diversion. In abject horror, Downy watched his brother pet the long, hairlike feathers that ran down Leoness's sleek reptilian neck.

"Fret not, Sir Downy," said Sage regarding his beloved banda. "She's a rare and beautiful creature of the noblest kind, with gryphon and Halouse dragon in her bloodline. Did you know that when a gryphon drinks from a lake or a river, the moment their blue beaks touch the water, the sacred fluid is imbued with valor, virtue, and truth?" As Sage spoke, he looked intently at Downy, who returned the gaze with suspicion. "'Tis true," said Sage, smiling, seeing the fissure of the Thessalian's prejudices shrink. "Such attributes are not born from imagination alone."

"I heard that they were protectors of kings who guard over treasure."

"There's truth in what you say, but the treasure they guarded was the Forest itself. To a gryphon, there was no greater treasure than the greens of leaves upon the Trees of their Forest. They were fierce protectors. They've not been seen for many an age," and so saying, his voice and thoughts drifted off.

Sage had captured the Thessalian's imagination. He was genuinely interested and asked, "And the dragons?"

"Ah, the dragons of the Halouse," said Sage, eagered by the question. "The elusive creatures are said to be good luck; let me assure you, they are indeed good luck. Did you know they are two-legged dragons with feathered wings similar to the gryphon? One can imagine the attraction to their union. They're such similar creatures," he mused, retreating into memories.

"I see," replied Downy. "Gallant creatures by your descriptions."

The change in the Thessalian's mindset pulled the elf back to the present moment in a tickled shock. "Aye! And look, in front of you, stands one of the descendants of both. She's worth luck, guardianship, and the anointing of water. Might be that a tinge of that valor, virtue, and truth has been imbued in you."

Downy was captivated. "I suppose I can courage a touch."

"Yes, brother," Sessile supported, demonstrating where best he might touch her.

Following his brother's guidance, the captain settled a wary hand upon her beak, and her eyes contracted and dilated. "How do you read her?" he asked, with curiosity arising from confidence.

"For Leoness, there's not much to read," Sage replied, chuckling. "She's an honest, odd girl. Aren't you?" he finished, cooing to the banda with a stream of sweet talk, which led Leoness to give a series of gleeful, burping honks.

Downy smiled cautiously. His was a thin smile as though unsure whether it ought to be present. His brother had no such issue and, so as now, beamed broadly. Sage felt most pleased, as did Leoness, who arched her neck under so much attention at one time. Contrary to the revered banda, Eyas, that noble hawk-in-miniature, chirped with what could only be irritation as she flew opposite the fire and fluffed to preen herself.

In the following moments, the company grew still and quiet. Time was bringing closer an end to the comfort that now encapsulated them.

Abi stirred from a brief nodding off and recognized the company's air upon regaining her bearings. Even so, she was not ready to give up her energies to the ethers, so she plotted for more time, tender though it was. "Lagacious," she said innocently, "tell one of your stories."

"Another?" Sage asked, making a pretense of not being inclined to engage in such activity while it was readily apparent to everyone that he was delighted to do so.

Leaf snorted to herself. Sage was an endless conundrum to observe. Downy fidgeted; he was not inclined to sit lazily for another tall tale, but his brother clapped in delight. Resigned, he grabbed a broken twig lying on the ground and drew vacantly in the sandy dirt. The great Daun situated herself comfortably. Stories were an important aspect of her culture. For Noblien, he was polite and attentive, however generally indifferent to a tale's point of purpose. Sure, he could read the lips of the storyteller and infer the inflections relayed, but he yearned more for a mountainside's accounts through the colors, smells, plants, and animals and the feel of the breeze.

"Well, let's see," Sage began, a gleam in his eyes.

A long time ago, when I was a youngling, I met with a most unusual encounter. You see, I'd been tromping about all night with my cousins and had roamed farther than the rest over a not-too-distant hillock in the wee hours of the morning's first rays. There, as the hillock flattened out across its highest rising point, stood a row of gigantic spiders with gleaming tusks of ivory and obsidian. Strange a sight. Yet stranger still, the creatures all stood facing the rising sun and made a most curious sound, like a swarm of bees in the distance, a rising and falling of auumms, deep and rhythmic. So, I crouched low and steady to watch and listen.

Once every gleaming point of the sun's rays rested well above the horizon, the spiders ended their meditations and began to graze on the grasses. Their long, golden-haired legs and amber-colored backs blended perfectly, although for what purpose such intimidating creatures would need to camouflage themselves is a mystery. These creatures greatly confused me because most spiders I knew of were small and hung in webs. But the spiders I was watching were nearly as giant as elephants and foraged upon blades of grass—like deer—click-clattering their mouth pinchers as they went, their fangs tapping, and their massive tusks ebbing and flowing with their steps like pendulums.

One particularly large spider turned its gaze toward me with an uneasy frequency. Yet, it did not ever hold an aggressive look. Quite the contrary, it seemed curiously meek and strangely . . . beautiful. Still, it was intimidating to have a spider creature of no small size look directly at you with all those large black eyes. Slowly, it made its way closer to me. Unlike the others, the long, silken hair about its body was nearly entirely grey, and it lumbered more than the others. Then, I noticed it didn't have eight legs but seven; it was missing an entire limb. Closer and closer, it meandered over to me. Its long pincers made easy work of slashing the grass. It chomped and chomped above its heavy breathing. And it was much bigger than it had looked when it was next to the others, and it had looked gargantuan before! All its feet tapped closer and closer to my person, but despite having so many, I could tell that it knew precisely where it was placing each foot. I was scared, but I was much more curious by then.

The creature made a long sigh and tossed a mouthful of grass down on top of me. I stared at it in confusion. Again, it sighed and thrust more grass on me.

"Now, now," said one of the creatures farther away, "take care not to frighten the little being."

The silver one next to me grunted.

Upon hearing these words, I popped up like a daisy. "You speak with words?"

"What else would we speak with?" the creature said, with a deep, husky voice one might imagine coming from a bear if a bear could talk.

I stood there considering his words as I watched the other spiders teeter away beyond eyeshot, far faster and easier than their size would suppose them able to do. It left my stomach with no small amount of unease.

"Well, pardon me for saying," I said, "but spiders where I come from do not speak. Also, they prey upon more than grass."

The creature balked. "Spiders? No child, we are the Ibus. The Ibus are as old as the Trees. You will not know of us because we do not exist."

It was my turn to balk. "Don't exist? Then how, sir, am I speaking with you now?"

"You may thank the Turnanillies for our communion."

"Turna—what? Okay, how are you here if you don't exist?"

"Hmmm. I don't know," he replied slowly, thinking hard. "Because we are divine beings, shields of the scablands."

"Shields of the what? I hardly know what you mean."

"Titles that describe our purpose; we are knights, defenders of what does not exist."

"And what doesn't exist?" I asked, proud of the question because I felt sure I'd stumped him.

"Excellent question," he replied, satisfaction radiating in his voice. "Tree chewers, walking-bones, and ghostmoms mostly. I think ghostmoms are the scariest."

I was dumbfounded.

"Oh dear, pardon me. I have not properly introduced myself. It's much the pleasure to meet you," the creature said, bowing. "My name is Montephoebius Longmire, son of Montague Whilom and Cedartulip Delovely, my lineage of the Woolbloom line. You may simply call me Montephoebius."

"'Tis nice to meet you. My name is Sage. What were you all doing earlier?"

"Ah. The Ibus seek out the Sun's first rays and auumm."

"Why?"

"Because we like to auumm. It feels very good inside."

"Why do you auumm during the sunrise?"

"You ask many questions. How old are you?"

"I don't know."

"Well, you're obviously the age that asks endless questions. I suppose that is why the ghostmom is here."

"A ghostmom! Here?"

"Yes."

I noticed the air had become heavy with the smell of sulfur. Montephoebius snapped his fangs just as a wailing hit my ears. He raised himself slowly, balancing his body on the two back legs of his right side and the one back leg of his left. The rest of his foremost legs spread outstretched into the air and took a deadly slice at a vagary yet seen by me. Then I saw the puckered face of a scowling woman with ocher eyes.

"Give me the child," it said, hissing, arms outstretched toward me. "He must come home now."

"Be off," Montephoebius replied with a snarl. "Sage, do not meet her gaze."

"Oh tender, tender, delicate child, come to mommy," it said, its smile curdling.

Montephoebius's hackles bristled, and his fangs bit the air. The ghostmom hissed as a whoosh fell against us, and it was gone. I realized I was standing underneath Montephoebius's towering legs and sheepishly peeked out from the safety beneath him.

"It did not fight?" I asked.

He replied. "Not this time. 'Tis a ghostmom's preference to steal, but one can ne'er be too sure. They're terrible creatures. It thought it'd taken us by surprise. If you ever encounter another, be careful not to meet its gaze, for it will entrance you. And watch that it doesn't spit on you.

"I like to catch them in my fangs and shake them a bit. Then, I like to plant them. You see, 'tis an Ibus custom to plant foul creatures like ghostmoms. This is what I do; I walk in circles, give it one last shake, and plop it, right into the sod of earth, up to the waist it goes. Then I tap and tend the ground like so."

While recounting the tale, Sage tapped his feet and demonstrated to the group as best he could what a seven-legged, giant spider might do to tend the soil; no one could argue against the Coyotl being a supreme storyteller. Leaf and Sessile were enthralled. His demonstration complete, and well satisfied by his captive audience, he continued in his best impersonation of the gruff voice of his character:

"Whatever creature an Ibus plants will begin to turn into a Tree immediately. Their skin hardens, and leaves unravel, sprouting atop their head. And for a long time, the foul creature will know the power of stillness."

Sage paused the story for effect, and Sessile clapped and cheered heartily in the brief silence. At this response, Sage relinquished his role as storyteller and burst into a tumbling laugh, contagious to everyone in its delightfulness. "And that, my good company, is one of many tales of the preeminent Montephoebius."

The campfires were now hot with red-orange embers, crackling and popping as if joining the multitude of ongoing conversations. Many grumbies came forward to offer gifts of rubbing stones for their journey. The stones and gems of Shee were renowned for their unique properties and energies. To be gifted one was a special honor, and the grumbies had a unique talent for deciding exactly what type of stone an individual would best benefit from.

One grumby, with a continually waggling ear and a listing set of whiskers, approached Sage with an outstretched hand and presented him with a crystal river stone, an adamant, set upon a silver armlet. The crystal pulsed as he accepted it, and he instinctively held the armlet tighter as if it might escape.

The grumby giggled. "Mohs makes good choice. It likes you."

"Your name is Mohs?" Sage asked, to which the grumby nodded as she watched him affix the ornament around his left arm. "Thank you, Mohs. Thank you very much," and so saying, he took in the last moments of Shee within her smile.

❧ ✦ ☙

Tree rings are the outline of hugs given to a growing Tree by the Forest. They are memories of love, representations of support and encouragement. Sometimes, they appear narrow and small, but those are the rings the Tree absorbed into its sentient being when times were difficult. This night was like a narrow Tree ring for the company. The grumbies sensed the need and gave their embraces and encouragement openly, all the energy therein becoming a bulwark of strength and hope in the company's spirits.

When the time arrived, Sage took one last look back at the Land of Shee and then, without a word, walked into the rush of balsam air winnowing through the delicate aperture of the last gateway of Shee. The others followed. Confident were everyone's steps, grateful were the last glances, and full were everyone's hearts with gratitude, hope, and well wishes.

◅ Chapter 21 ▻

Nails screech and grind,
Teeth clutch in fright,
Eyes terrified of the war in sight.

—Excerpt from the Dragons of Chickasaw

The Gauss made an audible sucking sound out of the corner of its mouth as it looked over the trampled foliage interspersed with streaky paths of brittle earth, burned and charred. The other Gauss walked mindlessly along, continuing their assault by their mere presence of being, thudding through their existence, meaningless and heavy: breathing, eating, voids. To disorganize, displace, and emotionally torture was their point of purpose. Even the Four Directions and the scents on the wind were made empty. And to render empty was to make the land a monochrome of sallow, a reflection of their kind.

The brute looked at its hand and sighed, pulling out a stained cloth tucked within its keeper. Slowly unfolding the raveled threads of linen, it stared with mulling eyes at the wilted clover pressed within. Its kind would move on, disrupt the vegetation of another land, make tender what was strong, thinking they were strong for having stripped it. The

Gauss could not reason out this concept, for such contemplation was still a vagary. Cerebral acuity above basic sensibilities had ne'er been fostered; it had been suppressed, and for many of its kind, it simply did not exist as more than a spark.

Still, this Gauss, regarding a simple clover, was perceiving with more than instinct and on the brink of reasoning, even questioning. Thus far, however, any deeper grasp into the realm of cognition would induce a spiral of despair. It only held an emphatic inkling that the desiccated clover held within its palm was a balsam of refuge, though the notions of balsam or refuge were utterly unknown.

Another Gauss bumped into it hard. Snarling, it clenched its fist. The clover was then enveloped in a grip of force and the stench of death. Yet, it was also pressed against a spirit gaining self-awareness. And as if recognizing such emerging traits, Nature quietly set forth a multitude of the tiniest leaves, as red as rich blood, imitations of the heart, peeking through the crisp, trodden earth—a sign of persistence if not outright defiance.

Swallowing the limacine rheum constantly and thickly running down its throat, the clover-Gauss plodded on with the others, a herd of speechless grunters whose purpose seemed only to feel the sting of the fire whips that lashed them onward. The Gauss did not know the name of the fire demons or question whether the continual duress they issued aligned with the proper order of their two species. A cascade might follow if just one Gauss could perceive enough to lash out. Perception, no matter the level of intelligence, is one of Nature's most fantastic totems. The Gauss might be well content to forage peaceably and alone. Their kind had ne'er been allowed to know.

The Ashindi, for their point of purpose, were not made entirely by Nature. They were an artifice of mental perception foreign to the elements of time and place, cruel in derivation and devoid of the fibers familiar to the organic aspects of living matter. The Earth and the heavens derive from the same components, whether similar or vastly different, remaining one and the same—made of the stars. But the Ashindi did not arise from the universe's precepts, not completely. From obscurity, their kind were like tentacles reaching out for a world ne'er meant for their dwelling. Nevertheless, they would take it for their own, force the matrix of life to conform to new tenets unaligned with eons of natural adaptation, and subjugate the Earth to its imploding disaster. There was only one possible salvation.

☙ ✦ ❧

Gathering their senses, the company stood slightly dazed from the jarring footfalls between dimensional space. Leaf looked behind her, a last glimpse into the Land of Shee, and raised her hand to Abi's blurring form.

"Where are we?" Tullkaee asked.

"North of Seayr," Downy speculated, inordinately confident and scanning the horizon.

"Why answer thus when you've no idea?" Sage asked, genuinely bewildered.

"Because it was a woman who asked," replied Tullkaee.

"Tush!" Downy scoffed.

Sessile sniffed the air. "Nah, brother. This isn't home."

Noblien knelt, knitting his brow. "He's right."

"Why would Abi direct us off course?" asked Leaf.

"Nay, LeadLeaf," said Sage, "that would not be her intent. Let us pause for a few moments and gain our bearings. Take in the sun, the landscape, the smells."

Leaf watched Noblien cock his head as if listening for an answer from the earth, and yet she knew he could hear naught. Insecurity sent her fingertips to the heart of the Sakatu, which felt warm and was beginning to thrum under her touch. Remaining still, she observed the

Puman, who grabbed a handful of earth and rubbed it into his palm. His eyes narrowed in consideration of the impossible as a rising trill vibrated into her hand and arm. Noblien's eyes widened.

"This is not our realm."

"Ha!" Downy said. "What jape do you play?"

Sage ran a hand through his hair and turned away, looking over the geography before him. The characteristics of this place were nearly identical. The difference was but a notion that one could not quite catch in recollection, yet it was there, taunting, chafing at the mind. He closed the windows to his spirit, and a marked incongruity shook his senses. It was entirely too quiet. There arose no chime work of faerie kind, that tinkering sound, feathering the backdrop of all their lives. Reopening his eyes, he studied the hills and wondered how he had not immediately noticed! These hills did not cradle a wealth of towering Trees that were old and gnarled. Trees, yes, but the giants of Laurantis were not within sight.

He could sense his mind slamming against his consciousness, the voices plying at his grip on reality. Gritting his teeth, the Coyotl fought the infamous battle to control his bearing, thoughts, and feelings. To the best of his ability, he would ne'er give in, but the struggle seemed incessant, and at times, he felt as though he was chasing sunlight. His left hand shook, and Leaf grasped it. Heartsease swallowed his nerves and gave distraction enough to allow his mental faculties to tamp off the abyss ever calling him away. He gazed down at her in gratitude and beheld a fragile smile he sought to remedy with a wink and a squeeze of her hand. They became at once a grounding, steadying influence on each other.

At the same moment, more than a breeze but less than a wind clipped around the company's ankles and stretched out above the long, bunched grasses toward the rising sun in the east. The moment made the Fierce-Eyed Elf stand stock-still. His eyes searched as his fingers spread apart to feel the air.

Eyas, the wee ave of soaring spirit, flew under his chin and alighted atop his quiver, chirping with zeal. Leoness joined her song with a discordant bray, ruffling the feathers of her entire body and snaking her neck. Both acted like foundlings reacting to life's scents, sounds, and sensations when new and invigorating.

"I believe," said Noblien, "we are set to encounter an elemental, perhaps even a wind."

Downy looked confused and began to utter a complaint of disbelief when a tight, crisp wind swirled around the company. The air was cold but controlled, fierce yet soothing, and throughout the mystery unfolding, ne'er chilled them. A fog began to billow and swirl before condensing into a male form, a tall figure with haunting blue eyes that looked like the sastrugi of the Cold Territories, snow dunes to infinity. His lips were long and thin like his nose, his forehead was broad and deeply furrowed, and his smile was genuine yet not overtight.

"Boreas!" Noblien cried out, as surprised as glad to see the wind giant.

Sage was not so eager in glad tidings or impressed by the whirling elemental. The winds were fickle, jealous creatures that had haunted him as a child, and he crossed his arms in unconscious defense. However, the Coyotl had ne'er met the North wind. While strong and fierce by nature, Boreas was a shy wind that let his reputation precede him to avoid unnecessary social interactions. He felt that almost all such interactions were superfluous. Yet here, this group of individuals had perplexed him and stopped him in his tracks, curiosity ever the enticer.

"Noblien Troyelle?" asked the wind, even more shocked than the other. "How are you here?"

"Well," answered Noblien, pausing to assume some semblance of order to his response, then quickly giving up. "Where is here exactly?"

"Wait, wait, wait," repeated Downy, trying to sort his thoughts. "You asked how and not why."

"Why would not concern me. I'm a wind. How is distinctly in my interest."

"You know him?" said Sage, incredulous and slanting his gaze back and forth between the Puman and the ghostly wind, irked by the practical answers given under these circumstances and by the arrogance in the wind's answer to Downy.

Boreas cast his eyes upon Sage without moving. "'Tis an honor to meet the Veriha's last tear," and so saying, tucked his chin in a barely perceptible nod, his eyes stealing away from their subject, directed humbly to the ground.

At this moment, Sessile stepped forward, and to this, the North wind jerked back ferally. He had forgotten himself and now stood taller, defensive after believing he had let down his guard. Tullkaee began to open her mouth to speak in reverence for meeting an actual wind and sympathy for having seen him so startled. However, Leoness, in all her pride of banda-being, and too, unable to forbear her excitement any longer, greeted the wind with a sound most akin to a dragon's belch. Tullkaee was decidedly appalled and, in a look of mild exasperation, looked to Noblien for aide. But it was Sage who preempted everyone's further attempts to converse.

"I may have come to be from a tear, but I am more than my beginnings and prefer to be regarded as such."

"Pardons," replied the Northern Gale in dismay.

"The intent does not negate the result," said Sage.

Leaf scowled at the Coyotl's tone, recalling their own introductions, and made way to displace the electricity in the air by gently recalling its memory aloud. "Sage, I remember when Bristleton introduced us. I was LittleLeaf LeadTree . . . and Lastborn. I was filled with much unease when you knelt before me. Yet, I didn't meet you with hostility. I constrained my intolerance so that I might respect your intent."

The Coyotl's expression softened immediately. "How can I be so much older and so less wise?" He faced Boreas, sighing with clenched teeth, but earnestness was present in his demeanor. "We are well met by the North wind," he said, inclining his head. "I am Sage Lagacious, an elf of the Coyotls. The wee sensible vessel to my right is LeadLeaf, Treean of Alderelm. This is the noble huntress, Tullkaee of the Dauns, and brothers Sessile and Downy, Thessalians who have resided for a time in the kingdom of Seayr. Leoness, the banda afore you is like family to me. You know Noblien—a story I'm eager to hear."

The wind smiled thinly yet with sincerity. "He is an acquaintance of my daughter."

Sage's countenance brimmed with delight to hear this, so Noblien placed a hand on the Coyotl's shoulder and stepped in front of him. "Boreas, we are well met indeed. We were sent here by the inhabitants of Shee, although here was not the intention."

"Aha, and now there's the sense of how," he said, nodding approvingly.

"Aye, but more is the predicament we now face. Leaf is the carrier of the Sakatu." The gentle wind giant furrowed his woolly long brows as Noblien continued. "We were advised by the wise alchemist, Abi, of the grumbies to travel to the White Mountain for its protection."

"The elementals do not generally tangle in the delights or woes of worldly matters. Yet, we're aware of more sensitivities than any might imagine. You understand this as one who holds the love of a season within your heart. 'Tis still so?"

Noblien's posture wavered. 'Twas for none to miss, and the North wind stood supremely satisfied.

"Good," and so saying, Boreas mulled over the company. "The unseen is as real as the air." He inhaled deeply, and a steady breeze wrapped the company's senses. "One knows the air is there, breathes it to stay alive, yet cannot touch it. Do you understand this?"

Sage narrowed his eyes. "Unsurprisingly, a wind has just told us that the air is important."

Noblien missed what the Coyotl had just said but saw Tullkaee punch the side of his arm in no light measure. Noblien's jowls gritted. It was not difficult to imagine what he had just uttered. Sage was not an elf of exuding patience, and communicating with an elemental was to dive headlong into a thick syrup cloud from whence riddles are born, and patience necessitates. He saw Boreas sigh and recognized that the wind's gentle spirit would not reckon with such incivilities for long before abandoning them altogether.

Leaf spoke up. "You're telling us that the unseen is important." The Cold Giant beamed, ear to ear, his cheeks at once rosy as though a warmth had just washed over him. "But why are you telling us this?"

Pointing to the Sakatu woven around her neck and the length of one arm, he said, "Because that is the epitome of Nature's essence. Important, powerful . . . but unseen. All the elements that make up its essence and every aspect it holds are invisible. Whether it resides in another world or the confines of a remote abyss, its life force is unaffected."

"I don't understand," Leaf said.

"He's saying," Sage said, "that 'tis not necessary to find our way back."

The wind looked dissatisfied. "That's only part of what I'm trying to convey. This place is essentially the Earthen realm—a bud, as it were, of the world you know. The fibers between the two are thin, one being a mere extension of the other, a continuation of the layers upon which the elementals traverse. Mind you, there are no History Keepers of the Ancient Forests, or many other winds aside myself; however, I quite like it, as does Nivia Nivom," he said, glancing at Noblien.

Leaf looked up at the Puman, who had put his hand to his heart. "Niveus?" she asked softly.

"This place has its charm and mystery," Boreas continued. "I am in empathy over your plight. This is not where you had hoped to return, howbeit," he said, pausing and sighing while watching the Coyotl out of the corner of his eye, "what I'm trying to point out is that, well . . . there are many white mountains hither and thither. Oh, and the tallest you would ever want to blow across resides along those hinterlands to the southwest."

The meaning of what he said hit each of them hard, leaving little room to breathe. They had presumed that taking the Sakatu to a white mountain was by nature of reason, Alderelm. Now, they were trodden with the prospect that it may or may not be, and yet, so much importance stood on their decisions, dilemmas, and outcomes.

Sage itched under his skin. His Coyotl blood was boiling to protect the world he loved while serving the obligation that very source put to him. With eyes wild and green, he searched the elemental's face.

"Wind Spirit," he said, coughing out of a suppression of much more. "Might be when your tailwind sends you hie, 'tis with a message to the Ancient Forests that the Sakatu is safe and Emerus indeed lives. In that, there is much good to strengthen them."

Boreas knew the words did not match the grief expressed plainly within his spirit, and respect was manifested for this bedraggled elf standing before him. "I will," he replied, and with a tacit glance at Noblien, he gave a nod and evaporated into a whoosh of icy air.

The company stood silent, absorbing its shock and contemplating its fate. The land was open, even welcoming, and the sun was high, with few clouds to shroud its omniscience, but nevertheless, they felt the cold of isolation.

"Could you not open this eve to the Earthen realm as you did to Shee?" asked Downy.

The Coyotl's complexion soured as he mulled over the question, for he had been entertaining the same consideration. "Opening the gateway to Shee took a good part of me, yet it was merely a hidden doorway. An eve between worlds is altogether and wholly different."

"Hmmm," Downy mused. "But that gentleman described these two Earthen places as the same."

Sage huffed. "Passable by elementals, to be sure, but by an elf?"

"Not even with your kind's gift of shapeshifting?" asked Tullkae.

"Or the enchantments of the Faiyum?" added Noblien.

"The power of transformation," corrected the Coyotl, with a scoff released in the last word. "There's no shapeshifting involved. That'd be unnatural," and so saying, he pulled up his trousers and rubbed his chin. "I could try, but there's no known spot where simply transforming into my Coyotl form might affect an eve to another world. Otherwise, in Llaurantis, I'd have been unwittingly opening eves right and left." He paused, considering what he had just said. "Hmm, Coyotls would be a powerful nuisance," he laughed. "In Shee, Thai Mielle and I chased that fickle gateway, and upon finding it, we used our trick to open the door. And still, as I have said, that was no easy task."

Leaf remembered. She had felt the Trees supporting him and knew the precarious nature of the Coyotl's mental balance more than the others might themselves suspect. She was not eager to see him subject himself to the danger of it again, even to get home.

"Well," said Leaf, wanting to buffer the burden she was witnessing the group place on Sage and also wishing to contribute to the working out of their predicament. "What if we returned to our realm only to realize that the white mountain we seek was, in fact, here in this realm all along?"

Tullkae grunted a long sigh. "We think only of getting home and forget our task."

"Aye, LeadLeaf," said Sage, fiddling with the arm bracelet that bore the adamant given to him by Mohs back in Shee. "We think only of home without realizing our return could end up as a gross sidestep."

Noblien said little and studied everyone. "Tullkaee, what of your family?"

"I raised strong daughters."

The company's energy drew back before welling up in a unified strength under the weight of her reply, for she had given it without hesitation or a whiff of doubt. The noble Daun was not resigned; she was committed.

"So, our task," said Downy, "is not finding our way home but taking the article she carries—"

"The Sakatu," said Noblien.

The Thessalian took the correction with a curt nod. "Taking the Sakatu to a white mountain. But how are we to know which white mountain and, back to the first issue, whether or not 'tis here?"

"I think I know," said Leaf, raising her head to show the veins of green twine lace in curls up under her chin and behind her ears. She then pulled up a sleeve and revealed her arm. The company was stunned.

"This is a significant change," said Sage in a graveled whisper, "in a short time."

"I feel as though I'm becoming a part of it."

"What does this mean?" asked Sessile, reaching to touch her arm.

"I don't know," Leaf answered, the Sakatu's sinews tickling under his petting.

Sessile leaned back on his heels, thinking. "When I touch it, I smell horses," and so saying, he walked off toward the southwest.

Leaf felt her collarbone, that heart of the World Tree Seed, and intuition stepped her off behind the sweet ostler. Noblien hoped his sense of danger could be depended upon in this realm. For now, the world was serene, naught to mark itself to his alarm. So, he and the others began to follow, except for Sage. He eyed the foreign, yet familiar horizon lined with crimson beyond the skeletal outlines of distant Trees and looked to Leoness.

"I'll be above," he called out, running to the honking banda who, after a breath-holding start, turned her gangly run into flight.

Noblien eyed them out. The pair were at ease in the upper currents, and he nodded with satisfaction. The group had eyes in the sky. *This is good*, he thought, watching them shrink into the distant sky.

❧ Chapter 22 ❧

Timpernickels and polka dots,
Parsel startles and wimsalwats
Are a turnanillies favorite desserts.

—Montephoebius, the Ibus, tells a story to Mohs, a faerie born from a
shooting star, about turnanillies, the creators of sweet dreams

Marching behind Sessile's unfaltering footfalls, the company traveled
across the youngling realm for the length of the day. Basins of
wildflowers and trickling springs gave way to an arboreal scape of
mountain foothills that seemed to welcome them with an overbrimming
joy of scent and color and, in this way, beckoned them further forward.
The glow of the mountain range that loomed behind this plush scene of
wonderment was so vast across the entire horizon that everyone mistook
it for a skyline of woolly clouds. The realization that the distant view was
instead a wide breadth of ever-rising alpine peaks induced a long groan
from Tullkaee, who thought it of no great luck that their tracks must
always continue uphill. So far, at least, the incline had been subtle, and

for that, she was grateful. Still, she bemoaned their plight, for however slight their current ascension, those distant mountains were monsters.

The day continued to reveal itself graciously with a sweet stillness, and the company was thus able to absorb the new realm with the awe and curiosity of younglings newly exploring. The scents were sweetly aromatic and marked with subtly rich terpenes, earthy and full. The fragrance instilled a secure delight, akin to a sylph's first giggle on discovering the air streams, especially Tilnook, the warm upper-river current of gentle swiftness. The Ancient Trees always reveled in reaching a height where that meandering force could kiss their crowns. Such was the appeal of this new land, and when a group of delicately limbed herbivores strode into view, 'twas yet another charming facet of the land born out.

The spotted, short-horned creatures walked away a short distance upon seeing the company, heads alert and curious. Smelling the air, they returned cautiously to their foraging grounds, their muzzles rapidly tearing away the patches of surrounding greens. Sessile crouched to observe them, intuitively aware that his great height might be threatening. Leaf was awed at his inherent ability to understand creatures of the wild.

A shadow passed overhead, and gazing skyward, Leaf beheld Leoness and Sage scouring the upper currents and lowering for a nearby landing. The Coyotl chose a small distance away, but the clamor of wings, honking, and shouts from the elf set the small group of foragers to rummage elsewhere.

As Sage approached the group, Leaf marveled at his hair, wild and fluffed, curled spindles flailing in all directions. She smiled. He had brought the winds down with him. His ever-expansive smile, more crooked than usual, greeted the company with his typical puckish swagger.

"Sessile, are those creatures the horses we search for?"

The gentle giant of a man replied with a sweetly innocent chortle, unaware of the elf's jesting. "Those aren't horses."

Sage had meant naught but a lighthearted jest, but upon realizing that Sessile translated all communications in the most literal sense, he grimaced at his error and smiled tenderly. "Sessile, you are a good man."

The Coyotl then pivoted to where he had seen Noblien standing when he and Leoness descended. The Puman had been making wide circles around the company as they progressed that day, and now he stood quite a way to the east of everyone. The cautious nature of Noblien's manner was typical for the Puman elves. Sage reckoned his solemn mien might cast its own shadow, protracted and even more portentous. He grinned at his imagination and then smiled fully upon recalling how methodically Flumen had also come across as downcast. Father and son were very much alike, and he laughed outright as he cobbled more memories together; they were good for the first time in a long time.

As Sage headed over to him, the corner of the Puman's mouth curled inwards, and he tilted his head so that he could gaze at the Coyotl directly, yet askew. *'Tis a setup*, Sage thought. He had figured out most of Noblien's mannerisms and habits, and this particular posturing was enlisted when readying a rebuke.

"You don't run to greet my return?" said Sage, grinning.

A smile of sorts extended across Noblien's mouth, yet further indulgence to the Coyotl's wisecrack was not offered. "Well?" he asked in eager impatience. "What did you see?"

"Those peaks are unlike any I've encountered," Sage replied. "They're in large part glossed with shale, in crumpling heaps. Lawks, Thai Mielle, it would not seem meet for the World Tree Seed, except," and so saying, he lowered his voice, "they're supremely beautiful."

"Is there a white mountain among them?"

Sage rubbed his forehead. "Each and every mountain is of itself a white mountain. We've only got to pick one. From the mightiest to the smallest, their brilliance extends from the feldspar and quartz that cover them and radiate as if a world of miniature stars is held within them. Yet for all this, which would otherwise sound pleasing, there's little soil to provide for life."

Noblien shifted his weight and looked away. "It's becoming a part of her. Our time is running short."

"Mmm," Sage replied. "I'm see."

"I do not have answers, but Leadleaf is alive, and the Sakatu is safe," said Tullkaee, having approached to stand by their sides and having spoken with such resolve as to have awoken the two elves from a dream. "Our path is forward."

Noblien groaned with a reluctant nod as Downy and Sessile joined them.

"Leoness can take us one by one into the new wilderness of our fate," said Sage.

Sessile was overjoyed upon hearing this and clapped, looking at his brother excitedly. Downy, however, scowled, though he tried to disguise his discomfort with the posturing of one weighing the matter seriously. Several times, he started to speak and halted before trying again.

"What happens," Downy said at last, "when the Sakatu is placed upon the mountain?"

"None know," said Noblien, casting his keen eyes out toward Leaf, who was still some distance away, enjoying the views and in no rush for the day to take on any burdens.

The elf felt a change, a shift in the energy that streamed through the plane of this new dimensional space. Here was a dram of solace brought, for he now knew the senses of his Puman kind remained within this alternate world just beyond the eves. Yet, he was also alerted as to why they pressed him, and in this regard, his foremost attention concentrated more carefully on the Treean.

"LittleLeaf," he called, an audible inhale whistling into his lungs akin to a gasp yet deeper and fraught with more worry than shock or fear. "Are you ...?" And before finishing the inquiry, he was sprinting to her side, much to the shock of the rest.

The horror unfolding was unfathomable, yet it exposed the undeniable truth, and time stood still, searing the moment into the group's consciousness. The young Treean stood, an incipient discomfiture ornamented in the posture, a teetering where her expression cast such a look of fear toward the group as to be recognized forthwith as an unspoken call for help. She was falling and not reacting to catch or block the descent, for her legs had transformed into an umber of sere bark, deeply furrowed and creased, immovable.

Since first meeting the dear Treean, the Fierce-Eyed Elf had always stayed close by, even though he felt powerless to stop this coming cataclysm. And now, he stood maddeningly too far away. He could not let her fall; he would not allow her to fall.

Leaf watched Noblien run toward her. His face was thin and stretched. She could see every nuanced detail of his expression, even the capillaries straining under the whites of his eyes. She hurt to see it, even as she was consumed with panic, for she battled to command her implacably immobile limbs. Nevertheless, his arms caught her in a cradle before the ground met her descent.

The subsequent tinge in the air held the straightforward yet numinous power of the will. For on random and mysterious occasions, the most indomitable intents can succeed in pressing the ethers of the universe to bend their course.

"Leaf," whispered Noblien, wiping away one of her tears and surveying her condition. "Oh, dear Leaf."

Leaf's mental wherewithal was strangely hyper-focused. She studied his hair, every strand of red individually highlighting the shadows of his war knives, whose long, curved hilts peeked from underneath his quiver. She surmised they were made of walnut, smooth and well-worn by his grasp. She took a reflexive and unsteady inhale as if startled. Her mind was opening to such unique intrigue.

Noblien's eyes searched hers as he spoke to Sage in the Elvish tongue, his voice graveled and rasping.

"Nay," replied Sage, "You go with her—trust in Leoness. She is steadfast. We'll not be long to your side."

"You're going to fly her?" Downy was at once disbelieving and appalled. "You don't even know where the white mountain is! What are you doing?"

Neither elf acknowledged the Thessalian's apprehensions. Although his misgivings were for a good cause, the Puman was too preoccupied to ascertain whether any of the group was speaking and focus on lip-reading. As for the Coyotl, he was also too overwhelmed to pause on further deliberations. The moment was now, for better or worse; there was no more time for other considerations. To pause in action was to succumb to the fear of the present moment, and he would not cave to that emotion today, not while the Treean depended on them. He could hear Bristleton's voice:

"We trust our most sacred gift to you."

Sage called to Leoness, who trotted over wide-eyed and mildly hesitant. Everyone's demeanor reeked of urgency, and her concern was mixed with confusion. Sage stroked her neck, laying his forehead on her mane. He spoke words the others could not hear. She blinked slowly, a huffling sound burbling from deep within her chest. He patted her and stepped away to hold Leaf as Noblien climbed on.

"Can she bend her legs?" Tullkaee asked.

Noblien flinched.

"They must be yet a little pliable," replied Sage. "Trees bend in the wind or break."

Noblien's eyes burned at these words. "Not their trunks."

"The young Tree trunks most certainly do," said Sage. "Trust me."

Tullkaee helped lift her into Noblien's arms. She was heavier, their little whiff of air was much heavier, and under the astonishment, their eyes widened. Leaf moaned. It was the first sound she had made. Sessile cried to hear it, stomping and shaking his hands.

"Easy, brother," Downy said.

"Do you have her?" asked Tullkaee, looking desperately at Noblien.

"Aye," he nodded, feeling the bulk of Leoness build up under him.

Leaf squeezed her hand around Noblien's arm, and in a simultaneous response, Noblien tightened his legs for Leoness to fly. The timid banda danced in place and arched her wings.

"Go, odd girl," said Sage under his breath, and she alighted with a gentle, nearly apathetic whispered whoosh.

Noblien relaxed under the realization that the banda, while land-awkward, was made of tamed power and purposeful gentleness within the ethers. The rhythmic swaying of her long wing beats was soothing and soft. She did not swing and veer or thrash and dart; she glided and soared as she mounted over the layers of air as if she were an element of the wind herself. She was the essence of majesty upon the heavens—a noble lioness of the welkin blue.

As the upper currents greeted the fronds and branched brambles of Leaf's hair, the Treean began to sense a memory, still faint, tug at her. It was like a reminiscence tapping upon the edges of her consciousness, and in this way, it felt peculiar, even given the current circumstances. More recollections clamored for her awareness. And as Leoness sailed, immeasurable memories washed over her, complementing each other like harmonies intertwined around a melody. She wondered if she was dreaming as voices filled her head. The utterances rose and fell with organized chaos, adding rich layers to the rush of mental images bombarding her perceptions.

One voice was distantly familiar above the rest. It carried a broadening melancholy, its fibers heavy and slow, determined and reverberating, and every story it laid out was with bellowing intonations. Leaf concentrated, focused on her mental sundial to spark the recognition she itched for. She strained to hear more, called for clarity, and finally grasped it. Miriam! These were the expressions of Alderelm relaying the annals of history.

◄◊ ◆ ◊►

In the distance, the mountains looked like any range distantly surveyed, grand and beautiful. Yet now, as they drew closer, their mammoth proportions humbled the elf who had in his long life explored all of Earth's mountains, his stalking Puman keenness drawn to them. However, those were but foothills next to these white-rock castles.

"Aelin-lumen," he said in marvel.

Rummaging through his spirit for intuition, self-doubt ever the shade of such insight, he scanned for a location to land. He leaned to the left, and Leoness, feeling the shift in his weight, angled the direction of their flight accordingly. She glided smoothly, gentle in her adjustments, and with grace and softness in her wing strokes and altitude adjustments. Noblien was grateful for this.

On the side of one of the mountains at about three-quarters of its great height was a half-moon indentation surrounded by some scant foliage—plants and shrubs. The mountain of this unique mark stood as high as the others but would assuredly require more steps to traverse, for it was rounded rather than angular. This aspect created the optical illusion of it being smaller. Noblien took further note of its advanced eastward position. He smiled. She was older than the others, and her neighbors would cast no long shadows over her reverence. The overall effect further disguised the peak's prominence, which intrigued him.

"Leaf, I believe this is the Sakatu's mountain."

Alderelm

Leaf perceived Noblien's voice very distantly. She fought to focus on his words, but she was experiencing all the world that ever was simultaneously, for the Sakatu's essence was melding into hers. It was no small struggle to focus on the present while simultaneously sustaining history's memories. For the Ancient Ones rode the past and present at once, and the Sakatu was their embodiment now infused into her very being. Moreover, the sacred, white-barked Trees that the Sakatu represented in totality did not simply hold unemotional historical narratives. Instead, they carved the intricacies of the living experience and the corresponding emotions into the memory of their deep, barked grooves. Hence, Leaf demonstrated enormous strength in turning even a vague ear to Noblien, for she absorbed so much transformative knowledge at that moment.

Revelations were revealed before her mind's eye; she reviewed the day of her birth, the day the Sakatu was given to Alderelm for safekeeping. This coincidence did not go unnoticed by the elders, who decided that the two had been drawn together for a purpose. This is why Leaf had been named LittleLeaf of the LeadTree, the Sakatu's keeper. They could not know that Leaf would be their Lastborn or that the Sakatu, even dormant, retained awareness. Indeed, while the seed's perceptions were sluggish, they were also visceral and thus spilled into Leaf's dreams. The two were connected from the beginning; a chimera formed from their spirits that intertwined long ago, and the physical attributes of their bond manifested last. Leaf recognized it all now; even her wanderlust, so at odds for a Treean, had been partly driven by the yearnings of memories she could not retrieve or recall. Moreover, when the Sakatu felt the effects of Leaf's tortured submersion into the waters of the Lethe, it sensed that the world was in danger, for Leaf was its world. And not seeing her separate from itself, it did begin to grow.

❦ ✦ ❧

To the crescent contour of the fractured mountainside did Noblien, through the whirling tranquility of the Elvish speech, convey his intention to the eager banda who yawped in reply. Descending in soft spirals, Leoness cut through the currents like silk. Noblien spoke to her with gratitude until she alighted next to a wind-dwarfed conifer. There, she circled, pattering her clawed feet until Noblien's patient use of the Elvish tongue of old soothed her apprehensive excitement.

"Well done, my grand Leoness, Goddess of the Thermals," he said, lifting his right leg over her thrumming feathered mane to slide off her left side, Leaf in his arms. "Well done indeed."

"Oh, Leaf," said Noblien, setting her down on the ground and wrapping her in his cross scarf, that long, linen cloth tied around his waist and chest. "What do you think of this little mountain?"

"Good," she whispered, nodding.

Noblien raised his eyebrows. "Well met, my dear LittleLeaf. 'Tis good to hear your voice again."

She smiled. "Stony, rough as it sounds?"

"Aye. 'Tis still the stars' glitter to me," he replied, enticing a smile from her. "How do you feel?"

"Strange, but right. I hear every story that the Sakatu holds. I've even heard Miriam."

Noblien looked with sadness, and Leaf, seeing this, shook her head. "I don't know what will happen, but I wouldn't change this path. Trust me when I say this. Do not pity me. I'm freer than when I hungered for the wilds that exploration satiates. I see the world through the long-stemmed hearts of the Old Woods. I can feel their experiences. And I can hear the Trees speak. Noblien, I've tasted, smelled, seen, felt, and heard the realities of Earth's plights as well as her most beautiful successes and greatest loves. So do not pity me."

"All right," he said, smiling. "You are not pitied. Let me send Leoness for the others."

Noblien turned toward the gentle banda, a small smile resting within the corner of his mouth, its favorite place to hide. Leoness was honking gracelessly at Eyas, who was now flitting and jinking, joyfully investigating the new surroundings.

"Leoness," he said, as her head craned toward him with wrapped adoration. "You are a most gallant and noble creature. Thank you," and so saying, the Fierce-Eyed Elf placed his hand over his heart and bowed. She nudged him, and he held her face in his hands. The pupils of her gold eyes constricted as she cocked her head and croaked. Eyas dove down around her head, landing neatly on Noblien's shoulder. He chuckled softly. "Aye, you've a right to be proud. Bring the others, dearest Baroness of the Cloud Seas, and you will be rewarded with much gratitude."

She skipped awkwardly to the side, arched her wings, and leaped into the ethers, becoming at once an elegance of Nature again. Noblien marveled as he watched her go. She was a kind, magical creature who oscillated between being the epitome of grace and the embodiment of ungainliness. In both cases, he considered her a delightful gem.

❧ ◆ ☙

One by one, the group was again joined and set camp around the Treean.

"Leaf!" cried Sessile. "We're close ta the herd!"

"Knave brother," replied Downy. "After flying on that fantastic, feathered beast, you're still on about the Haevonen?"

"Why do you both speak so differently?" asked Sage.

Downy's countenance turned ashen as though a grey gauze had been draped over it. "We were raised apart. I was shored away while Sessile was apprenticed as an ostler. Our parents thought it best, given his childlike fortitude. I returned to the shores of Llaurantis to find him."

"Ah, so this is how you learned the ways of the Thessalian and met your mad king," said Sage. "Not a common story."

Downy's aura instantly lit up, and the noble cast of his mien brightened. "All true, save he is no longer my king. Just another lost fool."

"A dangerous one," added Tullkaee.

"Indeed," said Noblien.

And though all agreed, no hostility was directed at Downy. Everyone was experiencing a shared understanding in all their life's journeys, for better or worse, which ultimately brought them together. Noblien reflected on this as he watched the capable soldier, an extremely flawed man in his opinion, tenderly adjust the cowl around his brother's head. This juxtaposition of seemingly contradictory personal attributes gave him much pause and induced a quiet sigh.

Tullkaee lit her pipe, the initial glimmer fading into the warm scents of white sage and bearberry. Smiles spread across the group, and they all conversed. There was a strange beauty to their being brought together as one. The company felt inexplicably secure on this faraway mountainside, and the late afternoon hours passed in shared stories, teasing, and relative ease, for the Sakatu was safe. However, their spirits rested on the edge of a precipice, and each of them, in one turn or another, turned a nonchalant eye toward their Treean to study her changes.

Her eyes had a near-unblinking gaze, the irises being stretched and drawn leaflike in serrated edges, although the green vibrancy remained unchanged. Her shoulders bore the look of ridged bark made in plates of irregular shape. The cinnamon color was vibrant, folded inwards along her sternum toward her heart. Twines grew from her clavicles and intertwined behind her ears, thus joining the nettle-twigs of her locks permanently bound into mottled plaits that seemed to serve as fern fodder. She had evolved into a strikingly grown presence; less childlike was her demeanor, a calmness flowing outwards like the full moon's reflection on a Forest lake. She had accepted her fate and done so with the fortitude of grace. The beauty radiating from her was an awe-inspiring tidal force of simple aspects, such as the flower buds pursing their petal kisses around her head. The Sakatu and Leaf were stronger and made whole together; the others sensed what they could not comprehend and were lulled to sleep under the security the pair exuded.

Throughout the rest of the night, Leaf rested peacefully but did not sleep and watched as the dawn began to unfold across the low sky, waking the Earth with rose-pink kisses. It was lovely. Peaceful. Quiet. Unthinkingly, she ran her finger over the Sakatu, which vibrated in subtle hums. She contemplated the setting stars, their journeys unseen, yet their paths still in motion.

Her thoughts jolted when Sage's sleeping breath became sharp and coarse. She turned to gaze at him, her eyes narrowing. He was sitting upright with clenched fists, staring forward, his gaze empty. She tilted her head, studying him with more concern, alarm beginning to well within her.

"Sage," she whispered.

She wanted to scoot closer to him and look up under those brown, unkempt locks to pull him away from what held him so unnaturally. Yet, move she could not. She glowered at her legs or at what had been her legs. They were becoming one in grooved bark Wood. Fascination at her transformation smacked her, but then frustration took the reins.

"Sage," she whispered again. "Come back."

He did not respond. He had fallen into the realm of his mind, catatonic to this world, alone in the grief his long life had accumulated, and she could not reach him. Noblien approached her from behind, and she was startled when he touched her shoulder.

"When will he come around?" she asked.

Noblien did not see her speak and so did not answer. Realizing this, the barest smile crossed her face like the susurration of a breeze. She reached for his hand as he stepped around to face her.

"Elves are the most mysterious creatures," she whispered distantly. "How did you know? Were you even asleep?"

"You, my dear Tree Goddess," Noblien said, his silver-grey eyes piercing her spirit, "can now understand the elven ways," and so saying, he tilted his head and paused. "Close your eyes and follow my breath. Travel with me in elven sleep."

Colors inundated her vision, dizzying in their vibrancy and breadth, where patterns shaped into a cool warmness. Concentrating, she realized that the mirage of color was Noblien. Pieces of his hair flowed forward as the tint-winds pressed their backs. The color blooms of heather and flax emanated as a representation of his personage.

"Relax," he said, disturbing the hues tiding around them.

"Sage is not relaxed," she replied, with a brushstroke of innocence in her inflection.

"Humph, you can see why this is an issue," he pointed out. "Now, my dear LittleLeaf, relax into the difference afore you. Let go of all you think you know, of your perceptions of how the world is supposed to be. You are now one of the History Keepers, and there are some events for which there are no words to convey their meaning. Feel their reality."

A rainbow of color churned, bubbling into a shape, the shape forming a sound, the sound tracing an image for the benefit of her mind. Yet alas, clarity stayed out of her reach.

"If this is elven sleep, I understand why Sage gets stuck."

"When one is familiar with a way of life, one experiences more clarity within it with less effort," he replied between tight lips. "Waking dreams are simply different for you, that is all. For Sage, well, he travels over that horizon. I have tried to follow, to help him from slipping in these ways, and have succeeded twice, but tonight, I could not follow. He's on his own."

Leaf strained her eyes over the orange thickness that Noblien described as the horizon and sighed. Defeat tapped her shoulder, but she shrugged it off. And as the others slowly awakened, Leaf persisted, both for Sage and for the knowledge that fed her.

Ellis McCauley

WHITE SAGE

White Sage. 1. A small shrub with whitish, smooth, evergreen leaves that grow with numerous basal branches in dense clusters and have a resinous aroma. Often used in pipeweed. *2.* Recent Age. Salvia apiana is an evergreen perennial shrub native to the southwestern United States and northwestern Mexico consisting of whitish evergreen leaves thickly covered in hairs that trigger oil glands; when rubbed, oils and resins are released, producing a strong aroma. Flowers are white to pale lavender growing on a flower stalk. This plant is very sacred to many Native Americans who use it to burn (for cleansing and purifying the air) in sacred Native American ceremonies and who have asked non-Natives to refrain from its usage due to the potential for overharvesting.

BEARBERRY

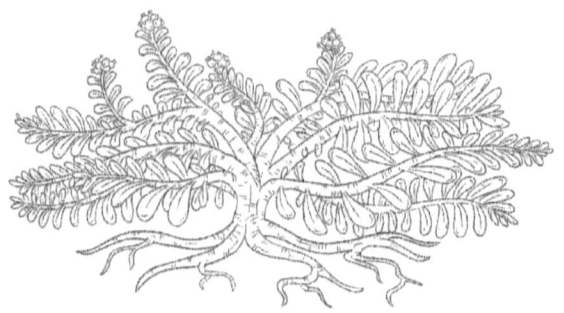

Bearberry. 1. *Low-lying evergreen plant with red berries and lantern-shaped pink-red flowers, used as a component in pipeweed by the Dauns called kinnikinnick and for making yellow dye.* **2.** *Recent Age. Identical to the physical description above. Of the genus Arctostaphylos, a circumboreal species of the subarctic Northern Hemisphere, used by the Blackfeet Nation as food and as a traditional medicinal, smoking mix (kinnikinnick), and dye by the First Nations.*

❧ Chapter 23 ❧

Soar unseen and silent like the air.

—Mother Owl to her owlets

The color of her gold-green eyes was faded beneath the mist clouds of long life. Despite this, they twinkled when she watched her elven babe cub. She was proud, especially of her youngling, who recoiled at the idea of her transition.

Sadly, Nature does not comprehend desires that are against the processes of life. There is no malice in her toils. She is a force. Whether Nature appears through life and beauty or death and destruction, each is the same to her. Nature is evolution, rejuvenation, and continuation, even when ugly, painful, and sad. We have only to keep up with her and take in the surreal beauty when it is brought.

And so, with the Coyotl elf by her side, she took her last inhale, striated and slow, her eyes ne'er deviating from his, peace apparent in her passing.

"I'm dreaming," whispered Sage, laying his head on her ribs.

Her fur smelled of summer earth—he would remember the scent

forever—and felt both soft and wiry, already losing the warmth of her body.

"Come back," he whispered, pressing his fingers deep into her coat, begging the spark of life to return.

A yip-yowl brought his head to alertness. He searched the landscape for the familiar call, but it was thereafter quiet.

Long and plaintively, he replied, his yip-yowl modulating in heartbreaking frequency and amplitude. "Woo-oo-woooo."

'Twas received with a corresponding answer more distant than before, and he wondered why the coyote retreated and whether distress chased its heels. He took a step to follow the call yet hesitated to look back at his mother; her body was no longer there. For a moment, he stood confused. His arms hung limply, and two of his fingers twitched. Yet this time, when another yip-yowl tore through the air, he hurtled after it.

To see Sage run was often to see two figures at once, for he rarely distinguished his transformational intention toward either elf or coyote. He was the oldest Coyotl and, as such, the rawest link between the two families. According to him, one kin did not serve the other; thus, he preferred a natural blending of the two.

The coyote calls led him to the banks of Beebark Creek. He knew the creek at once by its aroma. The cold water was crisp and tart with vanilla-earth scents, lined by resins of rock-baked algae and the woody balsams of shoreline flora. Memories washed over him; he stood at the basal roots of Alderelm's White Mountain, where he had first met Knowlton Hophornbeam, Ole Ironwood himself. To his fore, a clunking sound bit at his ear.

Chink-a-chank.

He reached for Timbriel, half forgetting that weaponry did not exist in the elven dreamscapes and was thus shocked when his reflexive instinct produced what was now coldly pressed into his palm. Confused, he swallowed hard, for he no longer knew what was real.

Fixedly, he stared at the blade. Knowlton's heritage sang out from within it while the engravings simultaneously caught and cast the surrounding light. Delving deeper into the blade's ensorcelled illuminations, the light of Timbrothiel revealed itself in the clustered brushwork of artisan glimmerings. The living lucency of a dying star obtained from the dragon that protected it did not suffer fools lightly.

The Coyotl's face cracked with a sidelong smirk, crooked and rueful. He found himself undecided as to whether he was now at his best or worst self, and he began twisting the blade in quick, successive hand twirls, fidgety in conflicted thoughts. He was at the foothill of Alderelm. How or why he had arrived was a vagary.

Chink-a-chank.

"That sound," he said, his irritation frustrating his thoughts. "Master yourself, you daft Coyotl," he murmured, closing the windows to his spirit and channeling his cognition toward the peaceful sounds of the Fignauts of Waterloo.

So often, those beautiful birds soothed his abysmal mind. He remembered them from his youth. Their wails and yodeling reiterations were a lullaby to all the creatures within earshot. He had enlisted this memory for longer than he could recall so his restless mind might be soothed of its aching memories. And now, he did so again, the hypnotic transference of peace to the body and mind for the spirit's wellbeing.

Having marshaled the better part of himself, he hurried to investigate the unnatural sounds emanating from his adopted Woodland when he was stung by a tingling from one of the tattoos on his hand. He looked down and beheld the source of his Faiyum powers, lighting not one symbol but two, then three. He pulled up his sleeve as tattoo after tattoo, those tracings of the Writs of Brighid impressed upon his babe skin by the leaves of the Tree of Cassen, awakened. He had ne'er experienced their magic in multitudes and stood at a loss.

Chink-a-chank.

His head shot up. The unnatural sound was unsettling. He crouched, blade in hand, and stepped forward with cautious boldness. Around Ponderosa and between Spruce, he discovered what he could not have imagined. While fascination feuded with disgust, the elf slowly lowered himself and blended with his surroundings to observe two Gauss aiding another whose limbs were bound in chains. He covered his nose to protect his senses as he watched the creatures take a few steps, halt, and strike the chains in futile attempts to free their companion. However, brute force was not enough to puzzle out their dilemma, so they walked and halted, struggled and struck. Sage's confusion overwhelmed him; his anger boiled, and his thoughts itched. Here was an absurdity poised to dismantle what little solidity remained to support his sanity. This could not be—the abominable fiends worked together.

Charging in a wellspring of angry grief, Sage screamed, "You cannot be here!"

He drew his sword high; he would cut the air in a whisper and smite the beasts to pieces gladly and with glee. He swung hard as one grunted in distress, its impressive bulk standing in intimidation. Sage halted and blinked. His mouth screwed up to the corner, his face becoming a contortion of bewildered repugnance.

"What are you doing? Fight!" he said. "Fight!"

Yet they only stood with vacuous expressions, blinking, save the one in a guarding posture. Impassively, it stared back at Sage, save for a glint reflected in one pupil, a sparkle that told of more goings-on within its ample skull than might be suspected of such a wretched creature. This gave the elf a strange unease. Sage squinted back at it. And while all his curiosity swelled, so did his unfathomable rage. He looked at the Gauss-in-chains, the suffering it endured, and he looked up at the switchbacks toward Alderelm. Screaming, he slashed at a sprawling sumac. He slashed and slashed for all his life's anguish. Slashed for the loss of his family, for the loss of the Veriha, for Alderelm, and for the Treeans . . . for Leaf. And turning back toward the Gauss with little warning, he rushed upon them. The guarding Gauss stood yet again against him, grasping his arm and holding it from following through with its hatchet work. And the instant the Gauss touched him, Sage froze, for a familiar tingling began to trickle through his body. His face curdling, he twisted and flicked his arm from the Gauss hold.

"Not you! She could not choose you."

Yet a flicker and a wisp of light upon the Gauss's finger told the story as disgust salted with betrayed anger pushed the elf in a stumbling backstep. The tattoo traced around and up the Gauss's index finger. Upon beholding it, the creature hollered in panic, flinging its finger as though the tattoo could be flicked away. Sage watched, and a growing pity for the beast brought the better part of his senses, once again, under his control.

"Nay, nay," Sage said, grabbing hold of the Gauss's arm firmly but with patience that surprised even himself. "Easy now. That there," and so saying, he pointed to the fresh tattoo, the Gauss's limacine eyes following, "is naught to fear. There's honor in it. You're one of the Faiyum now, unbelievably. But you don't understand what I'm saying, do you? Lawks, I must still be dreaming."

The Gauss stared at him, smacked its gums together, and released a heartbreaking sigh of resignation. Sage sighed, too. Eyeing the Gauss-in-chains, he approached with the silver tongue of elven reassurances. Timbriel's inner light pulsated under Sage's intention, brightening with each step. The chained brute widened its eyes, but it did not move to defend itself, nor did its companions move to the creature's defense. They risked their lives, hoping the elf's intentions had been deterred.

With one swoop-hack of agitated determination, the chains were broken. The bitter clang rang hollowly in the air. Released, the Gauss-in-chains huffed repeatedly, the other two joining the odd display. At no time in his long life had he seen Gauss act in such ways. He was conflicted and emotionally exhausted, his head dizzy with the ever-creeping submersion of his sanity; madness preferred to wedge its way against his better faculties under states of exhaustion like this. One day, he knew he would not be able to hold it off. Perhaps this would be the day.

Suppressing the thought, he ran away from the creatures and up the switchbacks toward Alderelm. The twinflowers, which had at all other times lit the paths in plenty, were now sparsely laid, and those were dulled. The Forest smelled of smoke and ash. And it was hauntingly quiet. Few were the chirps of birds, quiet were the buzzing of insects, and lacking were the melodies of flutes. But more than all the surrounding travesties was the absence of the towering white trunks growing toward the highest reaches of the sky. The Ancient Ones were toppled, crushed against the earth's soil, and turned up on their sides, their roots spreading unnaturally in the air. The white-barked mountain of Alderelm was gone.

Outlined figures of Treean form remained inlaid within the bark of many a sacred trunk. 'Twas a horrifying scene that the elf could not acknowledge in the processes of his mind. Keeping a brisk pace, he bent his eyes downward to avoid the sight of further heartbreak. Straight to the Tarn of Lumen, he strode, an old skip and limp reappearing in his gait. At last, by her side, he sat, lightly stirring the waters with his fingertips. To this, her reflections revealed the evils that had transpired—the Treeans had fought bravely, the Hawken elves ne'er leaving their sides.

'Twas the Ancient Ones who had taken it upon themselves to enlist a primeval magic, the magic of the Forest's pith itself, one that had given them their capacity for song and made them the History Keepers. This magic of old took the Trees' specialness and, with it, tilled the soil with the evils that assaulted them. Yet it also turned their roots upward toward the sky and their beloved Treeans into their Wood rings.

The magic of the Forest was gone.

The Sacred Ones had passed all they ever were on to LittleLeaf of the LeadTrees and returned their energies to Mother Nature. It was the purest of sacrifices.

As the visions dimmed, Sage cupped the Lumen's liquid ethers into his hands and watched as it ran through his fingers. He was devastated, and many of his tears blended into the water's confines. He stared, unfocused, until a cloud haze of color began to swirl. Then he positioned himself more upright, cocked his head, and watched in mystified incertitude as the likeness of a buffalo wisped together in a vision of watery reflections.

A loud crack in the foliage caused him to lift his head, although his eyes stayed their focus on the crystalline illumination for longer than one may suppose a battle-worn elf might abide for caution's sake. When he did turn, half his heart in the action, he beheld the three Gauss from the base of the Forest. Their heaving forms stared at him with an expression of dry curiosity, and at their side was a detail that he had heretofore not noticed—a cairn resting before one of the Ancient One's upturned root crowns. Sage's mind buzzed as he strode over to take a closer look, the Gauss marked out by the Faiyum's sigil grunting upon his approach.

"You did this?" Sage asked, scratching his head, marveling at the cairn's impossible balance of positions and slowly noticing that there were stone structures of seemingly impossible placement precariously adorning other upturned remnants of the Ancient Trees.

The Gauss bared its teeth and flapped its lips before raising its calloused mauler and unfurling a carefully pressed clover. Sage gaped at the dried petals so neatly pressed in perfection and wondered how the coarseness of such brutish, large hands held a flora of such delicacy so gingerly.

The Gauss now sniffed the air and curled its upper lip under its nostril. The Coyotl did not know what purpose that gesture served. Yet, as the creature folded the clover back within the dirty, bare threads of its encasement and placed it steadily within his palm, Sage comprehended and nodded in appreciation of so fine a gift, even while grappling against the instinct to recoil.

Sage could read the windows of the spirit as intuitively as he could feel a coming change in the weather. And while he did not consider himself an expert in many skills, despite his bravado to the contrary, he knew he could uniquely reach across the thresholds of an individual's psyche to interpret their deepest core. An individual's inner light was always unique, either hiding or bold, flickering brilliantly or shyly glimmering. There was no end to a spirit's inner expression, but that he could identify its essence, he felt certain.

So it was that the Coyotl now looked past the rheumy and sagging features of this creature of endless revelations and into the flecks and aberrations of its eyes for the hint that might explain why the Writs of Brighid had marked it as one of the Faiyum. And there, in the farthest corner, steady and unwavering, was an undecorated stream of character, neither bright nor dull, unhindered by ego. Swiftly, Sage grabbed the Gauss's broad hand and traced his fingers carefully around the lines of the creature's newly marked sigil, which meant kindred.

"Vell no 'ta bur'nighn," Sage said.

The Gauss flapped its lips and revealed its blunted, unkempt teeth, which showed the tannins of age. Yet Sage did not turn away. Snorting, the Gauss pawed the ground, circled, and sat down, moving its jaw in apparent contentment akin to chewing cud.

Sage contemplated the mirrors of the mind. His fists tightened as he shut his eyes. He could remember when he had been a mere thought within a tear. Yet he strained to recall the reason behind a singular pain that stayed pinned behind memory's capsule. He could almost grasp the memory that scratched to get out, and as images flooded, flashing in his mind's eye, he finally recalled it: He had not been the only teardrop. The Wonder had entrusted two wayward teardrops to the destiny of the future Earth.

Whispers of the Veriha were beyond the comprehension of life in the Earthen realm, save the elementals. Still, Sage grasped an inkling of a fragment of the Wonder's words at this moment, and when he reopened the windows to his spirit, they were as grey as a stormy summer sky.

"Sage!" Leaf's voice echoed.

The Coyotl searched for the anchor of his purpose. "LeadLeaf?"

SUMAC

Sumac. 1. A large, feathery, deciduous shrub with pinnately compound leaves and sharp-toothed leaflets. Its bright-red fruits grow in clusters and are used as a tea throughout Llaurantis. The roots are steeped in water and used for skin ailments. Its roots also make a lustrous yellow dye and fine tobacco smoke. **2.** Recent Age. In the genus Rhus, is any of about 35 species of flowering dioecious shrubs and small trees. The flowers grow in dense panicles or spikes. Each flower is very small and has five petals. The fruits are reddish drupes that form dense clusters at the branch tips. In North America, the smooth sumac (R. glabra), three-leaf sumac (R. trilobata), and staghorn sumac (R. typhina) are sometimes used to make a beverage termed "sumac-ade" or "Indian lemonade". This drink is made by soaking the drupes in cool water, rubbing them to extract the essence, straining the liquid through a cotton cloth, and sweetening it. Native Americans also use the leaves and drupes of these sumacs in traditional smoking mixtures.

❧ Chapter 24 ❧

The skies will tie together,
The loneliness of our hearts,
For we are not alone,
Ne'er aye truly apart.

—The stars of Sethmoire to their reflections on the Baltide Lakes

Blooms upon the fairest of flowers, delicate in every intricacy, could not exist in *more exquisite quality than those before him now,* Sage thought as Leaf's eyes of emeralds searched his. Blooms, he realized, were growing from within the corkscrewed stems of her matted plaits, which were metamorphosing into long, bark-crusted stems. He was well accustomed to the wide assortment of flora within Treean hair nests. However, Leaf's crown had grown from nettle-twigs into a stretching canopy of leaf, flower, and cone while patterned grooves of bark furrowed up her cheeks and nose toward the cascading undergrowth of her hairline. She was more beautiful in the transformation than the heartbreak brought in the recognition of it.

She stared into Sage's eyes with a knowing transcendence. At first, her expression was concerned, but as he twitched and fidgeted, she became secure that he was okay and himself.

"You're awake," she said with a smile.

"So," Sage said with a sigh and a disconcerted half smile, "'twas all a dream."

"It was no dream," replied Leaf, her eyes alight.

Noblien knelt beside them, his countenance becoming one of suspended incredulity. He turned to Leaf, who nodded in affirmation of his unspoken question.

"By the wonders," he said in awe.

The Coyotl had not noticed the Puman's bemused expression. He was still richly confused. "How do you know it wasn't a dream?" said Sage, stuttering, running both hands over his face. "And if it wasn't, what was it?"

"All this time, 'twas you," said Noblien.

Sage blinked. "What're you talking about?"

"How you've sufficiently harangued me," continued Noblien, beginning to smile with a wistful reverence at the irony of life's courses. "My friend, you've awoken with many of your tattoos glowing as hot as a brand just off the fire. But more interesting, if such could be the case, is the change in your eyes—for they're now grey, by lawks—even your pupils are grey," and so saying, he placed two fingers to his forehead in respect. "Fair greetings, Thai Mielle."

Sage was rarely without words, but now he stared at the Puman slack-jawed. Tullkae, Downy, and Sessile scooted closer and huddled around the others, amazed at what was transpiring.

"Your eyes look like ice," said Sessile, pointing to Noblien. "And your eyes," he continued, turning to Sage, "are the color of a storm. My eyes are blue, the color of the sky," he finished, pleased with himself and grinning in childlike fashion.

"Bosh! How can this be?" asked Sage, his voice hollow as though lost far and away.

"Why would Thai Mielle not be you?" posited Noblien.

"Thai Mielle," Sage repeated, disgruntled by the reference. "I'm not, though," he said, standing and beginning to pace.

"What do you mean you're not?" Noblien asked, challenge edged in the question.

Sage squinched up his face. "In my thought-dreams, I remembered my moments as a tear ere I took form. And there was another! I was not the only tear! There was another like me."

"This cannot be, can it?" asked Noblien.

"What does it mean that you weren't the only tear?" asked Sessile, eager for a story.

"It means there's another elven ketyl," mumbled Noblien as Sage continued pacing. "One unknown all this time."

Sage ran his hands through his hair. "Aye," and so saying, he recalled the meeting of the Gauss at the edge of Alderelm's borders, the anguish of his discoveries welling him over with grief. His face twitched with pain. "Oh, LeadLeaf. Alderelm—"

"The Ancient Ones and all my kin are right here," she said, pointing to her heart.

Noblien took a step backward, the presence of grief rising upon his visage. "What are you saying?"

Leaf blinked, the tawny-gold folds interlacing the green of her eyes, expressing a rue of age far surpassing her own. "The Ancient Ones embraced my kin and many of the Hawkens before turning their roots skyward. In so doing, Alderelm absorbed the darknesses of Llaurantis."

Noblien turned to Sage, disbelief confounding his expression. Sage dropped his head in acknowledgment.

"I beheld Alderelm," he began, his rusty voice quivering. "She's a horrific scene of tangled Tree roots. I sought out the Tarn of Lumen, and she revealed the story. The Sacred Ones enlisted the most ancient of power-essence. A magic created by the Veriha and heretofore only called upon by those supernal beings. I hadn't thought the Trees knew of it, but of course, as the History Keepers, they would've marked those spells to memory. Lawks, calling on such magic would've taken all of their intent in unison."

"They're gone?" choked Noblien. He was silent for a long moment, tears welling in his eyes. "Then we've failed," he murmured, his voice dropping with his spirit.

Leaf balked. "Alderelm has sent Grimaul back into the Caves of Geul. The Ashindi are vanquished. And the Sakatu is safe."

Noblien glanced at Leaf skeptically, for she spoke less and less as the little Treean he had given himself to protect and more as the culmination of all the Trees. To talk to her was beginning to feel like discourse with an entire Forest, not a Treean youngling.

"The Sakatu would not be safe if you all had not kept me safe."

Tullkaee was not one to be described as tender, yet when she next spoke, the touch of a mother laced her inflections, and her words were a buoy of comfort. "What has happened is a tragedy," she began in hesitant contemplation, "but there is a beauty to it. The Great Trees saw a future without their Treeans and knew Leaf would be alone without her kind. The future held certain heartbreak; they knew this as sure as the sun sets and the moon rises. The Great Trees were strong in spirit, and when enemies surrounded them, they did not lose hope. Instead, they chose their fate. They died on their terms for a noble cause with and for those they loved. The death of Alderelm is as beautiful as her life. And in their death, the Trees and Treeans became one. Even their Lastborn became a blending of Tree and Treean so that your kinds," she said, looking at Leaf, "will never be apart."

Leaf smiled, and therein, the youthful, innocent Leaf of Alderelm returned to the forefront of expression for a moment's whisper.

Noblien placed his hand on her cheek. "Oh, my dear LeadLeaf."

"You called me LeadLeaf!" and so saying, her countenance softened, reminded of the moment when they first met, and upon this reminiscence, her face changed. "Sage, you must tend to the Umbra Trees! They'll be utterly terrified and alone. Vow to their safekeeping. Promise me."

"I would do whatever you asked and more," Sage replied. "Yet for this, I know not how to return. Nor how I accomplished the feat originally."

"Nor I," said Leaf. "The Trees have no history on such matters."

"I suspect," said Noblien, scratching his chin, "that the power of your experience, which is demonstrated in your glowing tattoos and most certainly in the change in your eyes, will have endowed you all the more with the talents necessary. I wonder if being Thai Mielle is part of your Faiyum gifts," he said, touching his forehead where his sigil resided. "An elf born of a Veriha's tear, raised by coyotes, and marked by a Tree that carries the Writs of Brighid and is the source of an entire elven ketyl–lawks. I'm reminded," he continued, with a rare smile of full proportions, contemplative as it was, "of a poem you sang to us, which seems so long ago now. How did it go? Camas and beetle runes, welkin blue and cricket tunes, honeysouke, sweet the air, sunset waters, mountains fair," and so saying, he paused in thought. "Ah yes, Vestal vow under Tree flowers, 'tis that time of waking hour." The Puman looked at the others and raised his eyebrows. "Let surprise not take you. 'Tis an elven composition well known."

Sage's brows knit, and he was returned in thought to his encounter with the Gauss.

Noblien continued, noticing the change in the Coyotl's countenance. "Honestly, all this is a tale made for younglings. I believe the stars are aligned."

Sage moaned. "I encountered three creatures in Alderelm. The Faiyum marked one of them with a sigil."

"A creature anointed as a member of the Faiyum?" asked Downy, bewildered if not wholly envious.

"Aye. I had a mind to end its life's burden."

"Do you seek to end every creature's course upon Earth who has just been unwillingly enlisted as Faiyum?"

"Nay," answered Sage. "Just this one."

"Are you all certain this is Thai Mielle?" asked Downy. "Confoundations!"

Sage's complexion turned ashen, his fogged eyes darkening if it were possible. "The creature was a Gauss."

"A Gauss?" rasped Noblien, alarm blended with disbelief where his eyes reflected a disgusted horror.

"Not only a Gauss, but elven kin . . . the other tear."

"Nay, nay," replied Noblien, the revelations smothering him.

"I certainly question my memory, often in fact," Sage said, with a flick of his hand toward his head and an expression of frustration, "however, I'd ne'er doubt the Writs of Brighid. The Gauss, marked as a Faiyum, was anointed as he protected another from my sword. The moment he grasped my arm and held it from its downward swing, my Faiyum senses twinged. The sigil given was kindred. My memories unbound soon thereafter.

"The Gauss were lost from the very beginning. They were bullied and used for their heavy constitution. I cannot imagine what their ketyl has endured to have evolved so wretchedly. And I'm ashamed of having ne'er recognized them for what they really were. Against my prejudices and anger, there was no hope. These Gauss were more than deadheaded evil all along. I'm filled with much grief and turmoil."

"The weight of your burden is not yours alone," whispered Noblien, his shock tempered by the Coyotl's words. "Your turmoil is thus shared. Tell me, what is their ketyl?"

"Buffalo."

"Buffalo?" repeated Noblien.

"A most noble creature," asserted Tullkaee, her mind's eye seeing the mighty figure before her.

"Eons without guidance or purpose—I thought of them as creatures of rote function at best. However, my recent encounter refutes such judgment, although they do not speak. Lawks ta buoy, they do not know they are elves. They are utterly lost. And after so much damage has been done to them and by them, how are we to reconcile, much less teach and bring them into the fold? Certainly, 'tis our obligation to do so, to try. Yet I fear little will come by way of welcoming them and for good cause."

"I'm sorry," said Downy, identifying with the elves' predicament in a way none might think to imagine.

"Thai Mielle," said Tullkaee, unfettered by pity, "you will return to the Earthen realm and show them the way of the elves."

"Yet back to the start . . . I know not how," said Sage, running a hand through his hair.

"I do not think you need to know how," replied Tullkaee. "Like before, you simply will."

"Tullkaee is right," said Leaf, her voice crackling like the rustling of leaves, much to the concern of the others. "You believe in the Writs of Brighid, so don't let worry block your path."

There was much for the company to brew on, and silence blanketed them as the wind picked up. The others noticed Leaf had closed her eyes and decided that Downy, Sessile, and Tullkaee would venture about the mountain to scavenge for sustenance while she rested.

Tullkaee committed her axe to its sleeve and strung her bow with an eager, avid fondness. Downy wondered whether her expression was for the weapon or the hunt when, in truth, it was for the simple chore of satiating hunger.

Noblien looked out over the fat-gorged mountain. He exhaled, lamenting, and thus, inadvertently betrayed his usual overriding sereneness. Sage approached and stood next to him, their shoulders touching.

"Time," Sage said. "We've either too much of it or not enough."

Noblien grunted in agreement. He was not in the mood for flippant chattering. His heart was pained by the knowledge that he would soon lose his newfound friend and joyful irritant. In the Coyotl, Noblien had found something he did not know he had been missing.

"What will the others do?" Sage asked, squinting against the sun's pleated rays, which now struck several mountain ridges. "They've bravely traveled with us to be trapped beyond an eve unto a new world."

"The Thessalian and his brother have a new start here. They will explore and make new lives. They will live. Yet to our noble Daun, does pity strike the stability of my mind."

"Aye, mine as well." Sage nodded.

"To be separated from one's family, one's children—one does not simply pick up and start anew."

"Not anew, but she shall forge a path, nonetheless," said Sage. "If anyone is strong enough, 'tis Tullkae though my heart aches for her."

Noblien glanced back at Leaf. Leoness had curled her large, feathered form around her and breathed deeply in sleep. He smiled inwardly on seeing this and studied Leaf's condition with a peculiar mixture of pride and sadness before assurance granted his leave to turn back to the open view of the infinite sky and land before them. He sighed with a long exhale.

Sage watched him and swallowed hard. "What of you?"

Noblien was shocked Sage would ask this question. "I will stay with Leaf," he replied matter-of-factly.

"Loyalty," said Sage, eyeing the sigil on the Puman's forehead. "Although, she'll be a metamorphosis, a Tree by all looks and gatherings. Does she need watching over . . . as a Tree . . . in a new realm across the eves from former dangers?"

"Aye. She'll need protecting," Noblien snapped, immediately embarrassed at the emotion revealed in the answer. "These realms are inextricably tied, now more than ever. I'd not trust that because she resides in a Tree form, she is excluded from danger," he continued, the calmness of his tone returned. "More importantly, I'll not leave her alone. I'll always stand guard."

"Ah," said Sage. "The Pumans always take a stand for those in need."

Noblien rolled his eyes. "Nay, don't flatter me. Look. I'm truly at home in the solitude of the mountains. I'm at home here as anywhere else."

Sage was unconvinced and scowled as Eyas, that little warbird of giant heart, swooshed by the pair, playing in a curled breeze swept up from lower ridges.

"I'm at peace with this guardianship," insisted Noblien. "Honestly, LittleLeaf LeadTree has been my point of purpose since the waters of the Sasa called me hence. But more, Sage, she's still a child; whatever form she has, she's a child in this universe, and I'll not leave her alone."

"I see," said Sage, regarding his friend with respect. "The Treeans would be infinitely comforted, and the Ancient Ones would send songs throughout the earth in your honor. Aye, that's what they'd do. I will anoint you on Alderelm's behalf," he said, pulling Timbriel from its scabbard as Noblien's jaw tensed in no small amount of embarrassed discomfort. "I believe Knowlton would expect it," Sage continued, his rusty voice cracking while his mischievous, glinting eyes clouded over. "Now, don't scoff. I'll make the words pretty.

"I, Sage Lagacious, adopted son of Alderelm with the inherent permission granted in the holding of Heartwood Knowlton Hophornbeam's sword, Timbriel, recognize this Puman, Noblien, son of Flumen and Erato, descended from the long and noble Troyelle line, and member of the Faiyum, as official guardian of their most beloved Treean, LittleLeaf LeadTree, holder and essence of the World Tree Seed, known affectionately as the Sakatu. Herein, the honor entitled through history will be given forevermore and after," and so saying, Sage paused for effect before raising his voice and adding, "and more . . . let it be known that the title of official guardian was granted deservedly from he who calls this elf, friend, and who holds him in his heart as no less than a brother."

The Fierce-Eyed Elf's countenance softened as he lowered the windows of his spirit, humbled and obliged. After a respectful moment, he lifted his gaze back toward the Coyotl, his eyes always cutting to the threads of Sage's very fiber even as they were softened under the brimming of tears. The moment that followed between the pair did not contain words, yet the precious time was overflowing with tacit recognition and respect for the other.

During this time, Leaf's coarse-barked face cracked into a narrow smile—her last physical act as a Treean, for thenceforth, she was transformed completely. A Tree of the World, the ascendant of the Trees of Knowledge, she rode the tides of Tree songs while communing with the world at large. Her yearnings were at last slaked; she was free. Her roots, as divine and branched as the boughs above, dove into the depths of her new mountain abode, a multitude of blossoms, the merest size of tinker faeries, unfurling in celebration. The wind curled about her boughs, soughing joyously. Neither elf had yet to notice her change.

"When next I step into the elven mist of dreams," murmured Sage. "I believe the intent of my heart to recover the lost ketyl of the Buffalo will drive the power of the Faiyum within me to do what should be impossible. And when I cross the eve, methinks the old magic will be hard-pressed into such a feat again unless it is to your calling."

The Puman placed his index finger on his forehead in acknowledgment and smiled. "I shall catch word of your antics through the winds and the seasons."

Sage grinned at the Puman's jab. "I didn't want to bring the subject up, but what of your heart's affairs? The season? None can miss it."

A haunted shadow, gaunt in its longing, fell atop Noblien's

countenance like a death shroud. "Our kinds were not destined to be together."

"Ha!" said Sage sarcastically. "Please."

"Ah," returned Noblien. "So, you test me for old time's sake?"

"Nay," Sage replied, shaking his head. "Yet how be it that your fair sylphan mother found your proud elven father? And how be it that the North wind himself met with Nava-Lena, elf of the Eastern Lands, their love producing your fair damsel," and so saying, he ticked the corner of his temple with his finger, a knowing crooked smile ever wide and parted. "Nay," he repeated, long and drawn. "Do not profess such ludicrous outbursts as our kinds and destiny," he said.

"Oh!" Noblien said wryly. "So, we shan't speak on matters of fate . . . Thai Mielle?"

Sage maintained his smile. "Lawks, I'll miss you," and so saying, his expression tightened. "Do not sacrifice yourself needlessly. You're already a martyr."

Noblien shook his head. "'Tis not martyrdom that keeps us apart. Her nature is more season than elf; like the elementals, she flits and fades with the ethers. To tether an elemental is not love."

"Aye. I realize these facts. Still. Love always finds a way."

"Ah, you're a romantic!"

"My weakness has been found out." Sage laughed.

"My friend, you've more than one," countered Noblien, gazing back to check on Leaf. His heart dropped, and he gasped, "Oh, my dear Treean."

Sage turned to see the cause of the Puman's reaction, and he too gasped, a wheezing puff of breath as one just hit in the gut. Long did her bough arms stretch toward the sky in delicate swan neck arches where teardrop leaves of the darkest green fluttered with the wind, tinkling bell songs in their new glory. Her hair now hardened in ripples of rough, blue-veined bark that formed a groove where her trunk parted and gave way to the limbs of her crown. There was such beauty and wonder in her Tree form. Five petaled flowers opened in triumph, the rosy color of dawn on a crisp spring morning. She was glorious.

"Leaf," Noblien whispered, approaching her, "your heart is free, young one." The currents of the Yelm, that rolling current of the universe, struck outwards from the depths of his eyes as he searched for some awareness within her. Seeing none, he closed the windows to his spirit, sending an elven blessing on high.

⊷ Chapter 25 ⊶

Time is the keeper of love . . . all else diminishes.

—Opus

If there was an occasion when the company realized their time together had come to an end, this was it. As the others returned, a heavy silence enveloped them, nearly muffling their breaths like a nightfall's snow mutes the cadence of the morning's echoes. The hushed atmosphere surrounding this moment had a resonance, like a gonged bell traversing the reverberations of its triumph. A sublime beauty was cast out from their grief, and the passion from the resulting anguish lit the back of Nature's eye with the unfolding of bright new beginnings.

Tullkaee untied the feather in her hair and carefully tied it to one of Leaf's boughs. She stood there for some time quietly. The feather twirled in a lift of wind soon passed.

"I will make a home as a Daun in the Land of the Sakatu, and I will continue the traditions of my people, remembering the power of Trees." The inner glimmerings of Tullkaee's obsidian eyes turned their focus to Sage and pierced his spirit . . . and very nearly his heart. "You will find a way to communicate our journeys to my daughters?"

"By the Seven Stars, I swear it. And I ask for a task from you."

She stared back at him askance, suspicion rippling the fierceness of her presence.

"Check in on my odd girl. She'll be apart from her kind, and she knows not this world."

"I will do this," she stated, eyeing Leoness, who responded in delight to her brief attention by stretching her stance to a great height and spreading her wings so that she might briefly flap the harrowing appendages ahead of refolding and tucking them away with a ruffling of her head and neck feathers.

"Noble huntress," said Sage, his ever-darting eyes for this moment riveted and penetrating. "It has been much the pleasure."

Noblien stepped forward and extended his arm to hers, which she mirrored, each holding the other's forearm in a gesture of heartfelt respect. "It has been an honor."

"May we meet again," said Downy, nodding and holding Sessile's shoulders to steady the gentle giant now beginning the throes of agitation.

Tullkaee studied him before releasing a smile that resided more in the twinkle of her eyes than in the upward extension of her lips. The expression stunned Downy to a moment of immovability while the sun broke through the thick white clouds, turbulent and rising into columns. Tullkaee looked skyward. The upper air currents were intensifying, yet it felt strangely warm and hospitable, soothing her trepidation.

"We go with you," said Sessile.

"This you are welcome to do," replied Tullkaee, looking toward Downy.

Sessile crinkled his face in affirmation and, ignoring his brother, turned to Noblien, who had stepped away from the group to survey the uncharted lands stretching long into the horizon.

"You stay'in?" Sessile asked.

"Speak so he sees you, master ostler," said Sage with a wink.

Sessile moved right in front of the Puman, to which Noblien reacted by taking a step back and kindly looking at the large man.

"You've rare eyes. Not because they're like ice but because they're amicable. See, most people's eyes are the same as every'n else's—sometimes pleasant 'n glittery-like, 'n other times cold 'n burning, just depending on their moods. 'Tis not bad in of itself, just the way it is, right? Human, elf, or fae, 'tis the same. But thine eyes is kind by nature. Whether you're serious, worried, or even sad, thine eyes is kind. Rarer than aught else, I'd say. You're tried and true, and 'tis right proper you're stay'in with her."

Noblien smiled. "Thank you, Sessile—'Tis kind of you to say. I know you'll look after your brother, and I wish you happiness."

"We'll check in on you if you'll have it," said Downy, after which Noblien bowed his head in reply. "I had hoped we would've had an opportunity to fight side by side, but I'm grateful for this journey, nonetheless. 'Tis a new beginning for us."

"There's Haevonen here," Sessile said.

"But Haverdome is a long way from here, my friend," replied Noblien.

Sessile shrugged. "That's no matter as to the fact they're here. I feel it in my bones, smell it in the air, and hear their whinnies."

Downy chuckled. "Well then, we'll seek them out, brother."

"I'd love to see um again," said Sessile.

"I know you would, master ostler," replied Sage. "They were magnificent to behold, ne'er had they a better caretaker than yourself."

Sessile blushed. "They were in a bad state, yet they cared for me."

"I believe you are the Heppocrene," Noblien said, "this world seeks."

All stood for a moment in silent discomfort. Tullkaee was not one for such complexities and, sensing the change in the moment, turned away with a nod to the others.

"Leoness could take you below or to whatever lands appeal," said Sage after her.

"I would then not know my way back," she replied with a glint in her eyes.

"Fair enough," nodded Sage as the Puman's lips spread into a broad, thin smile. "What of you?" he asked, looking toward the captain and his brother.

Downy held his hands out and backed away laughing. "Never again, Lord Elf. My brother and I go with Tullkaee and familiarize ourselves with these new lands."

The speed in which the three departed increased, for a decision had been met with farewells and proper courtesy, and now was the time to descend the mountain and approach their future destinies anew. Also, none wanted to dissuade the Coyotl again. Their intention not to ride his dear banda was indeed heartfelt. Sage realized this fact from the start but could not release one last inner joke at their expense.

Noblien and Sage watched the three briefly, then sat near Leaf and delved into solemn, elven contemplations. However, Sage had little use for such elven applications and, in short order, was pacing.

"You're ready?" Noblien asked, looking up at the Coyotl.

"I am," Sage replied, looking like a figure wary of moldering away any longer.

None could look so pathetic in a mere moment's inaction, thought Noblien. He would ne'er lose the incredulity he felt over the energy the Coyotl required to necessitate his very existence. And how he would miss it.

"Do you have a task for me as well?"

"Nay," Noblien replied.

"No message to convey?"

"Nay," Noblien repeated flatly and, seeing his friend's dissatisfaction, added, "Niveus will know of my whereabouts through Boreas. Do not worry yourself."

Sage eyed the Puman long and hard, his fogged grey eyes piercing into the depths of the Puman's silver etchings, pathways to the inner spirit, finding little therein to satisfy his unease. Only could he perceive the past's reiteration of a youngling crying out for his father, and in this, he was unsure whether his insecurities deceived him, for he felt an endless pit of guilt in abandoning him to his fate again. What would Flumen think? He felt a sense of failing the noble elf before him and the lost elven ketyl of Buffalo. His heart was wrenched whichever way he turned.

"Thai Mielle," said Noblien, smiling patiently, "settle your worrit where I'm concerned. I can hear naught but all the blades of fountain grass waving their plumes of faerie tails and professing their glad tidings of your return. You are needed. Return without the heavy heart I see afore me."

Sage's ever-capricious nature most certainly evolved as a saving trait for the sanctuary of his wild mind, and now, as Noblien watched the Coyotl's struggle, he hoped for that whimsy to win out yet again. Sage closed his eyes. Noblien stood steadfast.

At last, there it was—the wide, crooked, and heartwarmingly mischievous smile of a half-crazed Coyotl. The world may or may not survive without the many inexplicable pillars of wonder woven elaborately together in the ecosystem of life. But it most emphatically depended upon the vantage of that smile to their underpinnings.

Sage placed his hand on Noblien's shoulder. "Thank you," and so saying, tilted his head as he watched Leoness snore next to Leaf's foot-roots. "Give me a moment. I need a word with my odd girl."

Sage took to her side and watched her breathing as he laid a hand atop her head. The mottled mix of fine hair feathers was of a softness rare to touch. Leoness stretched and yawned, blinking up at him and seeing it was Sage, sat upright with a vigorous shake of her entire body. Sage laughed, the lilt of a yodel echoed the rein, and rubbed her soapstone beak. "Ah," he sighed. "You grand, glorious, fluffy peahen. Your talent for finding me in my greatest need is uncanny, if not unprecedented. You've always found me. This time, odd girl . . . we'll be two worlds apart. I wish you could understand me. I'm not keen on abandoning you in a foreign realm, but I'm desperately needed from whence we came. Leoness, you are the grandest banda in two worlds now. Get into mischief and keep an eye on those mortals."

Leoness sighed with a contented huffling and returned her head to Leaf's foot-roots. The Coyotl cocked his head and squinted an eye in hesitation, for he had an itch within his rawest instincts that held off this final goodbye. "Leoness?"

She popped her head up in response and gazed at him adoringly.

"You feel LeadLeaf's presence, don't you?" The banda snortled and gurgled at him, a banda's equivalent of a cat purr. "That's my girl," he said, kissing her beak. "Be that you feel mine when I'm gone, for I'm leaving in presence only."

Rubbing his hands together, he stole a look back at Noblien. As he did so, the Puman's little warbird sliced by Sage's ear before alighting on Noblien's shoulder. The wee ave followed with a brilliantly executed song-salute. The tenacity expressed in every action and attribute of her robust spirit induced a joyous laugh, which the Coyotl was most easily given to.

"Alas and aye, I'll miss you too, mighty Eyas. Watch over your kin when opportunity allows," said he, nodding toward Leoness and settling his expression in a thoughtful pose. "You know, Noblien, she's quite the companion. It is an interesting coincidence that both our companions are fliers. Albeit of differing wingtips," he said as he finished laughing.

"I hadn't thought of it, but I suppose you're quite right."

"We've both the longevity beyond the keen of outcomes, haven't we?" Sage asked. "So, who's to say?"

Noblien's eyes twinkled briefly before their inner light diminished. "Indeed, perhaps we shall meet again."

The two stood awkwardly in their silence. There was naught more to express, yet neither was eager for the next phase of life to be thrust upon their persons. They had spent a lifetime apart after a moment together. And although there could not be two more differing personas, they were good together, and each knew it. Strange though it was, they could feel the bone-numbing familiarity and unconditional acceptance, even in the face of desperate exasperation, that was family.

"Well, slapdash to waking dreams," Sage said.

"Would you like to be alone?"

"Elven sleep is a wicked game for the likes of me," Sage replied. "Aye, stand your presence by my side."

"It'd be my honor."

"And sing to me."

At that moment, the Coyotl took a step away from the Puman, but he was still shoved squarely with the heel end of Noblien's hand, for he endlessly underestimated the Puman's quickness when he spied annoyance. With a primal growl and a whistling exhalation, Noblien stepped in for a second go; Sage deftly countered the attempt with hearty laughter.

"You'll definitely miss me."

As Sage traveled the waves of elves, the Puman stayed close. He stared out over the lands, his many red stranded locks burning against the setting sun as his grey eyes reflected the penetrating gaze of his kind. His visage held the signs of exhaustion, though his posture held stoic and firm. When Leoness honked, he turned around, and the misty remnant of Sage's personage was only a mirage. Noblien squinted and began to walk closer, his heart glad and heavy in the new silence. Leoness huffed over the impression of Sage's footprints. She sniffed and scampered with a cricket-like clucking. The sound was searching and mournful; she could no more sense the Coyotl to find from whence his need might beckon. She looked at Noblien with wide, searching eyes, and he cooed to her in Elvish, placing his arm around her neck. The banda sighed, walked back under Leaf's boughs, and curled herself tightly. Chirping, Eyas flew and perched upon one of the banda's soft-turned horns, tucking her head under her wing.

Noblien turned back to gaze at the horizon. He thought of Tullkaee, Downy, and Sessile while ruminating on Sage's coming challenges. *Life is certainly a twisting path of discoveries on a switchback of seemingly impossible heights whose beauty and intrigue keep one climbing*, he thought, taking a deep breath of the breeze. They were each of them onto new adventures, wiser for the entanglement of each other's lives and the experiences gained therein, strengthened by the energies that bound them together even when apart, and emboldened through what they had learned from one another. And now, a genuine descendant of the Great History Keepers grew unscathed and untouched upon an unnamed mountain in an unknown world, watched over by a Puman elf and a banda of the Old World. Their accounts would live on . . . for they had only just begun.

Ellis McCauley

FOUNTAIN GRASS

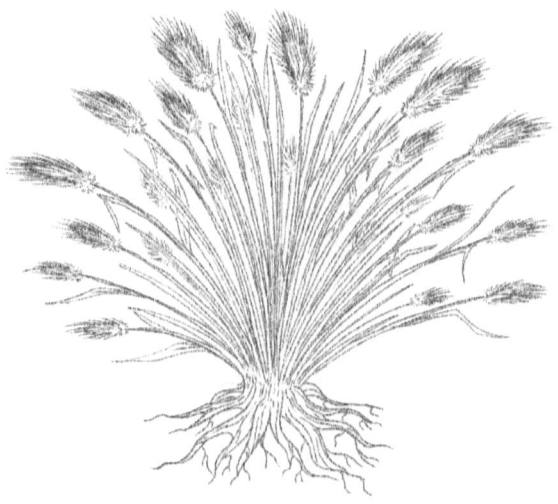

Fountain Grass. 1. A perennial plant in the grass family. In late summer, it has fairy tail plumes of white, pink, copper, or purple. The seeds are hidden in the bristles of the fuzzy inflorescences, or fairy tail plumes, and are primarily dispersed by the wind, remaining viable in the soil for six years or longer. *2.* Recent Age. No change from above. Of the genus, Pennisetum.

◄ Epilogue ►

There is a Tree named Methuselah high in the milky clouds of the White Mountains, holding the tablet of time and carving out her passages. The stars, the sun, and the wind are her companions.

Many millennia ago, her home resided within the long-graced boughs of a mountain Forest known as Alderelm. More than a Forest, Alderelm was the spirit and very quintessence of story—the wonders, delights, grandeurs, and tragedies accumulated throughout history in anecdotes and rumors spun in long yarns and short accounts so legends and myths might then comprehend them. Within this magical place of faerie tunes, beetle runes, and the heady scents of resin and warm-spiced terpenes, LittleLeaf LeadTree's story began. Now, where the earth-colored hues of complimenting subtleties touch the light of the air, Methuselah's tale continues through the threads of all of ours.

✌ Appendix ✾

Abi. Renowned alchemist and seer of the grumbies of Shee.

Adamant. 1. A crystal stone set in silver and worn on the left arm. It endows the wearer with courage and the ability to expel venom and remove anger. It is believed to be worn by the Grey-Eyed Elf. 2. *Recent Age.* Adamantine is called the metal of the gods. In mythology, it is an unbreakable, untarnishable, and lightweight material.

Aelin-lumen. 1. Elvish calling for the Tarn of Lumen in Alderelm. 2. Slang. Elven expression of serenity and peace of place. 3. *Recent Age.* (Aelin). JRR Tolkien's Elvish word for tarn.

Age of Laurentia. The period after Mulheteämult and when this story takes place.

Age of Ursham. 1. The period following the departure of the Veriha and leading up to Mulheteämult. 2. *Recent Age.* Ursham is a name of Islamic origin and means "flower of heaven."

Alderelm. 1. One of the seven Ancient Forests of Earth, residing in the West Lands, also known as Llaurantis and home of the faerie kind, Treeans.

Alus. A grumby with high weaving skills and sister to Abi.

Ama. 1. Of the elemental's language, meaning "winter."

Aman. 1. First and longest age of Earth, a time of beauty, innocence, and balance, ending on the Eluvium. 2. *Recent Age.* J.R.R Tolkien's name for the land in the West; "Blessed, free from evil.".

Anastomose. 1. Common calling for the language of the Trees of Harbored Memory. 2. *Recent Age.* Union of branches, as of rivers or veins of leaves.

Ancient Ones. The white-barked Trees of Harbored Memory, the Sacred Ones within the seven Ancient Forests, each an amalgam of Earth's Trees in totality.

Ashindi. 1. Ghouls of fire and smoke. 2. *Recent Age.* Similar to the Navajo word *chindi*, meaning devil. 3. *Recent Age.* Similar to the Cherokee word *asgina*, meaning malevolent spirit.

Atanta. The matriarch mare of the Haevonens and goddess of horses.

Baal. 1. Essence of Earth and spirit-giver of the Veriha. 2. *Recent Age.* (Bay-ell) a Semitic term that means "lord" or "owner," which evolved into the name of Nature gods before the rise of monotheism, where the term represented the god of fertility and weather, specifically rainstorms. Baal is considered a false idol by the Hebrews and known in the bible as the antagonist of the Israelite cult of Yahweh.

Banda. A large bird of prey, a cross between the extinct gryphons of Llaurantis (the Western Lands) and the Halouse breed of dragons prevalent in the MiddleLands.

Barsil Orbs. Also known as death beetles, originating from another world known to the West Lands as Barsil. The orbs tend to congregate where the newly dead have fallen and produce colors of tranquility and dancing light. Their purpose is a mystery.

Basswood Tree. 1. Found in the Land of Shee and marked by their wide, mushroom-shaped canopies and active limb-vines wherein the grumbies homes reside. 2. *Recent Age.* The Basswood is a subspecies of the Linden family with asymmetrical and lopsided heart-shaped leaves, the largest of all broadleaf Trees. Also known as the Bee Tree.

Battles of Nirmossa. Very rarely accounted for, these battles occurred after the Brekenridge Foils.

Bigdebar. An Ancient One, often called the Gentle Giant of Oaks, resided on the western slope of Alderelm next to Nertle.

Blue Borough. The only central township of the Puman elves, nestled within the Upper Palisades of Ether in the northeastern corner of Llaurantis on the east-west ridges of Uma-tànash Mountain.

Blue Fish Cave. The body of water surrounding the grumby borough of Shee. When properly summoned, it can create a water tunnel for passage to the further shore.

Bodark. Brother of Bristleton and Treean artisan who fell in love with Kaurì, one of the Sacred Ones of Alderelm.

Boreas. 1. One of the four wind elementals, the North wind, gentle and aloof. 2. *Recent Age.* The Greek god of the North wind and winter.

Braemarian. Dwarven kind of the MiddleLands.

Brekenridge Foils. A series of events that culminated in a tragic outburst from Baal, resulting in LittleLeaf LeadTree's scars.

Bristleton. Treean border guard, also called a marchwarden, and guardian of LittleLeaf LeadTree.

Buffalo. Forgotten ketyl of elves, spirit keepers of the wild ox. 2. *Recent Age.* The American bison (Bison bison) native to North America, colloquially referred to as buffalo.

Camelop. 1. Extinct ketyl of elves, spirit keepers of the Camel. 2. *Recent Age.* Extinct species of camel that once roamed western North America.

Appendix

Charlock. 1. The name of Flumen of Faiyum's legendary bow, crafted by the sylphs. 2. *Recent Age.* A wild mustard with yellow flowers.

Charqui. Beef jerky of the Dauns.

Cimmerians. 1. The ghosts of elves who died. 2. *Recent Age.* In classical mythology, mentioned in the Odyssey, a people living at the edge of Oceanus, the stream that surrounds Earth, in a city of perpetual darkness near the entrance to Hades.

Cirrus. 1. A season, brother to Niveus. 2. *Recent Age. High, thin clouds.*

Cland. 1. A social unit of humans. 2. *Recent Age.* Old Irish (Scottish Gaelic) means "offshoot of a plant," "offspring," "family," and "clan."

Cloud. A social unit of sylphs.

Clove. 1. A social unit of faeries 2. *Recent Age.* Aromatic flower buds of a Tree in the family Myrtaceae, Syzygium aromaticum, native to the Maluku Islands and used as spice and fragrance.

Cocia Tree. Evergreen Trees with long flowing limbs. They grow along the edges of rivers in the Western Lands of Llaurantis.

Coyotl. 1. Ketyl of elves who are the spirit keepers of the coyote and possess the power of transformation. Unlike other elven ketyls, they do not have specific physical characteristics. 2. *Recent Age.* The Nahua word for coyote.

Crag of Leda. The highest point on the Blue Borough. It is a place of reverence for the Puman elves.

Daevas. 1. A meddling witch. 2. *Recent Age.* A maleficent supernatural being.

Daggus. A grumby of Shee, nephew to Abi, and skilled rider of flagbearers.

Dauns. 1. Cland of human kind, Daunans, who reside in the northwestern region of Llaurantis along the Western Seas.

Dohiyi Elonna. 1. Calling of the Legged Ones in Daunan legend. To the elves, they are known as the Crone-sages of the Scimitar 2. *Recent Age. Dohiyi* is Cherokee for "peace", while "Elonna" is a variant of the Greek word *Ilona*, which means "light."

Edassa. One of the last of four Umbra Trees to exist, residing at the base of Alderelm with the other Notturn Guards who make and hold the Bridge of Telldon, known in combination with the other three Umbrae as the four Bridge Keepers.

Elementals. Creature kind who regulates nature's seasons and winds.

Ell'oyn. Sylph of the Welkin sentinels apprenticed under Yoor'el.

Eluvium. 1. Marks the departure of the Veriha, the last day of the Age of Aman. 2. *Recent Age.* Residual deposits of soil, dust, and rock particles produced by action of the wind.

Elves. 1. Of six different yet similar kinds representing the animals who stood by the last departing Veriha; two more ketyls were born out of the last Veriha's tears. All elven ketyls are deeply and intrinsically tied to nature. 2. *Recent Age.* A mythical creature of mischief and magic.

Emerus. 1. A living stone known as the Singing Tree Stone maintaining the balance of nature, or of Earth herself. 2. *Recent Age.* The Latin word for "emerald."

Erato. 1. Noblien's mother, a sylph. 2. *Recent Age.* The muse of lyric, poetry, and mime in Greek myth.

Esa. Grumby of Shee known for her humor and quick wit.

Etherea. A stone-art replica of the dragon who long and peaceably shared residence with the dwarves of Notturn within the MiddleLands.

It shined so brightly that it replaced the Umbra Trees' need for sunlight.

Eurus. 1. The elemental East wind. 2. *Recent Age*. East wind.

Eve. Neutral point and fabric between worlds and dimensions.

Even Tide of Hanging Lanterns. A Puman "end of seasons" celebration that takes place between the fall and winter seasons when the wind settles down upon the Crag of Leda, the pinnacle point of the Blue Borough, which is nestled within the Upper Palisades of Ether.

Exacontalitus. A stone found in caves and places of the deep within which sixty colors may be found.

Eyas. 1. A small finch and companion to Noblien, Puman elf of the Troyelle house. 2. *Recent Age*. Nestling hawk.

Fae. Faerie.

Faerie. 1. Collective word for a variety of beings who share a common heritage and can be visually marked by their smaller stature and frame compared with that of elves, sylphs, elementals, lliath, and humans. 2. *Recent Age*. Mythical being of magic and small stature.

Faiyum. 1. Magical guild of elven guardians made up of mysteriously selected members from several different ketyls and argued either to be extinct or high lords in waiting. 2. *Recent Age*. Also, Fayaum is a desert oasis west of the Nile River in Egypt and the place of the first paved road.

Feeorin. 1. Elven word for grumbies. 2. *Recent Age*. Fairies.

Feiko Steppe. Grassland on the leeward side of Alderelm.

Fignauts. Species of faerie marked for their musical quality. 2. *Recent Age*. A bird species similar to the loon.

Appendix

First Lands. Land northwest of the White Mountain, where the Daunan people reside.

Flagbearers. 1. Horses bred, ridden, and loved by the grumbies. They have an average height of fourteen hands with a cob body type. 2. *Recent Age.* An extinct species of horse that occupied the steppe-like grasslands of Beringia known as the Yukon horse.

Flumbaran. Race of winged faeries with light-green skin residing in the west lands or Llaurantis (especially within the borealis flowers). They transform between two forms, large and small (ladybug size), and are known to be greedy, compulsive, forgetful, and thoughtless, but they never intend direct harm to anyone and are protective of nature.

Flumen of Faiyum. 1. Most skilled archer in elven memory, gifted his bow, the Charlock, by the sylphs; Father of Noblien. 2. *Recent Age.* The Latin word for "river."

Foehn Wind. 1. A warm, dry, gusty wind that periodically descends the leeward slopes of the mountains. 2. *Recent Age.* Identical.

Freemont. 1. Treean elder of Alderelm 2. *Recent Age.* Name of a Tree with the following common names: Fremont Cottonwood, Rio Grande Cottonwood, Meseta Cottonwood.

Fulguris. 1. Prophecy during the Age of Laurentia concerning a continuous season of harsh winter preluding an age of darkness. 2. *Recent Age.* A Latin word meaning lightning, flashing, or brightness.

Gauss. 1. Race of ghouls, yet perhaps more. 2. *Recent Age.* The centimeter-gram-second electromagnetic unit of magnetic flux density, equal to one Maxwell per square centimeter.

Gehenna. 1. Veil to the afterworld. 2. *Recent Age.* Hell.

Gemyne. Elf royal of the elk.

Geul. Spirit keeper of Pythium, the sphere of an underworld of malevolence.

Grimaul. The first gulaug, master of fiends.

Groundlings. Distantly related to goblins residing in ground tunnels.

Grumby. Isolated species of stout small beings, known to be either sweet and playful or irritable beyond all reason, distantly related to Flumbaran faeries; they live upon an invisible land called Shee.

Grundy. Grumby of tall stature (for his kind); excellent rocksmith.

Gulaugs. Archfiends, heralds of Geul, ruled under Grimaul.

Haards. Small claw-footed horses; ancestral lineage of the flagbearers.

Haevonens. Breed of wild horses residing in Llaurantis upon the fields of Haverdome, known for their brilliant red or black coats and immense size.

Halouse. A type of dragon of the MiddleLands.

Hardtack. 1. Treean elder of Alderelm and elder of the Mountain Mahoganies, branch of the Birch house. 2. *Recent Age.* Tree, common names: Birchleaf Mountain – mahogany (Hardtack). Able to withstand cutting, fire, drought, and heavy browsing.

Haverdome. First home of the Veriha, home to the Haevonen, a horse country southeast of the White Mountain known for its flowing red fields of hob knob grass.

Hawkens. Ketyl of elves, spirit keepers of the hawk. They typically have gold-green eyes and sharp-angled features of medium height and build. Their realm resides near the ethereal city.

Heartwood. An honorific used for the Treean elders of the Ancient Forests.

Appendix

Ibus. A mythical, non-mythical creature with eight legs and eyes, giant tusks, and long, flowing hair that *aums* at the rising sun. Protector of children and shields of the scablands.

Kaurì. Deceased Ancient One of Alderelm, remembered for her love of the sea and known for Nirmossa with the Treean, Bodark.

Ketyl. Subdivisions of elves united by their origins yet marked differently through certain traits and features of their totem animal.

Knowlton Hophornbeam. 1. Treean elder of Alderelm and the Birch house, referred to as "Ole Ironwood." 2. *Recent Age.* Tree, common name, Ironwood.

Kongoni. Daunan word for the foul spirit of ghouls and the underworld, an equivalent to Geul, in the common tongue, or Skloi, in Elvish.

Lawks. Elvish expression for awe.

Lemnoss. Ancient Forest residing in the MiddleLands.

Lemure(s). 1. Guides of death, specters of the cross-world. 2. *Recent Age.* In Roman mythology, lemures were shades of the restless dead; also, Linnaeus characterized lemurs after their ghostly looks, unearthly calls, and nocturnal proclivity.

Lemuria. 1. A river that flows from the northernmost edge of Llaurantis through the Red Valley of the Raven elves. 2. *Recent Age.* A proposed continent existing as a land bridge and believed to have sunk. Once posited as a place of human origins and later discredited.

Leoness. Sage Lagacious' beloved banda.

Lethe. Waters of oblivion.

Lethoss Mountains. Mountain range residing upon the MiddleLands.

Appendix

Linden Tree. Common Tree of Llaurantis.

Line storm. 1. Equinoctial storm of fierce electrical energy. 2. *Recent Age.* Equinoctial storms of violent winds and rain.

LittleLeaf LeadTree or LittleLeaf of the LeadTrees. 1. Lastborn of the Treeans, holder of the Sakatu. 2. *Recent Age.* Tree, common names: Littleleaf Leadtree and Wahoo Tree.

Llaurantis. Land of West Earth.

Lliath. 1. Two-footed race of brown-haired beasts, six ells tall, living in the mountains of Quatch near Ghillie Dhu. 2. *Recent Age.* Am Fear Liath Mòr – the Grey Man, not unlike the Yeti, except existing within the Scottish Cairngorm Mountains.

Loyla. Mother elk of Alderelm.

MiddleLands. Region of land across the Eastern Seas from Llaurantis, home to the Ancient Forest of Lemnoss, the venerable halouse, and the bandas.

Mione. Grumby of Shee in charge of the beloved Flagbearers; excellent listener, easy to laugh, born with paralyzed antennae.

Miriam. Ancient Tree of Alderelm, LittleLeaf LeadTree's Tree.

Mohs. Apprentice of Abi. The giver of the adamant relayed in the Grey-Eyed Elf prophecies.

Montephoebius. A wise, seven-legged, well-aged Ibus.

Mulheteämult. Time period following the Age of Ursham and marking the emergence of human kind.

Nemus Hills. 1. Foothills on the eastern side of the White Mountain. 2. *Recent Age.* Latin for Tree or sacred grove.

Appendix

Nertle. An Ancient One resembling a Tortuosa Beech Tree and whose roots intermingle with Bigdebar's on the western slope of Alderelm.

Nimott. Very old Flumbaran faerie of Alderelm's council.

Nirmossa. True love across kin kind.

Niveus. 1. Season 'Of the Creatures,' whose elemental name is Nivia Nivom, known as Lady of Wold Reflections, Lady of Golden Sunsets, Season of Wold Reflections, Lady of Soft Dirge; her father is Boreas, the North wind and her mother was an elf of the Eastern Lands named Nava-Lena. She is half-sister to Cirrus and is the love of Noblien. 2. *Recent Age.* Latin for "snow."

Noblien of the Troyelle house. A Puman, who, unlike other Pumans, has fair skin and grey eyes. Known as the Fierce-Eyed Elf. His mother was a sylph mystic named Erato, his father a Puman elf named Flumen. Member of the Faiyum.

Notturn Guards. Also known as the four Bridge Keepers or the Guards of Notturn, these four Umbra Trees (Umbrae) reside on the border of Alderelm, having been retrieved, and thus saved from extinction, from the Lost Braemarian borough of Notturn after which they are named.

Notus. 1. The elemental South wind. 2. *Recent Age.* In Ancient Greek mythology, Notus is the god of the south wind, one of the Anemoi (wind gods), associated with storms of late summer and early autumn. Boreas and Zephyrus are his brothers.

Poem of Turkhyle. The last words of the Veriha, able only after their departure from Earth to be spoken by the seasons.

Puman. 1. Solitary and highly skilled warrior ketyl of elves, the spirit keepers of the Great Cat, preferring to reside within the high Woods and cliffs of Llaurantis. Most commonly of green eyes and gold hair. 2. *Recent Age.* Mountain lion.

Pythium. 1. Known as the Sphere of False Omens, the Gateway to the Underworld, or 'Other Realm of Earth' in which dwells various forms of fiends whose gateway is found within the Obsidian Fields of Llaurantis. Its spirit keeper is Geul. 2. *Recent Age.* a genus of parasitic oomycetes, most of which are parasitic to plants.

ᶦ**Quaternary.** 1. A random doubling in the girth of the White-Barked Ones, from whence creaks and groans join an explosive spurt of growth that heaves the mountain's balm far into the air. 2. *Recent Age.* System of rocks and sediment within the geological time of the second period of the Cenozoic Era, which was also characterized by the appearance and development of man.

Raven. Ketyl of elves, spirit keepers of the Raven, calling themselves the We'gyet. They are known for their intelligence and craftiness and for having black hair and eyes.

Sacred Ones. Trees of harbored memory residing within the seven Ancient Forests.

Sage Lagacious. Coyotl elf who was born by a Veriha's tear and, therefore, the first of his kind

Sakatu. The World Tree Seed is the amalgam of every Tree that has ever lived and, thus, contains the history, the culmination of individual stories, of all life on Earth.

Sasa. 1. River flowing on the western side of the White Mountain. 2. *Recent Age.* Cherokee word for "swan."

Sas'Dhu. 1. A lliath present at the council of Alderelm. Reluctant but ultimate friend of Sage Lagacious. 2. Recent Age. Not to be confused with or compared to the "Ghillie Dhu" which is a Scottish elf.

Sauktanumah. 1. A wizard of the MiddleLands and of Elven form of unknown ketyl, rumored to be one of the Faiyum. 2. *Recent Age.* The word "Sauk" refers to an Algonquian-speaking North American Indian Peoples of the Eastern Woodlands culture.

Appendix

Scimitar. 1. Extinct ketyl of elves; spirit keepers of the saber-toothed lion. 2. *Recent Age.* An extinct species of saber-toothed cat, living up to 10,000 years ago.

Scotch of the Downs. A human Captain of the Guard in the Land of Seayr, brother of Sessile of the Downs.

Seasons. Elemental beings who aide Earth in adaptations to the passage of the sun throughout the year; cousins to the sylphs, sprites, and winds.

Seayr. Realm of human kind (Seayrans) who reside on the western side of the White Mountain.

Sessile of the Downs. Human ostler of Seayr, brother of Scotch of the Downs (Downy).

Shee. 1. Invisible land of the grumbies. 2. *Recent Age.* Spelled Sidhe. Faeries of Ireland and the Highlands of Scotland.

Singing Tree Stone. A living stone of the Ancient Forests named Emerus that maintains the balance of nature.

Skloi. Elven calling for Geul, Spirit Keeper of the Pythium or the gateway to the underworld.

Spring of Tumoil. Living spring that feeds the Tarn of Lumen. Also referred to as "Tumoil."

Sunillum flood. A cataclysmic glacial lake flood that swept across eastern Llaurantis after the rupture of an ice dam on the Mellowamah River during the Age or Ursham.

Surgyle. Ancient Forest destroyed in the Age of Laurentia, the time of Alderelm's upturning.

Sylphs. 1. Tall, winged elemental beings of air, guided and loved by the stars. Distantly related to the seasons. 2. *Recent Age.* Beings of legend, invisible, female, winged, of the element air, never growing old and desiring only to fly in solitude with the birds.

Tarn of Lumen. 1. A small pond at the top of Alderelm, fed by the sentient spring, Tumoil, holding the healing qualities of restoration and wisdom. 2. *Recent Age.* A small mountain lake.

Thai Mielle. Thai means "grey" and "Mielle" means "eyes" in Elvish, the combination referring to the calling of the elf who will unite the Veriha's kin and call forth those wandering spirits of Haverdome to recognition and peace.

Thessalians. 1. Cland of humans residing within the MiddleLands. 2. *Recent Age.* Old World Paleolithic culture.

Timbriel. The sword of Heartwood Knowlton Hophornbeam's family branch which was anointed as the vessel of the living light of Timbrothiel.

Timbrothiel. The living radiance of a dying star obtained from the dragon that protected it, a water-dwelling dragon whose kind is called Physignathus. The star, the size of an average bullfrog, resided on Earth within the Sea of Barmoor, glowing in varying colors from violet-green to yellow white depending on its temper.

Tinker Faeries. Infinitesimal flying faerie kind of vivid light and color regarded as myth, although the History Keepers protect the secrecy of their existence because of how shy and rare they are and how much the Trees love their songs.

Tree of Cassen. A Tree as old as those within the seven Ancient Forests but not there residing nor possessing the characteristic white bark of those History Keepers; upon each leaf, she does, however, hold the hidden Writs of Brighid.

Treeans. Guardians of the Ancient Forest, as agile in the Trees as on the ground. Distantly related to faeries.

Appendix

Tullkaee. Human kind of the Dauns, daughter of Tukama, mother of Oshk and Maunt, Wiseone of her people, formidable warrior, and trusted companion.

Tumoil. Living spring that feeds the Tarn of Lumen.

Tumtum Tree. A Tree used as a symbolic representation of all the Ancient Trees in totality: it is an amalgamation of many Tree families, with peeling thin-layered bark, lustrous multicolored leaves, and a delightful vigor; its many corkscrewed limbs display an array of leaf shapes and sizes. Within it rests the secrets of energy and spirit song. 2. *Recent Age.* A Tree mentioned in Lewis Carroll's poem, *Jabberwocky.*

Tumult. A group of winds.

Tymen. Elvish word for "warrior."

Ullott. Flumbaran faerie of Alderelm's council.

Umbra Trees or Umbrae. Note: Umbra Trees are often referred to in the plural as "Umbrae"; a singular Tree is called an Umbra. 1. A species of Tree originally from the Lethoss Mountains of the MiddleLands, requiring only the light of Etherea for sustenance. 2. *Recent Age.* Similar to the archaic word, umbrage, meaning shadow or shade.

Vell. Elvish for "good" or "white," primarily when referring to a greater good.

Vell no 'ta bur'nighn. An elvish expression translated as "the pure is not buried."

Veriha. The Seven Wonders, original inhabitants of the Earth.

Wapiti. 1. Ketyl of elves, spirit keepers of the elk, generally tall with brown hair and skin. 2. *Recent Age.* Shawnee word for "large deer" or "white rump."

Appendix

Willow Elder. 1. Treean elder of Alderelm residing over the branches of Elder and Willow with some relation to the Hawthorns; the oldest and wisest Treean. 2. *Recent Age.* In ancient mythology, the Elder Tree is highly sacred, for it contains an indwelling matriarchal spirit known as the Elder Mother.

Writs of Brighid. Often misunderstood, the writs are written representations of the first spoken language, imbued with the living spirit of their meaning.

Wych. 1. River flowing on the Eastern side of the White Mountains. 2. *Recent Age.* An Old-World Elm Tree, also known as Witch Elm.

Yaguará. 1. Daunan word for "big cat." 2. *Recent Age.* South American Indian word for jaguar, meaning a beast that kills prey with a single bound.

Ylem. 1. A "veil" or "eve" of universal current. 2. *Recent Age.* The original matter from which the basic elements are said to have been formed after the explosion postulated in the Big Bang theory of cosmology.

Yolkai Estasan. 1. Daunan calling for Niveus. 2. *Recent Age.* Goddess of the Navajo, of land and seasons.

Yoor'el. Sylph of the Wyget sect, leader of the welkin sentinels, a loyal and fierce ally of the Sacred Forests, guided by Daedal, the blue star of Somatus.

Zephyr. The West wind.